Praise for #1 *New York Times* bestselling author Sherryl Woods

"Woods employs her signature elements—the Southern small-town atmosphere, the supportive network of friends and family, and the heartwarming romance—to great effect."

—*Booklist*

"Sherryl Woods always delights her readers—including me!"

—#1 *New York Times* bestselling author Debbie Macomber

"Woods is a master heartstring puller."

—*Publishers Weekly*

Praise for *USA TODAY* bestselling author Patricia Davids

"One of the best writers in the Amish fiction genre."

—Shelley Shepard Gray,
New York Times bestselling author

"Patricia writes with heart, integrity and hope. Her stories both entertain and edify—the perfect combination."

—Kim Vogel Sawyer, award-winning and bestselling author

With her roots firmly planted in the South, #1 *New York Times* bestselling author **Sherryl Woods** has written many of her more than one hundred books in that distinctive setting. Her Chesapeake Shores books have become a highly rated series success on Hallmark Channel and her Sweet Magnolias books have recently been released as a much-anticipated Netflix series. Sherryl divides her time between her childhood summer home overlooking the Potomac River in Colonial Beach, Virginia, and Florida's east coast.

USA TODAY bestselling author **Patricia Davids** was born in Kansas. After forty years as a NICU nurse, Pat switched careers to become an inspirational writer. She now enjoys laid-back life on a Kansas farm, spending time with her family and playing with her dog, Sugar, who thinks fetch should be a twenty-four-hour-a-day game. When not throwing a ball, Pat is happily dreaming up new stories where love and faith conquer all. Contact her at pat@patriciadavids.com.

#1 *New York Times* Bestselling Author

SHERRYL WOODS

HONOR

**HARLEQUIN
BESTSELLING
AUTHOR
COLLECTION**

**HARLEQUIN®
BESTSELLING
AUTHOR
COLLECTION**

Recycling programs
for this product may
not exist in your area.

ISBN-13: 978-1-335-49838-0

Honor
First published in 1992. This edition published in 2023.
Copyright © 1992 by Sherryl Woods

The Shepherd's Bride
First published in 2014. This edition published in 2023.
Copyright © 2014 by Patricia MacDonald

For questions and comments about the quality of this book,
please contact us at CustomerService@Harlequin.com.

Harlequin Enterprises ULC
22 Adelaide St. West, 41st Floor
Toronto, Ontario M5H 4E3, Canada
www.Harlequin.com

Printed in U.S.A.

CONTENTS

HONOR

Sherryl Woods

Prologue

Even at forty-eight Lacey Grainger Halloran was still one hell of a woman, her husband thought with pride and a sense of wonder as he watched her begin the long walk down the carpeted aisle of Whitehall Episcopal Church. She had never looked more stunning or more confident.

More than twenty-five years of marriage, Kevin Halloran thought. So many troubled times, shared and apart. Yet it felt as if they were starting out fresh, as if this were the very first ceremony in which they would make a commitment for life.

Last time, like so many of their friends in the mid-sixties, Kevin and Lacey had skipped the traditional prayer book, church wedding in favor of a hastily arranged outdoor ceremony atop a country hill alight with the colors of spring. Kevin's family, firmly en-

trenched in tradition, had been appalled. Throughout the brief service, with its unorthodox but heartfelt
vows, their faces had radiated disapproval. But at least
they had come.

Though Lacey had sworn it didn't matter, Kevin
had known that deep down she had feared his family
would stay away, publicly writing off the match as a
bad one. It had nearly broken his heart to see the relief
and hope in her eyes when she'd seen his parents join
the small gathering on that sunny hillside.

Today's ceremony, a renewal of their vows, was
every bit as significant as that first wedding day. His
father and his son stood next to him, each nervously
awaiting their own brides.

Kevin had been astonished to discover that long
ago his father had been deeply in love with a woman
whose name Kevin had never even heard mentioned.
Now, just a few years after his own mother's death, that
woman—Elizabeth Forsythe Newton—had reappeared
in his father's life. Today they would be wed as his
father had longed for them to be all those years ago.

With a sense of amazement, Kevin watched the
transformation of his father's stern face as his bride
began the walk down the aisle. After two long years
of sorrow and loneliness, Brandon Halloran looked
downright invigorated by life. His damn-the-world,
full-steam-ahead energy was back, and everyone was
having difficulty keeping up with him.

Something warm stole through Kevin as he realized that it was possible for love to endure through so
many years of separation.

Filled anew with a surprising sense of hope, Kevin

glanced at his son and caught the expression of open adoration in Jason's eyes as he waited for his wife to join him to renew their own vows. Within weeks Jason and Dana would be blessed with a child of their own—a boy if Kevin knew anything at all about the Halloran genes. The cycle would begin again.

All in all, it was quite a day for the Hallorans, Kevin thought as he took his wife's slender hand in his. Lacey was trembling, he realized with a faint sense of amazement. He gazed into her eyes, blue and bright with unshed tears, and realized anew how very deeply he cared for her and how devastated and lost he would have been had they not found their way back to each other.

Squeezing Lacey's hand for reassurance, Kevin began to speak. With his voice choked with emotion, he tried to find the words to tell her exactly what she meant to him, to express the strength he found in their marriage, had always found in her love. They were words he hadn't said nearly enough through the years, words he had almost lost the chance to say at all.

"Lacey, from the day I first saw you back in the fifth grade, there has been no one like you in my life. You have been my friend, my confidante, my lover and my wife. I am a better man for knowing you and loving you. I beg your forgiveness for the times I have forgotten that, for the times when I have lost sight of all that truly matters."

The memory of how hard his gentle Lacey had fought to save their relationship brought a smile to his lips. "I can't begin to find the words to tell you how much I admire the courage it took to shake up our marriage in the hope that we would find something even better. From now on I promise you days that will only get better with each passing year."

As a tear spilled down her cheek, he gently brushed it away, his own fingers trembling. Then he said in a voice that finally held steady, "I, Kevin, take thee, Lacey, a woman who has stood by me through hard times and good, who has provided love and under-standing, I take thee again to be my wedded wife. For the blessing of your undying love, I thank God. For the joy of our family, I thank you. And I promise to honor you and all that you have meant to me all the rest of my days."

As the solemn vows echoed in the old Boston church, his thoughts drifted back over those dark and lonely days when his own stupidity had almost cost him the most important thing in his life.

Chapter 1

"Dad, you're killing yourself."

Kevin Halloran tore his gaze away from the bleak Halloran Industries financial report he'd been working on for the past twelve hours and met his son's troubled eyes. "Jason, I am not having this discussion. Go home. It's after eight. Dana will be wondering where you are."

To Kevin's deep regret, his son defiantly removed his jacket and loosened his tie with the obvious intention of settling in for a lengthy chat. Kevin had a hunch they were headed over the same familiar turf. The sorry state of his marriage had been the primary topic of conversation for two weeks now. His son and his father couldn't seem to stop their meddling no matter how rudely he tried to cut them off.

Kevin reached for a cigarette, then caught Jason's

disapproving frown as his son eyed the mound of butts already overflowing the ashtray. Kevin drew his hand back and settled for another sip of cold, bitter coffee. The acid pitched in his stomach.

"Dana knows exactly where I am," Jason said, complacently ignoring his father's dismissal. "She sent me. We're both worried about you, Dad. You look like hell. You're smoking too much. You're living on caffeine. I doubt you're getting enough sleep. Face it, you haven't been yourself since Mother moved out of the house."

The cold knot that formed in Kevin's stomach every time he thought about home and Lacey came back with a savagery that stunned him.

"I don't want to talk about your mother," he countered bluntly and reached for the cigarette, after all. When it was lit and he'd drawn the smoke deep into his lungs, he deliberately forced his attention back to the stack of work on his desk.

If he buried himself in reports and figures, maybe, just maybe, Jason would give up and go away. More importantly, maybe he could forget the emptiness Lacey's leaving had created inside him, the echoing silence that greeted him each night when he returned home.

In theory it should have worked, but Kevin had discovered that theories and paperwork didn't mean a damn thing in the middle of another god-awful, lonely, silent night. That didn't mean he was willing to talk, not to Jason. Lacey had been the only person in his life to whom he could open up. She had had the most amazing knack for listening without making judgments.

Jason obviously thought that his cool, analytical

approach would help, but in Kevin's experience, talking about emotions never accomplished a thing. To his way of thinking, airing problems only exposed a man's weaknesses right at a time when he needed every shred of pride he had left.

Besides that, dissecting things a man couldn't change only made the hurt worse, Kevin thought, still careful to avoid Jason's increasingly impatient gaze. There were even times, in the dark, lonely hours of the night, when the pain became a blind rage, when he wanted to strike out, to break things. The only thing stopping him was the certain knowledge that he had only himself to blame for the way things were between him and Lacey. She'd made that clear enough before she'd gone.

"*I* want to talk," Jason said, still on the same relentless track despite his father's obvious unwillingness to open up.

His tone was deceptively mild. Kevin recognized the stubborn streak his son had inherited from a long line of mule-headed Halloran men. Even as Kevin glanced up, Jason was settling more comfortably into the chair opposite him, his jaw squared, his expression determined. He took Kevin's just-lit cigarette and deliberately ground it out, his hard look daring his father to challenge the action.

"Not once in all these months have you explained why Mother moved out," his son said.

"That's between your mother and me," Kevin responded stiffly, unwilling—unable—to say more. Then, because he needed desperately to know despite everything, he asked, "What has she told you?"

"About as much as you have," Jason admitted with obvious disgust at the continued parental secrecy. "Did you two make some sort of pact of silence, the way you always did when I was a kid?"

"We never did any such thing."

"Perhaps it wasn't a formal contract, drawn up by the Halloran legal staff, but it was a pact nonetheless. You never wanted me to guess that the two of you were quarreling. Instead, the house got quiet as a tomb for weeks on end." He shook his head. "It was awful."

Unable to bear his son's distraught expression, Kevin stood up, walked to the window and stared out at the Boston skyline in the distance. Lights were just now blinking on. Was one of them Lacey's? he wondered. What was she doing in that ridiculously cramped apartment of hers? How could she hope to find happiness there, when he'd given her everything a woman could possibly want and it hadn't been enough?

He sighed and turned back, just in time to hear Jason say, "When Dana's mad at me, she puts all her cards on the table, usually at the top of her lungs. There's not a chance in hell I won't know exactly what's on her mind. With the two of you, though, I don't know." He shrugged helplessly. "I think I'd have liked it better if you'd broken the china."

"And risked your grandfather's wrath?" Kevin retorted with a faint smile. "That china came over from England more than a century ago."

Jason didn't smile back at the weak attempt at humor. "I'm not interested in the china. I'm interested in what the hell happened to my parents' marriage."

Kevin sighed, a bone-deep weariness stealing

through him. "Son, if I knew that, maybe I could make it right."

When Jason started to probe more deeply, Kevin shook his head. "I will not talk about this," he warned with quiet finality. "Go home to your wife. She's expecting your baby. She needs you there."

"The baby's not due for another three months. I hardly think Dana's desperate for me to get home and watch her as if she might break. Besides, every time she gets the least little bit queasy, so do I. We're running out of crackers."

"Then buy some and go home," Kevin said flatly.

This time it was Jason who sighed. "Okay, but if you need to talk, Dad…"

Kevin might not be able to explain what had happened, or his own feelings, but he couldn't ignore the pain and confusion in Jason's tone. He relented as much as he could. "I'll come looking for you, son. I promise."

Finally, after several endless minutes, Jason nodded, his expression resigned. He stood in the doorway and said, "If you want her back, Dad, you're going to have to fight for her."

"I know that." What he didn't say was that he wasn't at all sure he had the energy left for the battle.

Jason left finally, shutting the office door very quietly behind him.

That careful exit, more than anything, told Kevin just how upset his son was. Jason slammed doors. From the time he'd been able to walk, he'd raced through life, hitting doors at full tilt, letting them crash behind him. The quiet closing of Kevin's door with its implied hint of defeat was just one more sign that both of their worlds had suddenly gone topsy-turvy.

When Jason had gone, Kevin leaned back in his chair and wondered why it had taken a crisis of this magnitude to begin to open the lines of communication with his son. If nothing else came from this damnable separation, at least perhaps he would have the new bond that had formed over the last few months between him and Jason.

After years of distance and a sense that they never connected, Kevin had been stunned to realize that his son truly did love him. It had been equally surprising to realize that Jason had matured so much. Kevin gave Dana a lot of credit for that. She had given Jason a sense of direction. Besides that, his daughter-in-law was every bit as determined as Lacey had once been to see that the Halloran family ties remained close-knit.

Jason, Dana, even Kevin's father used every opportunity to try to push him into reconciling with his wife. Right now, though, Kevin wasn't up to explaining that the choice wasn't his. He couldn't cope with explanations, period. The fact of the matter was that he couldn't cope with anything these days. There was an aching, leaden sensation in the middle of his chest that never seemed to go away.

If Jason didn't understand his separation from Lacey, it was a thousand times worse for him. How could a love that had begun in the fifth grade, a marriage that had lasted over twenty-five years, fall apart in a split second?

The day a year earlier when Lacey had moved out of their huge house and into a tiny apartment of her own, Kevin had been stunned. Sure, they'd had a few fights. She couldn't seem to understand the demands of running a business like Halloran Industries. In her own quiet way she had badgered him to let up, to spend more time with her, to think of his health.

The next thing he knew, Lacey was forcing his hand, trying to recapture a time long ago, a time when, as he saw it now, he'd avoided responsibility, rather than accepting it. Her harsh all-or-nothing ultimatum— Halloran Industries or a marriage—had taken him by surprise. His inability to make the decision she'd demanded had been answer enough, it seemed. In her view, with his silence, he had chosen the generations-old family textile business over her.

Lacey had made good on her threat, too. Kevin didn't have to understand her decision to know that it was final. Lacey appeared easygoing and flexible, but beneath that gentle facade was a stubborn streak a mile wide. He'd recognized it the first time he'd seen the defiant lift of her chin, despite the sheen of tears in her eleven-year-old eyes. That fierce determination, that willingness to spit in the eye of her own fears had made her a perfect match for a Halloran.

It was up to Lacey to explain her moving out to Jason, though. Kevin wasn't about to try. He would never be able to hide his anger or this raw, gut-wrenching feeling of utter helplessness that was totally alien to him. He might understand the most intricate details of business administration, but over the past year he'd come to realize he didn't know a damn thing about women, not even the one woman who'd captured his heart so very long ago.

And, to his profound regret given the circumstances, the woman who held it still.

"Mom, I just don't get it. What happened? Why did you move out? I thought you'd go back long ago. Haven't you made your point yet?"

How many times was Jason going to ask her that? Lacey Halloran wondered. How many times would she have to give the same stupid, evasive answer because she couldn't bear to get into the truth?

"Jason, that is between your father and me," she said, her tone gentle as she busied herself repotting a bright red geranium to keep her son from seeing how her hands shook. It wouldn't do at all for him to see how much she feared the empty days ahead, an emptiness she had brought on herself.

Lacey couldn't blame Jason for being confused. She'd felt that way herself for months now, maybe even years. She'd felt her relationship with Kevin sliding not just into a rut, but into some deep, dark ravine. Finally she couldn't take it any longer, couldn't bury the memories of the dear, rebellious young man who'd set himself up as her protector when they'd been barely eleven.

In those days Kevin had been noble and brave and adventurous. They'd roared through the sixties with spirit and love and idealism. Even now she wasn't sure exactly when he'd started to change or when she'd first noticed the shift in priorities, the abandonment of values they'd once shared.

Maybe it was when he'd caved in to pressure from his father to join Halloran Industries. Brandon had used every trick in the book to lure his son into taking his rightful place in the family business. He'd finally played on Kevin's guilt, convincing him that he was doing a disservice to his wife and son by not giving them everything they deserved. None of Lacey's protests had been able to allay Kevin's fear that his father was right.

Maybe it was after that, when he'd ignored her open distaste and bought that huge, monstrous house that was more like a mausoleum than a home. Kevin had wanted a place suitable for entertaining business associates, a palace for her, he'd said. Brandon's realtor had taken them to showcases. Ironically, Kevin had chosen the one most similar to the lonely status symbol of a house in which he'd been raised himself.

There were other symptoms of the chasm widening between them. Determined to prove himself, to exceed Brandon's high expectations, he'd begun spending longer and longer hours at the office. Lacey had even suspected, but never proven, that he was having an affair.

There were desperate times when she even pinpointed something as silly and unimportant as the moment when he'd traded folk songs and rock for classical music as an indication of all that was going wrong with their marriage.

Somewhere along the way, though, the life she'd anticipated with Kevin had changed. She had never expected to be caught up in a whirlwind of social, business and charitable demands. She had never expected to see Kevin's decency and strength lost to ambition.

As CEO of Halloran Industries, Kevin had become a respected member of Boston's elite establishment. But ideals they had once cherished, dreams they had worked for together, had been lost. Worst of all, Kevin seemed blind to the significance of the changes and the destruction of all they once held dear.

In the heat of that last, bitter argument, he had accused her of not keeping pace, of being unwilling to change, unable to accept the reality of getting ahead in a world that respected nothing so much as success.

If that was a flaw, so be it, Lacey thought, angrily snapping off a dead geranium leaf. What was so terrible about wanting to help others? Wanting to make a home for her family?

Wanting a husband to stop killing himself?

She sighed. Was there anything more important than love and family and commitment? It might be old-fashioned, but dammit she would fight to her dying breath to preserve those simple ideals, to get her husband to wake up before it was too late. She wanted that special, wonderful man she'd loved for so terribly long back again.

Even so, even though it had broken her heart to watch his rare, generous spirit wither and die, she might have forced herself to accept the changes if only Kevin had seemed happy. In lives otherwise rich with love, she might have accepted that no one ever stayed the same, if only his complexion hadn't taken on that deathly pallor.

Instead of being happy and energetic, he'd merely seemed driven. The effect on his health was devastating. He'd already suffered one heart attack, a mild one that the doctor described as a warning.

Rather than modifying his life-style, though, Kevin had become even more obsessed. They had argued again and again. Lacey had pleaded with him to stop killing himself, for him to at least try to make her see why he felt so driven. His response had been to avoid the arguments by spending even longer hours at the office. There had been one last explosive argument and then she had gone, unable to bear even one more day of watching him die before her eyes, one more lonely evening waiting for a call from some hospital emergency room.

Lacey couldn't say all that to Jason, though. He hadn't even been married an entire year yet himself. How could a mother explain the tarnish that eventually robbed love of its shine to a man for whom it still held a shimmering beauty? Instead she deliberately asked about Dana and watched his expression soften, heard the warmth steal back into his voice, replacing the despair that had been evident only moments before.

"Dana's glowing," he said. "She considers this pregnancy the grandest adventure in her life. Quite a statement given her decision to raise her brother on her own."

Lacey chuckled. "It certainly is an adventure. You're both happy about it, then? I wondered. It seemed a little soon. You have so many adjustments to make, especially with her brother living with you."

"To my astonishment, Sammy is no trouble at all. He spends every spare second with Granddad. The other night I found them crawling around under one of the looms at the plant. Granddad was trying to explain how to get a white-on-white pattern on damask."

"Does Sammy even know what damask is?" Lacey asked, trying to imagine the sixteen-year-old hellraiser with the outrageous haircut being familiar with fine fabrics.

"Actually that's how the subject came up in the first place, as I understand it. Sammy wanted to use Granddad's tablecloth for a ghost costume for some play."

The image brought a smile to her lips. "I can just imagine Brandon's reaction to that."

Jason shook his head. "No, you can't. He actually got the scissors for him. But before he'd let Sammy ruin the tablecloth, he insisted on showing him how it was made. Off they went to the plant, leaving dinner still sitting on the table. Needless to say, Sammy changed his mind once he saw that the cloth wasn't some old rag Granddad had gotten from a discount store."

Lacey tapped the soil gently around the geranium's roots, then put the pot aside and reached for another. The rich scent of earth and the pungent aroma of the flowers had begun to work their soothing magic. She could almost forget her life was no longer complete.

"I saw Dad last night," Jason said, all the laughter gone from his voice, replaced by a cautious note.

Lacey drew in a deep breath. Her hands stilled. The announcement brought a shuddering end to her tranquility. "How is he?" she asked finally.

"Terrible, though he won't admit it. Mom, you still love him. I can see that. And he's still crazy about you. How long are the two of you going to let this go on?"

"As long as it takes."

"As long as it takes to do what?" Jason demanded, his tone filled with frustration. "Do either of you have the faintest idea why you're apart?"

"We're apart because that's the way it has to be."

Before she could stop him, Jason crushed the bright red petals of a geranium between his fingers. She wasn't even sure he was aware of what he'd done until he glanced down. Then he impatiently tossed the mangled bloom aside.

"That doesn't make a damned bit of sense," he said, raking his fingers through blond hair the same shade his father's had been at that age.

"Stop." Lacey put her hand over his.

"Are you trying to find yourself? Is that what this is? Some crazy mid-life crisis?"

Lacey drew in a deep breath. "I couldn't watch it anymore," she admitted quietly, giving in to Jason's desperate need to understand something that was almost beyond explaining. "I couldn't sit by and watch your father destroy his health. I was dying bit by bit, right along with him. I tried everything I knew, but nothing worked."

Her son stared at her, his eyes filled with astonishment. "Are you saying that you wanted to shock him into letting up?"

Tears misted in her eyes. She blinked them away. "I hoped that our marriage would matter enough, that *I* would matter enough, to make him stop killing himself."

"But you *are* the only thing that matters to him."

She shook her head. "Not anymore. Not enough. Have you seen any signs that he's changing? Admit it, since I left, he's only working harder."

"Because he has no reason to go home. Don't you see? You've created a catch-22."

"So what should I do? Go home and watch him die? Give him permission to do it? I won't do that, Jason. I can't."

"Can't you talk about it? Compromise?"

"Not about this."

Jason ran his fingers through his hair again in the gesture he'd picked up from his wife. "Damn! What an awful mess."

"I'm sorry. I'm sorry you're caught in the middle. I would give anything for that not to be."

"I love you both. I want to see you happy again, the way you used to be."

Lacey's lips curved into a rueful smile. "No one wants that any more than I do. I promise you that."

They were still talking when the phone rang. Lacey picked it up and heard a cool, impersonal voice inform her that Kevin Halloran had just been brought into the hospital. "He's in the cardiac intensive care unit. He wanted you to know."

"Oh, God," she whispered softly, sinking into a chair, her own heart pounding.

"Mom, what is it? Is it Granddad? Dad?"

"Your father," she said, taking his hand, needing his strength to ask into the phone, "How is he? Will he make it?"

"His condition is critical."

Leaving had accomplished nothing, Lacey thought bitterly. Nothing.

Then, with a rush of panic, she tried to bring herself to face the very real possibility of losing forever the man she had loved nearly her whole life.

Chapter 2

The ten-mile ride across town to the hospital was the longest Lacey had ever taken, even though Jason drove like a maniac. His expression was grim, and she was certain she'd detected accusation in his eyes from the moment she'd told him about his father's heart attack. Whatever he thought, it was no worse than what she was mentally telling herself. She felt as if the guilt were smothering her.

The deep sadness, the sense of magic lost that had pervaded her entire being for so long had vanished in the brief seconds of that phone call, replaced by a gut-wrenching fear. Kevin couldn't die, not like this, not with so very much between them unresolved.

"It's my fault," she said when she could stand the silence no longer. "I moved out. Maybe if I'd stayed…"

But she knew deep down it wouldn't have mattered. Kevin had made up his mind to tempt fate.

And he'd lost. Dear God, she prayed, don't let him pay with his life. Make this just one more warning. Give him one more chance.

Jason glanced her way. "He's going to be okay, Mother. Stop beating yourself up over this. Casting blame isn't going to do Dad any good. Did the hospital call Granddad?"

She realized she hadn't asked, that she had no idea where Kevin had been when he'd had the heart attack or even how he'd gotten to the hospital. "I don't know. I don't know any more than what I've told you."

"Maybe Granddad was with him. Knowing the two of them, they were probably still at the office."

Jason seemed to take comfort from the possibility that Brandon had been with Kevin, that he might even now be with him. Lacey was less certain how she felt about seeing her father-in-law. She dreaded another confrontation. They'd already had one monumental set-to over her decision to move out.

Brandon had ranted and raved, even questioned her sanity. She knew it killed him that he couldn't manipulate them all like puppets on a string. She wasn't sure she could stand another meeting like that, especially tonight.

The bottom line, though, was that in his own way Brandon loved Kevin every bit as much as she did and wanted what was best for him. Unfortunately, they tended to differ on what that was.

Despite their differences, he had every right to be at Kevin's side. Knowing Brandon, though, he would

figure he had more of a right to be there than she did.
Maybe that was true. She didn't know anymore.

"It's my fault," she said again as Jason sped into the
parking lot by the emergency entrance and screeched
to a halt in the first space he could find.

"Stop it," Jason said impatiently, slamming the car
door and coming around to join her. "You did what
you thought you had to do. I may not agree with your
methods, but I know you did it out of love."

"Maybe I did it out of selfishness," she countered
and bit back a sob as guilt clogged her throat. "Maybe
I was only thinking of my needs, not his."

"You don't have a selfish bone in your body," Jason
said, taking her by the shoulders and giving her a gentle shake. He scanned her face. "Are you going to be
okay?"

Lacey drew in a deep breath. She slowly, con-
sciously pulled herself together and gave him a trem-
ulous smile. "I'm not the one in intensive care. I'll be
fine." She took his hand. "Let's go see your father."

Upstairs they found Brandon Halloran pacing the
long, empty corridor outside of cardiac intensive care.
Not even he could bluster his way past the restricted
visiting hours posted on the door. Pale and shaken,
his expression was bleak as he waited for word on his
son's condition.

Jason put an arm around his grandfather's shoulders
and steered him toward the waiting room, but Lacey
held back, uncertain of Brandon's mood.

Years ago, before she and Kevin had even married,
they had been the closest thing to enemies. Brandon
had blamed her for so much that was wrong with his

relationship with his son. Since then they'd forged a cautious friendship, which appeared to have splintered into a million pieces because she'd abandoned his beloved and only son.

Hesitant, Lacey stood in the doorway of the waiting room until Brandon held out his hand. Then she moved quickly, anxious for news, anxious for a little of Brandon's towering, unshakable strength. Clasping his firm but icy hand between her own, she asked, "How is he? What have they told you?"

"Not a damned thing," he grumbled. "As much money as I give to this place, you'd think I could get a straight answer out of someone."

"What happened?"

A shadow seemed to pass over his eyes as he remembered. "Found him at his desk, all slumped over. Thought for a minute he might be dead. The guard got the paramedics there and we brought him here."

"Was he conscious?" Lacey asked.

"Part of the time. Said he wanted to see you. I don't pretend to understand what's been wrong between the two of you, but I want you to put it aside for now," he said, giving her a warning look that Lacey recognized from a dozen different occasions.

Brandon Halloran had strong opinions on family loyalty and just about everything else. He wasn't afraid to voice them. He had the confidence of a man who'd done well with his life and knew it. In fact, he thought the world would be a whole lot better if everyone would just accept the wisdom of his plans for them. It had galled the daylights out of him that Lacey and

Kevin had dared to go their own way, at least in the beginning.

As much as she might have resented it once, Lacey found there was something almost comforting about the familiarity of his response to this crisis. That strength of purpose, that single-minded clarity of vision was welcome tonight in a way it never had been before. If there was any way in hell Brandon Halloran could buy salvation for his son, he would do it.

"I do love him," she said gently. "That's never been the problem."

Brandon scowled at her. "Well, I'll be damned if I know what is. I listened to all that double-talk you gave me months ago, chewed it over in my head every second since then and, by God, I still can't make a bit of sense of it. You got some sort of complaint about the life-style he gave you?"

"No," she whispered, stung by the harsh accusation. "Not the way you mean."

"I didn't notice you turning down the house, that fancy sports car."

Little did he know how she had fought both, Lacey thought but refused to say. Kevin had insisted. Brandon would never believe that, though. Even at the best of times in Brandon and Lacey's tenuous relationship, she'd been very much aware that he expected the worst of her, that he didn't entirely understand that someone could be motivated by something other than money and status, especially someone who'd brought nothing more than the strength of her love to a marriage.

"What then?" he demanded roughly. "Make me see

why a woman would walk out on a man who's provided her with everything money could buy."

"I only wanted my husband back," she told him, but she could see that Brandon couldn't fathom what she meant. He started to speak, but Jason cut him off.

"Granddad," he said, "this isn't the time."

The fight seemed to drain out of Brandon as quickly as it had stirred. "No. No, it's not." It was the closest he was likely to come to an apology. He asked Jason, "You called Dana yet?"

Jason shook his head. "I don't want to upset her."

"She'd want to be here," Lacey told him. "Go call. We'll be okay."

With Jason gone, the look she and Brandon exchanged was measuring. She suspected he was trying every bit as hard as she was to avoid starting another pointless argument. But the only way around it was small talk or silence. She didn't have the stomach for small talk. Neither, she suspected, did he.

"Damn, I hate this waiting," he said finally. "You want some coffee or something?"

Lacey shook her head. "Nothing."

"How do you suppose he ended up in a fix like this? He's a young man yet."

"It's not the first time," she reminded him. "If anything, he took worse care of himself after the first attack."

"And I suppose you're blaming that on me."

"Casting blame won't help," she said, repeating what Jason had said to try to comfort her. It didn't work on Brandon, either. He took up his impatient pacing again.

If someone didn't come out and talk to them soon, Brandon was likely to call up the hospital board's president and demand a change in administration, she thought. He'd wave another endowment under the president's nose for effect. Waiting was always hardest on a man who was used to making things happen.

Lacey hated it, too, because it gave her time to think, time to remember the way it had once been between her and Kevin, back at the very beginning.

It had been her first day at a new school. Worse, it was the middle of the year. Friendships had been made and she was an outsider. She was eleven years old, tall, skinny, shy and awkward.

She had been so sure that the other kids would make fun of her, that they would see that the clothes she wore were hand-me-downs, that her hair had been clipped impatiently by her mother, rather than in some fancy salon. She was terrified that they would discover that her last classmates had labeled her a brain and left her out of anything fun.

It had taken every ounce of bravery she'd possessed to slip into the classroom and scurry to a seat in the back, hoping no one would notice her. Then the teacher had singled her out, introduced her as a newcomer and made her move right smack to the middle of a room in which students had been seated in alphabetical order. She'd felt all those inquisitive, judgmental eyes on her and she'd wanted to cry.

She'd rushed too fast, trying to slide into her assigned seat without anyone taking further notice of her. Instead, she'd spilled her books in the process and had to listen to the taunting laughter that had made her feel more an outsider than ever. She'd kept her chin up, but hadn't been able to stop the tears from filling her eyes. She'd desperately tried to blink them away before anyone saw.

But a boy with tousled golden hair and a smile that revealed a chipped front tooth had seen. He had knelt down, picked up the books and placed them on her desk.

"Thank you, Kevin," Mrs. Niles had said, while the other boys in the room had made wisecracks about his gallantry.

Lacey had felt awful, knowing that he'd been embarrassed in front of his friends just for coming to her rescue. She had given him a hesitant smile and felt her eleven-year-old heart tumble at the impish, unworried grin he shot her in return.

From that moment on Kevin Halloran had been her protector, her knight in shining armor. He'd withstood a lot of teasing for befriending her. He'd fought a lot of playground battles on her behalf, had chosen her for teams when others wouldn't, had badgered her to try out for cheerleading when she'd known she wasn't pretty enough or popular enough to make it. To her amazement, he'd been right. She had cheered loudest and longest when he'd raced for the goal line.

Later, he'd ignored a lot of wealthy, admiring teenaged girls to date her, apparently preferring their quiet, serious talks to the adolescent wiles of her peers.

Then he'd dared to fall in love with her.

Brandon Halloran had thrown one of his inimitable fits about the engagement. He'd declared that no son of his was going to marry some little nobody who was only after his money. He'd vowed to do everything in his power to see that they split up. In the lowest moment of her life, he had offered her a bribe. When that hadn't worked, he'd sent Kevin off to college at Stanford, hoping that distance would accomplish what his ranting and threats had not.

None of it had dimmed Kevin and Lacey's determination or their love. Sometimes it astonished Lacey that at that age they had stood firm against the power of Brandon's opposition. In anyone else it might have been sheer stubbornness, but with Kevin it had been a deeply ingrained conviction that Lacey brought something into his life that he could never hope to find with another woman. At least that's what he'd told her when he'd insisted that they would get married with or without his parents' approval. He'd defiantly exchanged his class ring for a tiny chip of a diamond, rather than use parental funds for something splashier.

Where had that steadfast sense of commitment gone? The love hadn't died. As she sat in a corner of the cold, dimly lit hospital waiting room, terrified of losing him forever this time, Lacey could admit that much. She also knew that they couldn't go on as they had been, drifting farther and farther apart with each day that passed, fighting bitterly at every turn.

Jason returned just as Dr. Lincoln Westlake came out of the cardiac unit. Lacey froze at the sight of his grim expression. Even Brandon looked uncertain. It was Jason who finally dared to ask how Kevin was doing.

"I won't lie to you. He's in pretty bad shape. If I had to guess, I'd say he didn't take that last attack seriously and did everything in his power to ensure he'd have another one."

Brandon gazed at him in astonishment. "Are you saying he tried to bring this on?"

"In a way."

"That's absurd. Why that would be the next best thing to suicide."

"Mr. Halloran, your son is a bright man. He knew the risks and he did nothing to minimize them." He glanced at Lacey, and his tone gentled. "Did he?"

She sighed. The truth was that he'd even canceled half a dozen follow-up appointments with the doctor. She'd finally given up trying to make them.

"No. Nothing," she admitted. Damn him, she said to herself. Damn Kevin Halloran for trying to play God with his own life!

"Can I see him?" she asked, when she could keep her voice steady.

"For five minutes. He's resting now and I don't want you to wake him. If he's to have any chance at all, he needs to stay as quiet as possible."

Lacey nodded. "Thanks, Linc. If anyone can pull him through this, I know you can."

"I'm going to do my damnedest. If he'll give me a little help, we might have a chance. You come on in, when you're ready."

As he walked away, Lacey started toward the cardiac unit after him. Brandon stepped into her path. "Remember what the doctor said, girl. Don't you go upsetting him!"

"Granddad!" Jason warned.

Lacey put her hand on her son's arm. "It's okay,"

She met Brandon's gaze evenly and saw the worry and exhaustion in his eyes. "I'll tell him that you're here and that you're praying for him."

Brandon nodded, then sighed heavily and sank into one of the cushioned chairs. He motioned for Jason to sit next to him, then looked up at her. "You tell him we're all praying for him," he said.

Lacey nodded. She pressed the button that allowed the automatic doors to the unit to swish silently open, then stepped into a high-tech wonderland that was both magnificent and frightening.

Like the spokes of a wheel, small, softly lit rooms surrounded a central desk banked with monitors. Hushed voices competed with beeping equipment and the steady gurgle of oxygen.

She spotted Linc through one of the doorways, a chart in his hand, his troubled gaze riveted on the bed. Drawing in a deep breath, she walked to the doorway. Linc gave her a reassuring smile and motioned her in. Her steps were halting, but she finally approached the bed.

It took every last ounce of her courage to glance past the tangle of wires, IV tubes and oxygen to her husband.

Against the startling white of the pillow, Kevin's handsome, angular face had a grayish cast. His golden hair, shot now with silver, was mussed, its impeccable cut wasted. Without the armor of his custom-tailored suit, his designer shirt and silk tie, he looked vulnerable, every inch a mortal, rather than the invincible hero she'd always thought him to be.

He was so terribly still, she thought, fighting panic.

The man who had always seemed so alive, so filled
with energy looked like a shadow, quiet and lifeless.
Her gaze shifted desperately to a monitor and fixed
on the steady rhythm. She had no idea what the up-
and-down movement of the lines meant except that
they were proof her husband was still clinging to life.

Lacey stepped closer and took Kevin's one free
hand, curving her fingers around his, trying to share
her warmth with him. Her own heart lurched anew
at his vulnerability, then filled to overflowing, first
with love, then with rage—at him and at her own im-
potence.

Damn you, Kevin, she thought. *You were always my
strength. I'm not sure I know how to be yours.*

She whispered, "Fight, Kevin. Dammit, you have to
live. You have a grandchild on the way. You have to be
here to teach him how to ride a bicycle, how to throw
a ball. You know I'm not good at things like that."

She closed her eyes and thought of all the plans
they'd made. She kept her voice low as she reminded
him, willed him to live to see them come true.

"Don't you remember how we always looked forward to spoiling our grandchildren? There were so
many things we were going to do. We were going to
spend long, lazy days walking on the beach. We were
going to read Shakespeare's sonnets and visit Walden
Pond. Don't you dare make me do those things alone."

She felt Linc's hand on her shoulder. "That's enough
for now," he said gently. "Let him rest."

"Not yet," she pleaded, terrified Kevin would slip
away if she weren't there to hold on to him. "Another

minute, please. I won't say another word. Just let me stay."

Linc studied her silently, then nodded. He reached for a tissue and handed it to her. "Another minute," he agreed. "No more."

Lacey brushed away the tears she hadn't even realized were there until she had the tissue in her hand. Very much aware of her vow to remain silent, she tried bargaining in her mind with Kevin and then with God.

With her gaze riveted on her husband's face, she was aware of the first subtle blink of his lashes. Hope burst inside her. *That's it,* she cried in her heart. *You can do it, Kevin. I know you can.*

She knew her minute's reprieve was long over, but she didn't budge, waiting. It was a minute more and then another before Kevin's eyes finally blinked open and his gaze searched the room before finally focusing on her.

He managed a feeble smile that was only a faint shadow of the smile that had captivated her heart all those years ago. Even so, Lacey's heart filled to bursting and she felt tears of relief spill down her cheeks. In that instant she knew beyond a doubt that whatever it took, her husband was going to make it. He would fight to live.

But the struggle to save their marriage was yet to come.

Chapter 3

Lacey spent a long, uneasy night in the hospital waiting room, refusing to go home, desperately needing the few precious minutes every couple of hours that Linc allowed her to visit Kevin. She couldn't rid herself of that first sense of shock at his pallor, that initial horror that he might give up and slip away. Fear welled up inside her and abated only when she was by his side, willing her strength into him.

It had been nearly midnight when she had insisted that Jason take Dana home. She tried futilely to get Brandon to go with them. She was worried about the exhaustion that had shadowed his eyes. It reminded her all too vividly of those first grief-stricken weeks after he had lost his wife. For all that Brandon thought otherwise, he was not invincible.

Now, even though he was resting, he looked miscrably uncomfortable on the waiting room's too-short sofa. Lacey couldn't help thinking he would have been far better off in his own bed, in his own home with Mrs. Farnsworth, his housekeeper of thirty years, fussing over him. Still, she could understand his need to stay close to Kevin. Despite all she and Kevin had been through lately—all the bitterness and recriminations— she'd felt the same way.

Though Kevin hadn't awakened again through the long night, Lacey had been comforted simply by seeing him, by listening to the steady sound of the monitor tracking his heartbeat. Now, her throat dry, her stomach growling, she went off in search of tea and toast for herself and her father-in-law. If Brandon was going to insist on staying until the crisis passed, he would need all his strength.

Brandon was awake when Lacey returned, his cheek bearing the pattern of the sofa's piping, his clothes rumpled to a state that would have given his personal tailor palpitations. His eyes were brighter, though.

"Wondered where you'd gone," he said, accepting the cup of tea and ignoring the toast.

Even in this crisis he obviously had no intention of veering from his Spartan routine, Lacey thought with a mix of admiration and frustration. No wonder Kevin found his father such a tough act to follow.

"The doctor was by a minute ago," he said, interrupting her thoughts. "Can't believe that boy who used to climb trees in my backyard is a cardiologist these days. You suppose we ought to call in someone else?"

"Linc is one of the best and you know it."

"I suppose." He still looked doubtful.

"What did he say?"

"He thinks the worst is past. If Kevin stays stable another forty-eight hours, he'll consider moving him to a private room."

"And then what?" she asked, more to herself than Brandon.

His sharp gaze pinned her, the blue eyes glinting with a challenge. "Then we'll all do whatever it takes to help Kevin get his health back. All of us, you hear me?"

Lacey shook her head ruefully. An order like that was all too typical of her father-in-law. "Brandon, you can't bully us into a happy marriage."

He scowled and waved a finger under her nose. "Maybe not, but I can damn well see that you stick it out until this crisis is past."

Determined not to let him see how his threat disturbed her, Lacey returned his fierce expression.

"I will not argue with you about this," she said, carefully setting her tea on the table, then turning and walking away. Maybe it was the cowardly thing to do, but she couldn't see any other choice. The stress of the present on both of them was bad enough without battling over the future.

Outside the hospital, where winter hadn't quite given way to spring, a bed of purple crocuses were forcing their way through the still-icy earth. Lacey circled the grounds, holding her thin jacket closed against the damp breeze. The nip in the air cleared her head. She reminded herself that for all his blustering, Brandon couldn't control whatever decision she and Kevin reached about their marriage.

That decision, however, was far in the future. Brandon was right about one thing: the most important task now was to see that Kevin pulled through, that he took this latest warning more seriously than he had the last. She, more than anyone, wanted to see his masculine vitality restored, to see his pallor replaced by the healthy glow he'd once had.

She recalled the way he'd looked on their wedding day, his hair too long by his father's standards and tousled by a spring breeze. Used to seeing him in jeans and denim jackets, she'd thought he looked outrageously sexy and impressive in custom-tailored gray slacks and a blue dress shirt. She'd never guessed he owned clothes like that, though it stood to reason he would, given the family's business in textiles and their social standing. Usually, though, Kevin had rebelled at anything that hinted at his privileged background.

Most of all, Lacey recalled the expression of adoration on his face when she'd joined him on that blustery hillside. She had been so proud to become his wife, so touched by the tender vows he'd written himself. The emotions she had felt that day had only deepened with time. In the end she had loved him enough to leave, loved him enough to risk everything she cared about on the one slim chance that the desperate measure would force him to face the dangers of his present life-style.

Steeped in bittersweet memories, Lacey walked until it was time to go back in to see Kevin. She avoided the waiting room and Brandon, going instead straight to the cardiac unit.

She found Kevin with his eyes closed, his expres-

sion more peaceful. His jaw was shadowed by the first
faint stubble of a beard that under other circumstances
she might have found sexy because of its ruggedly sensual look. It would have reminded her of the rebellious,
bearded young man who'd marched for peace at a time
when his father was backing the Vietnam War. Today
it only reminded her of how sick he was, because that
shadow emphasized his pallor.

Seated by his bed, his hand in hers, Lacey's thoughts
began drifting back again. She was startled when she
heard him whisper her name.

"Lacey, is that you?"

"It's me, Kevin."

"You stayed," he said, gently squeezing her hand.
He sounded surprised.

"I stayed," she murmured, then added wearily, "but
dammit, Kevin Halloran, did you have to go to this
extreme just to get my attention?"

"You're here, aren't you?" he responded with that
familiar teasing note in his weakened voice. His tone
sobered. "What's Linc saying?"

"He says you're going to be all right, if you take
care of yourself and slow down."

A faint twinkle sparked in his eyes as his gaze met
hers. "Sounds like a fate worse than death."

"Don't you dare joke about it," she said furiously,
jerking her hand from his and poking it into her pocket.
"You scared the daylights out of all of us."

"Does Jason know? He came to see me at the office. Was it last night? Or before? I've lost track of
the time."

"It was two nights ago. He came to see me last night. He was with me when the hospital called."

"I'm afraid we had words."

"So he mentioned. He's frustrated and confused. He wants to help, but he doesn't know how."

Kevin sighed heavily. "That makes two of us."

Lacey bit back a retort that would match the faint edge of bitterness in his. If she started saying all that was on her mind—the whole jumble of fury and regrets— Linc would throw her out of intensive care.

"Lace?"

She met Kevin's troubled gaze. "Yes."

"You haven't forgiven me, have you?"

Faced with that unblinking, uncompromising stare, she could only shake her head. Instead of saying more, she deliberately changed the subject.

"Your father is outside. He's been here all night. In fact, he was driving the staff crazy because he had to wait to find out what was going on. I think he thought he ought to be in here telling them how to get the oxygen started."

Lacey waited for Kevin's familiar grinning response to tales of his father's efforts to manage life on his terms. Instead he winced. Lacey caught his effort to hide it and asked, "Are you in pain? Should I call the nurse?"

He grimaced. "I feel as if I've been run over by a truck."

"You look like it, too."

He reached for her hand again and when she finally placed it in his, he held on tight. "You were right, weren't you, Lace?"

"About what?"

"The work. I got my priorities all screwed up."

Lacey hadn't wanted to wring an admission from Kevin like this. Besides, the truth of the matter was that work was only part of the problem. Worse was the fact that the man who'd been her lover and best friend had too often seemed little more than a stranger.

"Now's not the time to talk about that," she told him.

"Can we talk about it, though?" he said, a sense of urgency in his voice.

"I always thought we could talk about anything," she replied softly, unable to hide the regret.

Blue eyes pinned her. "Until I shut you out," he said.

"I never said that."

"But it's the truth. I did. I'm sorry."

"Kevin—"

"I want us to start over. When I get out of here, I want to go away, take a long vacation and make things right between us again. I've missed you these past months, more than I can say." His voice faltered. "I just... I wanted you to know."

When she didn't say a word, couldn't squeeze a sound around the tears that clogged her throat, he prodded, "Lace, what do you think? Can we give it a try?"

A part of her thought it was too late. A part of her wanted to scream that this sudden change of attitude was too easy, a quick reaction to a health crisis that would pass as soon as he felt more like himself again.

And yet a part of her yearned for the way it used to be between them, wanted to believe it was possible to recapture the richness of their love.

"We'll talk about it when you're out of here," she said evasively.

Every bit as stubborn as his father, Kevin wouldn't let it go that easily. "You won't back out?"

Lacey drew in a deep breath and met his gaze evenly. "Of talking?" she asked. "No. I won't back out."

Kevin sighed then, obviously content with that much of a commitment. His eyes slowly drifted closed. He was still clinging to her hand, the touch apparently as much comfort for him as it was for her.

Kevin knew he was going to have a fight on his hands. He'd seen that much in Lacey's brilliant blue eyes, even when she'd reluctantly agreed to talk about the future. For some reason a fight didn't scare him anymore, not half as much as the thought of losing her forever.

Besides, nothing about his relationship with Lacey had ever been easy, not from the day he'd told his parents about her, anyway. Before that, they had spent long, quiet hours talking, sharing innermost thoughts that no boy dared to share with his buddies. Lacey's gentle smiles had brought sunshine into his life from the day they'd met.

More than simply his friend, she was his social conscience. She was the first person to make him realize that not everyone was as fortunate as he was, that he had an obligation to look beyond his own narrow world. From the first moment she had looked at him like a hero, he'd wanted to prove himself worthy of her.

Then Brandon had started throwing his weight

around, threatening Lacey, scowling at Kevin, swearing that the Halloran name would be sullied forever if he dared to marry a woman lacking the requisite Boston pedigree.

The truth of the matter was that Brandon had been afraid. He'd spent his whole life making plans for the day when Kevin would take his rightful place at Halloran Industries. But Kevin hadn't been interested. Brandon had blamed Lacey for that. He'd accused her of ruining his son's life, of forcing him to choose between her and his heritage.

Infuriated by the unjust accusation, Lacey had faced Brandon down, her shoulders squared, her chin jutting out, her eyes filled with fire. Only her hands, clenched at her sides, gave away her nervousness.

Her voice steady, she had said, "You're the one making him choose. I want Kevin to be happy. If Halloran Industries makes him happy, it's fine with me. But he says he wants to do something else with his life."

Kevin had never been more proud of her. Brandon had appeared stunned by her spunk and by her blunt words. He'd turned to Kevin. "Is what she's saying right? You don't want to work with me?"

"It's not that, Dad. You think of Halloran Industries as some sort of family dynasty. I need to prove myself. I don't want something that's handed to me."

"You're just one of those damned hippies. Just look at you. Your hair's too long. You dress like a bum."

"I dress like everyone else."

"Not like everyone else in *this* family," Brandon said in disgust. "You think we should be ashamed of having money. Well, dammit, I worked for every penny we have. So did your granddad, and you will, too."

"You're acting as if clothes are the only things that matter. What about having a social conscience? Doesn't that matter at all to you?"

Brandon slammed his fist down on his desk. "You act as if you invented it. You'll have to work for what you get at Halloran, same as I did. And you'll be expected to share with the community, the same way I have, the way your granddad did."

"It won't be the same and you know it. You think writing a check covers you for all eternity. What about fighting for what's right, fighting to make a difference? That's what I care about. That's what I want to do with my life. I just can't see myself making fancy fabrics for the wealthy when people are going hungry."

"And what about the people who have food on their tables every night because we provide them with jobs? You think that doesn't count for anything?"

Kevin had been at a loss to argue that point. Somehow he'd been so certain back then that he could find ways to make his life count, to better things for thousands, rather than the mere hundred or so employed by Halloran Industries.

Lacey had stood by him when he'd walked away from the Halloran money, turned his back on his family. As he remembered, he thought perhaps those were the best years of their lives. They had struggled. At times they hadn't had two nickels to rub together, but it had been okay because they'd had dreams and they'd had each other.

They'd worked side by side to help people who

didn't have nearly as much, people who didn't believe in themselves.

Educated in business and drawn by an idealistic notion of making the world a better place, Kevin had applied his skills in a series of low-paying and ofttimes unrewarding public service jobs. For several years he found the sacrifices he made worthwhile. He was filled with satisfaction and hope. He'd never once been tempted to touch his trust fund for himself.

Then he'd realized that for every instance in which he made a difference, there were a dozen more about which he could do nothing. Increasingly frustrated after nearly fifteen years of struggling, he was finally ready to listen when his father pressed him yet again about joining Halloran Industries.

It hadn't been difficult for Kevin to justify his eventual acceptance of the offer. Perhaps from a position of power, he would be able to make the changes in society that up to now had eluded him. And, as Brandon pointed out with distressing accuracy, his beautiful Lacey and his wonderful son did not deserve to live like paupers just so Kevin could make some obviously misguided political statement.

Like so many other idealistic children of the sixties, he figured he had finally grown up.

Kevin also recognized that Brandon's request was his awkward way of apologizing for misjudging Lacey, his way of making amends for years lost. Whether Brandon had made the gesture for himself or for Kevin's mother, Kevin felt he owed it to his father and to his own family to try to make it work. Lacey had been elated by the reconciliation, if not by the decision to join Halloran Industries.

Kevin had joined the company more than a decade ago and there had been no regrets on his part, not at first, anyway. He threw himself into the job the only way he knew how—heart and soul. Only now, with his marriage and his very life at stake, was he beginning to understand what Lacey had been saying all along, that the cost might have been too high.

When he'd awakened earlier to find Lacey standing beside his hospital bed, he'd been reminded of those early days. He'd seen the familiar tenderness and compassion in her eyes. He'd detected the faint trace of fear that had reminded him of the scared girl who'd stolen his heart when he'd been a mere boy.

He had wanted more than anything to tell her everything would be all right as he had so often in years past. But for the first time in his life, he wasn't so sure he could rectify things. He just knew he had to try, that the vows he'd taken nearly thirty years ago still meant something to him.

Kevin could only pray that they still meant something to Lacey, as well.

Chapter 4

Lacey heard the phone ringing through a bone-deep haze of exhaustion. The shrill sound brought her instantly awake.

Kevin! Something had happened to Kevin, she thought as she fumbled frantically for the phone, her heart hammering.

"Yes, hello," she said, her voice still scratchy with sleep.

"Lacey, it's Dana. I'm sorry if I woke you."

Lacey tried to shake off her grogginess. "It's okay, dear. I was just taking a nap. I didn't get much sleep at the hospital last night. Is there news? Is Kevin okay?"

"He's doing well," her daughter-in-law reassured her. "Jason called about an hour ago. He'd been in to see him earlier. He said Kevin looked a hundred percent better than he did when we left last night. What about you, though? Are you okay? Yesterday must have been—" she hesitated, then said "—well, it must have been difficult with things the way they've been between you and Kevin."

The last part was said in an uncertain rush, as if Dana wasn't sure she should even broach the subject of Lacey's relationship with her husband.

Hoping to avoid any further probing, Lacey deliberately injected a cheerful note in her voice. "Other than being tired, I'm just fine."

The reply was greeted with a skeptical silence. "Could we have lunch?" Dana asked finally. "I'll pick something up and bring it over, if you don't feel like going out."

"Maybe another time," Lacey said evasively. Dana had an uncanny knack for getting to the heart of things. Her directness was one of her charms, but Lacey wasn't sure she was ready to talk about what she was feeling— not until she understood it more clearly herself.

Before last night, it had been months since Lacey had seen Kevin. Then to see him in a hospital bed. It had been her worst nightmare come true. Anxiety, anger and love had each taken turns, leaving her thoroughly drained and confused. How could she feel so much for a man she didn't even think she knew anymore?

"Are you anxious to get back to the hospital?" Dana questioned.

Lacey might have grabbed at the excuse, if she hadn't known the implications. "No. Actually I hadn't planned to stop by until this evening."

"Then there's no reason for me not to come over,"

her daughter-in-law declared decisively. "I won't let you put me off. You need someone to talk to and it might as well be me. Who knows these Halloran men better than you and I do? I'll be there in an hour."

She hung up before Lacey could think of a single thing to say to keep her away. Besides, maybe Dana was right. She did need to sort things out, and Dana knew as much as anyone what these Halloran men were like once they started with their bulldozer tactics.

Brandon's warning, combined with Kevin's plea for another chance had taken their toll. Lacey was already dreading going back to the hospital, fearing that she would succumb to the combined pressure without giving the decision nearly enough thought. Maybe Dana could help her to stiffen her resolve.

A shower did its part to revive her. By the time the doorbell rang, she'd swept her hair back in a French braid and pulled on gray wool slacks and the cheerfully bright, blue sweater Dana had given her last Christmas.

At the door Dana shrugged out of her coat, then looked Lacey over from head to toe and nodded in satisfaction. "Everyone should have a mother-in-law who looks like you. You're a walking advertisement for my designs."

Lacey grinned. "You look pretty snappy yourself. How much longer do you figure you'll be able to wear that outfit?"

"About another hour, if I skip lunch," Dana complained as she headed for the kitchen with her armload of carryout food. "I couldn't get the waistband snapped as it is. Fortunately the sweater covers the gap. If I'm this bad with three months to go, what will I look like by the time I deliver? Jason will have to roll me to the hospital on one of those carts they use for moving heavy crates."

"Believe me, he'll be too excited to worry about how you look." She studied Dana's sweater, a bold swirl of hot pink on a neon green background. "A new design? Just looking at you cheers me up."

"That's the idea. It's for the mass market line. What do you think?"

"I think you're going to make a fortune for that designer who's added them to his collection and for Halloran Industries. Brandon must be ecstatic."

Dana rolled her eyes as she spread a selection of deli salads on the kitchen table. "Actually Brandon is more interested in the timetable for producing his great grandchild. I swear he would take Lemaze classes with me if Jason would let him. Jason has already had to stop him from checking the references of the instructors."

"That man needs to find a woman of his own. Maybe then he'd stop meddling in all our lives," Lacey said as she put plastic plates, mismatched stainless flatware and paper napkins on the table.

Dana's eyebrows rose a fraction. "Still roughing it?"

"It is a far cry from the Halloran china and silver, isn't it? You should have seen Kevin's expression when he saw it."

"He's been here, then?"

"Yes, when I first moved in. He left convinced that I'd lost my mind. Brandon agreed. Jason, also, probably, though he's too polite to say it to my face."

"Well, we know why Kevin would hate it. As for

Brandon, he can't imagine anyone not being madly in love with his son or grandson. He also thinks the Halloran life-style is the primary selling point. I agree with you that he needs to find some woman and fall in love again. Better yet, he should have to fight to win her over. I told him exactly that just the other day."

"What did he say?"

"That a girl my age shouldn't be meddling in the love life of her elders. I don't think he saw the irony."

"He wouldn't," Lacey agreed. "Brandon thinks his interference is a God-given right as patriarch of the Halloran clan."

Dana's expression turned quizzical. "Do I detect a note of bitterness?"

"Bitterness, resignation, maybe a little frustration."

"He's been cross-examining you about the separation again, hasn't he?"

"Brandon, Jason, even Kevin from his hospital bed. None of them seem to get it, even after all this time."

"I do," Dana said with such quiet compassion that it brought tears to Lacey's eyes.

She blamed the rare display of emotion on stress and gave her daughter-in-law a watery, grateful smile. "I think maybe you do. I didn't leave out of spite. I don't hate Kevin."

"Quite the contrary would be my guess," Dana said. "It hurts, doesn't it? It hurts to see someone you love changing before your eyes and feeling totally helpless to stop it."

Not for the first time, Lacey was astounded by Dana's insightfulness. "For a young woman, you sound very wise."

Dana shrugged off the compliment. "I watched my mother fade and then die after my father walked out on us. Then I saw Sammy turn from a wonderful kid into a teenager destined for real trouble. No matter what I said or did, it never made a difference. In the end all I could do was love them, anyway. Thank God Jason came along when he did. He's the one who finally got through to Sammy."

Lacey patted her hand. "I'm sorry I never knew your mother. She must have been something for you to turn out to be so special."

Lacey caught the unexpected tears shimmering in Dana's eyes before she turned away. The rare show of emotion surprised Lacey. Her daughter-in-law always seemed so composed.

"Thanks for saying that," Dana murmured. "Sometimes I forget what she was like before she changed. It's good to be reminded that she wasn't always so defeated, that there was a time when she was terrific and fun to be around."

Finally she faced Lacey again, the tearful, faraway look in her eyes gone. "You never met my mother and yet you have an instinctive understanding of her. At the same time, I wonder if you see the side of Kevin that I see at work."

"Meaning?" Lacey questioned cautiously.

"Did you know that he personally went to the hospital to visit the child of one of the Halloran workers, when the boy was diagnosed with leukemia?"

Startled, Lacey shook her head. It was something the old Kevin would have done in the blink of an eye, but now? She wouldn't have believed it, if she hadn't known that Dana would never make up such a story.

"It's true," Dana said. "Jason told me he also gave the woman time off with pay to be with her son. And he sent the whole family off to Disney World for Christmas because the boy had always wanted to meet Mickey Mouse."

"Kevin did that?" Lacey asked softly.

"He did. From what I've seen since I started working there, Kevin likes to make everyone believe that he's all business, that the only thing he cares about is the bottom line. I don't think there's a worker at Halloran Industries, though, who hasn't been touched by his kindness at one time or another." She smiled at Lacey. "I thought you should know. Maybe it will help to put things in perspective."

Lacey nodded. "Thank you for telling me. Kevin never did."

"He wouldn't. He takes it for granted that it's part of his job. That's what I admire so much about him. He doesn't think that being considerate, that caring deeply about his employees' welfare is unusual. It's just the way he is."

"Yes," Lacey said, more shaken than she could say by the reminder of a generosity of spirit she had thought was lost, "it is the way he is."

Was it possible that things weren't quite as hopeless as she had imagined?

Kevin thought he detected something new and oddly hesitant in Lacey's blue eyes when she came to visit him that evening. She regarded him as if she weren't quite sure what to make of him. Her assessing glance puzzled him.

"I like your hair like that," he began tentatively, wondering if it was past time to be wooing her with compliments, no matter how sincerely spoken. He yearned for the right to brush back the silken strands that had escaped the pulled-back style. "You look like a girl again. That sweater becomes you, too. It matches your eyes. One of Dana's designs, I'll bet."

A blush of pink rose in her cheeks as she nodded, making him regret how long it had been since he'd told her how beautiful she was. "It's true," he continued. "Sometimes I look at you and it's as if time had stood still."

She grinned at that. "What's gotten into you today? Is there a little Irish blarney in that IV?"

"They don't tell me what sort of concoctions they put in there. Maybe it's truth serum. I do know I've felt a powerful need to see you. I worried you might not come back."

"I told you I would."

"Are you here because I'm at death's door or because you want to be here?"

She regarded him impatiently. "You are *not* at death's door, so don't try playing on my sympathy. You're going to be just fine."

"If I rest," he reminded her.

"Exactly."

"Who's going to make me?"

"You're a grown man. No one should have to make you listen to reason."

"Maybe I've forgotten what it's like to rest. Maybe

I need someone around to show me." He met her gaze and held it. "I need you, Lacey."

Her lips parted, but before she could speak, Brandon slipped into the room. Kevin managed a rueful grin. "Your timing's lousy, Dad."

Brandon looked from Kevin to Lacey and back again, then nodded in obvious satisfaction. "Interrupting your courting, am I? I'm sure you'll remember right where you left off. Just wanted to say goodbye before I go get some sleep. These old bones of mine can't take another night on that poor excuse of a sofa in the waiting room." He glanced at Lacey. "Remind me to order up some new furniture for this place."

"I'm sure they'll appreciate it," Lacey said, already edging toward the door. "Why don't I leave you two alone. I don't think Linc wants two of us in here at a time."

"Lacey," Kevin said, stopping her before she could flee, "I won't forget."

"Forget what?"

"I won't forget what we were talking about," he answered meaningfully.

She scurried out the door, reminding him of the only other time he could recall seeing her flustered—the day he'd asked her to marry him. She had wanted so desperately to say yes. He'd been able to read that much in her eyes. She'd tried to weigh that desire against the implications, from Brandon's wrath to the certain end of his future in the family business.

"Yes," she had said hesitantly, then before he could whoop for joy, "No. Oh, Kevin, I couldn't bear it if our being together ruined your relationship with your father."

"Dad will survive this little setback to his plans. He always does."

"But there's nothing more important than family."

"We'll have our own family. You and I. Our children. It'll be enough for me. Will it be enough for you?"

"All I've ever wanted in my life was to love you."

"Then that's our answer, isn't it?" Kevin had said with the naive faith only a twenty-year-old can have. "All I've ever wanted is to make you happy."

For so many years love had been enough. Only lately had he realized that sometimes marriage took more than love. It took patience and understanding and a willingness to struggle through the bad times. It took listening and sharing and compromise.

Kevin knew, then, what he had to do, what it would take to win Lacey back, to convince her that what they had now was just as strong as what they'd had back then.

When Jason came in later, Kevin asked him to make arrangements to open their house on Cape Cod. "Call the caretaker and have him stock the refrigerator and put in a supply of firewood. I'm going there when I get out."

Jason's expression was concerned. "Shouldn't you stay in town, closer to your doctor?"

"I need to get away. I can't bear the thought of going back to that huge house again. Your mother hates it. Did you know that?"

Jason looked startled. "She does?"

"Always has. I insisted on buying it after I went to work with your grandfather. I thought we needed to make a statement, live up to the corporate image, some such nonsense. She put up with it when you were growing up, but once you'd moved out, she started talking again about moving, getting something smaller."

Kevin took a deep breath as he made another decision. "I want you to put it on the market. Maybe then she'll see that I'm serious about wanting a reconciliation."

"Dad, are you sure? I thought you loved that house."

"I loved what I thought it represented. Turns out it's just a house, and a lonely one at that."

"Are you planning to stay on the Cape?"

"If I can convince your mother to stay there with me, I just may."

Jason grinned. "You always could twist her around your little finger."

Kevin shook his head ruefully. "No, son. You've got that backward. All it took was a smile and she could make me jump through hoops. Guess I'd forgotten that because in recent years I haven't given her much to smile about."

"Want to tell me what that means?"

He grinned at his son. "No."

Lacey would know and that was all that mattered.

The next morning Kevin waited impatiently for Lacey's visit. She didn't come. She wasn't there when he moved into a private room. Nor had she arrived by the time he got his pitiful excuse for a dinner.

When Jason arrived at seven-thirty, Kevin swallowed his pride and asked, "Have you seen your mother today?"

"No. Why? Hasn't she been here?"

Kevin shook his head. "You don't suppose she's sick?"

"I'll check on her on my way home."

"Go now."

"But I just got here."

"I'll feel better knowing that your mother is okay. Maybe the stress of the past few weeks caught up with her. That terrible flu is going around."

Jason threw up his hands. "Okay, I'll go, but I think you're worrying about nothing. Dana usually talks to her during the day. I'm sure if anything were wrong she would have let me know."

Kevin watched as Jason pulled his overcoat back on. "You'll call me?"

"I'll call you. Now stop worrying and eat your dinner."

Kevin glanced at the bland scoop of mashed potatoes and the colorless chunk of chicken. "This is not dinner. It's a form of torture dreamed up by Linc Westlake. I don't suppose you could sneak me some of Mrs. Willis's chicken and dumplings?" he inquired hopefully, thinking of Jason's housekeeper's delicious cooking.

Jason grinned at him. "I'll check with the doctor. If he says it's okay, I'm sure Mrs. Willis will be thrilled to make it for you. Get some rest, Dad. Don't tire yourself out with worrying. It won't help."

Jason had been gone less than twenty minutes when

the door opened and Lacey walked through, her expression harried.

"Hi," she said cheerfully. "You're looking better."

"Where have you been?" Kevin asked, unable to control the edge in his voice.

Lacey regarded him sharply. "You sound angry."

"Worried," he corrected. "And if I sound worried, it's because I was. I expected you hours ago."

"Expected?" she echoed softly.

Kevin heard the warning note in her voice, but couldn't keep himself from adding, "If I couldn't get by, you should have let me know. I just sent Jason to check on you."

"Why on earth would you do that?"

"I told you. I was worried."

Kevin could see that Lacey was fighting her temper. She'd always been independent. No doubt she'd grown more so during their separation, when she'd been accountable to no one for her actions. She drew in a deep breath and pulled a chair close to the bed. He noticed she didn't take off her coat, as if to indicate to him that she wasn't here to stay.

"Kevin," she began in that patient tone he'd heard her use on Jason when he was five and misbehaving, "I'm sure you are bored to tears in here," she continued, "but I can't be here every minute. I have other obligations."

"One of those committees, I'm sure."

The sarcastic barb brought sparks into her eyes. "May I remind you that I am on those committees because you thought it would be the thing for the wife of a Halloran to do."

He winced. "Sorry. You're right. Is that where you were?"

"No. As it happens, I've gotten involved with something else."

Something or some*one,* he couldn't help wondering. Kevin felt an ache deep inside as he realized that this was probably just one of many things he didn't know about how Lacey spent her time.

"Tell me," he said. He saw her slowly relax at the genuine note of interest in his voice.

"Another time," she said. "For now, tell me how you're feeling. You must have had a good day, since Linc moved you out of intensive care and into a private room so quickly."

"The day's better now that you're here."

Kevin reached for her hand. After a hesitation so light that only a man deeply in love with his wife would notice, she slipped her hand into his. Contentment swelled inside him and he realized with Lacey here he could sleep at last.

Later he would never be sure if Lacey's gentle kiss was real or something he had dreamed.

Chapter 5

Over the next several days Lacey realized her feelings about Kevin's continued rapid recovery were oddly mixed. Day by day his strength returned. It was almost as if he applied the same obsessive attention to healing that he did to everything else. It was both astonishing and reassuring to see.

Though Lacey hated herself for even thinking it, she couldn't help wondering what would happen when he was well, when she no longer would have these hospital visits as an excuse for seeing him. The prospect of letting go for the second time daunted her. And yet there was no going back, not on the basis of a few quick promises, which were all too likely to be broken. She'd made up her mind about that.

Unfortunately, there was a troubling and unmistakable glint of determination in Kevin's eyes every time he looked at her. She'd often seen that expression right before he or Brandon scored some business coup. Kevin was scheming and it made her very nervous. Worse, she had the sense that Jason was conspiring with him. Together, the two men she loved most in the world were formidable opponents.

"Okay, enough is enough. What are the two of you up to?" she demanded when she found them with their heads together at the end of Kevin's first week in the hospital.

Jason looked from her to his father and back again. Guilt was written all over his face. "I'm out of here," he said hurriedly, backing toward the door.

Hands on hips, Lacey stepped into his path. "Not so fast."

He gave her a quick peck on the cheek. "Gotta go, Mom. Dana's waiting for me in the car."

"She can wait another ten seconds."

"Couldn't you just ask Dad, if you want to know something?" he suggested hopefully. "He's the one with all the answers."

She glanced at Kevin and saw the old familiar twinkle in his eyes. It made her heart tumble, just as it always had. That twinkle was downright dangerous.

Lacey recalled the first time she'd seen that glint of mischief in his eyes. He'd used some super glue to seal their fifth-grade teacher's desk drawer shut. That drawer had held their report cards. Kevin hadn't been anxious to take his home.

Now he was scowling with mock ferocity at Jason. "Traitor," he murmured, but there was a note of laughter in his voice.

"Bye, Mom. See you, Dad. Good luck."

Lacey approached the bed cautiously. "Now just why would you be in need of luck?"

"I'm a sick man," he said in a pathetically weak tone that was so obviously feigned, Lacey almost burst out laughing.

"I need luck, prayers, whatever it takes," he added for good measure.

"Nice try," she said.

Kevin managed to look genuinely dismayed. "You don't believe me?"

"I don't believe you," she concurred. "Try again."

"Have you seen Linc today?"

Her gaze narrowed as the first faint suspicion flickered in her mind. "What does Linc have to do with this?"

"He's agreed to let me out of here on Sunday."

"Kevin, that's wonderful!" she blurted out instinctively before she caught the glimmer of satisfaction in his eyes.

"What's the rest?" she asked slowly.

He folded his hands across his chest and inquired complacently, "What makes you think there's anything more?"

"Oh, please. I know you. If it were a simple matter of getting out of here on Sunday, you wouldn't look so smug."

"Smug? I was aiming for helpless."

"You couldn't look helpless if you tried. Come on, spill it. What's the rest?"

"There's a condition to my release."

Lacey got an uneasy feeling in the pit of her stom

ach, as suspicion replaced amusement. "What condition?"

"That I have someone around to look after me."

She ignored the return of the obvious gleam in his eyes and asked briskly, "Isn't our housekeeper there?"

At the quick shake of his head, she very nearly moaned. He'd never liked the stiff, unyielding woman, but he'd never been willing to fire her, either. "Kevin, you haven't fought with her, have you?"

"Actually, I had Jason send her off to visit her sister in Florida."

"Tell her to come back. I'm sure she'd cooperate under the circumstances."

"Afraid not."

"Why?"

"Well, the truth of the matter is that I fired her."

"You what?"

"I was never there, anyway," he said defensively. "So you see, I can't go home."

"Then you'll go to your father's. Mrs. Farnsworth would love the chance to fuss over you."

"I suppose that would work," he said. "But you know Dad. It wouldn't be long before he'd want to have business discussions over breakfast, lunch and dinner."

There was more than a little truth in that, Lacey conceded reluctantly. She knew now exactly where Kevin was headed, had known all along that some version of this game would come up sooner or later. Even so, she didn't have a ready, convincing alternative.

"Jason has room," she said desperately.

"What about Sammy?" he countered neatly.

Obviously he'd planned this as skillfully as a master chess player, Lacey thought, trying to muster up her fading resolve as he went on.

"I'll need peace and quiet," Kevin added for good measure. "You can't expect a kid that age to be on good behavior for days on end. Besides, Dana shouldn't have to take care of a sick father-in-law when she's trying to prepare for a baby."

"I think she'll have plenty of time to prepare after you're fully recuperated," Lacey retorted dryly.

She didn't have a strong argument where Sammy was concerned, however. Kevin was right to be worried about Dana's younger brother. He would probably try to engage Kevin in heated video games. With her husband's spirit of competitiveness, he'd land right back in the hospital.

"You could be right about Sammy, though," she admitted reluctantly. "Maybe Jason could loan you Mrs. Willis and you could just stay at home."

"I have a better idea," Kevin said cheerfully.

"Why doesn't that surprise me," she muttered darkly, envisioning the two of them in her cramped little apartment or, worse yet, back in their own home.

"I thought you and I could go to the Cape. It would be peaceful there this time of year."

Peaceful? she thought, stunned by the suggestion. The two of them alone on Cape Cod? No, that wouldn't be peaceful. It would be lunacy.

Cape Cod was where they'd made love for the very first time. Cape Cod was where he'd proposed to her. Cape Cod was where Jason had been conceived. Cape Cod was chock-full of memories. She had no intention of subjecting herself to that kind of torture.

"No," she said adamantly, "absolutely not."

"It would be good for us, Lacey. You have to admit that."

Lacey felt as if the walls of the room were closing in on her. It wasn't just the early memories. Later, nostalgic for all they had shared on Cape Cod, they had bought a house there. It was the one outrageously expensive indulgence that she had approved of totally.

They had made a pact that no business problems could ever follow them there. That house had become their refuge, a place for quiet talks, long walks and slow, sensuous sex. Kevin had kept his part of the bargain— until the day he'd stopped going because he no longer had time for the simple pleasure of a relaxing, intimate vacation.

Of all the suggestions he might have made, this was the most wickedly clever. The memories they shared there were among their most powerfully seductive.

She met his gaze and saw that he knew exactly what he was asking of her.

"Please, Lacey," he coaxed. "You did promise we would talk."

She was shaking her head before the words were out of his mouth. "I didn't promise to move back in with you. It won't work, Kevin."

"It will if we want it to. I'm ready to try. What about you?" He studied her closely, then added, "Or have you given up on our marriage?"

There was no mistaking the dare. Lacey cursed the tidy way Kevin had backed her into a corner. He knew how desperately she wanted to salvage what they'd once had. If she turned him down, she was as much as admitting that she'd given up hope.

Or that she was afraid.

She couldn't deny the fear that curled within her at the thought of what might happen if she gave in to his plan. If she accepted, if she went to the Cape and nothing had changed, she wasn't sure she could bear the pain of another separation and inevitably a divorce.

Now at least the worst days were behind her. She'd begun picking up the pieces of her life, creating a world in which Kevin was no longer the center. She liked the strength she'd discovered within herself.

But if that strength were real, if she'd truly gained her independence, wouldn't she be able to cope no matter what happened? She could practically hear him taunting her with that, though in reality he said nothing. Maybe it was simply her brain arguing with her heart.

All of the questions and none of the answers flashed through her mind in no more than an instant. Lacey studied Kevin's face and saw the uncertainty, the wistfulness in his eyes. It mirrored what she felt in her heart, the hope that had never died.

"I'll go," she said finally. She'd thought the risk of leaving Kevin had been dangerous enough. The risk of going back was a thousand times greater. She had to try, though. She would never forgive herself if she didn't.

"Thank you," he said simply. And she knew from the way time seemed to stand still as she met his gaze that her decision had been the right one, the only one.

No matter how much it might hurt later.

* * *

Kevin had the entire, endless night to think about Lacey's answer. He knew what it had taken for her to overcome her reluctance. The look in her eyes had spoken volumes about the struggle that raged inside her. He swore that he would do whatever it took to overcome her doubts. He viewed the coming days as a honeymoon of sorts, a chance to put their marriage on a new, more solid footing.

And he began making careful plans.

"I'll take care of everything," Brandon announced the following morning when he learned of their arrangement, which he clearly viewed as permanent. "Over the years I've learned a thing or two about patching things up after a spat."

"I'm sure you have," Kevin agreed, recalling the flurry of expensive gifts that would pour in whenever his father and mother argued.

His mother would point to a piece of jewelry and say, "This was for the time he stayed the whole night through at the factory and forgot to call. And these earrings were for that time he didn't tell me he'd invited guests for dinner and showed up with two of his most important customers."

Kevin grinned at the memories, but held up his hand. "Slow down, Dad. I think I'll handle this one my way. Besides, Jason's already called the caretaker. The house will be ready for us."

"What about flowers? Never was a woman who could resist a few bouquets of flowers."

"Like the five dozen roses you sent Mom, when

you forgot your anniversary? Or the orchids that came when you missed her birthday?"

Brandon scowled at him. "Okay, so I had a lousy head for dates. Your mother loved those flowers just the same."

"Yes, she did," Kevin said softly, "because they came from you. Let me deal with Lacey my own way, Dad."

Brandon went on as if he hadn't heard a word Kevin was saying. "Maybe I ought to take a drive out there and check on things. You can't trust strangers to remember everything."

Kevin groaned as he envisioned his father standing in the doorway to welcome them. Lacey would no doubt turn tail and run. Although, on second thought, she might welcome a buffer between them. Either way, Kevin had no intention of letting Brandon meddle in this particular scenario.

"Forget it, Dad. For a man who spent years trying to keep us apart, you're suddenly awfully anxious for us to get back together."

Brandon didn't rise to the bait. "I'm not one bit afraid to admit I've made mistakes in my life. A few of them have been doozies. I know what I did back then to try to ruin what you two had was wrong. Lacey's a fine woman. You couldn't have done better."

"I know that. I'm glad you can see it now, too."

"You think this plan of yours is going to work?" he inquired, his brow furrowed. "Seems mighty chancy."

Kevin sighed. "It is a risk. If it doesn't work, I'll just have to come up with another idea. I'm not going to let her go without a fight, Dad. Not a second time.

Come on. Let's go for a walk around the corridor. I'm going to need all my strength back if I'm going into battle tomorrow."

As they walked the length of the hospital hallway, Kevin saw the elevator doors slide open. He paused and watched, unwilling to admit how much he was hoping Lacey would be among those getting off. When she emerged behind a group of nurses, he spotted her at once, astonished at how youthful she looked with her honey-blond hair skimming her shoulders, her cheeks tinted pink from the March winds.

She started toward his room, then noticed him out of the corner of her eye. She turned his way, a smile spreading slowly across her face.

"I like the fancy new pajamas," she said, grinning at the outrageously expensive pair Brandon had brought him from a British collection made with Halloran fabrics.

Kevin would never have worn them if the only alternative hadn't been one of those indecent hospital gowns. In fact, as he thought back, the last pair of pajamas he'd owned had had bunny rabbits on them and he'd been going to sleep with a pacifier.

"What's wrong with them?" Brandon demanded. "This is one of the finest cottons we make. Do you have any idea what they charge for these things?"

"Settle down, Dad. I'm sure Lacey is truly awed by the quality."

"Awed isn't quite the word I had in mind," she teased. "I think I saw a pair just like these in some forties movie with Claudette Colbert. Or was it Katharine Hepburn?"

"Okay, enough, you two," Brandon grumbled. He shot a pointed glance at Kevin. "You could be walking up and down these hallways with your bottom bare."

Kevin sneaked a look at Lacey, whose lips were twitching as she fought the urge to laugh. She refused to meet his gaze. Brandon sniffed.

"Think I'll go off and leave you two alone. It's obvious you don't need me around anymore."

"Goodbye, Dad."

Lacey gave him a peck on the cheek and murmured something Kevin couldn't quite hear. From the amusement that immediately sparked in his father's eyes, Kevin had a hunch it had something to do with the damned pajamas.

When she finally turned back to Kevin, her expression was as innocent as a new baby's.

"What'd you say to him?" Kevin demanded.

"That's our secret."

"I thought secrets were taboo in a healthy marriage."

"Some secrets are taboo. Others add spice."

"You and my father have a secret that's going to add spice to our marriage?"

She grinned at him impishly. "You never know."

He regarded her indignantly. "You know, Lacey Halloran, it has occurred to me that locking myself away in a house on the Cape with you could drive me nuts."

"Not my fault," she claimed innocently. "It was your idea."

"And you intend to make me pay for that, don't you?"

"The regimen I have planned for you will make basic training seem like child's play."

He watched the play of light on her streaked blond hair and the sparks of mischief in her eyes. "What does Linc have to say about this plan you have?"

"Who do you think gave it to me?"

She waved several booklets without allowing him to catch a glimpse of the titles. He had to take her word for it when she flipped through them.

"'Cholesterol Management.' 'Triglycerides and You.' 'Exercise for the Healthy Heart.' 'The Low-Fat Diet.' And my favorite, 'Heart-Friendly Fruits and Vegetables.' I can hardly wait."

"I could still go to Jason's, you know. Sammy's beginning to look like a saint compared to my wife."

"I hear he has the newest video game. You very well might want to reconsider," she said agreeably.

He stopped where he was and framed her face with his hands. He could feel the heat climb in her cheeks. "Not a chance, Mrs. Halloran. Not a chance."

Chapter 6

The promise of long, quiet, intimate days on Cape Cod with Kevin terrified Lacey. It was possible—likely, even—that their expectations were entirely different. Anticipation and worry made the drive from the hospital to the Cape seem longer than ever.

What if Kevin only intended to lure her back, but hadn't thought beyond the challenge of the chase? she worried, when the first deadly silence fell.

She had little doubt that he could seduce her, that he could scramble her emotions and turn her best intentions to mush. Even in the worst of times, she had responded all too easily to his touch. The loving had been wonderful, but toward the end it hadn't been nearly enough. Now it would be a short-term solution at best.

A trip like this was what Lacey had been longing

for, but now that Kevin had made the commitment to spend time with her, she wondered what would happen if they couldn't recapture what they had lost. In a last-ditch desperation, were they pinning too much on this time alone? Was she expecting something from Kevin that he couldn't possibly give?

As she clutched the steering wheel with white-knuckled intensity, her thoughts tumbled like bits of colored glass in a kaleidoscope, leaving her hopelessly confused.

Beside her, Kevin had settled back in the seat and closed his eyes, no more anxious to continue the struggle for nervous, meaningless small talk than she was.

With a bone-deep sorrow, Lacey couldn't help noticing the contrast to other trips they had made, times when the car had been filled with laughter and quiet conversation as they made the transition from their harried life-style in Boston to the relaxation of Cape Cod. Then even the silences had been lazy and comfortable. The anticipation had been sweet, not mixed with a vague sense of dread as it was now.

She breathed a sigh of relief when she finally pulled into the driveway of the rambling old house with its weathered gray shingles and white trim. A few hardy geraniums bloomed in the window boxes, the splashes of red against gray reminding her of an Andrew Wyeth painting she particularly loved.

She vividly recalled the precise moment when she and Kevin had first come upon this place, choosing it over all the others they had seen because of its haphazard wandering over a spectacular oceanfront piece of property. Later in the spring there would be daffodils and tulips everywhere and the scent of lilacs from a bush near the kitchen window.

Lacey glanced over and saw that Kevin was awake, his intense gaze closely examining the house that had once been so special to them.

"It looks neglected," he observed ruefully. "When was the last time we were out here?"

"Together?" she questioned pointedly. "Three years ago. We drove out for the day."

He regarded her with astonishment. "Surely that can't be."

"You've been too busy," she reminded him, trying— and failing—to keep the note of censure out of her voice.

He sighed. "That excuse must have worn thin. I remember how much you always loved coming here, especially this time of year before the summer crowds came back."

Kevin leaned closer, his breath fanning her face. He trailed his knuckles along her cheek, stirring her senses. She turned into the caress, and his fingers stroked her skin. The pad of his thumb skimmed provocatively over her lips.

"I'm sorry, Lace. I truly am."

She could tell from the look in his eyes that he really meant it, and something deep inside her shifted, making room for emotions she wasn't yet prepared to handle. Trying to ignore the trembly feeling he could still evoke in her, Lacey swallowed hard. She pulled away and summoned a smile.

"No more apologies, remember? We're here now." Her tone turned brisk. "We'd better get you inside.

Linc wasn't all that thrilled that you wanted to come here, rather than stay in Boston."

"He just hates the fact that he won't be able to run up my bill with all those house calls," Kevin said as he opened the door and got out, following her to the trunk.

Instinctively he reached for a bag as they began the familiar ritual of unloading the car. Worried about the strain on his still-healing heart, Lacey quickly waved him off. "I'll get these."

A rare flash of anger rose in his eyes, then died just as quickly. "You're right," he said stiffly. "I'll go unlock the door. I should be able to manage that much at least."

Lacey cursed the fact that she'd reminded him that for now he wasn't as vital and healthy as he'd always been. Kevin had never been able to cope with so much as a cold, hating the slightest sign of weakness in a body he'd always tested to the limits. He looked so strong, with his powerful shoulders and well-sculpted legs, that she herself could almost forget that inside he was not yet healed.

Tennis, sailing and, years earlier, football—he had played them all with demanding intensity. How difficult it must be for him now to defer the simplest tasks to her. Still, Linc's instructions had been specific, and she intended to follow them to the letter.

There was no sign of Kevin as she made the half dozen trips to carry their luggage inside. He had vanished as soon as he'd opened the front door for her.

After an instant's hesitation, Lacey placed his bags in the master bedroom and her own in the guest room across the hall. The width of that hall was no more than three feet, but she saw it as symbolic of the ever-widening chasm between them in their marriage.

Worried that Kevin was still not inside—on such a chilly, blustery day—his first out of the hospital—she went in search of him.

She found him at last in back of the house, standing atop of a distant sand dune. Wearing only a thin jacket, a knit shirt and jeans, he had his hands in his pockets, his shoulders hunched against the wind. He was staring out to a white-capped sea that roared its strength as it crashed against the shore.

Guessing a little of what he must be feeling, Lacey walked to his side, hesitated, then tucked her arm through his.

"It certainly is setting up a fuss today, isn't it?" she observed.

At first she didn't think he would answer her, either out of some lingering resentment or because he was lost in his own thoughts. Finally he glanced at her, then back to the ocean and said, "I'd forgotten what that sound is like, how it fills up your head, driving out all petty annoyances."

"Like a symphony. Isn't that what you told me once?"

Kevin shook his head, clearly bemused by the words. "Was I ever that poetic?"

"I thought you were."

He turned and met her gaze then. Lacey thought for a moment she could see straight into his soul. Such sadness. It made her ache to think of him hurting so deeply. Yet her own sorrow was just as deep, just as heart-wrenching.

"Past tense," he noted wearily.

This time she lifted her fingers to caress his cheek. "Don't," she said softly. "Please don't. We have to make a pact to stop looking back. We have to look ahead."

"I'm not sure I dare."

Surprised by the genuine note of dismay in his voice, she asked, "Why?"

"What if there's only emptiness? Without you, that's all it would be, you know."

Hearing him say the words, hearing him admit how much she meant to him should have made her feel deliriously happy. But she was no longer that shy, innocent girl who'd given her heart so freely. Instead, knowing all she did, she felt this terrible pressure—pressure to forget the differences that had brought them to this moment, this place.

A part of Lacey wanted to give in now and promise him that everything would be as it always had been. She desperately needed to believe that coming here had been enough to reassure her. But the part of her that listened to her brain, rather than her heart, knew it was far too soon for either of them to make a commitment like that. Despite the pretty words, Kevin was no more ready for promises than she was.

She touched his cheek again, her splayed fingers warm against his chilled flesh, the gesture meant to comfort, not to promise. Their gazes met, caught, lingered. The silent communication was filled with hope and wistful yearning.

"I'm going to start dinner," she told him after several seconds passed. "Don't stay out here too long.

It will be dark soon and the air is already cold and damp."

His gaze once again on the sea, he nodded and let her go.

Inside, Lacey found the refrigerator already well stocked with groceries, including a container of clam chowder left by the caretaker with a note saying it was from his grandmother. She poured it into a cast iron kettle on the stove, turned the flame on low and went to check more thoroughly on the rest of the house.

Everything had been readied for them. A fire had been laid and extra wood was stacked beside the hearth. Without the salty haze that would be back again within hours, the just-washed windows glistened with the last soft rays of sunlight. The wide plank floors had been rubbed to a soft glow, the furniture polished with something that smelled of lemons.

Best of all, a huge basket of her favorite spring flowers—daffodils, tulips and lily of the valley— added a cheerful finishing touch. Brandon's romantic idea, no doubt.

If Lacey hadn't known how long the house had stood empty, she might have believed she and Kevin had been here only yesterday. As it was, she hadn't been able to bear more than a quick day trip now and again. Alone, she had been all too vividly reminded of what she and Kevin had lost. The ache in her heart had been too much so she had never lingered.

Now she touched the automatic lighter to the kindling in the fireplace. Within minutes the flames had caught and a cozy warmth stole through the chilly room.

Back in the kitchen she grabbed a handful of silver

and a pair of placemats and set places on the coffee table in front of the fire. When they were here alone, they rarely ate in the formal dining room or even in the huge old kitchen, preferring the intimacy of meals in front of the fire's warmth. Only on the hottest days of summer did the routine vary and then they moved to the beach, where they could listen to the waves and watch the stars as they ate by candlelight.

Kevin came in just as she was pulling a loaf of crusty, homemade bread from the oven. His eyes lit up as he shrugged out of his jacket and tossed it over the back of a chair.

"Is that what I think it is?" he asked, coming closer to sniff the wonderful aroma.

"Mrs. Renfield's homemade bread," she confirmed. "And her New England clam chowder. Your favorites."

"What can I do to help?"

"If you'll take the bread in, I'll bring the soup. That should do it."

"I don't suppose she left one of her peach pies in the refrigerator."

"Sorry," Lacey said, amused at his immediately disappointed expression. "Looks like a cherry cobbler to me. And don't tell me you didn't know perfectly well that she was going to leave all this for you. You probably called her up and pleaded with her."

"I did no such thing."

"Then you had Jason do it."

He grinned at her. "Okay, maybe I did suggest he drop a few hints."

"Are you sure he didn't do more than that?"

"Such as?"

"Sending her a few bolts of that outrageously expensive fabric she loves so much."

Kevin grinned guiltily. "A few yards, not a few bolts."

"Do you realize that that seventy-five-year-old grandmother uses that cloth to whip up fancy pot holders for the church bazaar?"

"She does not," he said, his expression clearly scandalized at the waste.

Lacey picked up one of the pot holders she'd used to carry in the steaming bowls of chowder. "Recognize this?"

Kevin groaned. "Oh, dear Lord. Don't ever let Dad see that."

"Too late. He bought up every one she had at the bazaar last year. He was terrified one of Halloran's customers would see them and realize they were designing ball gowns made out of the same material."

Lacey felt her lips curving into a smile as Kevin's laughter bubbled forth. It had been so long since she'd heard him sound genuinely happy.

"Can you imagine Miriam Grayson discovering that her latest couture creation matched Mrs. Renfield's pot holders?" Kevin said, still chuckling. "Her designer would wind up skewered with one of her lethal, pearl-tipped hat pins."

"I believe Brandon mentioned the same scenario. For about thirty seconds he actually seemed tempted to risk it."

"I'm not surprised. Old Miriam is a pompous pain in the you-know-what. However, her designer is one of Halloran's best customers. Dad obviously had second thoughts the minute he envisioned the impact on the company's bottom line."

As silly and inconsequential as the conversation was, Lacey couldn't help thinking it was the first time in months that she and Kevin had actually shared so much carefree laughter. She would have to remember to thank Mrs. Renfield by slipping her a few yards of that emerald-green silk that would go so well with her bright eyes—after warning her to use it on a dress, not pot holders.

The tone of the evening seemed set after that. Kevin and Lacey reminisced about other trips and other neighbors. They recalled clam bakes and bake sales, art festivals and favorite restaurants. Here, unlike Boston, they had always felt part of the quiet, casual rhythm of the community, had had time for neighborly visits and lingering over tea.

Lacey felt Kevin's gaze on her and regarded him quizzically. "What?"

"This is the way I always think of you," he said, brushing a strand of her hair back and letting it spill through his fingers.

"How?" she said. Her breath caught in her throat as her pulse scrambled wildly.

"The firelight in your hair, your eyes sparkling, a smile on your lips. Are you happy to be here, Lacey?"

Unable to speak, she simply nodded.

"With me?"

That question was more difficult to answer honestly. Being here with Kevin was bittersweet at best. She could almost believe things were perfect. Almost.

And then she would remember.

He sighed. "Obviously, I shouldn't have pressed," he said, his voice tight.

Stricken by the hurt in his eyes, she said, "Kevin, this isn't a quick fix. It's a beginning."

He nodded, then stood up. "I'm more tired than I thought."

Lacey started to force him to stay, force him to confront the very real ordeal ahead of them. Then she bowed to the exhaustion on his face. "Your things are in the master bedroom."

"And yours?" he asked very slowly.

"Across the hall. I thought it was best."

"As always, I'm sure you're right," he retorted not attempting to conceal the sarcasm. He pivoted then and walked away, leaving Lacey alone to face the fire and the long, empty hours ahead before sleep would claim her.

Kevin stood at the window of the master bedroom, his eyes gazing blankly into the darkness of a moonless night. The sound of the waves did nothing to soothe him.

Maybe this had been a terrible idea, after all. Maybe instead of bringing him and Lacey closer, staying here would only remind her of what had gone wrong.

What did she want? he wondered angrily. Lacey had always expected him to live up to some impossible ideal, and he'd tried. Lord, how he had tried. But in the end, he'd proven himself to be a mere mortal. Maybe that would never be enough for her.

He listened as the door across the hall closed softly, and he found his hands balling into fists.

Rest, Linc had told him. How could he rest, when the woman he loved was holding him at a distance, when his body ached to feel her next to him again?

He hadn't grown used to the emptiness of their huge bed in Boston. Though this one was smaller, it would be just as cold and unwelcoming without her there beside him. He stared at it bleakly, and for one brief second he considered grabbing his blankets and sleeping in one of the other guest rooms.

Kevin saw the folly of that at once. He could sleep in any bed in the house and Lacey's nearness would taunt him. He would sense her presence in his very gut. The unmistakable, seductive scent of her favorite floral perfume was everywhere in this house. He would lie there surrounded by her, yet unable to touch her.

Exhaustion finally propelled him across the room. He stretched out on the bed, the sheet skimming his naked flesh and reminding him all too clearly of his wife's first, delicate caresses. The aching arousal was almost painful, but in its own way reassuring. If the attraction burned this brightly for him, surely it could not have died for Lacey. It would take time, that was all. Time to discover each other anew. Time to heal.

Time to fall in love all over again.

Chapter 7

If they had ended the previous evening walking on eggshells, the morning was starting out to be a hundred times worse. Lacey was so painfully careful and polite Kevin was sure he was going to scream.

Not that he could blame her after the way he'd treated her when he'd found out about the sleeping arrangements. Morning had given him a different perspective on how he'd handled things. Had he honestly expected her to tumble into his arms just because she'd agreed to come to the Cape with him? Hoped, maybe. Expected, no.

As he'd anticipated, their bed had seemed incredibly empty without her. He'd lain awake for hours wishing she were close enough to touch, wishing he could feel the soft feathering of her breath against his skin. He'd ached for just a hint of their old physical intimacy. To-

ward dawn he had reconciled himself to the unlikeli-
hood of that happening for weeks, maybe longer. Not
until she trusted him again.

Even though Kevin accepted much of the blame
for the way things were between them, the saccha-
rine politeness to which Lacey was now subjecting
him grated.

"More decaf?" she inquired, every bit as solicitous
as a well-trained waitress, and just as impersonal.

"No," he responded curtly. He blamed the surliness
in his tone on the hours he'd spent counting sheep and
trying not to think of Lacey in that bed across the hall.

"Another piece of toast?"

"I've had plenty."

"Did you want the A section of the paper?"

"No."

"Sports?"

"No."

Lacey nodded and retreated behind the local section. In self-defense Kevin grabbed the section atop
the stack in front of her. Business, he noted with a
modicum of enthusiasm. Maybe that would keep his
mind occupied. He could concentrate on mergers and
takeovers, instead of the way Lacey's ice-blue sweater
clung to her curves and brought out the color of her
eyes.

One of the hazards of being in the textile business,
he'd discovered long ago, was the need to scrutinize
fabrics. When they were worn by his wife, it was doubly difficult to focus his attention elsewhere.

Damn, he hated the last instruction Linc had given
him. No sex, the doctor had warned. At Kevin's horri-

fied expression, he'd added, "Soon, but absolutely not right away. A little patience won't hurt you."

That was easy for Linc to say. He wasn't seated across the table from a woman he hadn't held in his arms for months, a woman who had never seemed so desirable or so aloof. Kevin knew that if he could just hold Lacey, caress her, then the distance and uneasiness between them would melt away.

Instead, he was going to have to rely on his wits. The prospect daunted him. Maybe if he thought of this as a deal he needed to close, a strategy would come to him. The thought of Lacey's reaction to being compared with a business deal brought a smile to his lips.

She folded the last section of the paper and apparently caught him still grinning.

"What's so funny?"

"Nothing," he said hurriedly. "What would you like to do today?"

"Do?" she repeated blankly. "You're here to recuperate, not to fill up every spare minute. It's called relaxation. You do remember how that works, don't you?"

"Barely," he admitted.

She nodded and he could see from the amusement in her eyes that the dark mood had lifted. He wasn't deceiving himself, though. It could return as quickly as it had gone.

"Then lesson one is that we make no plans," Lacey said. "We do whatever we feel like doing. For starters, there's a stack of new books in the living room. And since it looks as if it's going to pour any minute, that makes this the perfect day to curl up in front of the fire with a good book."

"Sounds good to me. Did you bring that new management book? I haven't had time to get to it yet."

Lacey shot him a disapproving frown. "No management books. Try mysteries, political thrillers, maybe a biography, as long as it's not about some titan of industry. Remember when we used to spend all day sitting out back, doing nothing more than reading and sipping iced tea?"

"Vaguely. Are you sure I wasn't reading management books?"

She grinned. "Positive."

"Political tracts?"

"Afraid not."

"I was reading fiction?" He was incredulous.

She nodded. "At the beach you read fiction. Actually I take that back. If I recall correctly, you fell asleep with the books in your hands. I can't swear that you read any of them."

"No wonder not one single plot comes back to me."

She smiled, then, and leaned closer. To his surprise she laced her fingers through his.

"It's going to be okay," she promised. "This awkwardness will pass."

"Will it?" he questioned doubtfully. "Sometimes I feel as if I'm an amnesiac trying to recall a part of my life that's completely blanked out. You seem to have such a vivid recollection of the way things used to be."

Lacey sighed and withdrew her hand. "Maybe I do live too much in the past. Maybe it's wrong to want to go back. But I think about how perfectly attuned we were, how much we treasured quiet moments, and I can't help having regrets. Now we can't even get through a single evening without arguing."

Kevin couldn't deny the truth in that. "We aren't the same people we were when we met. Lacey, we were eleven years old. We were kids."

"We were the same way when we were twenty-one, even thirty-one," she reminded him, suddenly angry. "We were on the same wavelength. We shared everything. We could practically finish each other's sentences, though thank God we didn't. It all started to change—"

"When I went to work at Halloran," he finished for her, his own temper flaring. How long did she intend to throw that decision back in his face? "Why is going to work for my father so terrible? Jason's there, too. I don't hear you criticizing him for making that choice."

"It was his *choice,* Kevin. It was what he always wanted. You were railroaded into it by Brandon."

The last of Kevin's patience snapped. "Was our life so rosy before that? Don't you remember the way we had to squeeze every last penny out of every dollar we made? Don't you remember the nights I came home so frustrated and angry that my jaws ached from clenching my teeth? Don't you remember how we both woke up one day to the fact that no matter what we did, no matter how hard we worked to fight the system, the system wasn't going to change unless we worked within it?" He slammed his fist down on the table. "For God's sake, Lacey, we aren't idealistic children anymore."

Her eyes widened during his tirade, then slowly

filled with hurt. "Is that what you think, that I haven't grown up? Is that it, Kevin? If so, then maybe we're wasting our time here, after all."

Her jaw set, she picked up the breakfast dishes and carried them to the counter. Her back to him, he could see the deep sigh shudder through her in the instant before she slammed the dishes down so hard it was a wonder they didn't shatter. She grabbed her jacket from a peg by the back door and stormed out, leaving him filled with rage and the uneasy sense that this brief but cutting argument might well have been their last.

He hadn't meant to accuse her of immaturity. It wasn't that at all. But it was true that she tended to cling to ideals, rather than deal with the practicalities. Looking at Halloran's bottom line had put things into the right perspective for him. He'd been able to provide for his family, give them the way of life they deserved. He had helped Brandon to make the company even stronger, kept him from at least some of his own wild schemes that would have cut deeply into their profits. Jason would have a legacy now, as would his child. What more did Lacey want from him?

Kevin waited anxiously after that, starting each time he thought he heard a sound. He wanted to finish the argument, make her see his point of view for once.

His frayed nerves grew worse with each passing hour. By mid-morning, with rain pelting the windows with the force of sleet, he was worried sick. Where was she?

He consoled himself with the thought that no one would stay outdoors in weather like this. Surely she had taken refuge with one of the neighbors. He glanced repeatedly out the front window to reassure himself that the car was still in the driveway, that she'd hadn't taken it and fled.

When Lacey wasn't back by noon, worry turned to anger. She had to know what she was doing to him, he thought. She could have called, let him know that she was safe and dry.

As quickly as the fury rose, though, it abated. What if she weren't safe? What if she had fallen and hurt herself? What if she were cold and wet, stranded on the beach somewhere, caught by a rising tide? *What ifs* chased through his mind and turned the canned soup he'd forced himself to eat into acid in his stomach.

It was nearly one o'clock when Kevin heard Lacey's footsteps on the back porch. He threw open the door and found her standing there looking soaked and be-draggled. Even as he met her gaze, he saw her shiver, her whole body trembling violently. The patches of color in her cheeks were too vivid. Her lips had an unhealthy bluish tint. She looked as if she might keel over into his arms.

"My God," he murmured, pulling her inside. "Did you decide to go for a swim?"

Her teeth chattered as she tried to answer.

Fury evaporated as he focused on her needs. There would be time enough for recriminations later. "Never mind," he said. "Let's get you out of these clothes and into a warm tub."

He reached for her jacket, but she pushed his hands away. "To-o-o c-c-old," she murmured.

"Well, this soggy mess won't do much to change that. Come on, Lacey, take it off, I'll go get you a blanket and you can sit in front of the fire while I run the bath water."

Teeth still chattering, she nodded finally and began working at the buttons. Satisfied that she was going to follow instructions, Kevin went into the bedroom and pulled the quilt off his bed. When he got back to the kitchen with it, he halted in the doorway, his expression stunned.

Lacey had stripped down to her underwear—scraps of lace that hid nothing, including the fact that her nipples had peaked into hard buds from the chill air. He drew in a ragged breath and forced himself to sacrifice his need to study every inch of her lovely, fragile body that had changed so little through the years. He wrapped her in the quilt and held her close until the violent shivering stopped.

With his chin resting on the quilt draped over her shoulders, he asked, "Better?"

"Much," she said, her voice finally steady.

"Then go sit in front of the fire, okay?"

Lacey nodded, then turned to meet his gaze. "Thanks."

"For what?"

"For not telling me what a fool I am."

He grinned. "I'm saving that for later."

After an instant's pause she managed a wobbly grin of her own. "I should have known."

When the bath water had been drawn and the tub was filled with her favorite fragrant bubbles, he called her into the bathroom. She drew in a deep breath of the steamy air.

"Heaven," she declared.

"I'll warm up some soup for you. Don't stay too

long," he said, wishing he dared to linger, wishing she would invite him to join her in that oversized tub as she had so often in the past. Imagining her skin slick and sensitized beneath his touch made his body grow taut.

Her gaze rose to meet his, and he could tell from the smoldering look in her eyes that she remembered, too, and that she could see exactly what the memories were doing to him. "I won't be long," she promised.

Reluctantly Kevin closed the door, then leaned against it, suddenly weak with longing. Oh, how he ached for her. How badly he wanted to hold her, to caress her, to claim her once more as his own. The longing spread through him, a slow flame that warmed and lured. If he knew anything at all about his wife, she too was burning. She too was filled with a sweet, aching need that nothing short of tender caresses and uninhibited passion would satisfy.

He forced himself to go back into the kitchen, to throw Lacey's soggy clothes into the washer, to pour a healthy serving of soup into the saucepan on the stove. The routine got him through the worst of the wanting. He was even able to have a perfectly rational discussion with himself about the dangers of rushing things.

Not that it meant a hill of beans when Lacey walked back into the kitchen with her blond hair curling damply around her face, her skin glowing from the fragrant steam. His body told him exactly what he could do with all of his rationalizations.

The only thing that saved him from making an absolute fool of himself was the way his wife pounced on the soup as if she hadn't eaten in days. Only when she'd finished the entire bowl, sighed and leaned back to sip a cup of tea did he dare to speak.

"Where did you go this morning?" He was proud of the casual tone.

"For a walk on the beach."

"In the pouring rain? Were you that furious with me?"

She shrugged. "I was furious, but the truth of the matter is that it wasn't raining when I left. I was a couple of miles up the beach before it got really bad. I started to head back, but by then the tide had come in and I couldn't get around the point. When I realized it wasn't going to let up anytime soon, I climbed the cliff."

Kevin's eyes widened. "You're terrified of heights."

"I'm not so thrilled with the idea of catching pneumonia, either. I figured climbing was the lesser of two evils. I only panicked once when I made the mistake of looking down. It wasn't all that far, but it looked damned treacherous and slippery."

"It *is* treacherous and slippery. You could have broken your neck."

"But I didn't," she said, looking pleased with herself.

He hesitated, then finally said, "Should we talk about what happened this morning?"

Her smile faded. "Not now. I'm exhausted."

Though he was reluctant to put the discussion off any longer, he nodded. "Go on and take a nap then. I'll clean up here."

She shook her head. "I think I'll go sit in front of the fire instead."

She stood up and started for the door, then turned back. "Kevin?"

He stopped halfway between the table and the sink. "Yes?"

"Will you come join me when you're finished?"

Irritated that even this small overture aroused him to a state of aching desire, he nearly refused. Then he caught the wistfulness in her eyes and realized that to deny them both a moment's pleasure was absurd.

"I'll be there in a minute," he promised.

Lacey wasn't entirely sure what impulse had made her ask Kevin to join her in the living room. Goodness knew the man had infuriated her earlier with the suggestion that she was behaving immaturely just because she wanted her husband healthy and happy again. Of course, she'd only added proof to his claim by running out. She should have stayed and talked, held her temper and listened to his explanation. That was the only way this was going to work.

They needed so desperately to talk. She needed to comprehend why he'd been so quick to condemn her attitude. He needed to understand exactly what she was trying to recapture. They both needed to discover if there was any common ground left at all. They couldn't do that without putting all their cards on the table, even the ones most likely to hurt.

She was too tired now to get into it again, but asking Kevin to join her in the living room had been an overture, at least. It had been impossible to miss the longing in his eyes when he'd come upon her in the middle of the kitchen with nothing but bra and panties keeping her decent. That longing had turned to desire as he'd stood beside the tub watching her lower herself into the foam of lilac-scented bubbles. Lacey knew exactly what Kevin was feeling, because it had taken every ounce of willpower she possessed to refrain from inviting him to share the bath with her.

All the talking and listening would have to wait, though. Now she wanted nothing more than to curl up on the sofa and stare at the mesmerizing flames. She wanted only to let the fire's heat soak into her bones.

As it did, she could feel herself relaxing, feel her eyes drifting shut. She blinked and forced herself awake. She wanted to stay awake until Kevin was by her side, but tension, exercise and fear had exhausted her. Her eyes closed again.

She had only the vaguest sense when Kevin joined her on the sofa. When he whispered her name, she thought she responded, but couldn't be sure. Then she felt herself being resettled in his arms, and it was as if she'd come home at last. A sigh trembled on her lips, and then she slept as she hadn't slept in all the lonely months they'd been apart.

Chapter 8

Kevin stood in the doorway of the kitchen watching the play of sunlight on Lacey's hair. She'd left it loose, not bothering to tame the haphazard curls that framed her face. It shimmered with silver and gold highlights, reminding him of the way it had looked on their wedding day.

There was something radiant and serene about her today, just as there had been then. However she felt about yesterday's disagreements, she had obviously pushed them out of her mind. She looked beautiful, despite the fact that she was elbow-deep in dirt that was still damp from the previous day's rain.

"What on earth are you doing?" he inquired as she scowled fiercely at something she saw.

In response, a clump of weeds flew over her shoulder and landed at his feet.

"I'm trying to make some order out of this mess. The weeds have taken over," she muttered without turning to look at him.

"Why don't you call Rick Renfield and have him do it? Isn't that what we pay him for?"

"We pay him to keep an eye on the house, to make sure the pipes don't freeze, to see that the grass is cut. I doubt he knows the first thing about gardening."

"And you do?"

Lacey turned, then, and swiped a strand of hair out of her face with the back of her wrist. The impatient gesture left a beguiling streak of dirt across her cheek. The curly wisp promptly blew forward again.

Unable to resist, Kevin walked closer and knelt down. His fingers brushed the silken strand back, then lingered against her sun-kissed skin. With the pad of his thumb, he wiped away the smudge of dirt. He could almost swear he felt her tremble at the innocent caress.

She gazed up at him and his heart stilled.

"You've forgotten that I was the one who put in all the flower beds at our first house," she said. "I landscaped that entire yard."

He regarded her with a faint sense of puzzlement. "I thought you just did that because we didn't have the money back then to hire somebody."

"I did it because I enjoyed it," she said almost angrily, backing away from his touch. "When we moved, you hired a gardener and I never had the chance again. Tomas wouldn't even let me near the rose bushes to clip them for the house, much less indulge me by letting me plant something."

"Why didn't you say something?"

"To him?"

"No. To me."

"I did," she said. "You never listened."

He heard the weary resignation in her tone and winced. "I'm sorry. I guess I thought you'd prefer to spend your time on all those committees you were forever joining."

"And you were wrong," she said curtly. "I joined those committees because you wanted me to and because there was nothing left for me to do at home. We had a gardener and a housekeeper. If Jason had been younger, you probably would have insisted on a nanny."

Kevin stood up and shoved his hands into his pockets. "Most women would kill to have full-time household help, especially with a house as large as ours and with all the entertaining we needed to do."

"I am *not* most women."

For emphasis she jammed a trowel into the rain-softened earth and muttered something more, something he couldn't quite make out. He decided it was just as well. He doubted it was complimentary.

Again Kevin wished that their first tentative steps toward a reconciliation weren't so incredibly awkward. So many things seemed to be blurted out in anger, complaints long buried. Once minor, now they seemed almost insurmountable.

He wondered if Lacey was right. Had she told him all this before? Had he failed to listen, sure that he was giving her what she wanted, rather than what he thought she deserved?

There were times he felt as if he were learning about

this woman all over again, rather than simply picking up the threads of a relationship that had weathered more than a quarter of a century. He tried to accept that it was going to take time, that two people who had apparently lost the ability to communicate what was in their hearts weren't going to relearn the skill overnight.

"I was thinking of going for a walk on the beach," Kevin said finally, unwilling to pursue the dangerous direction of their conversation on such a beautiful afternoon. They needed time just to be together, not a nonstop confrontation.

"It's a beautiful day for it," Lacey said, then added sternly, "Remember not to overdo it. Even though you've made remarkable progress, Linc wants you to take it easy."

That said, she seemed to be waiting, but for what, he wondered. An invitation? Surely she knew she was welcome. Then again, nothing could be taken for granted as it once had been. "Want to come along?" he asked.

For an instant he thought she was going to refuse, using the gardening as an excuse. He could see the refusal forming on her lips when she turned her face up to meet his gaze, then something shifted. Her mouth curved into a faint smile.

"Sure," she said, taking off her gardening gloves and tossing them aside. "Let me get a sweater. The wind is probably colder down by the water."

Kevin nodded and watched her go inside. When she emerged, a bulky red sweater topped her snug-fitting jeans. He had a hunch it was one of his daughter-in-law's designs. It was certainly far bolder than what

Lacey usually wore in town. There she tended to stick to cashmere and pearls, as understated and elegant as any society matron in the city.

In fact, with his hours at work and his business commitments, he had seen her more often in sleek designer evening wear than anything casual. With her quiet grace, her stunning figure and youthful complexion, she had done the name of Halloran proud, after all. Even Brandon had admitted that.

Kevin thought it was odd that he was only now realizing that he liked her better this way. It reminded him of the girl he'd fallen in love with, the girl in hand-me-downs who'd felt the needs of others so deeply, the girl who'd learned to overcome her shyness in order to fight for the things in which she believed with all her heart.

Including their marriage.

As much as it troubled and angered him, Kevin knew that's what Lacey had been doing when she'd walked out the door of their Boston home months ago. She hadn't left in defeat or even fury. She had left with the hope that her daring ultimatum would get his attention as nothing else had.

If it hadn't been for this most recent heart attack, he wondered if they would be here today or whether his stubborn refusal to acknowledge the validity of her claims would still be keeping them apart.

Knowing that somehow he had to fight for each precious moment until he could regain her trust, he held out his hand. After an instant's hesitation, she took it. They climbed over the dunes to reach the hard-packed sand by the water's edge.

The ocean was quieter today, its pace late-afternoon lazy as it shimmered silver gray in the sun. He felt good holding his wife's hand again as the sun's warmth kissed their shoulders and a cool breeze fanned their faces.

"Remember," he began at the same time she did. He glanced into her eyes and saw the laughter lurking in the blue depths. "You first."

"I was just remembering the first time we came here."

"To this house or to the Cape?"

"To this house. Your hand shook the whole time you were writing out the check for the deposit. I think in the back of your mind you viewed it as selling out to the establishment. You spent the whole weekend looking as if you expected the activist brigade to catch you and make you turn in your young idealist credentials. I was terrified you were going to back out."

"I still get a pang every now and then," he admitted candidly. "Especially when I think of how many people are homeless."

"Which explains why, the very next week, you donated money to create a homeless shelter. For a few anxious days I was afraid you were going to try to donate this place."

"Back then if it hadn't been for the zoning problems, I probably would have."

"And now?"

"I'm grateful you talked me into it. It's the one place where I feel as if we connect."

Lacey nodded. "I feel that, too. It's because it's the

one place where we have only happy memories. We never allowed our differences to follow us here."

Kevin returned her gaze evenly, pained by the depth of hurt that shadowed her blue eyes.

"And when the differences got to be too much to put aside, I just stopped coming," he admitted, certain that she would be angered or at the very least hurt by the brutal honesty. To his surprise she was nodding as if it were something she'd realized long ago.

"I know," she confirmed softly. "That made me saddest of all. We've lost three years here, years we can never get back. We missed the flowers blooming in the spring, the lazy summer days, the change of the leaves in the fall. Even before we were married, Cape Cod was where we always came to witness the changing of the seasons. Now the seasons just rush by."

"Don't," he whispered, pausing by the edge of the water and cupping her chin. "Don't count them as lost. We can learn from them. We can build on a foundation that's all the stronger for having weathered this crisis."

As tears welled in Lacey's eyes, Kevin drew her slowly into his arms, holding her loosely. At first she was stiff, but in no more than a heartbeat she began to relax, her arms circling his waist, her head resting against his chest, where he was sure she could hear his heart thunder.

The scents of salt water and flowery perfume swirled around him as he gave himself over to the sensations that just holding her stirred. His blood roared in his veins, then slowed as contentment stole over him. When had he last felt this peaceful? Months ago? Years?

"When you say it like that," she murmured, the words muffled against his chest, "I can almost believe we will work things out."

"Believe it, Lacey. I want it with all my heart."

"So do I."

But they both knew that wanting alone was not nearly enough.

Lacey was standing in front of the kitchen counter up to her elbows in bread dough and flour. She studied the mess and wondered what had possessed her to try to bake bread, when the best bakery in the universe was less than a mile away, to say nothing of Mrs. Renfield, who would gladly trade one of her home-baked loaves for more of that fancy material.

Maybe it had something to do with the confession she'd made the day before. It was true that she had resented giving up the claim to her own kitchen, her own gardens. She had spoken out, but obviously not forcefully enough if Kevin had no memory of it. Maybe she had just given up, once it was clear that he'd made up his mind. Maybe it was her own fault, as much as his. For all of his talents, he wasn't a mind reader. If she had capitulated, he must have thought it was simply because he'd convinced her.

Maybe she was baking bread because she was still shaken by the way she had felt with Kevin's arms around her. Each time he touched her, each time he gazed into her eyes, each time she felt his kindness surrounding her like the warmth of a quilt, he stripped away some of her defenses. After that, Lacey had desperately needed a project that would give her time to re-group. What better way to do that than tackling something she'd never tried before?

Just as she was resolving never to give in so easily again to his persuasive arguments or his touches, she heard Kevin's muffled chuckle behind her and whirled on him. She shook a warning finger at him, sending out a fine mist of flour.

"Don't say it. Don't even think it."

His eyes sparkled with amusement. "I was just admiring your domesticity. I suppose this is one of those other things I robbed you of by hiring a housekeeper."

She heard the note of good-natured teasing in his tone, but she was in no mood for it, not with this mess spread out around her. "Do you recall my ever baking bread?"

"Nope."

"That's right. I never once attempted it, even before you hired the housekeeper. Thank goodness you never wanted to live in one of those communes where everyone baked their own bread and lived off the vegetables they grew themselves."

"Without toxic pesticides, of course."

She grinned. "Of course."

"So why are you baking bread now?"

"Because I should have learned," she said, aware as she said it how ridiculous she sounded.

"Excuse me?" Kevin queried, justifiably confused by her convoluted logic.

"I know how you like home-baked bread. It was something I always meant to learn, but first one thing and then another came along and I never did."

"So you're learning now?"

She swiped her hand across her face. "More or less. I stopped by Mrs. Renfield's while you were resting this afternoon and asked her for the recipe."

"Maybe you should have asked her for another loaf of bread."

Lacey scowled at Kevin for echoing her own thoughts. "Go away."

He nodded agreeably. "No problem. When should I come back?"

"Try breakfast. I figure I ought to have some semblance of bread figured out by then."

"We haven't had dinner yet."

"Don't you think I know that? I forgot about all that rising and kneading and stuff. It takes time."

"I'd really like some dinner." At her fierce expression, he quickly amended, "Not right away, but soon. Say, by eight?"

"So order a pizza," she growled.

His eyes lit up. "A pizza! Great idea." He reached for the phone.

"Wait!"

He turned back. "I knew it was too good to be true. No pizza, huh?"

"Chinese. Call for Chinese. Nothing fried, nothing with eggs. That should be healthy enough. I think there's a menu from a carryout place by the phone in the living room."

He then left her alone to pummel the damn dough and rue the precise moment when she'd had this brainstorm. She slammed her fist into the doughy mound sending a spray of flour into the air. There was a certain amount of satisfaction in the action. Maybe she ought to recommend it to Kevin as a way to work off tension at the end of a long day at Halloran Industries.

Lacey thought she had the bread under control by the time Kevin came back. She'd actually put the dough into bread pans to rise for the last time. She stood back and admired them, breathing in the yeasty scent. Suddenly she realized she was starved.

"What did you order?" she asked him as he came over to examine the end result of her labors thus far.

"Chow mein, lemon chicken and for you fried rice with shrimp."

"Sounds heavenly."

"I placed another order while I was in there, too," he said, tossing a catalog onto the table. "Check out page five and see what you think."

Lacey's gaze narrowed as she picked up the brochure from a store famous for its kitchenware. She flipped the first couple of pages until she found the item he'd circled: an outrageously expensive automatic bread maker.

"You didn't," she said, laughter bubbling up as she looked at his smug expression.

"I did. If baking bread is going to make you happy, you might as well have the right equipment."

"There are some who'd say this is cheating."

"I prefer to think of it as modernization."

She grinned at him. "I'm not sure your motive is all that altruistic. I suspect you're just hoping I'll convert so you'll have some chance of getting your meals on time."

"Not me," he said piously. "I could live on love."

"I suppose that's why we're having Chinese carry-out tonight."

"Exactly. I *love* Chinese carryout."

Lacey caught the devilish twinkle in his eyes and suddenly felt warm all over. In moments like this she felt the deep, abiding pull of her love for Kevin all over again. She knew a lot of women who would regard a kitchen appliance as a sorry excuse for a romantic gift. She also knew that she would always see it as the first concrete evidence that the sensitive, considerate man she'd fallen in love with still existed.

Chapter 9

Lacey drove into town for a much-needed break from Kevin's gentle attentiveness. After nearly two weeks, she was finding it more and more difficult to ignore her mounting desires and keep her resolve.

Simply wandering the aisles of the grocery store kept her mind on more mundane matters. It was virtually impossible to feel particularly romantic in the frozen food section of the supermarket. It was also good to see other people, many of whom she recognized from past trips.

She had just turned the corner of the canned goods aisle, when she ran into Mrs. Renfield. Dressed in a blue-flowered cotton blouse, a matching sweater the shade of Texas bluebonnets, gray slacks and sensible black shoes, the seventy-five-year-old widow didn't look a day over sixty. There was scarcely a wrinkle on her face, a testament to the floppy-brimmed hat she always wore to work in her garden and to walk on the beach. Though her gray hair looked as if it might have been chopped off with hedge clippers, the short style was actually very becoming.

"Lacey, dear, how wonderful to see you. How did your bread turn out?"

"It was edible," Lacey said ruefully. "But it wasn't nearly as good as yours."

The older woman waved off the compliment. "You'll get the hang of it soon enough. Wouldn't you and Kevin like to drop by for tea this afternoon? I've just made another cherry cobbler. I know how much you both love it. There's even enough for Jason and that new wife of his. Are you expecting them anytime soon?"

"Maybe this weekend, in fact. Kevin mentioned after he talked to Jason this morning that they hoped to drive out on Saturday morning."

"Then you must come by and collect the cobbler. Besides, I haven't seen Kevin once since the two of you came out here."

"I know," Lacey said. "He's been sticking pretty close to home. He's still trying to get his strength back."

"Well, there's nothing better for that than fresh salt air and a brisk walk on the beach. You bring him by for tea and I'll tell him so myself."

Lacey grinned at her. "If I were you, I'd keep my advice to myself. Kevin is getting tired of being told what to do."

"Fiddle-faddle. He can grumble all he wants at me.

I can take it. I raised six boys and you'd better believe they all still listen when I have something to say."

"I'm sure they do. I'll see how Kevin's feeling when I get home. I'll call if we can make it over. If not today, soon. I promise."

Mrs. Renfield regarded Lacey intently and patted her hand. "My dear, you mustn't take it to heart when he loses his temper. Men never can deal with being sick. They take it out on whoever's closest to them."

With that reassurance given, the elderly woman was on her way, pushing her grocery cart briskly down the aisle without a backward glance. She was stopped twice more by friends before she reached the end of the row.

How had she known? Lacey wondered. How had a woman she knew only slightly guessed that Kevin was scowling impatiently every time Lacey dared to mention that he was pushing himself too hard?

She shrugged finally. Maybe it wasn't some odd psychic power. Maybe it was simply a matter of understanding the nature of the beast. After all, from the time Jason was old enough to talk, he'd always been a bear, too. He moaned and groaned so pathetically, it might have broken her heart if she hadn't known that he was dealing with a cold or measles and not something fatal. She thought it was poetic justice that he was suffering from morning sickness right along with Dana.

As for Kevin, the worst of it was probably over. Day by day his strength was clearly coming back. After the first week, she had been able to see it in the energy he found to walk on the beach every morning and afternoon. He'd begun to tackle small chores around the house with some semblance of his old enthusiasm.

Lacey might have worried more about the demands he was placing on his still-healing heart, if he hadn't balanced it all with quiet hours of reading. Just last night a techno-thriller had kept him up until the wee hours of the morning. She had seen the light under his door each time she'd awakened. Today at breakfast he'd been anxious to discuss every detail of the fast-paced plot with her.

With Kevin's energy increasing, she wondered how much longer she would be able to keep him idle on the Cape, how much longer before they would have to face making a final decision about their marriage. She knew he'd started making daily phone calls to Brandon and to Jason, though he tried to mask them as nothing more than casual chats. The fact that he felt the need to hide his business calls worried her almost as much as the increasing activity. If he couldn't confide even that, how could they expect to communicate about the really important issues facing them?

When Lacey came home from the store an hour later to find Kevin atop a ladder, clinging to the roof, she felt her heart climb in her throat. As she watched, he saw her and waved, his expression cheerful, his balance at the top of that ladder more precarious than ever.

"I'll be down in a minute," he called as she left the car door open and rushed across the yard to steady the ladder for his descent.

When he finally reached the ground and her own pulse rate slowed to something close to normal, she whirled on him. "Kevin Halloran, are you out of your mind?" Hands on hips, she stood toe-to-toe with him. "What did you think you were doing?"

"Checking the drainpipe for leaves," he replied nonchalantly. He dropped a casual kiss on her forehead. "No big deal."

Lacey felt her temper climb. "No big deal. *No big deal!* You could have fallen and no one would have been here to help. You're not supposed to go up and down steps, much less ladders. What if you'd gotten dizzy?" she demanded, listening to the hysterical rise of her voice, but unable to control it.

"I would have held on until the dizziness passed," he said so calmly that she nearly missed the glint of anger in his eye. "You have to stop hovering over me, Lacey. I can't take much more of it. I won't let you make me out to be an invalid."

She felt as if he'd slapped her. Unshed tears stung her eyes.

"Hovering?" she repeated furiously, Mrs. Renfield's wise advice a distant memory. "Is that what I've been doing? Well, I'm sorry. I thought I was just thinking about your welfare. I thought I was just trying to make sure that you recuperated the way Linc wanted you to. I'm sorry all to hell for worrying about you!"

If she'd had the groceries in her arms, she would have thrown them at him. Instead, she turned and stomped off, only to have him catch her by the arm and twirl her around to meet his equally furious gaze.

Before Lacey could catch her breath, Kevin's lips were on hers, hard and urgent. There was a raw, primitive anger behind the kiss, a battle for possession and control

She had known the kiss was coming for days now, known that their mutual desire could be banked only so long. She wanted desperately to fight his claim, but her body's needs wouldn't let her. She had hungered for far too long to feel Kevin's mouth on hers, to feel his heat rising, drawing her closer with the certain lure of an old lover. Day by day that hunger had grown, controlled only by stern lectures and rigid willpower.

Now, with the decision taken out of her control, her hands fisted, clinging to the rough denim of his shirt. He dragged her closer until their bodies fit together as naturally as two pieces of a puzzle. Her mouth opened too eagerly for the sweet invasion of his tongue. Within seconds the punishing kiss became a bold, urgent caress that set off a fire low inside her. Her blood rushed to a wilder rhythm.

It had been so long, so terribly long, since she had felt this alluring heat, since his clean, masculine scent had teased her senses. Her responses were instinctive, as doubts and warnings fled. This was the way she and Kevin had once been together—sensual creatures who stirred to passion with the most innocent touch, the most casual glance. This had been the crowning glory of their love, a lure so powerful that nothing, *nothing* could have stood in their way.

Thinking, as she had, that it had been lost, she exhilarated in the sensations pulsing through her body, the quick rise of heat, the questing hunger, the aching need. And all because of a kiss—a single, long, deep, slow kiss.

She moaned as he drew away, moaned and clung to

his shoulders, her knees weak, her breathing uneven, her emotions in turmoil.

Reluctant to end the moment, Lacey was slow to open her eyes, slow to search Kevin's expression for some sign of what he was feeling. Even so, it was impossible to miss the naked longing in his eyes, the ragged rise and fall of his chest, the still-angry set to his lips.

"I want you," he said, his voice gruff. "I want you more than I've ever imagined wanting a woman." He took her hand and pressed it against him. "This is what you do to me still, after all this time."

Lacey swallowed hard against the emotions that were crowding in her chest. Her fingers lingered against the roughness of denim, lingered against the evidence of her own powerful sensuality. If she could still affect him like this, if she could still make him yearn to touch and caress and love, weren't all things possible?

Maybe. Maybe not, she thought with a sigh as she slowly withdrew. At her age she knew better than to equate passion with the forever kind of love. Knew better, but wished just the same. Oh, how she wished that these few moments of uncensored desire were proof that she and Kevin were almost there, almost back to the way they had been.

As if the rare display of vulnerability had cost him dearly, Kevin refused to go to Mrs. Renfield's for tea, but insisted Lacey accept the invitation. Lacey went through the motions, listening to the latest gossip, pretending that everything in her own life was fine, accepting the cobbler because it would have hurt the older woman's feelings to turn it down.

When she returned, Kevin was careful to avoid her, as if he feared, as she did, that the raw emotions that had rushed to the surface earlier would disrupt their tenuous hold on an atmosphere of calm.

If they dared to allow passion to run its natural course, would they ever take the time to search their hearts for the answers they needed to make their marriage work? Lacey knew that soul-searching talks were something they had to do. The time was fast approaching when their discussions would have to reach deep, in order to bring all the old hurts into the open. Without such brutally painful honesty, they would never clear the air once and for all.

Lacey spent the last hours of daylight trying to stay out of Kevin's path, not yet ready for a confrontation that would rip open wounds just now healing. Nor was she ready for more of the bittersweet temptation she felt each time he was near—a temptation that taunted all the more now that she knew it was based on reality, not memories.

Kevin retreated emotionally as well as physically. Perhaps, she thought, because his own pride was at stake. He had shown himself to be vulnerable, and she doubted he would allow her to see his need again. Like boxers they had gone to their respective corners to soothe their wounds and prepare for the next round.

That night their unspoken truce was still uneasy. The conversation at dinner was stilted and confined to the barest attempt at politeness. More than once Kevin

looked as if he wanted to say something more important than "Pass the pepper," but each time he snapped
his mouth closed, leaving the words unsaid. He left the
table before dessert, declaring that the cobbler should
be saved for Jason and Dana.

Lacey and Kevin sat on opposite sides of the living
room, unopened books in their hands, both of them
staring at the fire. It was Lacey, nerves unbearably
taut, who finally broke the silence.

"I picked up a movie at the video store earlier.
Would you like to watch it?"

Kevin shrugged. "We might as well. You put it on.
I'll be back in a minute."

When he hadn't returned after a few minutes, she
went looking for him. She found him in the kitchen
with the refrigerator door open wide. He was scanning
the newly filled shelves.

"What are you looking for?" she asked.

"Something to eat while we watch the movie."

She knew what he meant by that. To his way of
thinking, carrot sticks, apples and celery were not
snacks. A bowl of chocolate chip ice cream, a bigger bowl of buttered popcorn or a handful of crackers with cheddar cheese went with old movies. So did
Mrs. Renfield's latest cherry cobbler, which just an
hour earlier Kevin had vowed to save. Yet in the midst
of a snack attack, she doubted he would remember
the promise.

Lacey also knew that she dare not offer advice on
the subject of his diet. He'd already indicated what he
thought of her interference. She consoled herself with a
reminder that Kevin was a grown man. If he was going

to improve his health, it would have to be a conscious choice on his part. It was time to let go of her own need to protect him, a need based on her desperate fear of losing him. It was no easier than Jason's first day at school or his departure for college. In so many ways it was more important than either.

Kevin glanced back at her, his expression defensive. "No comment?" he inquired.

"None."

He muttered something under his breath, reached into the refrigerator and withdrew the carrot sticks. Lacey let out the breath she'd been holding. Kevin put a handful of the carrots on a plate, regarded them with disgust and slammed the refrigerator door.

"This better be one helluva a movie," he grumbled as he stalked past her.

"Bogart and Bacall," she reminded him. "How could it be anything else?"

In no time at all Kevin was so absorbed in the film that he didn't even reach for the remaining carrots. Just as Lacey had finally begun to relax, the phone rang. She grabbed it as Kevin cut off the VCR and headed for the kitchen.

"Lacey, it's Paula. Is this a bad time?"

"No, it's fine." Unless Kevin was using it as an excuse to sneak the last of that cobbler, she thought. "What's up?"

"We could really use your help tomorrow. Is there any chance at all you can get to Boston?"

Lacey had a hunch it would be good to allow Kevin some space, more than she'd given him even today. Not only that, she knew she could do with a real break. The nonstop tension of fighting Kevin and her own emotions was beginning to get to her.

"I may be late, but I'll be there," she promised.

"Are you okay? You sound funny," Paula said, quick to pick up on Lacey's mood.

"I'm just tired. I'll get a good night's sleep and be fine by the time I see you."

"If you say so," her friend said skeptically. "Is Kevin okay?"

"Getting better all the time," she responded honestly.

"And you don't intend to say any more than that with him there," Paula replied. "Okay, I'll let you go for now, but be prepared to discuss this in depth tomorrow."

Lacey's laugh was strained. "Don't threaten me, pal. I could stay here tomorrow. They're predicting seventy degrees and sunny, a perfect day for the beach."

"But I know you won't let me down. See you."

Lacey was slow to hang up. She should tell Kevin about the remarkable housing project in which Paula had involved her. Paula and her husband Dave had never lost the idealistic fervor that had once gripped Kevin and Lacey. Tonight would be the perfect opportunity to fill Kevin in on what their old friends had been doing. Maybe he would even want to ride into town with her, take a look at a project that really worked.

When he hadn't rejoined her ten minutes later, she got up and went to look for him. He wasn't in the kitchen so she walked down the hall and saw that the door to his room was closed.

She opened it a crack. "Kevin," she said softly, as worry sneaked up on her.

After a moment's silence, during which all she heard was the quickened beating of her own heart, he said, "Yes?"

"Are you okay?"

"Just tired," he answered tersely.

His tone concerned her almost as much as the admission. "You're sure that's all it is?"

"Yes. Good night, Lacey."

There was no doubt that he had dismissed her.

"Good night, Kevin," she said, an unmistakable strain in her voice. She sighed and reluctantly closed the door.

She tried watching the rest of the old movie, but couldn't keep her attention focused on the flickering black-and-white images. Finally she gave up.

In her own room, with the book she'd been reading discarded, she stared at the ceiling and wondered how they could possibly hope to salvage their marriage when more often than not they treated each other like strangers, no doubt because neither of them dared to force the issues they really needed to resolve. Instead they skirted their problems, like drivers avoiding dangerous potholes.

No more, she vowed with determination—most likely because she knew already that tomorrow offered yet another reprieve. She would use the time in Boston to think through the best way to broach things with Kevin. She would organize her thoughts, if not her emotions.

Her plan decided, Lacey tried to sleep. Unfortunately the emotions she'd vowed to dismiss wouldn't release their hold so easily. Every sigh of the wind, each creak of the bedsprings, every crash of waves was enough to bring her wide awake again.

And awake, Kevin's face was always there, and the memories of his caresses were as tantalizing as the reality.

When dawn broke at last, she couldn't wait to run.

Chapter 10

After the unending tension of the previous evening and the sleepless night, swinging a hammer actually felt good to Lacey. Admittedly she was doing it with more energy than accuracy, but she relished the pull on her muscles, the warmth of the sun on her shoulders.

All around her were the sounds of electric saws, hammers and the blare of sixties rock 'n' roll. The hammering seemed to take on the rhythm of the music.

Simply being among a group that was mostly strangers made it easier not to think about Kevin. During their time on Cape Cod, there had been too many bold glances that unnerved her, too many innocent caresses that tempted, too many whispered words designed to lure.

Especially yesterday. That kiss had very nearly been her undoing. Lacey felt as if she'd been walking a tightrope, trying to maintain her equilibrium above a sea of temptations.

Now with sweat beading on her brow and tracking between her breasts, she put all of those confusing sensations out of her mind to concentrate on the task at hand. It was either that or risk slamming the hammer on her thumb instead of hitting the nails she was supposed to drive into place in the drywall. She'd already done that twice. The result was a throbbing, black and blue thumb, but she was determined not to quit until her assigned section of the house was complete. She knew how anxiously some family was waiting for the day they could move in.

When Paula Gethers had called months ago and pleaded with her to pitch in on a unique housing project that would ultimately provide renovated, low-income homes, the concept had intrigued Lacey. And the timing couldn't have been better. She had just left Kevin, and her days were filled with endless hours of loneliness and regrets.

When Paula had said she didn't want Lacey to do fund-raising, didn't want her to write a check, Lacey had regarded her skeptically.

"What then?"

"I need you to hit nails, paint, maybe lay some tiles. Who knows, maybe I'll have you learn to install plumbing."

Lacey had burst out laughing at that. "You've got to be kidding."

Paula had shaken her head. "Nope. Come take a look."

Lacey had gone that day and been relegated to

wielding a paintbrush. She'd ended up with more paint in her hair and on her clothes than on the walls, but she'd been hooked.

The calls had come steadily after that until Lacey was involved almost as closely with the project as her old friend. Last night's call had been more welcome than all the others because it provided her with an excuse to put that much-needed space between herself and Kevin.

At one time she had been on a dozen different committees, all of them demanding, all of them worthwhile. With none of them, though, had she felt such an immediate sense of satisfaction. Never before had she been able to stand back at the end of the day and look at the results of her labors and see so clearly that her contribution of time and energy truly made a difference for some family. Lacey felt good knowing that each house might become a first home for a family previously relegated to a ramshackle public-housing project.

Admittedly there had also been a sense of poignancy. Maybe if such a program had existed years ago, there would have been help for her own family. They had lived in a cramped, run-down, rented apartment, unable to afford anything better, yet too well-off to qualify for assistance.

Lacey would never forget the first time she had gone home with Kevin. She had circled the huge Halloran home as if it were a museum, studying the paintings in Brandon's collection with a sense of awe. The furnishings were perfect, down to the last crystal vase and the matching gold lighter and cigarette case. It was the first time she had truly realized how very different their lives were, and it had terrified her.

For weeks after the visit, she had tried to break things off, tried to put some distance between them. Kevin would have none of it. Intuitively he had known how she felt and even at eighteen he had been determined.

To her horror, he had spoken to her mother and wrangled an invitation to her home for dinner. There, amidst the garage-sale collection of furnishings and the strong aroma of garlic, he had looked as out of place as a Renoir amidst paintings on velvet.

If he had been appalled, though, he hid it well. He had been lavish with his praise of her mother's cooking. With the composure of someone who'd been brought up with all the social graces, he had talked about unemployment with her father, an assembly line worker who feared each and every day would be his last on the job.

Slowly Lacey had relaxed as his charm had touched them all. The evening had been a resounding success. Only later had she realized that that night had been the start of Kevin's transition from being solely her protector to his commitment to broader change for society itself. His fervor had ignited her own and they both had developed a sense of purpose that was all the stronger because it was something they shared.

How long ago that all seemed now. Lacey tugged at the red bandanna she'd tied around her neck and pulled it free, then used it to mop her brow. If Kevin could only see her now, she thought. He wouldn't believe the streaks of dirt, the paint and sawdust that clung to her hair, the aching muscles that were proof that on this project at least she was pulling her own weight.

She wasn't sure why she hadn't forced the issue last night and told him where she intended to spend the day. Because he'd slipped away during her conversation with Paula, then taken refuge in his room, she had felt more defeated than she had in a long time. When he'd dismissed her at the doorway, she'd consoled herself that there would be time to explain in the morning.

But when morning came, she had been almost relieved to discover that he was still asleep. Rather than waking him, she'd left an innocuous note on the kitchen table beside a bowl of high-fiber cereal.

"Had to go into town. Back by dinner. L."

A zillion years ago, he would have known where she was going, would have cared about a project like this, would have been among the first to volunteer. Her subconscious decision to keep it to herself now spoke volumes about how she felt his priorities had changed.

Or, more likely, how she feared his reaction would disappoint her. If he showed no interest or, worse yet, if he belittled the effort, it would be irrefutable proof of how much he had changed.

Maybe she was selling him short, though. Maybe if she gave him a chance, he would share in her excitement. There was only one way to find out. She vowed then and there to tell him every detail over dinner. And if his response was only to pull out his pen and write a check, at least the cause would benefit.

"When was the last time you actually hit a nail?" Paula inquired, her low, throaty voice filled with amusement. She sounded as if she ought to do sultry voiceovers for commercials, rather than spend her days on a construction site. "If everyone worked at this rate, the house wouldn't be ready until next year," she said.

Lacey glanced at her old friend and laughed. "What can I say? Volunteer help starts slacking off when the sun goes down."

"We're a good hour from sunset, lady." Paula handed her a soft drink and settled on the bottom rung of a ladder. "You okay? You looked lost in thought, a little sad."

"I was just wondering what Kevin would think if he could see me now."

"Probably that you'd lost your marbles. That's what Dave thinks about me, and he's been right here every day. He still can't believe that a woman who used to get her nails done twice a week when she was in high school now has none and isn't hysterical over it." She held up her hands, displaying the blunt-cut nails that were free of polish. Tiny cuts and specks of paint had turned them into a worker's hands. "They may not be as pretty, but I figure I've earned every battle scar."

She regarded Lacey closely. "Why haven't you told Kevin about this?"

"I'm not sure," Lacey admitted. "I was just thinking that I'd tell him tonight."

"You might have a glass of brandy nearby in case he swoons from shock the way Dave did. Or you could just bring him by sometime," she suggested slyly. "That's how I sold Dave and you and just about everyone else who's gotten involved."

Lacey grinned. "A pretty sneaky trick, if you ask me."

"I'll use whatever it takes if it means getting these

houses fixed up faster. I've fine-tuned my approach to the contractors so they start saying yes when they see me coming. You should have heard the number I pulled on the mayor. I've never been more eloquent, if I do say so myself."

"Has he committed any city funds yet?"

Paula shook her head. "I'm not counting on the city for anything. This is all about private citizens helping each other. I wanted him to cough up his own bucks and a few weekends of his time. I figured he'd be the ideal role model for all the other politicians and give this program some much-needed visibility."

"Did he agree?"

"It's an election year. Just imagine the photo opportunities," she said dryly. She glanced at her watch. "If you're going back out to the Cape tonight, you'd better get started. It will be dark soon and we'll have to shut down for the night, anyway."

Lacey nodded. "I'll try to get back later in the week, by next weekend for sure."

"Who knows? Maybe you'll have Kevin along."

"Yes. Who knows," she said, but she couldn't mask her very real doubts.

If the furious expression on Kevin's face when she drove up was any indication, Lacey figured she'd better not count on him for much of anything. As she crossed the lawn, he opened the screen door and stepped outside.

When she was close enough, he waved her note under her nose. "What is this?"

She immediately bristled at his curt tone. "The note I left for you."

"Is this supposed to give me the first clue about where to find you? What if there'd been an emergency? What if I'd wanted to get in touch with you? Was I supposed to call all over Boston and hope I lucked out?"

She stopped in mid-step and studied him, worry washing through her. "Was there an emergency? Are you okay?"

"Dammit, this is not about my health. It's about your lack of consideration. It's about your running off without so much as a word to let me know where you were going and when you'd be back."

Lacey swallowed the angry retort that rose automatically to her lips. Maybe now he would know how she felt more often than not, shut out and filled with loneliness and longing.

"Well," he demanded, "what do you have to say for yourself?"

"Nothing," she said softly. "You're obviously too upset to listen to reason."

"Don't you dare patronize me."

"We'll discuss it over dinner," she said with deliberate calm as she left him standing in the front hall.

"Oh, no," he said, catching up with her in the doorway to the kitchen and moving quickly into her path. "We'll discuss it *now*."

Lacey drew in a deep breath and lifted her gaze to clash with his. "Kevin, for the past decade you have not once beat me home in the evenings. I have always left a note just in case. Today I did the same thing. I told you I had gone out, and I told you when I'd be home.

I figured you wouldn't be any more interested in the details than you usually are."

Despite her best efforts, she hadn't been able to keep the bitterness out at the end. He looked stunned.

"Not interested?" he repeated softly. "I'm always interested in everything you do."

"No," she said evenly. "That was true once, but not recently. As long as I was there to greet you every evening, as long as I never disrupted your plans, you never once asked a question about how I spent my days."

"I assumed you went to those meetings," he muttered defensively.

"*Those meetings,* as you refer to them, were a sorry substitute for having any real purpose in my life. I know that I am as much to blame for allowing that to happen as you are, but the fact of the matter is that for too long now I have been frustrated, lonely and bored to tears. While you've been climbing the corporate ladder of success, I've been searching for some niche I could fill. Thanks to Paula, I've found it."

For an instant he looked puzzled. Puzzlement slowly turned to incredulity. "Paula Gethers? The one who used to organize peace marches? I didn't know the two of you even saw each other anymore."

"Actually we see each other quite a lot. I'm helping her to renovate houses."

Kevin's mouth dropped open. "You're what?" he asked, not even trying to hide his astonishment and disbelief.

"Renovating houses," she repeated a bit more emphatically.

"You mean hiring contractors, decorators, that sort of thing?"

"No. I mean picking up hammers and paintbrushes and screwdrivers." She held out her hands for his inspection.

He took her hands and examined them, slowly taking in the specks of paint that had escaped her cleaning, the blister on one finger, the black and blue under the nail of her thumb.

"My God," he breathed softly, as he gently smoothed his fingers over the rough spots. "You're serious, aren't you?"

Lacey withdrew her hand before his touch made her forget how irritated she was. "Never more so," she said with a hint of defiance.

"But why? You could hire anyone you wanted to do that sort of work."

"Not for this. There's no money involved. The work is done by volunteers. The materials are donated. Then the houses are turned over to needy families. Paula's more familiar with the financial arrangements made with the families, but I do know they have to help with the construction."

The last traces of anger vanished from Kevin's eyes. Lacey could tell the exact instant when his imagination caught fire. Her breath caught in her throat. A radiant burst of hope spilled through her.

"Sit down and tell me," he said, urging her to the table. He poured them each a cup of coffee and sat down opposite her. "How does it work? Who's involved?"

Kevin's sudden burst of enthusiasm was catching,

reminding her of long-ago nights when they had sat just like this for hours on end. Her words tumbled over each other as she shared her excitement about the program with him. All the things she had longed to describe to him for so long came pouring out.

"I was there the day they turned over the first house I'd worked on," she said. "A single mother was moving in with her three kids. There were tears in her eyes as she walked from room to room just touching things. She said she'd never before seen anyplace so clean."

Tears welled up in Lacey's eyes as she remembered that day. "Oh, Kevin, if only you could have been there. Knowing that that house was hers filled her with so much pride and so much determination. You could see it in her face. This is the kind of social program that really works, that doesn't spend a fortune on overhead. It gets down to one of the very first basics of life, shelter."

"I want to see for myself," Kevin said when she was finally done. He got up and began to pace, just as he always had when he was trying to work out a complex problem. "Maybe there's some way Halloran can get involved," he said finally. "We could donate fabric for draperies, underwrite some of the costs to buy up land or old houses. What do you think? Would that help?"

Lacey felt a wellspring of emotion rise up inside her. *This* was the Kevin she'd fallen in love with. *This* was the man who was touched by the plight of others and wanted desperately to help.

"Thank you," she said, feeling as if a boulder had lodged in her throat.

He seemed puzzled by her emotion. "Lacey, it's

only some fabric and a few dollars. Halloran makes donations like that all the time."

She shook her head. "You're wrong. It's much more."

"I don't understand."

"Kevin, it's more proof that the man I fell in love with still exists. Don't you see? If we could work together on this, it would be a start, a new beginning for us."

As understanding dawned, he clasped her hands in his and lifted them to his mouth. He kissed each speck of paint, each blemish until Lacey was sure the earth was falling away beneath her. She wanted to fling her arms around him, wanted to welcome him back from the cold, uncaring, distant place it seemed he'd gone without her. She held back only by reminding herself that this was only a beginning.

They were up until midnight making plans. Dinner was no more than sandwiches hastily slapped together and eaten distractedly. When neither of them could hold their eyes open a minute longer, they were still reluctant to go to bed. In the hallway between their rooms, their gazes caught and held.

Lacey raised her fingers to caress his cheek. "I love you," she dared to say for the first time in months.

"And I love you," he echoed. He glanced toward the door of the master bedroom, then back to her. "Lace?"

Her heart hammered in her chest at the invitation. To spend the night in his bed again, in his arms, would be just this side of heaven. But something inside her whispered that it was still too soon, that to give in to the provocative promise in his eyes would risk everything.

"I can't," she said finally.

She saw the quick hurt in his eyes and wished she could take the words back, but it was too late. Already he was retreating.

How many more times could she bring herself to say no? she wondered. How many more times could Kevin hear it without distancing himself from her for good? Would she even know when it was time to put her heart and soul on the line, no matter what?

The elusive answer to those questions kept her awake most of the night. When the early morning hours came, the questions were still there. And the answers were no clearer.

Chapter 11

So many times during the night Kevin was tempted to get up and go across the hall. It was three o'clock when he knew he could no longer deny himself. Lacey was still his wife. He still loved her with all his heart. And he knew in his gut that the longer they allowed this foolishness of separate bedrooms to go on, the more difficult it would be to end.

The longing in Lacey's eyes tonight had been unmistakable. Whatever was holding her back mystified him. She wasn't the type to play games. She never had been. Even when they had made love for the very first time, there had been no coy pretenses between them.

His thoughts drifted back to that long-ago night. It had been here on Cape Cod, the summer after their freshman year in college. Vacation was almost over and they faced another long year of being apart, thanks to his father's determined interference.

They had come to the beach for the weekend with friends, but had quickly abandoned them in favor of privacy. They had gone for a walk on the beach, their way lit by the full moon. When they found a secluded cove, he had spread a blanket on the still-warm sand. Other nights, other summers, they had done no more than sit and talk, often until dawn, but somehow both of them knew that this night would be different. The love that had blossomed between them with a slow, sweet dawning needed expression in a new and exciting way.

Lacey had made the first bold move. With his eyes riveted on her, she had slowly removed her clothes. She had been a virgin, yet there had been no shyness in her that night. She had stood before him, naked in the moonlight, proud, her eyes filled with love.

"Make love to me," she had whispered.

Uncertain, he was the one to hesitate. He had always been so sure that he was the stronger one, but that night Lacey had proved him wrong. She had been bold and daring, while he thought his heart would split in two with the sheer joy of making her his.

Slowly, tenderly he had claimed her, enchanted by the velvet softness of her flesh, intoxicated by the taste of her. He had wanted her for so long, needed her forever it seemed. His hands trembled as they cupped her breasts. His pulse raced as he touched her moist warmth. She had been so hot, so ready for him, so eager to guide him into her.

As he sank into her that very first time, she had

cried out his name, not in pain as he had feared, but in unmistakable exhilaration. Surrounded by her heat, thrilled by her pleasure, he had felt his own pleasure build and build until he too came apart in a shattering climax that was beyond anything he had ever imagined.

Just thinking about it now aroused him to a state of breathless, aching anticipation. It was past time for patience, past time for half measures. He stood up and crossed the room in three strides. At the door he hesitated, then shook off his doubts. No, he was right about this. He had to be.

He paused again at the guest room door, then opened it slowly. Inside, a beam of moonlight streamed through the window casting a silvery glow over Lacey's complexion. She was wearing a gown of French lace and Halloran's finest pale pink satin. It was one he had given to her for their last anniversary. Though she preferred a classic, elegant look in public, she had always loved impractical, frothy concoctions for sleeping. In this one, she looked more feminine, more tantalizing than ever.

Tenderness welled up inside him, as he guessed how restless she had been. The sheets were in a tangle. The gown had ridden up to bare one glorious, tempting thigh. Kevin sucked in a ragged breath as desire pulsed through him. She was so incredibly beautiful, so inviting.

And so exhausted, he realized as he inched closer and glimpsed the shadows under her eyes. It was little wonder after the day she had spent working with

Paula…and after the torment he had put her through for far longer than that.

Honor warred with need. This time, to his regret, honor won.

Reluctantly Kevin settled for a whisper-light caress of her shoulder, as he shifted one fallen strap of her gown back into place. Fingertips skimmed over cool, silken flesh, lingered as his pulse skipped, then raced.

Lacey's breath hitched at the touch. He held his own breath in an agony of anticipation, waiting to see if she would wake, hoping against hope that she would. He told himself he would be blameless then.

When she didn't awaken, when the pattern of her breathing became slow and steady again, he sighed.

Tomorrow, he promised himself. Tomorrow they would find their way back into each other's arms.

Lacey spent the morning trying to figure out why Kevin suddenly seemed so nostalgic. It was as if he'd spent the whole night lost in memories, caught up in the same sweetly tormenting dreams that she had had when she'd finally fallen into a restless slumber.

Today it seemed as if he were using those memories to rekindle the desire that had always surged between them like a palpable force.

"What's gotten into you?" she murmured, when his hand curved around the nape of her neck for just an instant as he returned to the breakfast table. The casual touch sent her pulse scrambling. She tried to cover it by spreading jam on her toast.

"I don't know what you mean," he said, pouring

himself a second cup of coffee, his expression all smug male innocence.

She regarded him with disbelief, then finally shrugged. "Perhaps it's just my imagination playing tricks with me."

He nodded, rather quickly she thought.

"I'm sure that's it," he agreed, but the gleam in his eyes contradicted the too-casual response.

Her gaze narrowed. "Are you sure you have no idea what I'm talking about?"

His eyes widened. "None. Did you sleep well?"

"I tossed and turned a bit. You?"

"I was a bit restless myself. I looked in on you," he said in a voice that sounded a bit husky.

Surprised, she didn't know what to say, finally settling for a simple, "Oh?"

She reached hurriedly for a section of the Boston paper so she could hide the flush of embarrassment that she could feel creeping into her cheeks. Kevin nudged the paper aside.

"Lacey." His voice was soft and slow as honey, but it held a definite note of command.

She swallowed hard, then forced herself to meet his gaze. "Yes?"

"You looked very beautiful."

This time there was no hiding the heat that climbed into her cheeks. "Kevin Halloran, if I didn't know better, I'd think you were trying to rattle me."

He grinned at that. "Then you obviously don't know me at all. Actually my intentions aren't nearly that honorable. I want to seduce you."

Lacey felt every muscle in her body clench, not just

at his words, though those were disturbing enough, but at the spark of satisfaction in his eyes.

"Am I having any luck?" he asked, his tone light.

"The offer is tempting," she admitted.

"That's good."

"It is the middle of the morning, though."

"And what is wrong with making love to my wife in the middle of the morning?"

"Not a thing," she murmured breathlessly, captivated by the possibilities.

She saw his whole body tense at that. He held out his hand. She was about to reach for it when reason intruded. There were a hundred reasons for going to bed with Kevin and a thousand more for saying no. She had remembered them all last night. Today it seemed she had to search her memory for just one.

"We can't, Kevin," she said desperately, thinking of Linc's insistent warning. "It's too soon."

Sudden anger turned his eyes a stormy shade of gray blue. "Too soon?" he repeated in a voice that throbbed with sarcasm. "Too soon for whom? We haven't made love in a year. Maybe more."

Though he had missed her meaning entirely, Lacey was too stunned by his harsh, bitterly accusing tone to explain. Instead, she snapped back, "And whose fault is that? Not mine, dammit. I wasn't the one who spent sixteen hours a day in an office and came home exhausted. I'm not the one who was so caught up in work that nothing else mattered."

"No," he said, his tone and his gaze as cold as a winter morning. "You were the one who walked out."

At that she shoved her chair back from the table and

forced herself to be silent. Arguing was no solution.
If anything it would only make matters worse. But all
of this tiptoeing around their problems for fear of upsetting Kevin was beginning to get to her. How many
times could she clamp her mouth shut, holding in her
hurt, her anger?

At the sink, Lacey gripped the edge of the counter
so tightly her knuckles turned white. She drew in a
deep, calming breath before she turned back to face
him.

"We have to talk about all of this, but only when
we can do it calmly."

"I'm not feeling one damn bit calm," he said furiously. "I am sick and tired of being made out to be the
bad guy here. I'm a human being, Lacey. Not some
storybook hero. I'm sure I've made more than my share
of mistakes, but so have you." He glared at her. "So,
my dear, have you."

Before Lacey could gather her wits for a comeback,
Kevin was gone, leaving her alone with her anger and
with the sad awareness that after all these days together, they were not one bit better off than they had
been months ago. They didn't understand each other
at all anymore.

Lacey was still in the kitchen, lingering over a last
cup of coffee, when she heard a car pull up outside.
She heard Kevin open the door and she wandered into
the hallway to see who'd come to visit.

Jason and Dana. Dear Lord, she had forgotten they
were coming. She viewed their arrival as a mixed blessing. They would serve as a buffer after this morning's

angry exchange. At the same time, their presence would create even more tension as she and Kevin both struggled to keep their son and daughter-in-law from seeing how little progress had actually been made toward a reconciliation.

As they hurried inside with their bags, Lacey was all too aware of the anxious glances they exchanged.

"Hi, Mom," Jason said, his voice too cheerful. His gaze searched her face. "You've gotten a little sun."

"I've been gardening," she said, putting her cup down to hug Jason and then Dana. She smiled at her daughter-in-law. "How are you feeling?"

"Much better. Jason's finally stopped getting morning sickness."

"Thank goodness," he murmured fervently.

"All men should have a taste of what it's like to carry a baby," Dana retorted. "It might make them more sympathetic."

"I'm sympathetic, all right. But we're only having the one. I can't go through this again."

"You!" Dana retorted indignantly. "At least you'll miss out on the labor pains."

Lacey decided she'd better step in before the familiar battle worsened. "Enough, you two. Where's Sammy?"

"We left him with Brandon," Dana said. "Sammy said something about teaching him to shoot down some kind of creatures."

"A video game created by a sadistic computer hack," Jason explained. "I was awake until three in the morning trying to save some princess from those same evil guys. They multiply like rabbits if you don't stay on your toes."

"Sounds intriguing," Lacey said. "You'll have to teach your father sometime."

"Not while he's recuperating," Dana warned. "It turns them into glassy-eyed monsters. I'm sure it can't be good for their blood pressure. I dared to interrupt Sammy and Jason for dinner the other night and they both jumped down my throat."

"I was winning for the first time in history," Jason explained. "I wasn't about to lose my competitive edge."

Dana rolled her eyes. "See what I mean?"

Jason put an arm around her waist and hugged her. "I love you, anyway," he said. "Where should I put our bags? The guest room across from yours and Dad's?"

Kevin deliberately turned away, leaving Lacey to respond. "No," she said, all too aware of the puzzled expression on Dana's face and on Jason's. There was no hiding the truth from them, though.

"Actually, my things are in there," she said briskly. "Use the yellow room at the end of the hall. It has the second best view in the house."

Jason shot her a sharp look, but fortunately he didn't make an issue of it. He picked up the bags. "I'll be right back. Dana, please go sit down."

"I've been sitting down," she reminded him very patiently. She regarded Lacey hopefully. "He will get over this, won't he?"

"Kevin never did. He watched me like a hawk all during the entire pregnancy. So did Brandon. It almost drove me wild."

"Fortunately Sammy and I made a pact. He'll keep Brandon busy and I will buy him the latest video games. Hopefully they won't release too many new ones between now and when this little one is born."

She patted her rounded belly. "Do you think there's any chance at all I'll have a girl?" she asked wistfully. "I would sure like to buy dolls, instead of footballs."

"The Halloran genes are against it," Kevin said. "I have to admit, though, that I wouldn't mind having a little girl to spoil rotten."

"There will be no spoiling of this child, girl or boy," Dana said firmly.

Lacey shook her head. "Then you married into the wrong family. The Halloran men take spoiling for granted, especially when it comes to grandchildren. I remember the first Christmas after I met Kevin. His grandfather was still alive then. He gave him the first ten-thousand-dollar installment on his trust fund."

"As I recall, I wasn't that impressed," Kevin countered. "I wanted a new ten-speed bike."

"That's okay. I was awed enough for both of us. I got a sweater and a doll that year. They were both second-hand."

Kevin smiled at her, his eyes gentle and filled with remembering. "You still have that doll, though, don't you? While I gave that money away long ago."

"To buy toys for the Salvation Army's Christmas drive," Lacey recalled. "You'd just turned twenty-one, which meant you could start drawing on the trust. I thought using the money to buy those toys was the sweetest thing you'd ever done."

"Dad thought I'd taken leave of my senses. You

were six months pregnant and I was giving away our savings to charity." He shook his head. "Talk about irresponsible."

"I didn't think it was irresponsible," Lacey argued. "We had enough. Those people didn't have anything."

"I agree with Lacey," Dana said, leaning down to give Kevin a kiss on his forehead. "It was a noble gesture."

Kevin reached up and patted her cheek. "That's all it was, a gesture. It didn't really solve anything."

Lacey lost patience. "It gave those families and kids a decent holiday, one they'll always remember. If more people made gestures like those, the world would be a better place. What's happened to you, Kevin? When did you become so cynical?"

"Cynical? No, Lacey. I grew up."

She was about to argue, when she saw the alarm in Dana's eyes. She bit back a sharp retort and shrugged. "I guess we still see some things differently," she said and stood up. "I think I'll get busy on lunch. Dana would you like to help me?"

Her daughter-in-law cast one last confused look at Kevin, then followed Lacey into the kitchen.

"Things aren't any better, are they?" Dana said as they prepared lunch.

"Better?" Lacey echoed with a catch in her voice. "If anything, they're worse than ever."

"But why? I don't understand. Anyone who looks at the two of you can see how much you still love each other."

Lacey shrugged. "When you get right down to it, love may not conquer all."

"Now who's sounding cynical?" Dana asked too gently.

Lacey had to fight off the tears that suddenly threatened. She tried to smile. "Come now, you didn't drive all the way out here just to be depressed. Let's have some lunch and then you and Jason can go for a walk on the beach. It's a beautiful day."

Dana looked as if she wanted to say more, but finally she took her cue from Lacey and busied herself with the lunch preparations.

They all ate much too quickly, anxious to put an end to the charade of cheer they tried to maintain. Jason had barely put his last bite of food in his mouth, when Dana stood up and grabbed his hand. "Let's take a walk."

Startled, he simply stared at her. "Before dessert?"

"Yes," she said firmly. With a shrug, he left the table and followed her from the room.

Kevin glanced across the table, his expression rueful. "I'll bet they can't wait to get back to Boston."

Lacey nodded. "I can't say that I blame them."

He hesitated, then finally looked straight into her eyes. "Do you want to leave, too? Was all of this a mistake?"

A sigh of regret shuddered through her as she thought about the question. "No," she said at last. "But I think we were expecting too much. We need to talk—" When he started to speak, she held up her hand. "No. I mean really talk. And we can't do that if I'm terrified of upsetting you."

"Is that really the problem?"

"It is a lot of it," she admitted. "Every time I think

that I'm ready to bring everything out into the open, I remember the way you looked in that intensive care unit. I caution myself to wait, just a little longer, just until Linc pronounces you fit again."

"Is that what you meant this morning when you said it was too soon for us to make love?" Kevin asked, his expression oddly hopeful.

"Yes. Then you took it wrong and the next thing I knew we were shouting. If only we could do this calmly and rationally, but unfortunately there's too much hurt and anger."

She couldn't miss his sigh of regret at her words. "What's going to happen to us, Lacey?" he said.

"We're going to survive all this," she said with sudden certainty. "If we can face it, if we can finally begin to be open and honest about our feelings, then we'll survive. We just have to be patient."

"Not one of my virtues, I'm afraid."

"No," she agreed with the beginnings of a smile. "But maybe it's time you learned a little about patience, for more reasons than one."

He reached for her hand and this time she took it and held on tight.

"You're the best reason I can think of, Lacey," he said quietly. "The very best."

Lacey felt her heart climb into her throat. "Maybe we should make a pact."

"We seem to be doing a lot of that."

"But this one could be the most important of all."

"What, then?"

"Could we pretend, just for a few days, that everything is okay between us? Maybe that would take the pressure off. As it is, we're too demanding of ourselves. Every conversation turns into some sort of cross-examination or psychoanalysis. Maybe we should just forget about all the problems and just be ourselves, have a little fun. We can save the serious talk for later."

Kevin looked skeptical. "Isn't that a little like hiding from reality?"

Lacey laughed. "It's a *lot* like hiding from reality, but so what? Nobody's on a timetable here, right? There's no law that says we must resolve every last problem by a certain date, is there?"

"I guess not," he said slowly. "I don't suppose this plan of yours includes moving back into the master bedroom?"

She stood up and pressed a kiss to his forehead. "Don't push your luck, pal."

"Medically speaking, you mean?"

His arm curved around her waist and tumbled her into his lap. Lacey gazed up into eyes that were suddenly filled with laughter. Serenity stole through her then, for the fist time in days.

"Medically speaking," she confirmed softly just before Kevin's mouth settled over hers in a kiss that was filled with tenderness and promise.

That was the way Jason and Dana found them, still at the kitchen table, still wrapped in each other's arms.

"This is an improvement," Jason commented approvingly from the doorway.

"Jason," Dana muttered urgently, tugging on his arm. "Leave them alone."

Lacey laughed. "Too late," she said as she stood up. "How about a game? Scrabble? Cards?"

"Cutthroat Scrabble," Kevin said with a hint of his old enthusiasm. They had spent many an evening engaged in just such battles before the age of video games.

Jason looked from his father to Lacey and back again, then nodded in satisfaction. "I'll get the board."

"And I'll get the snacks," Dana said.

Jason groaned. "Don't let her, Mom. The only things she likes these days are pickles and brownies."

Lacey patted her son's cheek. "Don't worry. We're fresh out of both."

"Don't be so sure," Jason retorted. "I'm relatively certain that's what she brought out here in that extra suitcase."

Kevin stood up. "Maybe I ought to get the snacks."

This time it was Lacey who groaned.

Kevin grinned at her. "Calm down, my love. There's enough celery and carrot sticks in the refrigerator to feed an army, to say nothing of one pregnant lady, one recuperating man and two nervous nellies."

The first word Lacey played on the Scrabble board was *joy*. It might not have earned as many points as some others she could have made, but it was definitely the one that best summed up the way she was feeling as she was surrounded by her family once again.

From the warm, tender expression in Kevin's eyes when he caught her gaze, it was a feeling he understood—and shared.

Chapter 12

Having Jason and Dana around did indeed take off the pressure, Kevin realized on Sunday. Witnessing his son and daughter-in-law's happiness spun a web of serenity around all of them.

Slowly he and Lacey had relaxed. Like old friends rediscovering shared interests, their laughter came more easily. And the looks they exchanged were filled with open awareness, rather than carefully banked accusation.

When they stood in the driveway to say goodbye, his arm curved naturally around Lacey's waist. And when Jason's car was out of sight, it seemed just as natural that their hands met and laced together.

"Feel like a walk on the beach?" he asked, reluctant to go back inside and risk spoiling the lazy, spellbinding mood. "We should have another hour or so of daylight."

"A walk sounds good," she said.

At the edge of the yard they slipped off their shoes, then crossed the dunes to reach the water's edge. The last of the day's sunlight slanted across the beach. Much of the wide stretch of sand had been cast in shadow, making the sand cool against their bare feet. For as far as Kevin could see, he and Lacey were alone in the early-evening shadows.

"Isn't this perfect, when it's like this?" Lacey asked with a sigh. "No one around. It's almost possible to believe that we're the only ones who know about this stretch of beach."

"Remind me to bring you back in mid-July," Kevin said, thinking of the crowds that descended with the first full days of summer and remained until Labor Day at least.

"And spoil the illusion? No way."

They walked as far as they could before the tide caught up with them and forced them to turn back. For the first time in months the silence that fell between them was comfortable, rather than strained. Neither of them seemed to feel the need to cover the quiet time with awkward conversation.

Kevin glanced over and caught the slow curving of Lacey's lips. "A penny for your thoughts," he said.

"At today's rate of inflation? You've got to be kidding," she said, repeating a joke that they'd shared over the years whenever one of them tried to pry into the other's secret thoughts.

"How much are your thoughts going for these days?"

She seemed to consider the question carefully. "A hundred dollars easy."

He reached in his back pocket and pulled out his wallet. He found the hundred-dollar bill he'd tucked there and offered it to her. "These thoughts of yours better be good."

"In whose opinion?" she countered, nabbing the money and tucking it into her pocket.

"Mine. Pay up."

She grinned at him with a wicked gleam in her eyes. "Chicken," she said succinctly.

"I beg your pardon?"

"I was thinking about chicken. Do you realize that there are at least a hundred different ways to fix chicken? And that's before you get into the ethnic variations."

Kevin regarded her intently. "I just paid one hundred dollars for a dissertation on chicken recipes?" He held out his hand. "I don't think so. I expected something terribly revealing about your romantic soul. Give the money back. You took it under false pretenses."

"Try to get it," she challenged and took off running.

Her pace was lightning quick at first as he stood flat-footed and stared after her in delighted astonishment. Then he took off after her. He was aware of the precise moment when she slowed down just enough to be caught. He fell on top of her as they tumbled onto the sand.

"You let me catch you," he accused, all too aware of the press of her breasts against his chest and the famil-

iar fit of their lower bodies. He captured her hands and
pinned them over her head. Her eyes were filled with
laughter and her breath was coming in soft, ragged
puffs that fanned his face.

"Maybe I did and maybe I didn't," she taunted.

"Lacey Grainger Halloran, you are a tease."

She wriggled beneath him, just enough to confirm
the accusation. There was an unmistakable flare of
excitement in her eyes, though she did her damnedest
to look innocent.

"Me?" she murmured.

"Yes, you," he said softly, and then he lowered
his mouth to cover hers. Her lips were soft and moist
enough to have him forgetting to be sensible and slow
and careful. Her mouth tempted, like the lure of a
flame, and the heat it sent spiraling through him was
devastating.

Their bodies strained together, hers arching into
his in a way that had him aching with an arousal so
hard, so demanding that he thought it very likely he
might embarrass himself as he hadn't since the first
time he'd experimented with sex.

Kevin fought for calm by rolling over on his back,
taking Lacey with him so that he could see her face
and the gathering stars in the evening sky at the same
time.

"Good Lord, woman, what you do to me." he murmured, his hands lightly brushing the sand from her
face, then lingering to caress.

"I know," she said, her expression dreamy and open
for once. "It's the same for me with you. Sometimes

you touch me and I think I'll fly apart. It's always been that way."

"Always?" he teased. "In the fifth grade you had the hots for me?"

She laughed at that. "Of course, only then I thought it was an allergy. I had a hunch a doctor could cure it, but I never quite got around to checking."

"Thank God," he said fervently.

"What about you?" she questioned, smoothing her fingers along the curve of his jaw. "Did I make you come unglued in the fifth grade?"

"Only when you hit that home run during the spring baseball tournament. I was ready to marry you after that."

"Fortunately there are laws about that sort of thing."

"I'm glad we waited as long as we did," he said, his hands stroking over the backs of her thighs and up over her still-perfect bottom. Even through a layer of denim, she tempted. "I wouldn't have missed the sweet anticipation of those years for anything."

"Me, neither," she whispered, twining her arms around his neck and fitting her head into the curve of his shoulder. "Me, neither."

They stayed right where they were, snuggled comfortably together, for what seemed an eternity. Neither of them was willing to move and risk losing the rare and special mood. Despite thick sweaters and jeans, they were both cold and damp through to their bones by the time they finally made the effort to stand up and go inside.

"How about soup?" Lacey suggested as they stood in front of the fire to warm up.

"Chicken noodle, no doubt," he said.

She scowled at him, but her eyes were bright with laughter. "I was thinking of that white bean soup you like so much. It's thick and hearty, the perfect thing for a night like this. Of course, I could manage chicken noodle from a can, if that's your preference."

"Is there any of that bread you made left?"

"Yes."

"Then the white bean soup and bread sounds great."

"Here, in front of the fire?"

"Yes."

He followed her into the kitchen and helped with chopping onions and gathering silverware. There was something reassuring and cozy about working side by side to prepare a meal. How long had it been since they had done that? Before he'd hired the housekeeper certainly. And long before that? Maybe so.

Possibly from the first moment he'd gone to work at Halloran, when he'd realized that Lacey didn't really want to hear how his days at his father's company had gone.

Before that, early in their marriage they had both rushed in after six and divided up the chores so they could get dinner on the table at a decent hour. Lacey had cooked. He had set the table. And they had used the time to compare notes on everything they'd done while apart.

Occasionally he had fixed dinner and let her catch up on laundry. Without any particular planning, they had had the ultimate liberated household, Kevin realized now with amusement. Still, the rhythm of their evenings had been satisfying in some elusive way he couldn't begin to explain. There had been a closeness, a unity. How had he forgotten that?

The phone rang just as Lacey was ready to ladle up the soup. "I'll get it," he offered and picked up the receiver.

"Kevin?"

"Hey, Dad, how are you?"

He glanced at Lacey and saw her shoulders stiffen almost imperceptibly.

"Fine, now that that rapscallion of Dana's has gone home. That boy wears me out."

"Are you sure it isn't the other way around? What did you two do all weekend?"

"Played some fool video game. A lot of nonsense, if you ask me."

"You must have lost," Kevin guessed.

"The boy whipped the daylights out of me," his father admitted with an indignant huff. "No respect for his elders."

"You wanted Sammy to let you win?"

"Of course not, but he didn't have to humiliate me."

Brandon cleared his throat, always a prelude to saying something he figured the other person didn't want to hear. Kevin waited, his nerves tensed.

"I didn't call up there to discuss video games," his father announced. "Just wanted to see how things are going."

"*Things,*" he mocked, realizing where the conversation was headed, "are going fine."

"You ready to get back to work?"

"Dad, don't start."

"I'm not pushing, son. Just asking."

"With you, it's hard to tell the difference."

Brandon uttered a long-suffering sigh. "It sure is hard to get an ounce of respect in this family."

Kevin ignored the play for sympathy. Finally his father said, "You and Lacey doing okay?"

Now they were really getting down to the reason for the call. Kevin studied his wife out of the corner of his eye. There was no mistaking the tense set of her shoulders now. It was as if she could hear her father-in-law's end of the conversation, rather than just Kevin's innocuous replies.

"Okay," he said, wondering if he was stretching the truth.

"Hear she was staying across the hall."

"Dad! That is none of your business." Only Lacey's presence kept him from saying more. He would speak to Jason first thing tomorrow about spreading tales, especially to Brandon. Jason had had his own bitter experience with his grandfather's meddling. He should have known better.

"Of course it's my business. Your happiness will always be my concern."

"Drop it," Kevin warned.

"Okay, okay. The papers on that deal for the new looms are due in tomorrow. Shall I send 'em on out there?"

Kevin hesitated. Those papers were likely to be like waving a red flag under Lacey's nose. On the other hand, what harm could there possibly be in looking through a contract? Somebody besides Brandon needed to look at the fine print. His father wanted those new looms too badly to worry about whether they were being taken to the cleaners on the deal.

"Send them out," he said finally. "Dad, I've got to go now. Lacey has dinner ready."

"You give her my love, then," his father said. "And tell her to get the hell back in her own bed where she belongs. Better yet, put her on and I'll tell her myself."

Kevin groaned. "You will do nothing of the kind. Good night, Dad."

When he'd hung up, Lacey put their bowls of soup on trays, along with the warm bread. They carried the meal into the living room and settled down on the sofa in front of the fire.

For the first time in the last twenty-four hours the silence that fell between them was uneasy. Kevin was more disappointed than surprised.

"Okay," he said finally, putting his spoon down carefully. "What's on your mind?"

"Who says anything is on my mind?" Lacey asked stiffly.

"Lacey, being evasive won't help anything."

"Okay, what did Brandon want this time?"

"He just called to say hello."

She regarded him doubtfully. "It certainly took him long enough to spit one word out."

"You know what I meant," Kevin said, his irritation beginning to mount. "What is it with you and my father? I thought all that animosity was a thing of the past. I thought you'd forgiven him years ago."

"I did."

"Then why do you react like this every time he calls up?"

"He's trying to get you to start working again, isn't he? Doesn't he realize that the whole purpose of your coming out here was to recuperate?"

With her gaze pinned on him, he couldn't manage a convenient lie. "It's just some papers. It'll take me an hour or two."

"Just some papers. An hour or two," Lacey repeated. "Can't you see that's just the tip of the iceberg with Brandon? Next he'll be pulling up here with an attaché case filled with more papers and a fax machine."

"So what if he does?" Kevin snapped. "I have to get back to work sooner or later. I'll be a helluva lot more relaxed here than I would be back in Boston."

Lacey didn't respond to that.

Kevin threw down his napkin. "On second thought, maybe Boston would be simpler. I wouldn't have to worry about you looking over my shoulder making judgments, would I?"

He stood up and started for the door. "I'm going for a walk."

"Kevin," Lacey called after him.

The last thing he heard before he slammed the front door was her muttered curse.

"Damn," Lacey muttered for the tenth time as she paced and waited for Kevin to come back. How had a simple phone call reopened every wound and shattered the cautious tranquility they had finally managed to achieve?

Because it had been from Brandon, of course. She had heard more than enough to realize he had work for Kevin to do. If she hadn't guessed, Kevin's guilty expression would have told her. She suspected there was more—probably unwanted advice about their marriage, if she knew Brandon.

Even so, it had been stupid to force the issue with Kevin. She couldn't keep jumping down his throat over every little thing.

What on earth was wrong with her? Was she so terrified of losing him that she wanted to wrap him in a cloak of that protective bubble wrap and watch over him for the rest of their lives? What kind of life would that be for either of them? Longer, maybe, but rife with tension.

She was going to have to get a grip on herself. She was going to have to ignore her obviously futile plan to hold reality at bay and start talking. No matter how much the words hurt. No matter how angry they got. They could not allow their pain to fester any longer. Tonight had been proof of that. After a wonderful day of pretending that everything was normal again in their marriage, they had slammed into reality with one phone call.

Lacey was waiting in the living room when Kevin finally came in. She heard him start down the hall and called out to him. For an instant she was afraid he would ignore her, but finally she heard a cautious movement, then a quiet, "Yes?"

"Will you join me?"

"I don't think so," he said. "I'm tired. I'm going to bed."

"Please, Kevin."

"Why, Lacey? What's the point?"

"Our marriage is the point."

"Right now I don't give our marriage a snowball's chance in hell," he said with bleak finality. "Maybe I'll have a different view in the morning, but I wouldn't hold my breath, if I were you."

He was gone before she could force a single word past the tears that clogged her throat.

Chapter 13

All the pretense, all the games had to end, Lacey reminded herself as she sat at the kitchen table in the morning. She had made a pot of tea and laced it liberally with milk. She didn't need the jagged edginess of too much caffeine on top of everything else today. Her nerves were already shot and it was barely six a.m.

She could hear the first faint sounds of the birds as dawn finally broke beyond the horizon. Black became gray, then purple, then softest pink as the sun edged its way up through the clouds. This was her favorite time of day, a time when anything seemed possible. She needed that sense of hope more than ever as she waited for Kevin to join her.

Lacey thought of all the emotions she'd kept hidden, all the desperate thoughts she had never dared to voice, and tried to pick one above all the others as a place to start.

It would be so much easier if healing could take place without all this airing of past betrayals, she thought wistfully. But it would be false healing, one that could never last.

Above all else, she wanted whatever happened today to be the beginning of forever. Her marriage would be salvaged today.

Or it wouldn't.

Either way, she would go on. Both of them would. They were too strong not to fight for happiness—together or apart.

Kevin was wide awake when he heard Lacey leave her room and go into the kitchen. It was still dark outside, too early to be up on a vacation day, far too early to begin dealing with anything that required soul-searching.

But this was no normal vacation, he reminded himself wearily. He couldn't begin to recall the last time he had taken one of those. As for soul-searching, what difference did it make if he went over and over things here in his head or voiced them aloud to Lacey?

Even so, as he lay on the bed, his hands behind his head, he was struck by an odd reluctance to get up and see what form their confrontation was likely to take. After last night, he doubted they would have anything pleasant to say to each other. There was the heavy sense of impending doom weighing him down. He no longer had any idea whether the fault for that was Lacey's or his own. He just knew, as he expected she did, that they couldn't go on this way.

He'd expected something simple to come of this trip, something magical. Instead he'd been faced with a hard dose of reality. For a man who prided himself on having outgrown so many naive attitudes, he'd clung to this one about his marriage for far too long.

He heard the whistle of the teakettle, a sure sign that Lacey's distress was as deep and dark as his own. She drank tea only when she needed comfort. He could visualize her sitting at the kitchen table, an old china cup cradled in her hands, her gaze fixed on the splashy display of daybreak, her thoughts...

Well, who knew where her thoughts were? He definitely didn't anymore, not with any certainty.

How he regretted that, he thought with a sigh. He regretted too damned much these days, it seemed.

Then fix it, a voice inside his head muttered. *Fix it now or forget it.*

With understandable reluctance, Kevin finally dragged himself out of bed and pulled on a comfortable pair of soft, well-worn jeans and a fisherman's knit sweater that he and Lacey had bought years ago on a trip to Ireland. He dragged on socks and sneakers, because of the chill in the air, though he would have preferred to be barefoot.

He took as long as he could brushing his teeth and shaving. He even ran a comb through his hair. It was a delaying tactic more than anything. His hair had always fallen where it damn well pleased, unless he tamed it often with a short cut. It had grown past taming over the last few weeks and there was too much silver amidst the blond. Funny how there were days when he truly forgot how old he was. Not that forty-eight was exactly ancient, but at times he felt no more than half that.

Kevin glanced at the bed, considered spending more time making it up, then admitted the one or two minutes it cost him wouldn't be enough to make much difference. He might as well get into the kitchen and face the music.

It was going to be even worse than he'd thought, he decided as he saw Lacey's exhausted expression. She was clinging to that cup of tea as if it were her only lifeline. Her streaked blond hair tumbled loose across her shoulders, inviting his touch, but the look in her eyes when she saw him was forbidding.

"Good morning," he said cautiously, noting that she'd chosen a bright yellow blouse as if to defy her mood.

"Good morning. Would you like breakfast? I could fix you something."

"Tea and toast will do. I'll fix it."

As he popped the bread into the toaster, poured the tea, then brought everything to the table, he stole surreptitious glances at her. She was as still as could be, but there was nothing calm about her. He sensed that turbulent emotions were seething just below the surface. Her gaze was mostly directed down at the tea, but he could see the sorrow and wariness whenever she dared to glance his way.

"Kevin."

"Lacey."

The blurted words were practically simultaneous. With his glance he indicated deference.

Given her chance she looked uncertain. "We can't go on like this. I thought we could, but I was wrong."

"I know," he agreed.

She looked at him then, straight into his eyes, and to his amazement she looked a little helpless and more than a little vulnerable.

"I don't know where to begin," she said finally.

"At the beginning," he suggested, too glibly, judging from the look she shot him.

"That was too long ago to count," she said, but her tone was just a bit lighter. "Can you remember what it was like when we first got married?"

"Yes. At least I think I can. Why don't you tell me what you remember."

"I remember getting up in the morning filled with excitement and anticipation. I remember rushing through the day, reminding myself of every detail so I could share it with you that night. I remember how we talked about everything, every nuance of our lives, every decision, every hope, every dream." She sighed wistfully. "I thought that was the way it would always be."

"I suppose I did, too," he admitted. "It wasn't very realistic of either of us."

"Maybe not."

"Is that all you want back, Lacey? Just the sharing?"

"No, of course not." Her gaze met his, then slipped away. "We had the same vision, then. Somewhere along the way that's what we lost."

"Did we?" he argued. "Don't we both still want the

world to be a better place? Don't we both care about family more than anything?"

"I thought we did."

"But?"

"We have such different ways of acting on it. You see a charity, and you need to write a check. You want a home, so you hire people to run it. You believe in family, but not in spending the time it takes to nurture one."

"So I'm still the one at fault," he said, unable to keep the impatience out of his voice. "Only me."

"Of course not," she said at once. "The difference between us is that I've tried every way I could think of to tell you what I need, but you've never once given me a clue about what you want from me anymore. Whatever the housekeeper fixes for dinner is fine. Whatever I wear is fine. However I spend my days is fine." Her tone mimicked him. Her chin rose another notch. "Even the sex began to seem more like habit than the spontaneous passion we used to have."

Kevin stared at her in astonishment. "That's ridiculous," he said defensively.

"Is it? Is it really?" She drew in a deep breath, then braced her hands against the table, almost as if she needed support for whatever she had to say. "Were you having an affair, Kevin?" she asked point blank. "That would explain so much."

Kevin felt as if she'd punched him in his midsection. Shocked, he simply stared at her. He couldn't imagine an accusation that would have thrown him more.

"Well?" she demanded defiantly.

"An affair? Where on earth would you get a ridiculous idea like that?"

"Come on, Kevin. Don't act too stunned. You wouldn't be the first man to have an affair. I can't even count the number of husbands we know who openly play around on their wives."

"Not me, dammit. Not me."

When she continued to look skeptical, he said, "Lacey, I can honestly say that I never even contemplated breaking our marriage vows, much less acted on the thought."

"Is that the truth, Kevin?" she asked softly, her gaze searching his.

He realized then that perhaps more than all the other complaints, all the other differences, this was the one at the root of all their troubles. She couldn't even bring herself to trust him anymore, not even on something as sacred as their marriage vows.

He could read the vulnerability in her eyes, the fear that he'd turned elsewhere for satisfaction, and the expression in her eyes made him ache.

"Darling, I love you. Only you. No matter what else has happened, that has never, ever changed. I've never wanted anyone the way I wanted you."

"Past tense," she observed ruefully.

"No," he swore, leaving his chair to gather her into his arms. She held herself so stiffly, refusing to yield to a comfort too easily offered.

"Present tense," he told her. "I want you now every bit as much as I did when we were a couple of kids discovering our hormones for the first time. Couldn't you tell that last night on the beach, or the night before that and the night before that?"

Apparently he had found the right words—or the right combination of words and touch, after all. He could see the relief slowly washing through her. The words, though, would never be enough. He had to show her how much he needed her, how beautiful he still found her.

"Come with me," he coaxed, brushing her hair back from her face. All thoughts of other issues, other problems faded in his need to convince her of this much at least. "Let me put this crazy notion of yours to rest forever."

Lacey was slow to accept, and he thought for a moment that she might not, using who-knew-what this time as an excuse. In that brief instant of hesitation, he weighed the future without her against the past and realized that nothing would ever be the same if he lost her.

Kevin slid his fingers through her hair until the silky curls tumbled free. The pad of his thumb traced her mouth, the full bottom lip that trembled beneath his touch.

"Please," he whispered, unable to hide the faint note of desperation. "I need you, Lacey. I need you now."

Her fingers came up and linked with his, and the shadows slid away from her eyes, revealing the sheen of tears. "I need you, too," she said.

He would have swept her into his arms in a romantic gesture if he hadn't caught the forbidding look on her face when she realized his intentions. He grinned ruefully. "It's only a few feet," he reminded her.

"Then surely my knees aren't so weak with longing that I can't walk there on my own," she said, surprising him with the dry humor.

His low chuckle slipped out and then they were both laughing. He slanted a kiss across her mouth, capturing the much too infrequent musical sound of her laughter and the taste of milky tea.

"You could always make me laugh," he said.

"I know," she said with a devilish twinkle in her eyes.

But then her hands were at work on the snap of his jeans and he no longer felt the least bit like laughing. He sucked in his breath when her fingers skimmed across denim seeking the already hard shaft beneath.

"Wait," Kevin said urgently, pulling her down to the bed with him and pinning her hands away from him. He touched his mouth to hers, savoring again the taste, the texture, the heat. Her lips, her tongue had always fascinated him. He could have spent hours absorbed in no more than the nuances of her kisses. But all the while, he worked to rid her of her blouse, her bra, her jeans and panties, just so he could skim fingertips over velvet flesh and tight golden curls.

Soft whispers turned to anxious moans as he came closer and closer to the moist warmth at the apex of her thighs. She struggled to free her hands and when he released her at long last, she used her hands to torment him, to stroke and caress, to soothe and inflame. She slid her hands under his sweater, tangling her fingers in the hairs on his chest, seeking masculine nipples, her gaze locked with his.

She shifted then, and he couldn't take his eyes off

the pale softness of her hands as they curved around him, stroking until he thought he would explode from the intensity.

Each of them battled to give, to shower the other with all the love, all the satisfaction that had been withheld for so long. And when the giving pulled them higher and higher, they had to release that last thread of control and learn to accept the unselfish offering.

Lacey came apart first, her body arching, her skin slick with sweat, her eyes filled with so much joy that Kevin was drawn along with her.

When both of them had caught their breath, when the caresses had slowed, he looked into her eyes and promised more. This time, joined together, they traveled even farther, soared even higher.

He couldn't recall a time when they had asked more of each other or given so much. It was proof, beyond all doubt, that what they had was strong enough to last a lifetime.

They slept then, close together, their breath mingling as morning turned to afternoon.

It was only later, in the aftermath of that extraordinary lovemaking, that Kevin said, "This was never, ever the problem between us, Lace."

He swept his hand over the curve of her hip, lingered on the fullness of her breast to prove his point. He knew at once when her body tensed, knew instinctively that his meaning had registered in a way that went beyond the reassuring simplicity of the words. He had unwittingly opened a new door, rather than closing an old one.

"Then what was it?" she demanded softly. "You

can't deny that for a time we never touched, not in any way that mattered. Were you just too busy? Too tired? What?"

Kevin tried to find the answers she needed to hear. He searched his heart for things he had never before been willing to put into words. Maybe even thoughts he'd never dared to acknowledge, even to himself.

"Too distracted is probably closer to the truth. I lost sight of what was important," he admitted slowly, as he carefully sorted through explanations.

"After all those years of rebelling, of making my own way, I got caught up in my father's dreams after all. Halloran Industries became important to me. I wanted to make it work. I wanted to have a legacy for our son."

Lacey sat up then, dragging the sheet around her and knotting it above her breasts. Sitting cross-legged before him, she watched him closely in the way that she had of trying to read his innermost, unspoken thoughts. Apparently she came up wanting, because she shook her head.

"But that doesn't explain it. Why should that have driven a wedge between us? I always wanted whatever it took to make you happy."

"You did," he agreed, "or at least you gave it lip service whenever I tried to discuss my decision about Halloran Industries with you."

"Lip service?" she repeated, obviously stung by the charge.

"Yes. As long as what I wanted didn't change too substantially, you went along with it. But along the way I did change substantially. Not necessarily for the best. My needs changed and, no matter what you said aloud, I could see the way you really felt about those changes. It was as if I'd betrayed you, as if I'd betrayed what we'd once fought so hard against. You kept your ideals. I caved in. The accusation was there every time I looked into your eyes."

As the full meaning of Kevin's words sank in, Lacey was shocked by his interpretation of what had gone on between them. "Did I ever say that?"

"You didn't have to. Like I said, it was in your eyes every time you looked at me. When I went to work for Dad, when I bought the house, I always sensed you were making a judgment and that I was coming up short."

"That was your own guilt talking, not me."

"Then why did you begin to withdraw?"

Withdraw? Her? How could that have been, she wondered. "I never meant to do that," she said with total honesty. "Kevin, I didn't hate your job or that house because they represented some evil standard of living. I worried because it seemed to me that you took the job for all the wrong reasons, that you took it because you thought it was your obligation to your father and to Jason and me."

"And the house? What about that?"

"I hated the house because it no longer seemed like our home, not the way our first house did. I couldn't keep the new one up, so we hired a maid and a house-keeper and a gardener. All the things I loved to do, all the things that I needed to do to take care of my family, to feel I was making a contribution were in the hands of strangers. I felt as if I'd been cast adrift."

Her claim hovered in the air until at last he said softly, wearily, "I never knew that."

"Because we never talked about it. That was my fault, I suppose. I should have explained how I felt."

Kevin caressed her cheek, the touch light and fleeting. "I just wanted you to have everything," he explained. "It never occurred to me that in giving you all that, I was taking away something that you felt was more precious."

"My identity," she said quietly. "How could you not have known, Kevin, that all I ever wanted was you?"

Something in Kevin's face shut down at her words. Lacey had meant them to be reassuring, but it was clear he hadn't taken them that way.

"What's wrong?" she asked, as an odd chill seemed to invade her.

For the longest time he didn't answer, and during that time she was sure she could hear every tick of the clock on the bedstand, feel every anxious beat of her heart.

Finally, his eyes troubled, he met her gaze. There was so much raw anguish in his face that she was trembling even before he spoke.

"I can't be your whole world, Lace. I just can't."

"But that's not what I meant," she protested.

He shook his head. "Isn't it? The pressure of that, it's more than I can handle."

Stunned by the bleak finality of his tone, she could only watch as he left the bed, grabbed his clothes and went into the bathroom. She was still helplessly staring after him when he left the house just moments later.

Chapter 14

No one was more stunned than Kevin at the words that had popped out of his mouth just before he'd left the house. Where had those thoughts come from? How had he gone for so many years without the vaguest sense that there was so much resentment buried deep inside him? A shrink would surely have a field day with that one.

As he walked on the beach, oblivious to the sun's heat and the pounding of the waves, Kevin tried hard not to remember the quick flash of hurt and confusion in Lacey's eyes. His implied accusation that her dependence on him had somehow weighed him down had been cruel, especially since he couldn't even explain what was behind it.

Hell, he was the one who'd carved out his role as her protector early on. He'd liked feeling ten feet tall when she looked to him for answers to everything from math lessons to politics. If some of that uneven balance had carried over into their marriage, wasn't that as much his fault as hers?

What worried him more than casting blame for that was the discovery that he had hidden such feelings from himself. Were they really buried in his subconscious or had they merely been a quick, defensive reaction to the guilt he'd accepted too readily for far too long?

Lacey was perfect. Their marriage was perfect. Wasn't that why he'd wanted so desperately to win her back? Surely he wasn't one of those men who clung to the past, simply because they couldn't bear the thought of change.

But if that were so, if he were convinced that everything was so perfect, why did he have this nagging sense that he'd been fooling himself? Had he simply grown comfortable in the role of martyr, accepting the blame heaped on him and feeling noble for ignoring his own doubts?

No, dammit! He did love Lacey. He tried that claim out in his head. It rang just as true as it ever had. Okay, then, he wasn't stark raving mad. He was just mixed up, confused, maybe a little exhausted from all the tension. He wasn't thinking clearly.

Hard as he tried, though, he couldn't easily dismiss what had happened. Those words had come from somewhere and he'd darned well better figure out where before he went back to face Lacey again. If their marriage hadn't always been so perfect, after all, he'd better be able to explain what had been lacking from his point of view. She knew what she thought of as his failings as clearly as if she'd carried an itemized list of his sins around in her head.

But no matter how desperately Kevin tried to find a precise, clear-cut answer, he couldn't. So, he thought with a sigh filled with regrets, it wasn't going to be so easy for them, after all. They were going to have to struggle for answers.

He supposed they were among the lucky ones. They still had the will to fight for their marriage. They had their love. They had this new-found honesty, as painful as it was. He hadn't a doubt in his head that they would make it, as long as they didn't shy away from the truth.

He walked until the sky dimmed and the wind picked up. The biting chill cut through his jacket, but worse was the chill he felt deep inside.

For years now he had not taken the time to be terribly introspective, but suddenly he had the sense that something very precious was on the line. He had to figure out exactly why there had been that vague anger behind his words, that hint of something too long repressed. Theories weren't the answer. He needed facts. He needed to pinpoint the cause, narrow it down to a specific moment or an evolution. He had to understand what was in his heart as clearly as what was in his head.

Kevin thought back to the early days of his marriage, days crammed with too much to do and so much tenderness and love. He and Lacey had both worked like demons at demanding, and often thankless, jobs. Then they had spent long hours side by side volunteering for causes they both believed in. Each night they had tumbled into bed, exhausted, but filled with exhilaration.

That period of their lives had been incredibly special. There was absolutely no doubt in his mind about that. Thinking about those days brought smiles, even laughter. Never pain.

But that time had been far too short, now that he thought about it. When Jason was born barely a year after the wedding, things began to change. Lacey took her maternity leave and seemed to blossom before his eyes as she took care of their son. She turned their cramped apartment into a real home, and there were tempting, creative dinners on the table.

Soon any thoughts of her returning to work, any time for volunteering vanished in a sea of household demands. They moved into the house Jason now owned. Nothing ever quite went back to the way it had been.

And he'd resented it, he realized with a sense of shock that actually brought him to a standstill. All these years he had resented the way things had changed, and yet he'd never said a word, hadn't even identified the cause of his mild dissatisfaction.

If he had changed as she had accused him of so often, then so had she. They had never once dealt with that.

He thought he understood why. Unlike Lacey, he had kept the resentment so deeply buried that only now could he recognize the subtle way it had affected everything between them.

If Lacey was going to conform to a more traditional pattern, if she was going to content herself with a home and motherhood, then why shouldn't he do the male equivalent of caving in? At least that must have been the subliminal message at work on him when he'd finally made the decision to go to work at Halloran Industries. How many decisions after that had been affected in the same way?

To top it off, he'd then had to deal with Lacey's unspoken disapproval, along with his own burden of guilt about becoming more and more like his father with each day that passed. He'd called it growing up, but obviously deep inside he'd never truly believed it.

Explaining all of this to her after all this time wasn't going to be easy. He needed some time to sort through it all himself, time to be sure that the answers he'd come up with were valid. Time, in fact, to discover if his marriage was something he really wanted to succeed.

The last seemed like blasphemy. Of course he wanted it to succeed. That was the one given in all this, the one thing he'd never questioned.

Until now, he reminded himself. Lord knows, he had questions now. Unfortunately he didn't have the luxury of time to find the answers, time to examine and come to terms with these raw new discoveries about himself. Lacey was waiting for him.

Kevin's pace picked up, almost in spite of all the doubts tumbling through his poor, pitiful, aching head. That alone should have told him something. He needed to get back to her, to share his thoughts and hear her re-action to them. Lacey had always had a knack for cut-ting through his self-delusion.

Until now, he reminded himself ruefully. Now when it probably meant more than anything.

When he got back to the house, he found her sitting in the living room, almost lost in the shadowy darkness. He flipped on a light and felt his heart wrench at the tears tracking down her cheeks. He wanted to go to her. He wanted to hold her, comfort her.

Instinctively he started toward her, then stopped himself. They needed to air these raw emotions, not soothe them away with meaningless promises.

"Are you okay?" he asked.

"Sure. Terrific," she said with a defiant lift of her chin. She couldn't hide the way it trembled, though. It reminded him of their first meeting so long ago, and his heart ached for her.

And for himself.

"I think maybe this had been the most difficult couple of hours in my entire life," he said finally, sinking into a chair across from her and dragging a hand through his hair.

Eyes shimmering with tears clashed with his. "It hasn't been much of a picnic for me, either."

"No, I'm sure it hasn't been. I'm sorry."

She shrugged. "For what? For being honest? I asked for it, didn't I?"

"But I think we both thought it was going to be a simple matter of airing a few gripes, vowing to try harder and then forgetting all about it."

"Yeah," she said, "silly us."

"There is a bright side," he told her, trying to earn a smile.

"Oh?"

"We haven't had to pay a fortune for shrinks to get to this point."

"Now that is something to stand up and cheer about," she said, her voice steadier at last.

Tears still clung to the ends of her lashes, but she looked stronger somehow, as if she could withstand anything. Perhaps he'd underestimated her ability to stand on her own and overestimated the depth of her need for him.

Whichever it was, Kevin knew in that instant that he had never loved Lacey more. Whatever faint, lingering doubts he had had about that had fled. His heart still turned over at the sight of her. His head still demanded that he protect her from the sort of hurt he himself had inflicted on her. Old habits obviously died hard.

"Feel like talking?" he asked. "Or should we take some time out? Go to a movie or something?"

She met his gaze evenly. "Hey, it couldn't get much worse than this. Let's get it all out now. I don't think I could concentrate on a movie, anyway."

Her glib words were sheer bravado, but Kevin knew there would never be a better time, that what he had to say would hurt whenever he said it. It was better to get everything out in the open now, so they could begin to pick up the pieces.

If there were any left to pick up. Dear God, why did that thought creep in so often? It terrified him. Like an earthquake, it seemed to shake the very foundation of his life.

He stared at the fire before he spoke, gathering courage, censoring harsh accusations. "It's funny," he began slowly. "I never knew that I felt quite so angry until the words came out of my mouth earlier."

Lacey regarded him intently, as if she were weighing his words. "I still don't understand," she said finally. "You talk about feeling pressured. Why? What did I ever do to make you feel that way? I built my life around making you happy."

"Exactly. Instead of caring about the world as you always had, you limited your concerns to just me and our family. I guess I felt that you had betrayed me long before it was the other way around."

"Betrayed you how?" she asked, looking wounded. "By loving you? By needing you?"

"By changing," he said simply.

"But I'm not the one who changed," she protested.

"Yes. Maybe you can't see it, but I can. You were always strong and independent. You always had this clear vision of what you wanted out of life, what we should be doing to make the world a better place to live. There we were, these two intrepid souls going off to tilt at windmills. We were so self-righteous, I suppose, thinking that we knew more than our parents, that we could fix all their mistakes."

"We did fix some things," she reminded him, a little sadly it seemed.

"Maybe some," he agreed. "Then we had Jason and everything changed. The entire focus of your world centered on our son and on me."

"We had a new baby, Kevin. What did you expect?"

"I'm not talking about the first month or even the first year. I could have understood that. But that absorption with our own narrow world didn't end. I began to feel pressured for the first time since I had known you. No man should ever have to carry the burden of being totally responsible for another person's happiness."

With a growing sense of shock and dismay, Lacey listened to Kevin's version of what had happened to their marriage and tried to reconcile it with her own. It wasn't that she could not accept part of the blame. It was simply that the way he described the changes in their relationship weren't the way she remembered things at all.

There had been so much magic once. There had been so many times over the past couple of weeks that she had thought for sure they were recapturing it. Now she knew that had been only a naive dream.

This time, magic wasn't quite enough. Lacey struggled with the fact that the life she'd chosen for herself—the role of homemaker in which she'd been so happy, could never be quite the same again. Jason was married now and her husband didn't need her to see to his every need, in fact resented her devotion.

Could it possibly be true that the very things she accused him of were true of her, as well? Was she no longer the generous person who thought only of helping others? Had she lost the vision they'd once shared, just as she believed he had? It had been only recently that she'd rediscovered a sense of activism in the form of the housing project in which Paula had involved her.

"Maybe I should leave, go back to Boston," she said finally, expressing a thought that had already come to her while Kevin had been gone. In fact, her mind was already made up despite the tentative way she'd phrased it.

Kevin regarded her angrily, as if the suggestion were yet another betrayal. "Leave? Now? Lacey, we're just starting to get somewhere. You can't run away now."

"It's not running. I just need to find some answers to questions I didn't even realize existed. What you've said makes a lot of sense. I was so busy bemoaning the fact that you were no longer the man I married that I never saw that I was no longer the woman you'd married. I need to go find Lacey Grainger again."

"Lacey Halloran," he corrected sharply. "I never meant for you to leave."

Lacey moved to his side, hunkered down and placed her hand over his. She caressed his knuckles, wishing she weren't responsible for the fact that he'd clenched his hands into tight, angry fists.

"I know leaving wasn't your idea. But I have a lot of thinking to do."

"And you can't do it here?"

"No," she said sadly. "When I'm with you, it's all I want and that's wrong. You've said so yourself."

Kevin sighed deeply, then looked resigned. "When will you go?"

"If it's okay with you, I'll wait until morning."

"Sure."

"Will you go back into town with me or do you want to stay out here?"

"I think I'll wait here. If I go back, I won't do the thinking I need to do, either. I'll end up going back to the office."

She nodded and stood up. "I'll go pack."

She was almost out the door when he said, "Lacey?"

"Yes?" she said without turning around.

"The one thing I know without question is that I do love you. I'll be here waiting for you when you're ready to talk again."

She felt the salty sting of tears. Her lower lip trembled. "I love you, too," she said in a voice that quavered slightly.

She couldn't quite bring herself to promise that she would be back. She had no idea where the coming days of self-discovery were likely to lead her.

Chapter 15

Naturally the most depressing day of Kevin's life had dawned sunny and mild. The beauty of the sunrise, the gentleness of the morning breeze seemed to mock him. A day like this should have been gray and gloomy, with the threat of a blizzard maybe. Barring that, a good, steady rain would have done.

Instead, he had to contend with clear skies and a temperature that beckoned. He'd tried his best to make it work to his advantage, but the time was fast approaching when Lacey would be pulling out of the driveway and heading back to Boston.

Saying goodbye to his wife—and quite possibly to his marriage—was one of the most difficult things Kevin ever had to do. It would be a thousand times harder this time than it had been months ago when Lacey had first made the decision to move to a place of her own. Or maybe he'd just forgotten the pain of that goodbye.

Already he had delayed her departure by several hours. He had talked her into one last walk on the beach in the glorious morning sunlight. Then he had convinced her that she had to eat before facing such a long drive. He'd insisted on a picnic on the beach. Then he'd asked her to pick up a few last-minute things in town so he wouldn't have to call on the neighbors. She had seized each excuse far more readily than a woman who was anxious to go.

Finally, though, he had run out of excuses. The only one left to him was a plea for her to reconsider leaving at all, and that one he had promised himself not to use. Though yesterday he had fought her going, he knew that she was right. They needed time apart to sort through everything, to figure out exactly who they were.

"You'll call when you get to town?" he asked as he carefully closed the car door.

"I'll call."

She glanced up at him, her blue eyes shimmering with unshed tears. She blinked hurriedly, then looked away. He could barely hear her when she asked, "You'll be careful? You'll take care of yourself?"

"Of course," he promised. "You don't think I'm going to undo all the good you've done with those nourishing soups, do you?"

"Are you sure you don't want me to take you to rent a car?"

"No. You'll be back before I need one," he said, though there was a forced sound to his optimism. He touched a finger to her chin and tilted her head up until he could gaze directly into her eyes. "I'll miss you."

"Me, too." She hesitated, then reached for the key and started the engine. "I should get started."

"Right. Drive carefully." He stepped back from the car.

"I always do."

He couldn't think of one more thing to say to make her linger. He reminded himself again that her decision to leave was the right one, the only one.

So why did he feel a lump the size of Texas lodged in his throat as he watched her go? Why did he feel this aching sense of abandonment, of loneliness and loss, when the car wasn't even out of sight?

Lacey prayed that she would be able to go back to Boston without anyone knowing. She didn't want Jason and Dana hovering. She certainly didn't want Brandon charging in to save the day. Why hadn't she extracted a promise from Kevin not to tell them? Hopefully he would have his own reasons for keeping quiet.

She turned the car radio on full blast, to an oldies station, hoping to drown out her thoughts. Instead, every song dragged her back down memory lane. She cried all the way home—big, sloppy tears that left her blouse soaking wet and her eyes red.

It was dark when she finally got back into town. She had never felt lonelier than she did when she turned the key in the lock of the apartment she had rented months earlier. She went through the living room, bedroom and kitchen switching on lights. She flipped on the ste-

reo because the silence seemed oppressive. This time,
at least, she was wise enough to avoid old favorites.

The apartment wasn't so bad, though after the home
she and Kevin had shared, it seemed little bigger than
one of their walk-in closets. The furniture was slightly
shabby, but comfortable. She reminded herself that in
many ways she had been happy during her months
here. There had been a contentment, though she'd always felt that something was missing. Not something
material, just Kevin.

Just Kevin, she thought mockingly, as if he were
no more important than a comfortable bed or a faded
print of some masterpiece. The truth of the matter,
though, was that she could have been happy here for
the rest of her days, if Kevin had been here to share
it. She supposed that was just one example of that dependence he'd complained about.

Enough, she decided. Tomorrow would be soon
enough to tackle the future. She concentrated instead
on settling in. It took her no time at all to put her clothes
away, to shove her suitcases into the back of the cramped
closet. Making herself a pot of tea wasted ten minutes
at best.

And then she had to face the fact that she was really
and truly alone. Always before she had known in the back
of her mind that leaving here and going home was her decision, that Kevin would welcome her back. It was entirely
possible after the talk they had had last night that he would
have second thoughts about resuming their marriage.

She was startled when the phone rang. She considered
not answering it, then worried that it might be Kevin.
He'd looked fine when she'd driven off, but something

could have happened since then. And he was the only one who knew she'd left the Cape, the only one who would expect to find her here.

"Hello," she said hesitantly.

"Lacey, it's me."

"Kevin. Are you okay?"

"Fine. More to the point, how are you? You promised to call."

"I'm fine," she said, clutching the phone tightly. So, she thought, they were reduced to polite chit-chat. "I'm sorry. I just got in a half hour ago. I was getting settled."

"Everything's okay, then? You've locked the door? Checked the windows?"

A smile crept up on her. "Yes. Kevin, this apartment is perfectly safe."

"Lacey, the security system consists of an old man who'd sell out his own mother for a bottle of booze."

"That's not true. Charley is very careful about who he lets in. Besides, he's not on at night."

As soon as the words were out of her mouth, she realized they'd been a mistake.

"What do you mean he's not on at night?" Kevin demanded. "Who is?"

"Actually, there's a buzzer system."

"My God."

"Kevin, it's fine."

"Sure, okay. I guess you know what you're doing," he said wearily.

"Thanks for checking on me, though," she said, reluctant now to cut the connection. Kevin's concern, even under these tense circumstances, made her feel warm and cherished.

But of course that was what this was all about—proving whether she could stand on her own two feet without him there to protect her. She wasn't sure which of them needed to know the answer to that the most.

Lacey spent the next day restocking her refrigerator, going through the mail and cleaning the apartment. It gave her one whole day of reprieve from thinking about the agonizing decision she had to make.

By afternoon, a late spring cold front was pushing through, bringing rain and icy winds. The skies turned dark and miserable by five o'clock, mirroring her mood.

By eight she was ready to scream. Fearful of what too much introspection might reveal, she picked up the phone and called Paula Gethers. She sensed that staying busy, that finding a new purpose to her life was going to be the most critical thing to come of the next days or weeks.

"How's the house coming?" Lacey asked without preamble, hoping to get her friend off on her favorite topic before she could pick up on any unwitting signals Lacey might be sending out.

"Okay," Paula said, then promptly added, "Lacey, what's wrong?"

So much for fooling an old friend. "Who says anything is wrong?" she said anyway.

"I do, and I'm never wrong about these things."

"Look, I was just wondering if you could use my help tomorrow. That's all."

"I can always use your help, but something tells me you want to hit nails so you won't break up the furniture."

"If you're suggesting I sound depressed, you're right."

"Actually, I would have said angry."

"Maybe that, too. But I don't want to talk about it," she said firmly. "Not now and definitely not tomorrow."

"Then I will see you first thing in the morning and I will keep my opinion of your sorry state of mind to myself."

Lacey sighed. "Thanks on all counts."

"Hon, you don't have to thank me for letting you work your buns off. As for the rest, you may not want to thank me after you've had time to think about it. You sound like you could use someone to talk to. Just remember, I'm here if you change your mind."

Paula said goodbye and hung up before Lacey could reply that the last thing she needed right now was more talk. She and Kevin had done enough of that to last a lifetime. Maybe if they hadn't spent so darn much time digging below the surface of their problems, she wouldn't be questioning the very foundation of her life right now.

She had built her life on loving and being loved by Kevin. Without him, what was left? Her relationship with her son and daughter-in-law to be sure, but they certainly didn't need her hanging around twenty-four hours a day.

Her thoughts were starting to be so depressing that she made the mistake of grabbing the phone without thought when it rang again. Any interruption would be better than more of these dark reminders of the state of her marriage.

The sound of Brandon's voice snapped her back to the present. Any interruption except this one, she corrected, wondering if she dared to hang up in his ear.

"Good. You're there. I'm coming over," he announced.

"Brandon, don't," she pleaded, then realized that she was talking to herself. Her father-in-law had already hung up.

If she hadn't been so furious, she might have laughed. Brandon was reacting totally in character. He was as predictable when it came to loving his family as, well, as she was. The comparison was the most amusing thing of all.

Lacey briefly considered fleeing, but figured a stint in the French Foreign Legion wouldn't take her far enough. She satisfied her need for some illusion of control by letting him lean on the buzzer downstairs for five full minutes before letting him in.

Brandon glared at her when she finally opened the door, then breezed straight past her, carelessly tossing his Halloran cashmere coat over the back of a chair. He left his umbrella dripping all over the kitchen floor, then stalked into the living room. It looked smaller than ever with him prowling from one end to the other, a disapproving scowl on his face. He rubbed his fingers over the cheap upholstery on the sofa and shook his head, his dismay unmistakable.

"I'm delighted to see you, too," she said dryly, when it looked as if it might be a long time before he got down to saying exactly what was on his mind.

"What's the point of making small talk? We both know why I'm here."

"I doubt that," Lacey retorted.

He shot her a puzzled glance as her implication sank in. "What the devil's that supposed to mean?"

"It means that you couldn't begin to know what's gone on between Kevin and me the last couple of days, not unless your son has broken a lifelong cardinal rule and confided in you."

"I know you're here and he's still on Cape Cod."

"And how did you discover that?"

"I drove out there today."

Lacey's eyebrows rose at that.

"I had some papers to drop off," he retorted without a trace of defensiveness. "Kevin tried to cover for your absence, but he's a lousy liar. That's enough to tell me you two fools still haven't settled your differences."

"Brandon, you can't charm me into doing what you want," Lacey said dryly.

He gave her a sharp glance. "I wasn't trying to charm you. Dammit all, can't you stop jumping down my throat for five minutes and listen to what I have to say?"

Lacey drew in a deep breath and apologized. "You're right," she said, sitting down opposite him. "Would you like something? A cup of tea, maybe?"

"I came here for a real heart-to-heart, not to see if you're up on your social graces."

"Fine. Say whatever you want to say."

He nodded in satisfaction. "Years ago I did you a grave disservice. Nobody's sorrier for that than I am. You and Kevin came pretty close to lighting up a room with the kind of love you had. When the two of you stood up to me, I thought there'd never come a day when something more powerful than me would come along and change that."

She found herself grinning at the high esteem in which he held his own power.

"What's so danged funny?" he grumbled.

"Nothing," she said. "Go on."

"I'm not here to ask you again what your differences are. Kevin's old enough to plead his own case."

To her astonishment, he actually looked uneasy. Before she could figure out what to make of that, he said, "I just want you to know if this has anything at all to do with those old days, I'm sorry for what happened and nothing would make me happier than to see the two of you back together."

Touched by the apology, even though it had come nearly three decades too late, Lacey found herself reaching for his hand and clasping it. "Brandon, this isn't about you. I swear it."

"Halloran Industries then? You never did want Kevin to work there."

"That's not true. I just wanted him to make his own choice, not to be bulldozed by you."

"Well, if it's not me and it's not my company, what is it?" he demanded as if the thought of anything else were totally preposterous.

Lacey burst out laughing at that. "And Kevin complained because *I* had a narrow world."

Brandon glowered at her. "What's that supposed to mean?"

"It means, you crotchety old man, that I adore the

single-minded purpose with which you protect what's yours. Kevin obviously inherited that from you."

Brandon was shaking his head. "You think he's anything like me?"

"A lot more than either of you suspect, I think. Thank you for coming by. It means a lot."

"You going back there in the morning?"

"No," she said firmly.

Brandon looked disappointed. "My powers of persuasion must be off a little."

"Don't worry. I'm just a tougher sell than your run-of-the-mill client."

"What are you going to do?"

"Tomorrow I'm going to build a house."

He regarded her as if she'd suddenly started speaking in Swahili. "Am I supposed to understand what that means?"

"No," she said, laughing.

"Good. I'd hate to think I'd started losing my wits, when I have some plans for the future I've been thinking about. If I could just get the two of you settled and get that great grandbaby born, I might start thinking about my own life."

This time it was Lacey's turn to be confused. "Am I supposed to know what you're talking about?"

He gave her a wink. "Nope. This business of keeping secrets goes both ways."

Lacey felt her spirits begin to climb just a little as she arrived at the housing site in the morning. The thought of what the half-finished house before her would mean to some family was gratifying. Maybe she couldn't do much to fix her own life, but she could do her part to help someone else get a new start.

She wandered around the house in search of Paula or Dave, so she could get an assignment. She found Paula atop a ladder. Her husband, his hair tied back in a ponytail, was holding the ladder steady with one hand. The other was sliding slowly up the back of Paula's denim-clad leg in an intimate caress.

Lacey felt the sting of tears as she listened to their familiar bickering. There wasn't a hostile note in the exchange, just the fond give and take of two people who'd found their own shorthand way of communicating.

When Dave's hand reached Paula's bottom, she turned and glared down at him. "You're not helping, David Gethers," she grumbled, but Lacey could clearly hear the amusement in her friend's voice.

"How can you say that?" he inquired innocently.

"Because I need to concentrate on what I'm doing here, instead of wondering where that roving hand of yours is heading."

"Don't you worry about that. You go right on doing whatever you need to do."

"If I have to come down off of this ladder," Paula warned with mock ferocity, "you are going to be one sorry man. Go check on the plumbers or something."

"It's the *or something* I'm interested in."

"Dave!"

"Okay, okay," he finally said with weary resignation. He turned and caught sight of Lacey.

"The woman is a trial," he grumbled. "Maybe you can explain to her that there are more important things than checking shingles or whatever she's doing up there."

Lacey laughed. "I doubt I'm the right person to be giving anyone advice on priorities."

Paula peered down at her and immediately descended. "Good. You're here."

"Ready, willing and able," Lacey confirmed. "What's my assignment?"

"First things first. Come with me," Paula steered her around the corner to an RV that served as a mobile office for the project. Inside, she held up a pot of coffee. "Want some?"

Lacey hesitated, sensing that Paula had more on her mind than deciding whether to hand her a paintbrush or a screwdriver.

"Sure, why not?" she said finally. She sat down on a corner of the office's one cluttered desk.

"So what did Kevin think when you told him about our project?" Paula asked.

"He was very excited," Lacey said honestly. "He wants to find a way to get Halloran Industries involved."

"So why aren't you whooping for joy? Did you expect him to turn up here first thing this morning with a tool kit?"

Lacey sighed and set the cup of coffee aside. "No, that's not it."

"What then? Are you two reconciling or not?"

"I don't know."

Paula shook her head. "I don't get it. You love him. He loves you. What could be simpler than that?"

"He wants me to have my own interests."

"Like this project?"

Lacey shrugged. "I suppose."

"Come on, girl. Pick up the pace here. I'm getting lost. What do you want?"

"Let me see if I can figure out how to say this. The best thing about our relationship from the very beginning was that we always shared everything. Now he goes off to Halloran and I come here. I guess if anything, I'm envious of what you and Dave have. You share the same concerns. You work side by side."

"Can I assume that Kevin does not want to come over here and hammer things?"

"He wants to write checks."

"Hey, we need people like that, too. Don't even think about complaining about that."

Even as she and Paula talked, Lacey was struck by the first spark of an idea. Suddenly she felt her energy returning and her spirits mending. She grabbed Paula by the shoulders and hugged her.

"You are a genius," she declared. "I've got to run."

"Hey, I have you down for painting the entire living room today."

Lacey opened her purse and took out the hundred-dollar bill Kevin had given her as a joke a few nights earlier. "Pay someone," she said, handing it over. "I have a long drive ahead of me."

Chapter 16

Lacey didn't waste a second before taking off for Cape Cod. Even though she was wearing paint-spattered jeans and an old blouse, she refused to go back to the apartment to change into something more presentable. What she had to say to Kevin was far more important than the way she looked. Half the time he didn't notice what she was wearing, anyway. She did pull off the bandanna she'd tied around her head and ran her fingers through her hair to get rid of the tangles. At least there was no paint in it.

As she drove she considered all the implications of her idea. She couldn't figure out why she hadn't had this brainstorm before. During all those lonely months when she'd had nothing to do but think, no solution to the real problems in her marriage had come to her—probably because she hadn't even know exactly what those problems were. She'd focused too much on Kevin's health and not on the reasons he might have had for driving himself so hard.

Now, after less than forty-eight miserable hours apart, she had recognized the perfect answer, one that had been staring her in the face all along.

Perhaps the reason it seemed so easy now was because of the time she and Kevin had spent together on Cape Cod. In all of that painful self-analysis, they had brought themselves right to the brink of discovery. They might not have reconciled, but they had certainly laid all of the groundwork.

She had to be right about this, she thought as she reversed the drive she'd made only two days before. This time she felt so much more hopeful, not just about fulfilling her own needs, but about finding common ground that she and Kevin could share again, about recapturing that sense of purpose that had made their relationship so special.

Excitement and anticipation spilled through her. She deliberately turned on the oldies station and sang along with all the nostalgic hits, laughing at the happy memories that came back to crowd out the sad.

Her mood lasted until she turned into the driveway and saw Brandon's huge tank of a luxury car parked beside the house. Why was he back out here today? she wondered with a sinking feeling in the pit of her stomach. Why was he here when she so desperately needed to be alone with Kevin to see if they could finally fix their lives?

She drew in a deep breath and reminded herself that she was the one who'd said quite plainly that she wouldn't be coming back this morning. She had no one to blame but herself if her father-in-law had taken that to mean that it was up to him to keep Kevin company.

Of course, it was unlikely that Brandon was inside making soup or playing cards with Kevin. It was far more likely that he'd brought along a stack of work on the pretense of keeping his son occupied.

Feeling oddly uncertain, Lacey looked down at her old clothes and wondered if she ought to drive to the nearest boutique and buy something new. She could already envision Brandon's disapproval. Only her desire to share her idea before she had second thoughts prevented her from leaving. That and an awareness that it was long past time when she had to impress her father-in-law. His visit last night had finally put them on a friendlier footing that she was sure would last and grow.

She walked slowly up the walk, then found herself ringing the doorbell, rather than using her key. It was Kevin who opened the door.

His face looked haggard, as if he hadn't been getting nearly enough sleep since she'd left. There was a faint stubble on his cheeks that she yearned to reach out and caress. As tired as he looked, he'd never seemed more desirable. She wanted to throw herself into his arms and hold on until the dark days had gone for good.

And there was no mistaking the sudden spark of hope in his eyes when he saw her.

"You're back," he began inanely.

She understood the awkwardness, because she was feeling it as well, that and so much more. Trepidation, hope, love.

"Did you forget your key?"

She shook her head. "No. It's in my purse. I wasn't sure if I should use it."

"Lacey, this is your house as much as mine. More, probably."

She shrugged. "I realized that Brandon was here. I thought maybe, I don't know. I thought maybe I should wait and come back later when we could talk."

"Don't be ridiculous."

Just then Brandon appeared in the doorway to the living room. He searched her face, and then, as if he'd seen something he approved of—maybe her new-found confidence—he nodded. He turned at once and went back. It was more discretion than he'd ever displayed before.

"Come on in," Kevin said. "Dad and I were just finishing up."

"That's right," Brandon said, when they'd joined him. "I'll be on my way in just a minute."

It was clear though, that he had been ensconced in the living room for some time. Files were spread on the coffee table. As Lacey walked in, he punched a long series of numbers into a calculator. He nodded in satisfaction, jotted them down and then stood up.

"I'll leave you two. I'm sure you have a lot to discuss," he said, sounding as if he couldn't wait to get away. "Kevin, your instincts were exactly right. Those figures look good. I'll tell Jason to get on with things."

"That sounds good," Kevin said distractedly, his gaze still fixed on Lacey.

"You don't have to rush off," Lacey felt compelled

to say to Brandon, though she wanted nothing more than to see him leave.

He grinned at her then. "You're a lousy liar, girl. Same as Kevin." He grabbed his coat and headed for the front door. "He's been trying to kick me out since I got here, but was too polite to come right out and say anything to my face."

"Drive carefully," she told him.

"Always do."

He left the room then, and Lacey stared out the front window while she waited for Kevin to come back. The last thing she overheard Brandon ask was when Kevin intended to get back to work.

"I'll have to let you know about that, Dad."

Lacey noticed Brandon had left the files and the calculator behind. She was tempted to toss the papers into the fireplace, but she left them on the coffee table, waiting to see what Kevin would do about them.

When he came back into the living room, his expression was cautious. "I'm surprised to see you back so soon," he began, his tone wary. He'd shoved his hands into the pockets of his jeans as if he couldn't quite figure out what else to do with them. He kept his distance, standing over by the fireplace, rather than joining her.

"No more surprised than I am to be back." She hesitated, then couldn't keep herself from asking, "You're not going to let Brandon push you into going back to work too soon, are you?"

He held up his hands. "Lacey, please don't start on that."

"I can't help it," she said, gesturing toward the mess

on the coffee table. "Just look at what he's brought. There's enough there to keep you busy for a month."

"It's just Dad's way of making sure I'm not too lonely out here. He needed an excuse to come back."

Lacey wrestled with the idea of Brandon making up excuses for any of his actions. She couldn't imagine it. Then again, in his relationship with his son, anything was possible. She suddenly realized that ever since Kevin had turned down that job at Halloran Industries years ago, Brandon quite probably had feared another rejection. He had never taken Kevin's presence at the company for granted.

At the same time, she and Kevin had taken each other for granted. They had operated for years now under the misguided notion that their relationship would always remain exactly the same. No wonder the past year had been so rocky.

"Are you ready to go back to work?" she asked finally.

"That depends."

"On?"

"What happens with us."

She shook her head. "No, you can't pin that decision on us, on me. What do you want to do with the rest of your life?"

She thought she knew the answer to that, but she had to hear him say it, had to know if the plan she'd devised made any sense at all.

"Actually, I do want to go back to Halloran," Kevin finally admitted with an obvious sigh of relief. "Tradition seems more important to me now. Working with my father and my son creates a bond that most men never have. I want that in my life. I didn't realize until recently how much I counted on that sense of continuity. I think I understand finally what it must have done to Dad when I walked away from it."

"Then you should go back."

He shook his head. "Not at the cost of destroying our marriage."

"Working at Halloran Industries could only destroy our marriage if we allow it to, if we attach some symbolic significance to it the way we did before," she said with a trace of impatience. "I think we're both past that. The important thing is to keep a balance in our lives, to keep the priorities straight. I don't want you obsessed with our marriage, any more than I want you obsessed with work. Isn't that what you were saying to me earlier?"

"Yes, but—"

"No," she said softly. "No *buts,* Kevin. This is about what you think is right for you."

"But I can't decide that in a vacuum. What do you need? What will make you happy?"

She turned to stare out the window as she searched for a way to explain what she was feeling, all the discoveries she'd made.

"I think maybe I actually have an answer to that," she said, finally turning back from the window and meeting his gaze. "I came back here so I could run it by you."

"So, tell me," he said.

Lacey drew in a deep breath. "I've been thinking, maybe we could form a Halloran Foundation, something we could work on together."

"Give away Halloran money?" Kevin teased, pretending to be scandalized by the very notion.

"Stop," she said. "I'm serious. You and your father have always been very generous, but this could be something we do in a more organized fashion."

Kevin's gaze was suddenly more intense. How many times had he looked just that way when they'd bounced ideas back and forth long ago? Her confidence had grown simply by seeing the way he respected what she thought.

"Go on," he said, the first hint of excitement in his voice. "I think I see where you're going with this."

Now, with that slim bit of encouragement, Lacey couldn't keep the enthusiasm out of her voice. "Okay. The way I see it, we'd set up a trust, an endowment, whatever. That would become the basis of the Foundation. That's where you and Brandon come in. You have to make the commitment to set aside the money to do this."

"And where do you fit in?"

"I thought I could evaluate applications, seek out the organizations and individuals that really need help, help establish programs. All those committees I've served on have taught me a lot about fund-raising and grant proposals and effectively run charities. I think I could weed out those that are poorly operated. I'd handle all the day-to-day things, the paperwork. The Halloran board would okay the grants."

Even as she talked, the tiny seed of an idea took root and flourished. She could see from the excitement in Kevin's eyes that he shared her enthusiasm.

"Yes," he said and added his ideas to hers until the

Foundation seemed more a reality than a sudden in-
spiration that had come to her only hours ago.

"Don't you see, Kevin? The best part would be that
we'd be doing it together, we'd share the same focus
again, even if it's only one small aspect of what you
do at Halloran."

He got up and moved to the window to stand behind
her. His arms circled her waist. "I think it's the most
wonderful, generous idea I've ever heard."

She turned in his arms until she could study him.
She searched his face. "Really?"

"Really," he said, pressing a tender kiss to her forehead. Lacey felt her heart tumble.

"Do you think Brandon will go for it?" she asked,
unable to keep the anxiety out of her voice.

"I think he'll love it."

"Kevin, I know this doesn't take care of everything.
I know it's not some magical solution for us, but it's
a start."

His lips touched hers then, capturing all the excitement and adding to it. Anticipation and joy touched
off a spark that sent fire dancing through her veins.

"God, I love you," Kevin murmured, when he finally pulled away. "There are so many things I want
to say to you, so many things we can do together, now
that we know our marriage is here to stay. That is what
you want, isn't it?"

"More than anything."

"What about the house?" he asked.

"Which house?" she asked, thoroughly puzzled by
the change in direction.

"The one in Boston. Jason told me there's an interested buyer."

Lacey just stared at him. "You put it on the market?"

He nodded. "Before I left the hospital."

"Why?"

"It was awfully cold and lonely without you. Frankly, I kind of like it here. You and me, walking on the beach, warming up in front of a fire."

His hands swept over her, slowly stroking until she could imagine those nights of loving in front of the fire as vividly as he could. Then it didn't matter at all that she'd worn paint-spattered clothes, because he was sliding them off her, kissing every inch of her bare flesh until the fire in the hearth was nothing compared to the one deep inside her.

"Oh, my beautiful Lacey," he whispered, his gaze locked on hers. "I was so afraid you wouldn't come back, so afraid that my stupid pride would keep me from coming after you."

"Would you have come after me?" she asked, her voice breathless as he skimmed his fingers over her breasts.

"Yes. I realized finally that I have no pride at all where you're concerned. You hadn't been gone fifteen minutes when I knew that I was wrong to let you go. The only way to work things out was to do it together."

"Of course, I did do some pretty incredible thinking while I was away from you," she taunted.

"But look how much more clearly you're thinking now that we're back together."

She moaned as his fingers slid lower, over her belly and beyond to the precise spot where she yearned to be touched. She arched into the teasing touch. "This doesn't have anything to do with thinking," she told him when she could manage enough breath to say anything.

"That's not what I heard," he told her. "Making love starts in the head."

She slid her hand up his thigh until she reached the hard evidence of his arousal. "But that's not where it finishes, is it?" she taunted.

"Lacey, dearest, darling…"

"Yes?"

"If you keep that up—"

"That is my intention," she said.

"Lacey!"

"You had something else in mind?" she inquired pleasantly.

Kevin groaned. "No. No, I think you've got it."

"Then come here, please."

She arched her back as he drove into her. He pulled back, then entered her more slowly, establishing a tantalizing pace that was just one shade shy of unbearable.

"You're getting even, aren't you?" she asked him as he withdrew again.

"Would I do that?" he inquired, a glint of amusement in his eyes.

"You would." She concentrated very hard on not letting him drive her over the brink until she could take him with her.

Unfortunately she found it very difficult to concentrate on anything but the sensations that were throbbing through her with increasing intensity. The excitement she'd felt about the Halloran Foundation was nothing compared to the excitement generated by this one Halloran man.

"Kevin," she murmured finally.

"Yes."

"I think it's time to stop playing games."

The spark of amusement in his eyes gave way to a dark, burning desire as he lifted her hips and drove into her one last, exquisitely slow time. She felt herself tightening around him, holding him deep inside her until there was nothing left to say, nothing left to do except give herself over to the thrill of coming apart in his embrace.

For the longest time after their passion was spent, they stayed right where they were, curled up in front of the fire, the reflection of the flames dancing over their perspiration-slicked skin.

"So what do you think?" Kevin asked eventually.

"About what?"

"The house."

After the past half hour, there was only one possible answer as far as Lacey could tell. "Maybe we could make do with an apartment in the city and live on the Cape. I don't think I want to give up what we found out here."

"I certainly don't want to give up times like this," Kevin agreed.

"Are we really okay, though? I'm not dreaming the way I feel right now, am I?"

"Lacey, if it's a dream, then I'm caught up in the same one."

"But will it last?"

"Who can say? I can only promise you that from

now on we'll never take each other for granted again. Maybe what happened to us was all for the best. We both learned to appreciate what we have, and next time we'll both fight harder before we risk losing it."

"Will there be a next time, then?" she asked.

"I'm afraid so. There will always be crises in a marriage. Most people these days opt out at the first sign of trouble. I don't want us ever to do that again."

"Is that your sense of Halloran honor talking?"

"No, Lacey, it's my love."

* * * * *

Also by Patricia Davids

HQN

The Matchmakers of Harts Haven

The Inn at Harts Haven
A Match Made at Christmas

The Amish of Cedar Grove

The Wish
The Hope
The Prayer

Love Inspired

Brides of Amish Country

The Inn at Hope Springs
Katie's Redemption
The Doctor's Blessing
An Amish Christmas
The Farmer Next Door
The Christmas Quilt
A Home for Hannah
A Hope Springs Christmas
Plain Admirer
Amish Christmas Joy
The Shepherd's Bride
The Amish Nanny
An Amish Family Christmas: A Plain Holiday
An Amish Christmas Journey
Amish Redemption

Visit her Author Profile page at Harlequin.com,
or patriciadavids.com, for more titles!

THE SHEPHERD'S BRIDE

Patricia Davids

This book is dedicated with endearing love
to my lambs, Kathy, Josh and Shantel.

He shall feed His flock like a shepherd:
He shall gather the lambs with His arm,
and carry them in His bosom, and shall gently lead
those that are with young.
—*Isaiah* 40:11

Chapter 1

"You can't be serious." Lizzie Barkman gaped at her older sister, Clara, in shock.

Seated on the edge of the bed in the room the four Barkman sisters shared, Clara kept her eyes downcast. "It's not such a bad thing."

Lizzie fell to her knees beside Clara and took hold of her icy hands. "It's not a bad thing. It's a horrible thing. You can't marry Rufus Kuhns. He's put two wives in the ground already. Besides, he's thirty years older than you are."

"Onkel wishes this."

"Then our uncle is crazy!"

Clara glanced fearfully at the door. "Hush. Do not earn a beating for my sake, sister."

Lizzie wasn't eager to feel the sting of their uncle's wooden rod across her back, but it was outrageous to imagine lovely, meek Clara paired with such an odious man. "Tell Onkel Morris you won't do it."

"He won't go against Rufus's wishes. He's too scared of losing our jobs and this house."

It was true. Their uncle wouldn't oppose Rufus. He didn't have the courage. Rufus Kuhns was a wealthy member of their small Plain community in northern Indiana. He owned the dairy farm where they all worked for the paltry wages he paid. He claimed that letting them live in the run-down house on his property more than made up for their low salaries. The house was little more than a hovel, although the girls tried their best to make it a home.

"Onkel says it is his duty to see us all wed. I'm twenty-five with no prospects. I'm afraid he is right about that."

The single women in their isolated Amish community outnumbered the single men three to one. Lizzie was twenty-three with no prospects in sight, either. Who would her uncle decide she should marry?

"Being single isn't such a bad thing, Clara. Look at my friend Mary Miller, the schoolteacher. She is happy enough."

Clara managed a smile. "It's all right, Lizzie. At least this way I have the hope of children of my own. If God wills it."

It hurt to see Clara so ready to accept her fate. Lizzie wouldn't give up so easily. "Rufus had no children with his previous wives. You don't have to do this. We can move away and support ourselves by making cheese to sell to the tourists. We'll grow old together and take care of each other."

Clara cupped Lizzie's cheek. "You are such a dreamer. What will happen to our little sisters if we do that?"

Greta and Betsy were outside finishing the evening milking. At seventeen, Betsy was the youngest. Greta was nearly twenty. They all worked hard on the dairy farm. With twenty-five cows to be milked by hand twice a day, there was more than enough work to go around. Without Clara and Lizzie to carry their share of the load, the burden on their sisters would double, for their uncle wouldn't pick up the slack.

Morris Barkman hadn't been blessed with children. He and his ailing wife took in his four nieces when their parents died in a buggy accident ten years before. He made no secret of the fact that his nieces were his burden to bear. He made sure everyone knew how generous he was and how difficult his life had been since his wife's passing.

Lizzie couldn't count the number of times she had been forced to hold her tongue when he shamed her in front of others for her laziness and ingratitude. Her uncle claimed to be a devout member of the Amish faith, but in her eyes, he was no better than the Pharisees in the Bible stories the bishop preached about during the church services.

She rose and paced the small room in frustration. There had to be a way out of this. "We can all move away and get a house together. Greta and Betsy, too."

"If we left without our uncle's permission, we would be shunned by everyone in our church. I could not bear that." Clara's voice fell to a whisper. "Besides, if I won't wed Rufus... Betsy is his second choice."

Lizzie gasped. "She's barely seventeen."

"You see now why I have to go through with it. Promise me you won't tell her she's the reason I'm doing this."

"I promise."

"I know you've been thinking about leaving us, Lizzie. I'm not as strong as you are. I can't do it, but you should go. Go now while you have the chance. I can bear anything if I know you are safe."

Lizzie didn't deny it. She had been thinking about leaving for years. She had even squirreled away a small amount of money for the day. Only the thought of never seeing her sisters again kept her from taking such a drastic step. She loved them dearly.

The bedroom door opened and the two younger Barkman girls came in. Greta was limping. Clara immediately went to her. "What happened?"

"She got kicked by that bad-tempered cow we all hate," Betsy said.

"She's not bad-tempered. She doesn't hear well. I startled her. It was my own fault. It's going to leave a bruise, but nothing is broken." Greta sat on the edge of the bed she shared with Betsy.

Clara insisted on inspecting her leg. It was already swollen and purple just above the knee. "Oh, that must hurt. I'll get some witch hazel for it."

As Clara left, Lizzie turned to her sisters. "Onkel is making Clara marry Rufus Kuhns."

"Are you joking? He's ancient." Greta looked as shocked as Lizzie was.

"It's better than being an old *maedel*," Betsy said. "We're never going to find husbands if we aren't allowed to attend singings and barn parties in other Amish communities."

Would she feel the same if she knew how easily she could trade places with Clara? Lizzie kept silent. She had given Clara her word. Betsy began to get ready for the night.

Greta did the same. "Rufus is a mean fellow."

Lizzie turned her back to give her sisters some privacy. "He's cruel to his horses and his cattle. I can't bear to think of Clara living with him."

"His last wife came to church with a bruised face more than once. She claimed she was accident-prone, but it makes a person wonder." Greta pulled on her nightgown.

"Shame on you, Greta. It's a sin to think evil thoughts about the man." Betsy climbed into bed, took off her black *kapp* and started to unwind her long brown hair.

Greta and Lizzie shared a speaking glance but kept silent. Neither of them wanted their oldest sister to find out if their suspicions were true. They remembered only too well the bruises their mother bore in silence when their father's temper flared.

Clara returned with a bottle of witch hazel and a cloth. "This will help with the pain."

Greta took the bottle from her. They had all used the remedy on bruises inflicted by their uncle over the years. He wouldn't stand up to Rufus, but he didn't have any qualms about taking his anger and frustration out on someone weaker. "You can't do it, Clara. You should go away."

"And never see you again? How could I do that?

Besides, where would I go? We have no family besides each other."

Lizzie met Greta's eyes. Greta gave a slight nod. After all, they were desperate. Lizzie said, "We have a grandfather."

"We do?" It was Betsy's turn to look shocked as she sat up in bed.

Clara shook her head. "*Nee*. He is dead to us."

"He is dead to Uncle Morris, not to me." Lizzie's mind began to whirl. Would their *daadi* help? They hadn't heard from him in years. Not since the death of their parents.

Greta rubbed the witch hazel on her knee. "We were told never to mention him."

"Mention who?" Betsy almost shouted.

They all hushed her. None of the sisters wished to stir their uncle's wrath. "Our mother's father lives in Hope Springs, Ohio."

Clara began getting ready for bed, too. "You think he does. He could be dead for all we know."

"We really have a grandfather? Why haven't I met him?" Betsy looked as if she might burst into tears.

Lizzie removed the straight pins that held her faded green dress closed down the front. "We moved away from Hope Springs when you were just a baby."

Clara slipped under the covers. "Papa and Grandfather Shetler had a terrible falling out when I was ten. Mama, Papa, Uncle Morris and his wife all moved away and eventually settled here."

"Grandfather raised sheep." Lizzie smiled at the memory of white lambs leaping for the sheer joy of it in green spring pastures. She hated it when her father made them move to this dreary place. She hung her dress beside her sisters' on the pegs that lined the wall and slipped into her nightgown.

"Do we have a grandmother, too?" Betsy asked.

Lizzie shook her head. "She died when our mother was a baby. I'm ready to put out the lamp. You know how Onkel hates it when we waste kerosene.

"Grandfather had a big white dog named Joker," Greta added wistfully. "I'm sure he's gone by now. Dogs don't live that long."

"But men do. I will write to him first thing in the morning and beg him to take you in, Clara." Lizzie sat down on her side of the bed and blew out the kerosene lamp, plunging the small bedroom into darkness.

Clara sighed. "This is crazy talk. Our uncle will forbid such a letter, Lizzie. You know that. Besides, I'm not going anywhere without my sisters."

Lizzie waited until Clara was settled under the covers with her. Quietly, she said, "You will go to Rufus Kuhns's home without us."

"I…know. I miss Mama so much at times like this."

Lizzie heard the painful catch in her sister's voice. She reached across to pull Clara close. "I do, too. I refuse to believe she made your beautiful star quilt for this sham of a marriage. She made your quilt to be her gift to you on a happy wedding day."

Their mother had lovingly stitched wedding quilts for each of her daughters. They lay packed away in the cedar chest in the corner. The quilts were different colors and personalized for each one of them. They were cherished by the girls as reminders of their mother's love.

Lizzie hardened her resolve. "We'll think of something. It's only the middle of March. We have until the wedding time in autumn. You'll see. We'll think of something before then."

"*Nee*. My wedding will take place the first week of May so I may help with spring planting."

Greta slipped into bed behind Lizzie. "That's not right. We can't prepare for a wedding in such a short time."

"Rufus doesn't want a big wedding. It will be only the bishop, Uncle Morris, you girls and Rufus."

Such a tiny, uncelebrated affair wasn't the wedding dream of any young woman. Lizzie felt the bed sag again and knew Betsy had joined them on the other side of Clara.

"I don't want you to leave us." Betsy's voice trembled as she spoke.

"I won't be far away. Why, you'll all be able to come for a visit whenever you want."

A visit. That was it! A plan began to form in Lizzie's mind. She was almost certain she had enough money saved to travel to Ohio on the bus. Their grandfather might ignore a letter, but if she went to see him in person, she could make him understand how dire the situation was.

It was an outrageous plan, but what choice did she have? None.

Clara couldn't marry Rufus. He would crush her gentle spirit and leave her an empty shell. Or worse.

Lizzie bit her bottom lip. She couldn't let that happen. Nor could she tell her sisters what she intended to do. She didn't want them to lie or cover for her. As much as it hurt, she would have to let them think she had run away.

Her younger sisters soon returned to their own bed. Before long, their even breathing told Lizzie they were asleep. Clara turned over and went to sleep, too.

Lizzie lay wide-awake.

If she went through with her plan, the only person she dared tell was Mary Miller. There was no love lost between the schoolteacher and their uncle. Besides, it wasn't as if Lizzie was leaving the Amish. She was simply traveling to another Amish community. If she wrote to her friend from Ohio, she was certain that Mary would relay messages to the girls. If their grandfather proved willing to take them in, Mary would help them leave.

Lizzie pressed her hand to her mouth. Would it work? Could she do it?

If she went, it would have to be tonight while the others were asleep. Before she lost her nerve. She closed her eyes and folded her hands.

Please, Lord, let this plan be Your will. Give me the strength to see it through.

She waited until it was well after midnight before she slipped from beneath the covers. The full moon outside cast a band of pale light across the floor. It gave her enough light to see by. She carefully withdrew an envelope with her money from beneath the mattress and pulled an old suitcase from under the bed. It took only five minutes to gather her few belongings. Then she moved to the cedar chest.

Kneeling in front of it, she lifted the lid. Clara's rose-and-mauve star quilt lay on top. Lizzie set it aside and pulled out the quilt in shades of blue and green that was to be her wedding quilt. Should she take it with her?

If she did, it would convince everyone she wasn't returning. If she left it, her sisters would know she was coming back.

Suddenly, Lizzie knew she couldn't venture out into the unknown without something tangible of her family to bring her comfort. She replaced Clara's quilt and softly closed the lid of the cedar chest.

Holding her shoes, her suitcase and her quilt, Lizzie tiptoed to the door of their room. She opened it with a trembling hand and glanced back at her sisters sleeping quietly in the darkness. Could she really go through with this?

Carl King scraped most of the mud off his boots and walked up to the front door of his boss's home. Joe Shetler had gone to purchase straw from a neighbor, but he would be back soon. After an exhausting morning spent struggling to pen and doctor one ornery and stubborn ewe, Carl had rounded up half the remaining sheep and moved them closer to the barns with the help of his dog, Duncan.

Tired, with his tongue lolling, the black-and-white English shepherd walked beside Carl toward the house. Carl reached down to pat his head. "You did good work this morning, fella. We'll start shearing them soon if the weather holds."

The sheep needed to spend at least one night inside the barn to make sure their wool was dry before being sheared. Damp wool would rot. There wasn't enough room in the barn for all two hundred head at once. The operation would take three to four days if all went well.

It was important to shear the ewes before they gave birth. If the weather turned bad during the lambing season, many of the shorn ewes would seek shelter in the sheds and barn rather than have their lambs out in the open where the wet and cold could kill the newborns. Having a good lamb crop was important, but Carl knew things rarely went off without a hitch.

Duncan ambled toward his water dish. At the moment, all Carl wanted was a hot cup of coffee. Joe always left a pot on the back of the stove so Carl could help himself.

He opened the front door and stopped dead in his tracks. An Amish woman stood at the kitchen sink. She had her back to him as she rummaged for something. She hadn't heard him come in.

He resisted the intense impulse to rush back outside. He didn't like being shut inside with anyone. He fought his growing discomfort. This was Joe's home. This woman didn't belong here.

"What are you doing?" he demanded. Joe didn't like anyone besides Carl in his house.

She shrieked and jumped a foot as she whirled around to face him. She pressed a hand to her heaving chest, leaving a patch of white soapsuds on her faded green dress. "You scared the life out of me."

He clenched his fists and stared at his feet. "I didn't mean to frighten you. Who are you and what are you doing here?"

"Who are you? You're not Joseph Shetler. I was told this was Joseph's house."

He glanced up and saw the defiant jut of her jaw. He folded his arms over his chest and pressed his lips into a tight line. He didn't say a word as he glared at her.

She was a slender little thing. The top of her head wouldn't reach his chin unless she stood on tiptoe. She was dressed Plain in a drab faded green calf-length dress with a matching cape and apron. She wore dark stockings and dark shoes. Her hair, on the other hand, was anything but drab. It was ginger-red and wisps of it curled near her temples and along her forehead. The rest was hidden beneath the black *kapp* she wore. Her eyes were an unusual hazel color with flecks of gold in their depths.

He didn't recognize her, but she could be a local. He made a point of avoiding people, so it wasn't surprising that he didn't know her.

She quickly realized he wasn't going to speak until she had answered his questions. She managed a nervous smile. "I'm sorry. My name is Elizabeth Barkman. People call me Lizzie. I'm Joe's granddaughter from Indiana. I was just straightening up a little while I waited for him to get home."

As far as Carl knew, Joe didn't have any family. "Joe doesn't have a granddaughter, and he doesn't like people in his house." He shoved his hands into his pockets as the need to escape the house left them shaking.

"Actually, he has four granddaughters. I can see why he doesn't like to have people in. This place is a mess. He certainly could use a housekeeper. I know an excellent one who is looking for a position."

Carl glanced around Joe's kitchen. It was cluttered

and dirty, unlike the clean and sparsely furnished shepherd's hut out in the pasture where he lived, but if Joe wanted to live like this, that was his business and not the business of this nosy, pushy woman. "This is how Joe likes it. You should leave."

"Where is my grandfather? Will he be back soon?" Her eyes darted around the room. He could see fear creeping in behind them. It had dawned on her that they were alone together on a remote farm.

Suddenly, he saw another room, dark and full of women huddled together. He could smell the fear in the air. They were all staring at him.

He blinked hard and the image vanished. His heart started pounding. The room began closing in on him. He needed air. He needed out. He'd seen enough fear in women's eyes to haunt him for a lifetime. He didn't need to add to that tally. He took a quick step back. "Joe will be along shortly." Turning, he started to open the door.

She said, "I didn't catch your name. Are you a friend of my grandfather's?"

He paused and gripped the doorknob tightly so she wouldn't see his hand shaking. "I'm Carl King. I work here." He walked out before she could ask anything else.

Once he was outside under the open sky, his sense of panic receded. He drew a deep, cleansing breath. His tremors grew less with each gulp of air he took. His pounding heart rate slowed.

It had been weeks since one of his spells. He'd started to believe they were gone for good, that perhaps God had forgiven him, but Joe's granddaughter had proved him wrong.

His dog trotted to his side and nosed his hand. He managed a little smile. "I'm okay, Duncan."

The dog whined. He seemed to know when his master was troubled. Carl focused on the silky feel of the dog's thick fur between his fingers. It helped ground him in the here and now and push back the shadows of the past.

That past lay like a beast inside him. The terror lurked, ready to spring out and drag him into the nightmares he suffered through nearly every night. He shouldn't be alive. He should have accepted death with peace in his heart, secure in the knowledge of God's love and eternal salvation. He hadn't.

He had his life, for what it was worth, but no peace.

Joe came into sight driving his wagon and team of draft horses. The wagon bed held two dozen bales of straw. He pulled the big dappled gray horses to a stop beside Carl. "Did you get that ewe penned and doctored?"

"I did."

"*Goot.* We'll get this hay stored in the big shed so we can have it handy to spread in the lambing pens when we need it. We can unload it as soon as I've had a bite to eat and a cup of coffee. Did you leave me any?"

"I haven't touched the pot. You have a visitor inside."

A small elderly man with a long gray beard and a dour expression, Joe climbed down from the wagon slowly. To Carl's eyes, he had grown frailer this past year. A frown creased his brow beneath the brim of the flat-topped straw hat he wore. He didn't like visitors. "Who is it?"

"She claims she's your granddaughter Lizzie Barkman."

All the color drained from Joe's face. He staggered backward until he bumped into the wheel of his wagon. "One of my daughter's girls? What does she want?"

Carl took a quick step toward Joe and grasped his elbow to steady him. "She didn't say. Are you okay?"

Joe shook off Carl's hand. "I'm fine. Put the horses away."

"Sure." Carl was used to Joe's brusque manners.

Joe nodded his thanks and began walking toward the house with unsteady steps. Carl waited until he had gone inside before leading the team toward the corral at the side of the barn. He'd worked with Joe for nearly four years. The old man had never mentioned he had a daughter and granddaughters.

Carl glanced back at the house. Joe wasn't the only one who kept secrets. Carl had his own.

Chapter 2

Lizzie had rehearsed a dozen different things to say when she first saw her grandfather, but his hired man's abrupt appearance had rattled her already frayed nerves. When her grandfather actually walked through the door, everything she had planned to say left her head. She stood silently as he looked her up and down.

He had changed a great deal from what she remembered. She used to think he was tall, but he was only average height and stooped with age. His beard was longer and streaked with gray now. It used to be black.

Nervously, she gestured toward the sink. "I hope you don't mind that I washed a few dishes. You have hot water right from the faucet. It isn't allowed in our home. Our landlord says it's worldly, but it makes doing the dishes a pleasure."

"You look just like your grandmother." His voice was exactly as she remembered.

She smiled. "Do I?"

"It's no good thing. She had red hair like yours. She was an unhappy, nagging woman. Why have you come? Have you brought sad news?"

"Nee," Lizzie said quickly. "My sisters are all well. We live in Indiana. Onkel Morris and all of us work on a dairy farm there."

Joe moved to the kitchen table and took a seat. "Did your uncle send you to me? He agreed to raise the lot of you. He can't change his mind now."

She sat across from him. *"Nee,* Onkel does not know I have come to see you."

"How did you get here?"

"I took the bus. I asked about you at the bus station in Hope Springs. An Amish woman waiting to board the bus told me how to find your farm. I walked from town."

He propped his elbows on the table and pressed his hands together. She noticed the dirt under his fingernails and the calluses on his rough hands. "How is it that you have come without your uncle's knowledge? Do you still reside with him or have you married?"

"None of us are married. Onkel Morris would have forbidden this meeting had he known of my plan."

"I see." He closed his eyes and rested his chin on his knuckles.

She didn't know if he was praying or simply waiting for more of an explanation. She rushed ahead, anxious that he hear exactly why she had made the trip. "I had to come. You are the only family we have.

We desperately need your help. Onkel Morris is forcing Clara to marry a terrible man. I fear for her if she goes through with it. I'm hoping—praying really—that you can find it in your heart to take her in. She is a good cook and she will keep your house spotless. Your house could use a woman's touch. Clara is an excellent housekeeper and as sweet-tempered as anyone. You must let her come. I'm begging you."

He was silent for so long that she wondered if he had fallen asleep the way old people sometimes did. Finally, he spoke. "My daughter chose to ignore my wishes in order to marry your father. She made it clear that he was more important than my feelings. I can only honor what I believe to be her wishes. I will not aid you in your disobedience to the man who has taken your father's place. You have come a long way for no reason. Carl will take you back to the bus station."

Lizzie couldn't believe her concerns were being dismissed out of hand. "Daadi, I beg you to reconsider. I did not come here lightly. I truly believe Clara is being sentenced to a life of misery, or worse."

Joe rose to his feet. "Do not let your girlish emotions blind you to the wisdom of your elders. It is vain and prideful to question your uncle's choice for your sister."

"It is our uncle who is blind if he thinks Clara will be happy with his choice. She won't be. He is a cruel man."

"If your uncle believes the match is a good thing, you must trust his judgment. There will be a bus going that way this afternoon. If you hurry, you can get a seat. Go home and beg his forgiveness for your foolishness. All will be well in the end, for it is as Gott wills."

"Please, Daadi, you have to help Clara."

He turned away and walked out the door, leaving Lizzie speechless as she stared after him.

Dejected, she slipped into her coat and glanced around the cluttered kitchen. If only he would realize how much better his life would be with Clara to care for him.

Was he right? Was her failure God's will?

With a heavy heart, she carried her suitcase and the box with her quilt in it out to the front porch. Her grandfather was nowhere in sight, but his hired man was leading a small white pony hitched to a cart in her direction.

He was a big, burly man with wide shoulders and narrow hips. He wore a black cowboy hat, jeans and a flannel shirt under a stained and worn sheepskin jacket. His hair was light brown and long enough to touch his collar, but it was clean. His size and stealth had frightened the wits out of her in the house earlier. Out in the open, he didn't appear as menacing, but he didn't smile and didn't meet her gaze.

He and her grandfather must get along famously with few words spoken and never a smile between them.

It was all well and good to imagine staying until her grandfather changed his mind, but the reality was much different. He had ordered her to go home. How could she make him understand if he wouldn't hear what she had to say? He hadn't even offered the simple hospitality of his home for the night. He wanted her gone as quickly as possible. She would have to go home in defeat unless she could find some way to support herself and bring her sisters to Hope Springs. She didn't know where to start. All her hopes had been pinned on her grandfather's compassion. Sadly, he didn't have any.

Carl stopped in front of the house and waited for her. She bit her lower lip. Was she really giving up so easily? "Where is my grandfather?"

"He's gone out to the pasture to move the rest of his sheep."

"When will he be back?"

"Hard to say."

"I'd like to speak to him again."

"Joe told me to take you to the bus station. It's plain to me that he was done talking."

She stamped her foot in frustration. "You don't understand. I can't go home."

He didn't say anything. He simply waited beside the pony. A brick wall would have shown more compassion. Defeated by his stoic silence, she descended the steps. He took her bag from her hand and placed it behind the seat of the cart. He reached for the box that contained her quilt and she reluctantly handed it over.

He waited until she had climbed aboard, then he took his place beside her on the wooden seat. With a flip of the reins, he set the pony in motion. She looked back once. The house, which had looked like a sanctuary when she first saw it, looked like the run-down farmstead it truly was. Tears stung her eyes. She tried not to let them fall, but she couldn't hold back a sniffle. She wiped her nose on the back of her sleeve.

* * *

Carl cringed at the sound of Lizzie's muffled sniffling. He would have been okay if she hadn't started crying.

He didn't want to involve himself in her troubles. Whatever it was, it was none of his business. He glanced her way and saw a tear slip down her cheek. She quickly wiped it away. She looked forlorn huddled on the seat next to him, like a lost lamb that couldn't find the flock.

He looked straight ahead. "I'm sorry things didn't turn out the way you wanted with your grandfather."

"He's a very uncaring man."

"Joe is okay."

"I'm glad you think so."

"He doesn't cotton to most people."

"I'm not most people. I'm his flesh and blood. He doesn't care that his own granddaughter is being forced into marriage with a hateful man."

Carl looked at her in surprise. "You're being forced to marry someone not of your choosing?"

"Not me. My sister Clara. Our uncle, my mother's brother, took us in after our parents died. Onkel Morris is making Clara marry a man more than twice her age."

"Amish marriages are not arranged. Your sister cannot be compelled to marry against her will."

"The man who wishes to marry Clara is our landlord and employer. He could turn us all out of his house to starve. My uncle is afraid of him." She crossed her arms over her chest.

"But you are not." He glanced at her with respect. It had taken a lot of courage for her to travel so far.

"I'm afraid of him, too. Sometimes, I think he enjoys making life miserable for others." Her voice faded away. She sniffled again.

The pony trotted quickly along the road as Carl pondered Lizzie's story. He had no way to help her and no words of wisdom to offer. Sometimes, life wasn't fair.

After a few minutes, she composed herself enough to ask, "Do you know of anyone who might want to hire a maid or a housekeeper?"

"No." He didn't go into town unless he had to. He didn't mingle with people.

"I would take any kind of work."

"There's an inn in town. They might know of work for you."

She managed a watery smile for him. "*Danki.* Something will turn up."

She was pretty when she smiled. Although her eyes were red-rimmed now, they were a beautiful hazel color. They shimmered with unshed tears in the afternoon light. Her face, with its oval shape, pale skin and sculpted high cheekbones, gave her a classical beauty, but a spray of freckles across her nose gave her a fresh, wholesome look that appealed to him.

It felt strange to have a woman seated beside him. It had been a long time since he had enjoyed the companionship of anyone other than Joe. Did she know he had been shunned? Joe should have told her. Carl wasn't sure how to bring up the subject.

He sat stiffly on the seat, making sure he didn't

touch her. If she were unaware of his shunning, he would see that she didn't inadvertently break the tenets of her faith. The sharp, staccato *clip-clop* of the pony's hooves on the blacktop, the creaking of the cart and Lizzie's occasional sniffles were the only sounds in the awkward silence until he crested the hill. A one-room Amish schoolhouse sat back from the road, and the cheerful sounds of children playing during recess reached him. A game of softball was under way.

One little girl in a blue dress and white *kapp* waved to him from her place in the outfield. He waved back when he recognized her. Joy Mast immediately dropped her oversize ball glove and ran toward him. He pulled the pony to a stop. Two boys from the other team ran after her.

"Hi, Carl. How is Duncan? Is he with you today?" She reached the cart and hung on to the side to catch her breath.

He relaxed as he grinned at her. He could be himself around Amish children. They hadn't been baptized and wouldn't be required to shun him. Joy had Down syndrome. Her father, Caleb Mast, had recently returned to the area and rejoined his Amish family. "Hello, Joy. Duncan is fine, but he is working today moving Joe's sheep, so he couldn't come for a visit. Has your father found work?"

"Yes, I mean, *ja,* at the sawmill. Mrs. Weaver is glad, too, because that silly boy Faron Martin couldn't keep his mind off his girlfriend long enough to do his work."

Carl heard a smothered chuckle from Lizzie. He

had to smile, too. "I'm not sure your grandmother and Mrs. Weaver want you repeating their conversations."

"Why not?"

The two boys reached her before Carl could explain. The oldest boy, Jacob Imhoff, spoke first. "Joy, you aren't supposed to run off without telling someone. You know that."

She hung her head. "I forgot."

Joy had a bad habit of wandering off and had frightened her family on several occasions by disappearing without letting anyone know where she was going.

The younger boy, her cousin David, took her hand. "That's okay. We aren't mad."

She peeked at him. "You're not?"

"Nee."

She gave him a sheepish smile. "I only wanted to talk to Carl."

A car buzzed past them on the highway. Jacob patted her shoulder. "We don't want you to get hit by one of the Englisch cars driving by so fast."

"This was my fault," Carl said quickly. "I should have turned into the lane to speak to Joy and not stopped out here on the road."

Joy stared at him solemnly. "It's okay. I forgive you."

If only he could gain forgiveness so easily for his past sins. He quickly changed the subject. "How is your puppy, Joy?"

"Pickles is a butterball with legs and a tail. She chews up everything. Mammi is getting mighty tired of it."

Joy could always make him smile. "Tell your grandmother to give your pup a soupbone to gnaw on. That will keep her sharp little teeth occupied for a few days."

Joy looked past him at Lizzie. "Is this your wife? She's pretty."

He sat bolt upright. "*Nee, sie ist nicht meine frau.* She's not my wife."

Lizzie watched a blush burn a fiery red path up Carl's neck and engulf his face. It was amusing to see such a big man discomforted by a child's innocent question, but she was more interested in his answer. He had denied that she was his wife in flawless Pennsylvania Dutch, the German dialect language spoken by the Amish.

Carl King might dress and act Englisch, but he had surely been raised Amish to speak the language so well.

He gathered the reins. "You should get back to your game, kids. I have to take this lady to the bus station."

He set the pony moving again, and a frown replaced the smile he had given so easily to the little girl. Lizzie liked him better when he was smiling.

"Your Pennsylvania Dutch is very good."

"I get by."

"Were you raised Amish?"

A muscle twitched in his clenched jaw. "I was."

"Several of the young men in our community have left before they were baptized, too."

"I left afterward."

Lizzie's eyes widened with shock. That meant he was in the Bann. Why had her grandfather allowed her to travel with him? Her uncle wouldn't even speak with an excommunicated person. A second later, she realized that she would very likely be placed in the Bann, too. Her uncle would not let her rebellious action go unpunished. She prayed her sisters were not suffering because of her.

She glanced at Carl and noted the tense set of his jaw. The rules of her faith were clear. She could not accept a ride from a shunned person. She was forbidden to do business with him, accept any favor from him or eat at the same table. Her grandfather had placed her in a very awkward situation. "Please stop the cart."

Carl's shoulders slumped. "As you wish."

He pulled the pony to a halt. "It is a long walk. You will miss the bus."

"Then I must drive. It is permitted for me to give you a lift, but I can't accept one from you."

"I know the rules." He laid down the reins and stepped over the bench seat to sit on the floor of the cart behind her.

She took the reins and slapped them against the pony's rump to get him moving. He broke into a brisk trot.

"How is it that you work for my grandfather? Has he left the church, too?"

"No."

"Does he know your circumstance?"

"Of course."

She grew more confused by the minute. "Surely the members of his congregation must object to his continued association with you."

"He hasn't mentioned it if they do."

She glanced toward him over her shoulder. "But they know, don't they?"

"You'd have to ask Joe about that."

As she was on her way to the bus depot, that wasn't likely to happen. "I would, but I doubt I'll see him again." She heard the bitterness in her voice and knew Carl heard it, too.

Her grandfather had made it crystal clear he wasn't interested in getting to know his granddaughters. His rejection hurt deeply, but she shouldn't have been surprised by it. To depend on any man's kindness was asking for heartache.

As the pony trotted along, Lizzie struggled to find forgiveness in her heart. Her grandfather was a man who needed prayers, not her harsh thoughts. She prayed for Carl, too, that he would repent his sins, whatever they were, and find his way back to God. His life must be lonely indeed.

As lonely as Clara's would be married to a man she didn't love and without her sisters around her. Lizzie had failed her miserably.

After they had traveled nearly a mile, Lizzie decided she didn't care to spend the rest of the trip in silence. It left her too much time to think about her failure. Conversation with a shunned person wasn't strictly forbidden. "Is Joy a relative?"

"A neighbor."

"She seems like a very sweet child."

"Yes."

"Who is Duncan?"

"My dog."

His curt answers made her think he'd left his good

humor back at the schoolyard. She gave up the idea of maintaining a conversation. She drew a deep breath and tried to come up with a new course of action that would save her sisters.

All she could think of was to find a job in town, but she didn't have enough money to rent a room. She had enough to pay for her bus fare home and that was it. She didn't even have enough left over to buy something to eat. Her stomach grumbled in protest. She hadn't eaten in more than a day. Nothing since her last supper at her uncle's house.

If she returned to his home, she would have to beg forgiveness and endure his chastisement in whatever form he chose. It would most likely be a whipping with his favorite willow cane, but he sometimes chose a leather strap. Stale bread and water for a week was another punishment he enjoyed handing out. She would be blessed if that were his choice. She shivered and pulled her coat tight across her chest.

"Are you cold?" Carl asked.

"A little." More than a little, she realized. There was a bite to the wind now that they were heading into it. A stubborn March was holding spring at bay.

Carl slipped off his coat and laid it on the seat. "Put this on."

She shook her head. "I can't take your coat."

"You are cold. I'm not."

She glanced back at him sitting braced against the side of the cart. "*Nee,* it wouldn't be right."

He studied her for a few seconds, then looked away. A dull flush of red stained his cheeks. "It is permitted if you do not take it from my hand."

"That's not what I meant. I don't wish to cause you discomfort."

"Watching you shiver causes me discomfort."

It was hard to argue with that logic. She picked up the thick coat and slipped it on. It retained his body heat and felt blissfully warm as she pulled it close. *"Danki."*

"You're welcome."

They rode in silence for the rest of the way into town. As they drove past the local inn, she turned to him. "I wish to stop here for a few minutes. Since my grandfather won't help us, I must try to find a job."

"He told me to take you to the bus station."

"I'll only be a few minutes."

He grudgingly nodded. "A few minutes and then we must go. I have work to do."

"Danki." She gave him a bright smile before she unwrapped herself from his coat and jumped down from the cart.

When she entered the inn, she found herself inside a lobby with ceilings that rose two stories above her. On one side of the room, glass shelves displayed an assortment of jams and jellies for sale. On the opposite wall, an impressive stone fireplace soared two stories high and was at least eight feet wide. Made in the old-world fashion using rounded river stones set in mortar, it boasted a massive timber for a mantel. A quilt hanger had been added near the top. A beautiful star quilt hung on display. Two more quilts folded over racks flanked the fireplace.

At the far end of the room was a waist-high counter. A matronly Amish woman stood behind it. Tall and big-boned with gray hair beneath her white *kapp,* she wore a soft blue dress that matched her eyes. "Good afternoon and *willkommen* to the Wadler Inn. I'm Naomi Wadler. How may I help you?"

Her friendly smile immediately put Lizzie at ease. "I'm looking for work. Anything will do. I'm not picky."

"I'm sorry. We don't have any openings right now. Are you new to the area? You look familiar. Have we met?"

Lizzie tried to hide her disappointment at not finding employment. "I don't think so. Might you know of someone looking for a chore girl or household helper?"

"I don't, dear. If I hear of anything, I'll be glad to let you know. Where are you staying?"

Lizzie glanced out the window. Carl was scowling in her direction. He motioned for her to come on. She turned back to Naomi. "That's okay. I thank you for your time. The quilts around the fireplace are lovely. Are they your work?"

"*Nee,* I display them for some of our local quilters. Many Englisch guests come to this area looking to buy quilts. These were done by a local woman named Rebecca Troyer. I'm always looking for quilts to buy if you have some to sell."

All she had was her mother's quilt, and it was too precious to part with. "My sister has a good hand with a needle. I'm afraid I don't, but I can cook, clean, tend a garden, milk cows. I can even help with little children."

Naomi gave her a sympathetic smile. "You should check over at the newspaper office, *Miller Press.* It's a few blocks from here. They may know of someone looking for work."

Lizzie started for the door. As she reached it, the woman called out, "I didn't get your name, child."

"I'm Lizzie Barkman. I have to go. Thank you again for your time." She left the inn and climbed into the cart again. "They don't have anything. I wish to stop at the newspaper office. There might be something in the help-wanted section of the paper."

"Joe can't move all the sheep without help. I should be there."

"It will only take a minute or two to read the want ads. I'll hurry, I promise. Which way is it?"

He gave her directions and she found the *Miller Press* office without difficulty. Inside, she quickly read through the ads, but didn't find anything she thought she could do. Most of them were requests for skilled labor. It looked as if going home was to be her fate, after all.

With lagging steps, she returned to the cart. She followed Carl's succinct directions to the center of town. When the bus station came into view, she felt the sting of tears again. She'd arrived that morning, tired but full of hope, certain that she could save her sister.

It had been a foolhardy plan at best. She stared at the building. "My sister was right. I'm nothing but a dreamer."

A short, bald man came out the door and locked it behind him. Carl took Lizzie's suitcase from the back of the cart and approached him. "This lady needs a ticket."

"Sorry, we're closed." The man didn't even look up. He started to walk off, but Carl blocked his way.

"She needs a ticket to Indiana."

The stationmaster took a step back. "You're too late. The westbound bus left five minutes ago. The next one is on Tuesday."

"Four days? How can that be?"

The little man raised his hands. "Look around. We're not exactly a transportation hub. Hope Springs is just down the road from Next-to-Nowhere. The bus going west departs at 3:00 p.m. on Tuesdays and Fridays." He stepped around Carl and walked away.

She wasn't going back today. She still had a chance to find a job. Lizzie looked skyward and breathed a quick prayer. "*Danki,* my Lord."

She wanted to shout for joy, but the grim look on Carl's face kept her silent. He scowled at her. "Joe isn't going to like this."

Chapter 3

"What is she doing back here? I told you to make sure she got on the bus!" Joe looked ready to spit nails.

Carl jumped down from the back of the cart and took Lizzie's suitcase and her box from behind the seat. He knew Joe would be upset. He wasn't looking forward to this conversation.

"She missed the bus. The next one going her way is on Tuesday. I couldn't very well leave her standing on the street corner, could I?"

"I don't see why not," Joe grumbled.

Lizzie got down for the cart and came up the steps to stand by her grandfather on the porch. "I'm sorry to inconvenience you, Daadi, but I didn't know what else to do. I don't have enough money to pay for a room at the inn until Tuesday and get a ticket home. I won't be any trouble."

"Too late for that," Carl muttered. She had already cost him half a day's work.

"What am I supposed to do with you now?" Joe demanded.

"I can sleep in the barn if you don't have room for me in the house."

She actually looked demure with her hands clasped before her and her eyes downcast. Carl wasn't fooled. She was tickled pink that she had missed the bus. He half wondered if she had insisted on making those job-hunting stops for just that reason. He had no proof of that, but he wasn't sure he would put it past her.

Joe sighed heavily. "I guess you can stay in your mother's old bedroom upstairs, but don't expect there to be clean sheets on the bed."

Lizzie smiled sweetly. "*Danki.* I'm not afraid of a little dust. If you really want me to leave, you could hire a driver to take me home."

Scowling, Joe snapped, "I'm not paying a hired driver to take you back. It would cost a fortune. You will leave on Tuesday. Since you're here, you might as well cook supper. You can cook, can't you?"

"Of course."

He gestured toward the door. "Come on, Carl. Those shearing pens won't set themselves up."

She shot Carl a sharp look and then leaned toward Joe. "Daadi, may I speak to you in private?"

Here it comes. She's going to pressure Joe to get rid of me.

Carl didn't want to leave. He enjoyed working with the sheep and with Joe. In this place, he had found a small measure of peace that didn't seem to exist anywhere else in the world. Would Lizzie make trouble for the old man if he allowed Carl to stay on?

Joe waved aside her request. "We'll speak after supper. My work can't wait any longer. Carl, did you pick up the mail, at least?"

He shook his head. "I forgot to mention it when we passed your mailbox."

Joe glared at Lizzie. "That's what comes of having a distraction around. I'll go myself."

"I'll go get your mail." Lizzie started to climb back onto the cart, but Joe stopped her.

"The pony has done enough work today. It won't hurt you to walk to the end of the lane, will it?"

She flushed and stepped away from the cart. "*Nee,* of course not. Shall I unhitch him and put him away?"

"Put him in the corral to the right of the barn and make sure you rub him down good."

"I will."

As she led the pony away, sympathy for her stirred in Carl. Joe wasn't usually so unkind. "I can take care of the horse, Joe."

"If she's going to stay, she's going to earn her keep while she's here. I don't know why she had to come in the first place." Joe stalked away with a deep frown on his face.

Carl followed him. The two men crossed to the largest shed and went inside. Numerous metal panels were stacked against the far wall. They were used to make pens of various sizes to hold the sheep both prior to shearing and afterward.

They had the first three pens assembled before Joe

spoke again. "You think I'm being too hard on her, don't you?"

"It's your business and none of mine."

"What did she have to say on your trip into town and back?"

"Not much. She's concerned that her sister is being made to marry against her will by their uncle Morris. It's not the way things are done around here."

"*Nee,* but it doesn't surprise me much. I never cared for Morris. I couldn't believe it when my daughter wanted to marry into that family. I tried to talk her out of it. I've never met a more shiftless lot. The men never worked harder than they had to, but they made sure the women did. In my eyes, they didn't treat their women with the respect they deserved."

"What do you mean?"

"They spoke harshly to them. They kept them away from other women. I saw fear in the eyes of Morris's wife more than once when he got upset with her."

"Do you believe there was physical abuse?"

"I thought so, but none of them would admit it. Such things weren't talked about back then. I went so far as to share my misgivings with the bishop. The family didn't take kindly to my interference."

"I imagine not."

"My daughter assured me her husband was a kind man, but I saw the signs. I saw the changes in her over the years. My son-in-law and I had some heated words about it. Then one day, the whole family up and moved away. I never saw them again. My daughter never even wrote to let me know where they had gone. Years later, I got one letter. It was from Morris telling me my Abigail and her husband were dead. He said a truck struck their buggy. Her husband died instantly, but Abigail lingered for another day."

Joe's voice tapered off as he struggled with his emotions. Carl had never seen him so upset. After giving the old man a few minutes to compose himself, Carl said, "I've never heard of the Amish having arranged marriages."

"They don't, but if you dig deep enough in any barrel, you'll find a few bad apples, even among the Amish. Morris was a bad apple. I don't know why my girl couldn't see that, but I was told she lived long enough after the accident to name Morris as guardian of her children. I'm not surprised he thinks he can pick their husbands."

"So, you aren't going to help Lizzie?"

Joe shook his head slowly. "I loved my daughter, Carl. I never got over her leaving the way she did, but she was a good mother. I have to ask myself what would she want me to do. Honestly, I think my daughter would want me to stay out of it. Life is not easy for any of us. I don't want Lizzie to think she can come running to me whenever it seems too hard for her."

"Do you really think that's what she's doing?" Carl asked gently.

"I don't know. Maybe."

Carl didn't agree, but then it wasn't his place to agree or disagree with Joe. It was his place to take care of the sheep.

"What else did she say?" Joe asked. He tried to sound indifferent, but Carl wasn't fooled.

"She wants to find a job around here."

Joe nodded but didn't comment. Carl drew a deep breath. "I had to tell her I'm in the Bann."

"*Ach,* that's none of her business." Joe kicked a stubborn panel into place and secured it with a length of wire.

"She asked. I couldn't lie."

Joe shared a rare, stilted smile. "It would astonish me if you did."

"Will she go to church services with you on Sunday?"

"*Ja,* I imagine so."

"Will my being here cause trouble for you?" He didn't want to leave, but he would. Joe had been good to him.

"Having her here is causing me trouble."

"You know what I mean." Joe could easily find himself shunned by his fellow church members for allowing Carl to work on his farm. The rules were clear about what was permitted and what wasn't with a shunned person. Joe had been bending the rules for more than two years to give Carl a place to live. A few people in Joe's church might suspect Carl was ex-Amish, but no one knew it for a fact. Only Lizzie. If she spread that information, it would change everything.

The old man sighed and laid a hand on Carl's shoulder. "*Sohn,* I know I'm not a good example. I don't like most people, but that's my fault and not theirs. Folks around here are generous and accepting of others. I've known Bishop Zook since he was a toddler. He's a kind and just man. I don't know your story, Carl, but I've come to know you. You seek solitude out among the flocks and in your small hut, but it does not bring you peace. 'Tis plain you carry a heavy burden. If you repent, if you ask forgiveness, it will be granted."

Carl looked away from the sympathy he didn't deserve. "Sometimes, forgiveness must be earned."

Joe's grip on Carl's shoulder tightened. "Our Lord Jesus earned it for us all by His death on the cross. However, it's your life. Live as you must. I've never pried and I never will."

"Thanks, but you didn't answer my question. Will my staying here cause trouble for you?"

Joe dusted his hands together. "I can handle any trouble my granddaughter tries to make."

Carl wasn't as confident.

The evening shadows were growing long by the time they finished setting up the runways and pens. Both men were tired, hot and sweaty, in spite of the cold weather. Carl found he was eager to see how Lizzie was faring. Was she a good cook? Joe wasn't. Carl managed, but he didn't enjoy the task.

The two men entered the kitchen and stopped in their tracks. They both looked around in surprise. The clutter had been cleared from the table. The wild heaps of dishes and pans in the sink had been tamed, washed and put away. The blue-and-white-checkered plastic tablecloth was glistening wet, as if she had just finished wiping it down. Even the floor had been swept and mopped. The scuffed old black-and-white linoleum looked better than Carl had ever seen it. There was a lingering scent of pine cleaner in the air, but it was the smell of simmering stew that made his mouth water.

Lizzie stood at the stove with her back to them.

"It's almost done. There's soap and a fresh towel at the sink for you."

She turned toward them and used her forearm to sweep back a few locks of bright red hair that had escaped from beneath her black *kapp*. Her cheeks were flushed from the heat of the oven. Carl was struck once again by how pretty she was and how natural she looked in Joe's kitchen.

If the aroma was anything to go by, this might be the best meal he'd had in months. His stomach growled in anticipation, but he didn't move. The arrangement he and Joe shared might be different now that Lizzie was with them. He locked eyes with Joe and waited for a sign from him.

Lizzie wasn't sure how to proceed. She'd never fixed a meal for a shunned person. If Carl sat at the table, she would have to eat standing at the counter or in the other room. Eating at the same table with someone in the Bann was forbidden. Had her grandfather been breaking the Ordnung by eating with Carl? If so, it was her solemn duty to inform his bishop of such an infraction. She quailed at the thought. Such a move on her part would ruin any chance of bringing her sisters to live with him.

She watched as her grandfather went to the sink beneath the window and washed the grime off his hands. He used the towel she'd placed there and left it lying on the counter so that Carl could use it, too.

Her *daadi* stepped to the table, moved aside one of the benches and flipped back the tablecloth. Puzzled, Lizzie wondered what he was doing. Then she saw it wasn't one large kitchen table. It was two smaller ones that had been pushed together. He pulled the tables a few inches apart, smoothed the cloth back into place and returned the bench to its original place.

She relaxed with relief. Her grandfather hadn't broken the Ordnung. It appeared that he and Carl maintained the separation dictated by the Amish faith even when no one was around.

She caught Carl's quick glance before he looked away. He said, "Is this arrangement suitable, or should I eat outside?"

He was trying to look as if it didn't matter, but she could tell that it did.

"If my grandfather feels this is acceptable, then it is." It was his home, and he had to follow the rules of his congregation. It wouldn't have been acceptable in her uncle's home. Her uncle wouldn't have allowed Carl inside the house. Her uncle expounded often about the dangers of associating with unclean people.

Joe took his place at the head of the table. Lizzie dished stew into a bowl and placed it in front of him. She dished up a second bowl and gave Carl a sympathetic look before she left it on the counter. She took a plate of golden-brown biscuits from the oven and set it on the table, too.

Carl washed up and carried his bowl to his table opposite her grandfather.

Lizzie got her own bowl and took a seat at her grandfather's left-hand side. When she was settled, he bowed his head and silently gave thanks to God for the meal. From the corner of her eye, she saw Carl bow his head, too.

What had he done that made him an outsider among them, and why was her grandfather risking being shunned himself by having him around?

The meal progressed in silence. Lizzie didn't mind; it was normal at her uncle's home, too. She and her sisters saved their conversations until they were getting ready for bed at night.

The unexpected weight of loneliness forced her spirits lower. She missed her sisters more than she thought possible. Tonight, she would be alone for the first time in her life. She didn't count her night on the bus, for she hadn't been alone for a minute on that horrible ride. She thought she was hungry, but her appetite ebbed away. She picked at her food and pushed it around in her bowl. A quick glance at her grandfather and Carl showed neither of them noticed. They ate with gusto. Maybe good food would convince them they needed a woman around the house full-time.

A woman, yes, but four women?

There was more than enough work to keep four women busy for months. The place was a mess. All the rooms needed a thorough cleaning. There was years of accumulated dust and cobwebs in every corner of the four bedrooms upstairs, although only one room contained a bed. The others held an accumulation of odds and ends, broken furniture and several plastic tubs filled with baby bottles. She assumed they were for the lambs.

The downstairs wasn't as bad, but it wasn't tidy, either.

She was afraid to speculate on the amount of mending that was needed. There was a pile of clothes in a huge laundry hamper beside the wringer washer on a small back porch. The few bits of clothing she had examined were both dirty and in need of repair. It was too bad that one of her days here was a Sunday. She wouldn't be able to engage in anything but the most necessary work on the Sabbath.

She'd simply have to rise early tomorrow and again on Monday and Tuesday mornings to get as much of the washing, mending and cleaning done as she could before her bus left. Her grandfather might not want her here, but she would do all that she could for him before she left, even if she disliked mending with a passion.

It was a shame that Clara hadn't come with her. Clara loved needlework. Her tiny stitches were much neater than Lizzie could manage. Each of the girls had a special talent. Lizzie liked to cook. Betsy was good with animals. Clara, like their mother, enjoyed sewing, quilting and knitting. Greta avoided housework whenever she could. She enjoyed being outside tending the orchard and the gardens.

Just thinking about them made a deep sadness settle in Lizzie's soul. She had failed miserably to help them thus far, but the good Lord had given her more time. She wouldn't waste it feeling sorry for herself.

She smiled at her grandfather. "I hope you like the stew. I do enjoy cooking. I couldn't help noticing your garden hasn't been prepared for spring planting yet. It's nearly time to get peas and potatoes planted. My sister Greta would be itching to spade up the dirt. The Lord blessed her with a green thumb for sure."

Her grandfather ran his last bite of biscuit around

the rim of his bowl to sop up any traces of gravy. "The planting will get done after the lambing."

"Of course. You probably know there's barely any preserved food left in the cellar. I used the last of the canned beef and carrots for tonight's meal. There will be only canned chicken for the next meals unless you can provide me with something fresh or allow me to go into town and purchase more food. What a shame it is to see an Amish cellar bare. At home, my sisters and I have hundreds of jars of meat, corn and vegetables. Do you like beets, Daadi?"

"Not particularly."

"I like snap peas better myself." She fell silent.

"There are plenty of eggs in the henhouse. We men know how to make do."

There had to be a way to convince him of her usefulness. Perhaps after he saw the results of her hard work over the next several days he would agree to let her stay.

Joe pushed his empty bowl away and brushed biscuit crumbs from his beard and vest. "You're a *goot* cook, I'll give you that."

"A mighty good cook. Thank you for the meal," Carl added.

"You're welcome." She wasn't used to being thanked for doing something that was her normal responsibility.

Her grandfather swallowed the last swig of his coffee and set the cup in his bowl. "I reckon it's time to start moving the flocks closer to the barns."

Carl nodded. "I can put the rams and the first of the ewes in the barn tomorrow in separate pens."

"No point penning them inside just yet. Monday will be soon enough. Shearing can start on Tuesday."

Lizzie brightened. Perhaps the sheep held the key to proving her usefulness. "Can I help with that? I'd love to learn more about sheep and about shearing them."

Joe huffed in disgust. "If you don't know sheep, you'll be no use to me."

She looked at Carl. He didn't say anything. She was foolish to hope for help in that direction. Suddenly, she remembered the mail she had collected earlier. There had been a letter for him. She went into the living room and returned with her grandfather's copy of the local newspaper and an envelope for Carl.

Her grandfather's eyes brighten. "*Ach,* my newspaper. *Danki.* I like reading it after supper."

She turned to Carl and held the letter toward him. "This came for you."

When he didn't take it, she laid it on the corner of the table and resumed her seat.

Rising to his feet, Carl picked up the letter, glanced at it and then carried his empty bowl to the sink. Turning to the stove, he lifted the lid on the firebox and dropped the letter in unopened. He left the house without another word.

After the screen door banged shut behind him, Lizzie gathered the rest of the dishes and carried them to the sink. She stared out the window at his retreating back as he walked toward the barn and the pasture gate beyond.

His dog came bounding across the yard and danced around him, seeking attention. He paused long enough to bend and pat the animal. Straightening, he glanced back once at the house before he walked on.

What had he done to cut himself off from his family, his friends and from his Amish faith? Why burn an unopened letter? Why live such a lonely life with only a dog and an old man for company? Carl King was an intriguing man. The longer she was around him, the more she wanted to uncover the answers about him.

"Out with your questions before you choke on them," her grandfather said, still seated at the table.

"I don't know what you mean." She began filling the sink with water.

"*Ja,* you do. You want to know about Carl."

She couldn't very well deny it when she was bursting with curiosity about the man. She shut off the water and faced her grandfather. "I don't understand how you can do business with him. It is forbidden."

"I do no business with him." He opened his paper and began to read.

She took a step toward him in disbelief and propped both hands on her hips. "How can you say that? He works for you. He's your hired man."

"I did not hire Carl. He works here because he wishes to do so. He lives in an empty hut on my property. He pays no rent, so I am neither landlord nor employer."

"You mean he works for nothing?"

Folding his paper in exasperation, he said, "Each year, when the lambs are sold, I leave one third of my profits here on the kitchen table, and I go to bed. In the morning, the money is always gone."

"So you do pay him?"

"I have never asked if he's the one who takes the money."

She crossed her arms over her chest. "Don't you think that is splitting hairs?"

"No doubt some people will say it is."

"Aren't you worried that you may be shunned for his continued presence here?"

He leaned back in his chair. "What would you have me do?"

"You must tell him that unless he repents, he must leave. What has he done to make all your church avoid him?"

"I have no idea."

"But all members of the church must agree to the shunning. How can you not know the reason? It is not a thing that is done lightly or in secret."

"In all my years, I have seen it done only a handful of times. It was very sad and distressful for those involved. Carl is not from around here. He has not been shunned by my congregation. I would not have known he was anything but an Englisch fellow in need of a meal and a bed if he hadn't told me. It seems to me that he holds our beliefs in high regard."

"Then for him to remain separated from the church is doubly wrong, and all the more reason to send him away."

Her grandfather let his chair down and leaned forward with his hands clasped on the table. "Child, why do we shun someone?"

"Because they have broken their vows to God and to the church by refusing to follow the Ordnung."

"You have missed the meaning of my question. What is the purpose of shunning an individual?"

"To make them see the error of their ways."

"That is true, but you have not mentioned the most important part. It is not to punish them. Shunning is done out of love for that person so that they may see what it is to be cut off from God and God's family by their sin. It is a difficult thing to do, to care for someone and yet turn away from them."

"But if they don't repent, we must turn away so that we do not share in that sin."

"If I give aid to a sinner, does that make me one?"

"Of course not. We are commanded to care for those in need, be they family or stranger."

"As the Good Samaritan did in the parable told by our Lord."

She could see where his questions were leading. "*Ja,* if you have given aid to Carl, that is as it should be."

A smile twitched at the corner of his mouth. "I'm glad you approve. The first time I met Carl, I discovered him sleeping in my barn. It had rained like mad in the night. His clothes were ragged and damp. They hung on his thin frame like a scarecrow's outfit. Everything he owned in the world he was wearing or had rolled up in a pack he was using as a pillow, except for a skinny puppy that lay beside him.

"Carl immediately got up, apologized for trespassing and said he was leaving. I offered him a meal. He declined, but said he would be grateful if I could spare something for the dog."

Lizzie's heart twisted with pity for Carl. To be

homeless and alone was no easy thing. "I assume you fed the dog?"

"I told Carl I had a little bacon I could fry up for the pup. I coaxed them both into the house and fried enough for all of us. I put a plate on the floor and that little Duncan gobbled it up before I got my hand out of the way. Bacon is still his favorite food. When I put two plates on the table was when Carl told me he could not eat with me."

"At least he was honest about it."

"If you had seen the look in that young man's eyes, you would know, as I do, that he cares deeply about our faith. He was starving, but he was willing to forgo food in order to keep me from unknowingly breaking the laws of our church."

"Yet, he never told you why he had been placed in the Bann?"

"*Nee,* he has not, and I do not ask. I told him I had an empty hut he could use for as long as he wanted. His dog took naturally to working the sheep and so did Carl. He has a tender heart for animals."

"What you did was a great kindness, Daadi, but Carl no longer requires physical aid."

"True. The man is neither hungry nor homeless, but his great wound is not yet healed. That's why I have not turned him away."

She scowled. "I saw no evidence of an injury."

Her grandfather shook his head sadly. "Then you have not looked into his eyes as I have done. Carl has a grave wound inside. Something in his past lies heavy on his mind and on his heart. My instincts tell me he will find his way back to God and to our faith when he has had time to heal. Then there will be great re-joicing in heaven and on earth."

Maybe she came by her daydreaming naturally, after all. "*If* it happens."

Her grandfather sighed, rose from his chair and headed toward his bedroom. Before he closed the door, he turned back to her. "It will happen. It's a shame you won't be here to see it when it does."

Chapter 4

He wouldn't go up to the house today.

Carl stood in the doorway of his one-room hut and stared at the smoke rising from Joe's chimney a quarter of a mile away. The chimney was all he could see of the house, for the barn sat between it and his abode.

It hadn't taken Carl long to decide that avoiding Lizzie would be his best course of action. It was clear how uncomfortable his presence made her last night. He didn't want her to endure more of the same.

Her presence made him uncomfortable, too.

She made him think about all he had lost the right to know. A home, a wife, the simple pleasure of sitting at a table with someone.

No, he wouldn't go up to the house, but he knew she was there.

Was she making breakfast? If it was half as good

as supper had been, it would be delicious. He couldn't remember the last time he'd had such light and fluffy biscuits.

Even for another biscuit, he wouldn't go up the hill.

He could make do with a slice of stale bread and cheese from his own tiny kitchen. He didn't need biscuits. He didn't even need coffee.

And he sure didn't need to see her again.

Lizzie Barkman's pretty face was etched in his mind like a carving in stone. All he had to do was close his eyes, and he could see her as clearly as if she were standing in front of him.

He hadn't slept well, but when he dozed, it was her face he saw in his dreams and not the usual faces from his nightmares.

In his dream last night, Lizzie had been smiling at him, beckoning him from a doorway to come inside a warm, snug house. He wanted to go in, but his feet had been frozen to the ground as snow swirled around him. Sometimes, the snow grew so thick it hid her face, but as soon as it cleared a little, she was still there waiting for him—a wonderful, warm vision in a cold, lonely world.

Carl shook his head to dispel the memory. No, he wouldn't go up to the house today. She wouldn't beckon him inside, and he shouldn't go in if she did. He was a forbidden one, an outcast by his own making.

He needed to stop feeling sorry for himself. He had work to do. He glanced toward the sturdy doghouse just outside his doorway. "Come on, Duncan. We have sheep to move today."

Duncan didn't appear. Carl leaned down to look

inside and saw the doghouse was empty. Puzzled, he glanced around the pasture. His dog was nowhere in sight. Carl cupped his hands around his mouth and hollered the dog's name. Duncan still didn't come.

This wasn't like him. The only time the dog occasionally roamed away from the farm was when school was in session. He liked to play fetch with the kids and visit with the teacher's pretty female shepherd. It was too early for the children or the teacher to be at school yet, so where was Duncan?

Maybe Joe had taken him and gone out after some of the sheep already. If that was the case, Carl had better see that the fences in the hilltop enclosure around the lambing sheds were in good repair.

He headed up to the barn and found Joe pitching hay down to the horses in the corral. If he hadn't gone after the sheep, where was the dog? "Joe, have you seen Duncan this morning?"

Joe paused and leaned on his pitchfork handle. "*Nee,* I have not. He's not with you?"

Carl shook his head. "He was gone when I got up."

"He'll be back. Lizzie should have breakfast ready in a few minutes. Tell her I'll be in when I'm done here." Joe resumed his work.

"I'm not hungry. I'm going to fix the fence in the little field at the top of the hill, and then I'll move the ewes in the south forty up to it. They'll be easier to move into the barn from there when it's time to shear them."

"All right."

Carl knew if he took two steps to the left, he'd have a good view of the house from around the corner of the barn. "It'll make it easier to keep an eye on them for any early lambs, too."

"It will." Joe kept pitching down forkfuls of hay.

"I don't expect any premature births from that group. They've all had lambs before without any trouble."

"I know."

Carl folded his arms tight across his chest and tried to ignore the overpowering urge to look and see if he could catch a glimpse of Lizzie. "We might have to cull a few of them. We've got five or six that are getting up there in years."

Joe stopped his work and leaned on his pitchfork again. "I'm not senile yet. I know my own sheep. I thought you were looking for your dog."

"I was. I am."

"Have you checked up at the house?"

"No." Carl unfolded his arms and slipped his hands into his front pockets.

"That granddaughter of mine was singing this morning. Could be the dog thought it was yowling, and he's gone to investigate."

"Is she a poor singer?" Somehow, Carl expected her to have a melodious voice to match her sweet smile.

"How do I know? I've been tone-deaf since I was born. It all sounds like yowling to me." Setting his pitchfork aside, Joe vanished into the recesses of the hayloft.

Now that he was unobserved, Carl took those two steps and glanced toward the house. He didn't see Lizzie, but Duncan sat just outside the screen door, intently watching something inside.

"Duncan. Here, boy!"

The dog glanced his way and went back to staring into the house. He barked once. Annoyed, Carl began walking toward him. "Duncan, get your sorry tail over here. We've got work to do."

The dog rose to his feet, but didn't leave his place.

Carl approached the house just as the screen door opened a crack. The dog wagged his tail vigorously. Carl saw Lizzie bend down and slip Duncan something to eat.

After deciding he wouldn't see her at all today, that tiny glimpse of her wasn't enough. He wanted to look upon her face again. Would she welcome his company or simply tolerate it?

It didn't matter. He had no business thinking it might.

What had Joe told her about him last night? Carl kept walking in spite of his better judgment telling him to go gather the flock without his dog.

By the time he reached the door, Lizzie had gone back inside, but the smell of frying bacon lingered in the air.

Carl stared down at his dog. "I see she's discovered your weakness."

Duncan licked his chops.

Carl grinned. "*Ja,* I've got a strong liking for bacon myself."

"Come in and have a seat before these eggs get cold. I hope you like them scrambled." Her cheerful voice drove away the last of his hesitation. She was going to be here for only a few days. Why shouldn't he enjoy her company and her cooking until she left?

He moved Duncan aside with his knee and pulled open the screen door. The dog followed him in and took his usual place beneath the bench Carl sat on. Duncan knew better than to beg for food, but he would happily snatch up any bits his master slipped to him. It was a morning ritual that had gone on for years.

The house smelled of bacon and fresh-baked bread. Lizzie must have been up for hours. She stood at the stove stirring something. There were two plates piled high with food already on the counter. Carl sat down and waited. "Joe will be in shortly."

She took her pan from the stove and poured creamy gravy into a serving boat on the counter beside her. "*Goot.* I ate earlier. I have a load of clothes in the washer I need to hang out. Having a propane-powered washer is so nice. At home, we do all the laundry by hand." Turning around, her eyes widened with shock. "No! Out, out, out!"

Carl leaped up from his seat. "I'm sorry. I thought it was all right if I ate here."

"You, yes. The dog, no."

It took him a second to process what she meant. "But Duncan normally eats with me at breakfast."

She plunked the gravy boat on the table. "Then he will be thrilled when I'm gone. But until I leave this house, I won't tolerate a dog in my kitchen at mealtime. Look what his muddy feet have done to my clean floor. Take him outside." She crossed her arms over her chest and glared at them both.

So much for basking in the glow of her smile this morning. Carl looked down and saw she was right. Muddy paw prints stood out in sharp contrast to the clean black-and-white squares. The dog must have gone down to the creek before coming to the house.

Duncan sank as flat against the floor as he could get. He knew he was in trouble, but Carl was sure he didn't understand why.

"Come on, fella. Outside with you."

Duncan didn't move.

Carl took hold of his collar and had to pull him out from under the table. His muddy feet left a long smear until Duncan realized he wasn't welcome. Then he bolted for the door and shot outside as Joe came, in nearly tripping the old gent.

"What's the matter with him?"

"His feet are muddy," Carl said. He left the kitchen and went out to the back porch. He returned with a mop and bucket. He started to wipe up the mess.

Already seated at the table, Joe said, "Leave the woman's work to the woman."

"It was my dog that made the mess." Carl met Lizzie's eyes. They were wide with surprise. Suddenly, she smiled at him. It was worth a week of mopping floors to behold. He leaned on the mop handle and smiled back.

Lizzie realized Carl's bold gaze was fixed on her. And why shouldn't it be? She wasn't behaving in the least like a modest maiden. She averted her eyes and schooled her features into what she hoped was a prim attitude. It was hard when his presence made her heart race. He was a handsome fellow, but she shouldn't be staring at him.

"Am I getting breakfast, or should I go out and get the rest of my work done?" Joe snapped.

"I'm sorry, Daadi. I have it right here." She hurried to bring both plates to the table. Keeping her eyes downcast, she said, "I'll take the mop out to the porch. I'm going that way. It was kind of you to help."

"It's no trouble. I'll take it out."

"As you wish." She scurried ahead of him out the back door and stopped when she had the tub of the wringer washer between them.

He emptied the pail out the back door and placed it with the mop in the corner. When he didn't go back inside the house, she realized he wanted to say more.

"Is there something else?" *Please let it be quick and then please let him go away.* He made her nervous, but in a strange edgy way that she didn't understand.

"I know you hope your grandfather will let you and your sisters live here. I can see you're trying to please him. I don't think Joe will change his mind, but there are a few things you should know about him."

"Such as?"

"He mentioned you were singing this morning."

So her grandfather had noticed. She brightened. "I was. Did he like it?"

"Joe is tone-deaf. Singing is just noise to him."

"Oh." That was a letdown. She hoped a happy attitude and a cheerful hymn would soften his heart.

"And there is something else," Carl said.

She crossed her arms. "What?"

"Don't jump to do his bidding. He doesn't like people who are spineless."

Indignation flared in her. "Are you saying I'm spineless?"

"No, not at all. It took courage to come here. Just stand your ground and don't pander to him."

She relaxed when she realized he was honestly trying to help. "I appreciate your advice. I imagine you think I'm being underhanded by seeking to worm my way into his affections."

"No, I don't. Just don't get your hopes up."

"I'm afraid hope is all I have at this point. If nothing changes by Tuesday afternoon, I will go home a failure. My sisters are all I have. My sisters and my faith in God. I can't believe our Lord wants Clara in an unhappy marriage any more than I do."

"I respect what you're trying to do, but Joe has lived alone for a long time. He's old and he's set in his ways."

"He has you around every day."

"I'm sort of like Duncan. I'm useful and tolerated because of that."

She shook her head. "You don't know my grandfather nearly as well as you think. He cares deeply about you. He cherishes the hope that you will one day find your way back to God and salvation."

There was no mistaking the sadness that filled Carl's eyes. "Then I reckon you aren't the only one who shouldn't get their hopes up. God isn't interested in my salvation."

He went back into the house and left Lizzie to puzzle over his words. What had happened to make him lose faith in God's goodness and mercy?

What a strange man Carl King was. He was polite and kind, he liked dogs and children, he was more helpful than most men she knew, and yet he seemed to believe God had abandoned him. Why?

If he had grown up in the Amish faith then surely he must know that God loved all His children. No sin was greater than God's ability to forgive.

With a tired sigh, she unloaded the washer and carried the wet clothes to the line outside. One by one, she hung the shirts, pants, sheets and pillowcases to dry in the fresh morning air until she had filled both clotheslines. She pulled a brown sock out of the basket and then had to search until she found its mate. They had both been neatly darned at the heels. She suspected it was Carl's work. She pinned them together on the clothesline. The next pair she put together had holes in both toes. More mending work for her.

She finished hanging up the load, and as she started for the back steps, movement caught her eye out in the pasture. Carl was striding toward the sheep dotting the far hillside. Duncan stayed close to his side until some unheard command sent him bolting toward the sheep in a wide, sweeping move.

As she watched, her grandfather joined them. The dog gathered the scattered flock into a bunch and began moving them toward the pens just beyond the barn. Carl and the dog worked together until the group was safely penned. After Joe swung the gate shut behind the last ewe, Carl knelt. Duncan raced to him and the two enjoyed a brief moment of play before Carl rose to his feet. He and her grandfather headed farther afield with the dog trotting behind them.

As intriguing as Carl was, she couldn't add him to

her list of people to be rescued. First and foremost, she was here to find a home and jobs for herself and her sisters. If there was any chance that her grandfather would change his mind, she had only these few days to prove how valuable she could be and how comfortable a woman in the house could make his life.

She went back to the washing machine and by late afternoon, the pile of clothing had dwindled to a few pieces that she considered rags. The pants that were dry had been folded and laid on her grandfather's bed. His shirts that were clean and mended hung from the pegs along his bedroom wall. The kitchen and bathroom towels had been sorted and put away. The socks that needed mending could wait until after supper. The jeans and shirt she knew were Carl's were piled on a chair in the living room where he was sure to see them.

Eggs from the henhouse and the last of the flour in the bin made a large batch of noodles that she simmered together with some of the canned chicken from the cellar. She discovered two jars of cherries and made an oatmeal-topped cobbler that she hoped would please both the men.

When everything was ready, she walked out onto the porch and rang the dinner bell hanging from one of the posts. A beautiful sunset was coloring the western sky with bands of gold and rose. Such powerful beauty before the darkness of night was another reminder of God's presence at the close of day.

Tomorrow would be a new day and a new chance to find a way to save her sisters.

* * *

Bright and early the next morning, Lizzie hurried to get in the buggy, where her grandfather was waiting impatiently. She said, "I hope I have not made us late."

The moment she was seated, Joe slapped the reins against the horse's rump. "Do not expect the horse to make up the time you've lost."

"I don't. Is the service far away?"

"*Nee,* it's less than two miles. It's at the home of Ike and Maggie Mast. I will tell you now that I don't stay for all the visiting and such afterward. We'll go home as soon as the service is over."

"But what about the meal?"

"I eat at home."

Lizzie hid her disappointment. Her family always stayed to eat and visit until late in the afternoon. Sunday service was a huge social event. She had hoped to meet as many local families as possible and see if anyone had work for her. Perhaps she could convince her grandfather to let her stay while he went home. "I would like to meet some of your neighbors and friends. I can walk home after the service."

"No point in getting friendly with people you'll never see again." He kept the horse at a steady trot until they came even with the small shepherd's hut that was set back a little way from the road. He stopped the buggy by the pasture gate and waited.

Lizzie realized he was waiting for Carl. When Carl didn't appear after a few minutes, her grandfather's shoulders slumped ever so slightly. He clicked his tongue and set the horse moving again.

Lizzie glanced back as they drove away. "You were hoping that he would join us."

"He will when he is ready. All things are in God's own time."

"Some people never come back to the Amish life."

"Carl will." He slapped the reins again and the horse broke into a fast trot.

Would Carl ever seek forgiveness, or would he remain an outcast? It seemed so sad. He respected their ways, but something kept him from accepting them. If only she knew more about his past, she might be able to help him, but it wasn't likely she would get to know him that well.

The journey to the preaching service took less than half an hour. When they arrived at the farm home set into the side of a tree-covered hill, Lizzie saw the yard was already filled with buggies. Her grandfather's congregation was a large one. Several young men came to take charge of the buggy and the horse.

Her grandfather got down without waiting for her. Lizzie clasped her hands with trepidation. It was the first time she had attended a prayer meeting at a church besides her own. She wouldn't know anyone here. It was an uncomfortable feeling, but one she was determined to overcome.

Today was for praising God and giving thanks to Him for His blessings.

The singing of the first hymn started by the time they reached the front doors. Inside the house, the living room held four rows of backless wooden benches with a wide center aisle dividing them. The women and girls sat on one side, while the men and boys sat on the other. Her grandfather walked straight ahead to where the married men and elders sat. She made her way to an empty spot on the women's side of the aisle near the back.

She gathered many curious glances. The only face she recognized was the woman from the inn, Naomi Wadler. Smiling and nodding to the woman, Lizzie took a seat and picked up a copy of the Ausbund.

The hymnal was the same one used in the services she attended at home. The weight of the book felt familiar in her hand and gave her a sense of comfort. She might be far from home, but she was never far from God.

When the first hymn ended, she joined in silent prayer with those around her.

Please, Lord, protect and keep my sisters. If it be Your will, let Grandfather change his mind and allow us to live with him. And please, Heavenly Father, help Carl King to find his way back to You. Amen.

When the Sunday prayer service was within walking distance, Carl followed Joe to the neighboring farms. He never went near the buildings, but often, like today, he found a place beneath a tree and settled himself to listen. The sound of solemn voices raised in song came to him on the light spring breeze. The hymns, hundreds of years old, were sung by the Amish everywhere. The words and the meaning remained unchanged by the passage of time. They were as familiar to him as the clothes on his back or the worn boots on his feet.

Sometimes, like now, he softly sang along. The birds

added their songs to the praising as the sun warmed the land. Spring was coming. A time of new births, a time of new beginnings. A time for the new lambs to join the flock.

For years, Carl had been waiting for a sign from God that he had been forgiven, that he could return to the fold of worshippers and be clean and whole again, but no sign had been forthcoming.

God had not yet forgiven him for killing a man.

Chapter 5

Lizzie sat patiently through the three-hour-long church service at the home of her grandfather's neighbors, Ike and Maggie Mast. She enjoyed the preaching, singing and prayers. The entire morning lifted her spirits.

When the last notes of the final hymn died away, Lizzie was immediately welcomed by a young woman seated near her, a redhead with a set of freckles that rivaled Lizzie's.

"Hello, and welcome to our church. I'm Sally Yoder. Did I see you arrive with Woolly Joe, or did my eyes deceive me? I didn't know he had any family."

"If you mean Joseph Shetler, then yes, I came with him. I'm his granddaughter from Indiana. I'm Lizzie Barkman."

"Are you Abigail's daughter?" someone asked from

behind her. Turning, Lizzie saw it was Naomi Wadler, the woman from the inn.

"*Ja,* my mother's name was Abigail. Did you know her?"

"Very well. No wonder I thought you looked familiar. You resemble her a great deal. How wonderful to see you all grown up. I'm sure you don't remember me, but when you were very young, your mother and I spent many happy hours together. We were dear friends. You have more sisters, don't you?"

"Yes, there are four of us."

"I'm so happy that Joseph has mended the breach with your family. He was deeply saddened when your mother moved away. He never really got over it. I was so sorry to learn of her death. You must come visit me at the inn so that we can catch up. I'd love to hear what Abigail's daughters are doing."

Lizzie didn't care to share information about her strained relationship with her grandfather. Instead, she changed the subject. "I'm still looking for work. Have you heard of anything?"

"I have, and it may be just the thing for you. Come meet Katie and Elam Sutter. Elam's mother mentioned the couple has been thinking of hiring a girl to live in and help with the children and the business."

Excited by the prospect, Lizzie asked, "What kind of business?"

"Elam runs a basket-weaving shop. He and his wife are opening a store to sell their wares here in Hope Springs in addition to taking them to Millersburg to be sold there. We have so many tourists stopping by these days that it makes sense to have a shop locally."

Sally said, "I've worked for Elam for ages, and I've known Katie for several years. They are wonderful people."

Naomi led Lizzie to a group of young mothers seated on a quilt on the lawn. They were keeping an eye on their toddlers playing nearby while several infants slept on the blanket beside them. "Katie, have you found a chore girl yet?" Naomi asked.

Katie picked up a little boy and rose to her feet. She deftly extracted a pebble from his mouth. He yowled in protest. "Jeremiah Sutter, rocks are not for eating. *Nee,* Naomi, I have not found anyone willing to take on my horde."

"They are not a horde. They are adorable. Katie, this is Lizzie Barkman, and she may be just the woman you and Elam are looking for if you don't scare her away."

Lizzie met Katie's gaze and liked what she saw. The young mother had black hair and intelligent dark eyes. Her coloring was a stark contrast to her son's blue-eyed blondness.

"I don't know anything about basket weaving, but I'm willing to learn. I have two younger sisters, so I know something about taking care of children."

Katie put her little boy down and tipped her head slightly as she regarded Lizzie. "You aren't from around here, are you?"

"I was originally. My family moved to Indiana when I was small. My grandfather is Joseph Shetler."

"I didn't realize that Woolly Joe had any family," Katie said.

Sally propped her hands on her hips and rocked back on her heels. "That's exactly what I said."

Naomi smiled sadly at Lizzie. "After your mother and father moved away, your grandfather became a recluse. I hope that will change now."

"I don't believe it will." Lizzie glanced toward the line of buggies. Sure enough, her grandfather was hitching up his horse. He was ready to go. He wouldn't be happy if she kept him waiting.

"I pray that his eyes will be opened and he will see how many of his old friends still care deeply about him and miss him." There was something oddly poignant in Naomi's tone. Lizzie looked at her closely, but Naomi's gaze was fixed on Joe.

After a moment, Naomi sighed and looked back to Katie. "I'll leave you women to get acquainted while I go help set up for the meal. It was wonderful talking to you, Lizzie. I'm serious. You must come by the inn so we can catch up. I want to hear all about Abigail's daughters."

As Naomi walked away, Sally leaned close to Katie. "Did I just hear what I thought I heard?"

Katie wore a puzzled expression, too. "If you just heard Naomi Wadler sighing over Woolly Joe Shetler, then yes."

Lizzie pointed at Katie's son. "Jeremiah just ate another rock."

Katie rolled her eyes. She grabbed her son and swiped a finger through his mouth to pull out a pebble. "Come by our farm on Tuesday of this week and meet my husband. If he agrees, we'll work out the details. How soon could you start?"

"As soon as you would like."

Lizzie could barely contain her excitement. Once she had a job, she would be able to send money home, enough to get all of her sisters to Hope Springs. She had no idea where they would all live, but she put her faith in God. He would provide. She bid the women goodbye and rushed across the yard to where her grandfather was waiting.

A man approached their buggy as they were preparing to leave. "Might I have a word with you, Joe?"

"If it's a short word." Reluctantly, her grandfather nodded toward her. "This is my granddaughter Lizzie Barkman. This fellow is Adrian Lapp."

Adrian smiled at her. "Pleased to meet you. Joe, has Carl King had any experience shearing alpacas?"

Her grandfather scratched his cheek. "I've never heard him mention it."

"But he does all your sheep, right?"

"He does."

"My wife didn't like the man I hired last year. She said he was too rough with them. She's very attached to her animals. I'm looking for someone local who is willing to take on the task."

Joe stroked his beard slowly. "I've heard that they spit on folks."

"Only if they are frightened or very upset. Normally, they are as gentle as lambs."

"I heard the one you call Myrtle spit on the bishop's wife."

Adrian smothered a grin as he glanced over his shoulder. "It was a very unfortunate incident."

To Lizzie's surprise, Joe chuckled. "I would have given a lot to see that."

"Faith would rather the whole thing be forgotten, but a number of people feel as you do. Myrtle spit on me, too, the first time we met. The smell fades in a few days."

"I'll make sure Carl knows that."

"If he's willing to take on the work, just have him drop by tomorrow and let me know. We're in a hurry to get them done, but I know you'll be shearing soon, too. It could wait until after lambing season if need be, but Faith is anxious to get started on a batch of new yarns before our baby arrives. Her orders are already coming in. She's going to need help if she is going to keep up with them."

Lizzie leaned forward. "Are you looking to hire someone?"

Adrian shrugged. "We've been talking about it."

"I have a sister who is looking for work. The pay doesn't have to be much if she can get room and board."

"Does she have experience with carding wool and spinning?"

"She does." It had been years ago, but Lizzie remembered Clara and her mother working together on the big wheel. Before their mother died and Uncle Morris sold it.

"I'll let my wife know. She isn't here today. She wasn't feeling well this morning. Why don't you come over with Carl if he decides he wants the job? That way, you and Faith can discuss it."

"I'll do that." Lizzie didn't want to get her hopes up,

but it was a promising lead. She glanced at her grandfather. "Before I go home on the bus."

"Which is Tuesday," he stated.

"But not until in the afternoon," she added. "Please tell your wife I'll stop by even if Carl decides not to take the work."

"All right, I will."

As Adrian walked away, her grandfather turned the buggy and headed down the lane. "I thought I told you to accept your uncle's wishes in the matter of your sister's marriage."

Lizzie remembered Carl's advice and spoke with firm resolve. "I appreciate your wise counsel, but my sister deserves a choice. Nothing good can come from marriage vows made without love."

Joe glanced at her but didn't say anything more. Lizzie relaxed when she realized he didn't intend to argue the point.

It had been a productive morning. So far, the Lord had provided two promising opportunities. Lizzie wasn't going to ignore them. She might be able to offer Clara a job and a place to live, but unless she could find something for all her sisters, Clara wouldn't take it. She wouldn't leave Betsy behind to marry Rufus Kuhns in her stead.

That evening after supper, Joe mentioned Adrian's offer to shear his alpacas to Carl.

Carl remained silent. Lizzie noticed that he didn't rush into making decisions. He always thought before he spoke. "The extra pay would come in handy. I've never clipped an alpaca, but it can't be too much different than a sheep. I'll give it a try. Can we spare the time tomorrow? We have the sorting pens to build yet."

"We can spare half a day. If we don't get them put together on Monday, Tuesday will be soon enough. Take the job if you want it."

Lizzie broached the subject that couldn't be avoided much longer. "Adrian Lapp cannot do business with you, Carl."

"True, but the man needs help. I'll find a way that is acceptable."

Joe said, "Lizzie will go with you. She can handle the money. Adrian's wife is looking for help with her yarn business."

Carl sat up straighter. "So you may not be leaving?"

"Not if I can find a job and a place to stay."

She thought for a moment that Carl looked happy at the prospect, but he quickly looked away.

Would it please him if she stayed in the area? It shouldn't matter, but for some reason, it did. "The spinning job with Faith Lapp is for my sister Clara. I go Tuesday morning to see if Elam Sutter will hire me to work in his basket-weaving business. It is my hope to bring all my sisters to live here."

Joe pushed his chair back from the table. "The next thing you know, I'm going to be surrounded by a gaggle of women. Well, I won't have it. I like my peace and quiet. You and your sisters can move anywhere you want, so long as you leave me be."

He stomped out of the kitchen and slammed his bedroom door behind him, leaving Carl and Lizzie alone.

"He doesn't mean that." Carl looked embarrassed by the outburst.

She began to gather the dishes. "I think he does. I've done everything I can think of to show him having a woman in his house is a good thing. I've cooked. I've cleaned until my fingers are raw. I've been quiet. I have stayed out of his way to the best of my ability, and still he treats me like a millstone around his neck."

"I appreciate your work, especially your good cooking. I'm sure Joe does, too. I don't think housekeeping skills will impress him enough to let you and your sisters stay here. Joe loves his solitude."

"And you do, too?"

He couldn't meet her gaze. "Yes, I do, too."

She felt so sad for them. They were two lonely men living apart from the world. It seemed that they both planned to remain that way.

Carl woke in the middle of the night bathed in sweat and shaking. He sat up gasping for air. Slowly, his nightmare faded. He wasn't in a grass hut in Africa. He was in a stone shepherd's hut in Ohio.

He had left the door open, and Duncan came in. The dog laid his muzzle on Carl's hand and whined. As soon as Carl's thundering heart slowed, he said, "It's okay, boy."

He had not been forgiven. Every time the events of the past played out in his nightmares, he knew God was reminding him of his sin.

He rose from the bed and got a glass of water. Walking to the door, he looked out at the star-strewn sky and wondered how much more he had to endure.

The events of that terrifying day were as clear to him as the water glass in his hand. He had gone to Africa to be with his sister, Sophia, on her wedding day.

Born with a burning desire to share God's salvation with the world, Sophia chose not to join the Amish faith of her parents, but to become a Mennonite and go out into the world to spread God's word.

His family, like all the Amish, did not believe in seeking converts, but they supported missions of mercy. Sophia's first mission trip took her to Africa. She fell in love with the land and the people, and eventually, with another young missionary. They chose to marry in the village they called home. Sophia wrote and begged that at least one member of her family come to attend her wedding. Carl, being the oldest and unmarried, chose to go.

Although the land and the people were strange, Carl quickly saw why his sister loved the place. He soon became a favorite with some of the village children, particularly a young girl named Christina.

She called him Kondoo Mtu, a name that meant "sheep man" or "shepherd" in her native tongue. His sister told him it was because *ja,* his word for *yes,* sounded like the noise the sheep and goats made. He sometimes wondered if that was why he had decided to stay on Joe's farm and become a true shepherd instead of a carpenter like his father.

The day before Sophia's wedding, Carl had gone out to help Christina find her lost goat when he heard the first gunfire. There had been talk of a civil war, but no one believed it would happen. The frightened child raced back to the camp. Sophia's home was on the edge of the village. Carl caught up with Christina and took her there. When he opened the door, he saw a dozen women from the village huddled together with his sister. The fear in their eyes was terrible to see.

Christina's mother stood up. "Run, Carl. Take my daughter and run away."

Christina began screaming, "Where's Daddy?" She bolted toward the fighting. Carl raced after her. He saw a dozen villagers lying dead in the street. Christina found the body of her father among them. She sobbed over him and begged him to get up.

As if in slow-motion, Carl saw it all again. A soldier came around the corner and spotted her. He raised his gun. Christina's father's rifle was lying in the dirt at Carl's feet. Carl had grown up hunting. He knew how to use a gun. With barely a thought, he snatched it up and fired.

A second later, he watched the surprise on the soldier's face fade away. The light went out of his eyes as he fell dead.

Carl couldn't get that picture out of his head.

He had killed a man.

Nonviolence was a pillar of the Amish faith. For centuries, they suffered persecution without reprisal as the Bible commanded.

But I say unto you, That ye resist not evil: but whosoever shall smite thee on thy right cheek, turn to him the other also.

It was a creed Carl believed in with all his heart, but his faith hadn't been strong enough. He did not face the death of that child, nor his own certain death, as he should have. God was the giver and taker of life, the judge of men, not Carl King.

He threw down the gun, grabbed Christina and hid as more soldiers scoured the area for him. He managed to make his way back to his sister's home, but he was too late. The women had been found by the soldiers looking for him.

He lived while everyone else died. He should have been brave enough to face his own death as his sister had done, with her Bible in her hands and peace in her soul. Instead, he'd broken a most sacred law: "Thou shalt not kill."

Each morning, he prayed for forgiveness. On those nights when his nightmare didn't come, he began to hope that God had taken pity on him.

But always, like tonight, the nightmare came back. He was forced to watch a man die by his hand over and over again and to know that his actions had cost his sister her life, too.

No, he had not been forgiven.

Later the next morning, Carl loaded his equipment in the back of the wagon and waited for Lizzie. He didn't have to wait long. She came rushing out of the house, still drying her hands on her apron.

She was out of breath by the time she reached him. "I hope I haven't kept you waiting. I had to get the breakfast dishes done and then I had to get something started for Grandfather's lunch. I pray that God wants Clara to work for Faith Lapp. I really do."

Her cheeks were rosy and her eyes sparkled with

excitement. How could someone who had been up before dawn and hard at work for hours look so fresh and adorable?

He dismissed the thought as unworthy the moment it occurred. He had no right to look upon an Amish maid with such delight. He laid the reins on the bench seat and scooted over.

Lizzie climbed aboard and picked them up. "You will have to tell me the way."

"Go past the school and turn right at the next road. Then it's about a mile."

"I'm excited to see an alpaca up close. Do they really spit at you? How far can they spit?" She was like a kid on her way to the county fair.

"I have no idea."

"My sister Greta would love to visit a farm with such exotic creatures. She loves animals. She has a special way with them, even the stubborn and mean ones."

"You should write and tell her all about it."

"That is exactly what I will do."

She grew silent and some of the happiness faded from her face.

"What's wrong?" he asked.

"I miss them. I've never been away from them before."

"You will see them again soon enough." He wanted to offer more comfort, a shoulder to cry on if she needed one, but he held himself rigid beside her.

"If I fail to get a job, then I must return home on the bus tomorrow afternoon. As much as I miss them, I don't want to go back and face them having accomplished nothing, for I know my leaving has caused great heartache."

"But it was a brave thing, nonetheless."

Lizzie thought Carl looked tired and sad this morning. She wondered why, but didn't wish to pry. She sensed that he needed comforting. After riding a while in silence, she glanced at him. "Are you okay?"

"I'm fine. I didn't sleep well, that's all."

He just needed cheering up. "I find a cup of herbal tea in the evenings helps me sleep like a babe. I haven't seen any in Grandfather's cupboards, but I'm sure you can buy some in town. I will write down the name for you, if you'd like."

"Thanks."

"If my constant chatter gets on your nerves, just shush me. I can take a hint."

He closed his eyes and rubbed his brow. "A little peace would be nice this morning."

"Absolutely. I understand completely. I often find I'm not at my best until almost noon. Isn't it a nice morning? March is such a funny month. A person would think winter is over when we have such a pretty day, but then, bang, the cold weather comes back."

"Lizzie."

"What, Carl?"

"Shush."

"Oh. Shush as in stop talking?"

"Is there another kind of shush?"

She opened her mouth, but he held up one hand. "No, don't explain. Shush as in stop talking."

She managed to be quiet for the rest of the trip,

but it was hard. How could she cheer him up if she couldn't speak to him?

When they reached the Lapp farm, she met Adrian and Faith's son, Kyle. A nine-year-old boy with bright red hair, freckles and an outgoing personality, he was happy to share his knowledge of shearing alpacas with everyone. Lizzie could have spent all day just gazing at the beautiful, graceful creatures. An adorable baby alpaca, which she learned from Kyle was called a cria, bounced around on stiff legs and darted under the adults standing in a small herd.

Inside the barn where the men were getting ready to work, Kyle indicated a number of bags stacked on nearby hay bales. "These bags are for the fleece. Alpacas have three kinds of fleece. There's prime—that's the best fiber. It's from their back and ribs. The fleece that we get off their thighs, neck and the legs is called seconds. The rest is called thirds and it isn't used by spinners. It's trash, but we keep some for batting inside the cria blankets if the babies are born during cold weather. Our little ones, the ones less than one year old, have prime all over because they've never been shorn."

"Is he bending your ear?" Faith asked as she entered the barn. She walked with a slight limp and wore a metal brace on her lower leg. Adrian came in with her, leading a white alpaca with a brown-and-white baby trotting at her heels.

"Not at all," Lizzie said with a smile for the boy. "I'm enjoying learning all about your beautiful animals."

The baby came to investigate the hem of Lizzie's

dress. She had never seen a more adorable creature. She looked at Faith. "Is it all right if I pet him?"

"Of course. We like to keep the ones we have as tame as possible so that they get used to handling. It makes working with them much easier. The important thing to remember is that they need to respect humans. We don't make pets of them. An alpaca that is spoiled with a lot of petting and treats can become aggressive when they are grown, especially the males. Once they have lost respect for a human, they can't be trusted."

"It's the same with sheep," Carl said. "It's often the bottle-fed lambs that become the most aggressive ones."

Kyle knelt and gathered the baby in his arms. "This is Jasper."

Lizzie stroked his velvety head. The mother watched them intently and made soft humming sounds to her baby. "I'm afraid I could not raise them. I would constantly want to hug them. They are so soft and they have the most beautiful eyes."

Carl walked around the mother. "If she was a sheep, I'd pick her up and set her on her rump to shear her. With those long legs, that looks a little tricky."

Adrian laughed. "I tried that the first time I attempted to shear Myrtle. She jumped straight up in the air a good four feet off the ground and sent me tumbling backward. Then she spit on me. Don't worry. We have a sock we use for a muzzle now. You'll be safe."

"I have it right here," Faith said and came up to put it on.

Carl tipped his cowboy hat back with one finger. "So how do we do this?"

Adrian led Myrtle forward until she was standing on a large rubber mat. "It's a three-person job. Someone needs to hold her head. That will be me. We put ropes around her legs and just stretch her out until she is flat on the ground. It looks a little awkward, but it doesn't hurt them. I will warn you, some of them really hate this, and they will scream. Others simply lie still until it's all over and never make a sound. Once we have this girl down on the ground, I'll tell you how we need the fleece to be cut. Kyle will gather the blanket as it comes off and put it in the bags. Are you ready to start?"

"As ready as I can get," Carl said with a lack of certainty.

Lizzie watched as Faith wrapped loops around each of Myrtle's legs, then she and Kyle pulled on the ropes until Myrtle was lying on her belly. Several of the other alpacas wandered over to watch what was happening. Having them and her baby nearby kept Myrtle quiet.

Carl followed Adrian's instructions and quickly learned the best way to shear the animal. In a matter of a few minutes, Myrtle was released and scrambled to her feet.

Lizzie giggled. "She looks positively ridiculous."

Myrtle's big woolly body was now skinny and scrawny except for the thick fleece that had been left around her head and a pom-pom at the end of her tail.

Kyle grabbed the rest of the fleece from the floor around Myrtle's feet. "They always looked shocked. Like, what just happened to me?"

Lizzie met Carl's gaze, and they both chuckled. He said, "She looks like that is exactly what she's thinking."

"Are you from Texas?" Kyle asked.

Lizzie perked up. Perhaps she would learn something about Carl's past today.

Carl frowned. "What makes you think that?"

Kyle pointed to his head. "Your cowboy hat. I'm from Texas. Lots of people wear hats like yours out there."

Kyle was from Texas? Lizzie glanced at his parents. Faith smiled and said, "*Ja,* our boy is a Texan. Confusing, isn't it? Tell them how you came to live in Ohio, Kyle."

The little boy grew solemn and crossed his arms over his chest. "It went like this. My dad, my first dad, was my aunt Faith's brother. He moved away from his Amish family and married my first mom. I was born in Texas. Are you with me? Then they died in a car accident. After that, I was really scared and sad. I lived in this home with other kids without parents.

"I didn't like it much, but I did like my foster mom. Her name was Becky. Anyway, a social-worker lady brought me here to Ohio to live with my aunt Faith. Then we met Adrian. He had the farm next to our house. Only, it's our farm now, and someone else lives in my aunt's house. A nice fellow named Gideon Troyer and his wife, Rebecca. He used to be a pilot.

"Anyway, Adrian became my new dad because he fell in love with my aunt and married her and they adopted me, so now they are my new *mamm* and *daed.* And that's how I got to be Amish.

"I do miss having a TV, but I like having alpacas a lot. I have one named Shadow. He's black as coal, and I get to keep all the money from his fleece when we sell it." Kyle's solemn expression dissolved into a wide grin.

Lizzie struggled to take in all of the information he had dished out so quickly. Faith laughed. "Did you get that?"

"I think so. Kyle is from Texas."

Adrian handed the lead rope to the boy. "Take Myrtle back to the pen and bring one of the others."

Kyle rushed to do as he had been asked. He was a charming child, but Lizzie was disappointed that she hadn't learned anything about where Carl was from.

Would she ever?

Chapter 6

Carl soon relaxed and grew more confident with each animal he sheared. As Adrian had said, some of the animals screamed in protest, but most lay quietly and allowed him to do his job without worrying about injuring them. He was spit at once but managed to jump aside, and only his boot took a direct hit. After that, Faith put muzzles on every animal.

Lizzie, of course, dissolved into laughter as he scraped his boot clean on a nearby hay bale. Each time she caught him looking at her after that, she pinched her nose and made a face.

He tried to keep his attention strictly on the task at hand, but having Lizzie working beside him made that difficult.

Her good humor never lagged as she pitched in to help without being asked. She was soon tying up alpacas as if she'd been doing it for years. When one was a particularly bad squirmer, Lizzie lay down on the ground beside him to help hold the animal still.

When she wasn't needed to help control the animals, she was helping to sort and bag the fleece. The whole time, she was smiling and cheerful, chuckling at the antics of the alpacas and making the morning one of the most pleasant he'd had in a long time.

When noon rolled around, Faith brought a picnic hamper down from the house. Lizzie followed with a large quilt over her arm and a pitcher of lemonade in her hand.

"Lizzie suggested we eat out here. I think a picnic is a wonderful idea. It's the first one of the year," Faith said as Adrian took the hamper from her.

Lizzie glanced at Carl and then looked away. "It's such a beautiful spring day that I thought it would be a shame to spend it eating at the table inside."

"Adrian, would you spread the quilt in a sunny place for us?" Faith indicated the spot she wanted and her husband quickly did as she asked.

Within a few minutes, they were all settled on the quilt except for Carl. He carried a bale of hay out and put it where he could sit and lean against the trunk of an apple tree.

Faith withdrew a plate full of ham sandwiches made with thick slices of homemade bread from the hamper. They all helped themselves as Lizzie poured glasses of fresh lemonade. She handed them out to everyone except Carl. When she approached, he was busy wiping his hands with a wet towel. "Just set it on the ground. I'll get it in a minute."

She caught his glance and nodded. It was acceptable.

"When do you plan to start shearing Joe's sheep?" Adrian asked.

"Tomorrow."

"How many sheep does Joe have?" Kyle asked as he examined the large clippers Carl had laid aside.

"He has four rams and about two hundred ewes."

Kyle's eyes widened. "And I thought shearing ten alpacas was a lot of work. How long will it take you?"

"If the weather holds and nothing goes wrong, we'll be done in three or four days."

Kyle was holding Carl's shears trying to squeeze the big scissor-like blades together. "Doesn't your hand get tired?"

Carl almost choked on his lemonade. "It does. By the end of the week, my hand is very tired. I'll show you how to use those. A good shearer can earn a tidy sum of cash in the spring."

Kyle handed them back. "No, thanks. I'm gonna farm with my dad and grow peaches. How did you learn? Did your dad shear sheep?"

"*Nee,* my father is a carpenter." A sharp stab of regret hit Carl. He hadn't seen his father since he left home when he was twenty-four years old. He would be twenty-nine this fall. Five years was a long time. When would he be able to go home? When would God grant him the forgiveness he craved?

"Where does he work?" Lizzie asked softly.

"Pennsylvania." He didn't share more details. "Lizzie mentioned you are looking for a spinner to work with you, Faith."

Faith smiled. "Lizzie has a sister who might be interested in the job."

"My oldest sister, Clara. She used to spin with our mother, but that was many years ago."

"Did she like it?" Adrian asked.

"She loved doing it, but our uncle sold the spinning wheel after our mother died."

Adrian pushed his straw hat back a little and regarded her intently. "Is she staying with Joe, too?"

"*Nee.* Clara is at home in Indiana, but I know she would come if she knew she had a job."

Adrian gave Faith a speaking glance and then said, "I would rather meet your sister first and see her skill level before we offer her a job. Faith's work has gained a good reputation among the shops that purchase her yarns. We don't want to start selling an inferior product."

Lizzie nodded. "I understand. It's just that it's very important that Clara have a job soon."

"And why is that?" Adrian asked.

Lizzie looked to Carl. He was pleased that she valued his opinion. He nodded. "Tell them."

She drew a deep breath. "My uncle is making Clara marry a cruel man. Rufus Khuns is our landlord. We live and work on his dairy farm. Clara doesn't want to marry him, but Onkel Morris is afraid Rufus will turn us out if she doesn't. He told Clara that he'll make our youngest sister wed Rufus if Clara won't. Betsy is barely seventeen."

"That's terrible. Oh, Adrian, we have to help them," Faith cried.

Adrian took his wife's hand in his and patted it.

"Calm yourself. Remember, the midwife said getting upset isn't good for your blood pressure."

"I know. And sitting for a long time at the wheel makes my feet swell, so I shouldn't do that, either. I will be glad when this babe makes an appearance."

Adrian turned to Lizzie. "Tell your sister she has a job here for as long as she needs one."

"But what about your other sisters?" Faith asked. "They can't stay and be abused in your uncle's home."

"I have a job interview tomorrow at Elam Sutter's home. Once Clara and I both have jobs, we'll be able to take care of our little sisters. I don't care what it takes. I won't leave them behind."

Faith reached over and squeezed Lizzie's hand. "Of course you can't. I will pray for the success of your mission every day."

Lizzie felt as if she had finally found people who understood what she faced. It was a deeply comforting feeling.

She and Faith carried the quilt and lunch items back to the house as the men returned to shear the final four alpacas. After the dishes were washed, Faith said, "Come see my spinning room. You will want to tell your sister about where she'll be working."

She led the way to a bright room that had been built off the kitchen on the east side of the house. In it were three spinning wheels of various sizes and dozens of skeins of yarn. The windows overlooked a small orchard where the shorn alpacas were gathering beneath the trees.

Lizzie admired the largest spinning wheel. "This

is the kind that my mother had. What a lovely place you have to work."

"Adrian built it for me when I first moved here. He knew how much I liked to watch my animals."

"He seems like a caring husband."

Faith cupped her hands over her pregnant belly. "He is a wonderful man. I never thought I would find someone like him. My first husband was a very demanding and hard man. Life was not…easy with him. It wasn't all his fault. He had a very tragic childhood. Then we had two little daughters who were stillborn early in our marriage, and he was never the same after that."

"I'm so sorry for your loss."

"*Danki.* I know they are with God in Heaven and I will see them again someday. You must tell your sister not to give up hope and not to marry without love. God brings special people into our lives exactly when we need them. If it is His will, your sister will find a man like my Adrian, and she will know the joy of being a true wife."

"I will tell her. Thank you for giving her a job. I can't believe how fortunate I've been since coming to Hope Springs."

"I felt the same way when I first arrived. So many people came to give me a hand getting my house and my farm in order. My husband and I had moved around a lot, so I'd never known the sense of community that exists here. You and your sisters will see. You'll be welcome by all."

"I hope so."

"You have not mentioned how Joe feels about your sisters coming here. Is he glad? I have only known him as the recluse who shuns the company of all others except for Carl."

"Grandfather doesn't want us here."

"How sad for you."

"Honestly, I think it is sad for him."

"You're right. We can't change how people feel. We can only do what we know to be right, and bringing your sisters here sounds right to me."

"Bless you for understanding."

"I do. Now, we must get back to the shearing or I'll find black thirds mixed in with my white firsts." She chuckled. "I have good men, but they still need supervision."

It didn't take long to finish shearing the rest of the animals. Faith led the last one back to their enclosure while Adrian pulled a wallet from his pocket.

He counted out the amount and held it toward Carl. "My wife is very satisfied with your work. I hope I can count on you for next year."

"If I'm still in the area. Give the money to Lizzie while I go wash up. They might be prized for their fleece, but it makes me itch." Carl walked to a nearby stock tank and began to rinse his arms.

Adrian seemed a bit surprised, but offered the payment to Lizzie. She accepted it and put it in her pocket.

Later, back at her grandfather's farm, she left the bills on the table and went down to the cellar for a jar of vegetables. When she came up, the money was gone. Carl had been as good as his word. Everything had been done carefully so as not to have Adrian or Faith unknowingly break their church's Ordnung.

Once again, Lizzie was puzzled by Carl's behavior.

Adrian and Faith had no idea that Carl was a shunned person. He could have gone about his business as an Englischer and no one would've been the wiser. Why did he take such great care to protect the people when he was no longer a member of their faith? If he cared so much, why didn't he ask forgiveness for his sin, whatever it was, and be welcomed into the church again?

It didn't make sense. Nothing about Carl made sense. And yet she spent a great deal of time thinking about him and wishing she could find a way to help.

When her grandfather came in for supper that evening, he hung his hat on the peg by the door as usual. "Carl won't be joining us."

"Why not?" She set a platter of noodles on the table.

"Said he wasn't hungry. How did the alpaca shearing go?"

"Fine. Is Carl unwell?"

"Not that I could see."

"Is it unusual for him to miss a meal?"

"He's a grown man. If he doesn't want to eat, he doesn't want to eat. Could be he's tired of your cooking."

She snatched the dish off the table. "There's nothing wrong with my cooking. If you don't want it, I'll feed yours to the dog."

"I never said I didn't want it," he admitted grudgingly.

She glared at him. "I'm a good cook."

"I said that before, didn't I?"

"Then you shouldn't suggest otherwise. It's hurtful."

It took him a few seconds, but finally, he said, "I didn't mean to hurt your feelings. Now can I eat?"

It was as close to an apology as she was likely to get. She set the platter on the table again and turned away to hide a smile. Her grandfather needed someone to stand up to his cantankerous ways. Carl was right about that.

She went to the window and looked out, but she couldn't see his hut beyond the barn. "Carl was quiet on the ride home from the Lapp farm. I didn't give it much thought. I assumed he was tired, but perhaps he was ill."

"I hope not. We need to get started on our beasts first thing in the morning. The lambs are due to start arriving in two to three weeks."

"I hope I can be here to see it." She turned around and went back to the table. "I remember watching the new lambs when I was little. They jumped, ran and played with each other, and it looked like they were having so much fun. Mother said they were leaping with joy."

"Did she?"

"She said the lambing season was the hardest work of the year, but it was all worth it."

A sad, faraway look came into his eyes. "*Ja,* my girl was right about that."

He bowed his head to pray and didn't speak again during the meal. He went to his room directly afterward, leaving Lizzie alone. Perhaps she had been wrong to mention her mother in front of him. It seemed to bring him pain.

She went to bed that night and lay under the quilt

her mother had made. Outside her open window, a chilly breeze blew by and carried the sounds of the night with it. An owl hooted nearby. In the distance, a sheep bleated and another answered. A dog barked somewhere.

This was her last night in the house where her mother had grown up. Tomorrow, if she got the job with Elam Sutter, she would stay with his family and work to bring her sisters to Hope Springs. If she wasn't hired, she would be forced to go home, back to Indiana. At least she'd found a job for Clara, but she wasn't sure her sister would take it if it meant leaving the rest of them.

She slipped out of bed and got to her knees. "Please, Lord, I'm begging You. Give me the strength and wisdom to find a place for all of us."

Knowing that she could do nothing more and that it was all in God's hands, she climbed into bed and quickly fell asleep.

Lizzie finished her chores the next morning and hurried outside. She was surprised to see Carl waiting with the pony already hitched to the cart. "*Danki,* Carl, but you should not do this for me."

"It's not a favor, Lizzie. It's part of the work I do here. Do you know how to get where you're going?"

"I have a general idea."

"I drew a map. It's on the seat if you need it."

"That was very thoughtful of you."

"Good luck. I hope you get the job."

"I shall know soon enough." She stood beside the

cart knowing that she should hurry, but she was reluctant to actually get under way.

What if it didn't work out? What if she was back here in two hours to pack and board the bus this afternoon? The thought was depressing.

Carl stepped close to her. "The journey of a thousand miles begins with a single step."

"I thought I took that first step when I walked out of my uncle's house last week."

"Then you are well on your way to where you want to be. This next step cannot be as difficult as that one."

She smiled softly. "You are right about that. You are right about a lot of things, Carl King."

"And I will be right if I tell you to hurry up and go or you won't get back in time to make us lunch."

She laughed. "I declare, you men think with your stomachs."

"I'm going to miss your cooking, Lizzie Barkman."

"I'm going to miss cooking for you."

"You will have Sundays off if Sutter gives you the job. Feel free to come out here and cook to your heart's content."

"That is only if I get the job."

"I don't know Elam Sutter, but he is a fool if he doesn't hire someone as hardworking as you are. Now, get going. Joe and I need to get our sheep sheared."

Lizzie climbed into the cart and picked up the reins. "At least you know they won't spit on you. See you soon."

She slapped the reins against the pony and left Carl standing in the yard watching her. When she reached the end of the lane, she looked back. She lifted a hand and waved. Carl saw her gesture and waved back.

Lizzie drove toward town with a light heart that had nothing to do with a job prospect. Her happy mood was because Carl cared about her comfort and because he said he would miss her if she left.

Lizzie arrived at the Sutter farm and was immediately welcomed by a little girl about four years old, followed by a puppy that reminded Lizzie of Duncan.

"Guder mariye," the little girl called out. She turned and shouted toward the house, "Mamm, we have company."

Lizzie stepped down from the cart. "Thank you. You must be Rachel."

"Ja, I am. Who are you?"

"My name is Lizzie Barkman, and I'm here to see your father about a job."

"Papa is in his workshop. Shall I get him?"

"That would be nice, *danki.*"

The little girl turned to her puppy and patted her leg. "Come on, Peanut Butter. Let's go find Papa."

Together they ran toward the barn. Lizzie heard the door of the house open and saw Katie come out with Jeremiah balanced on her hip. "Lizzie, I'm so glad you are here. Come in the house. My husband should be in shortly."

"Rachel just went to tell him that I'm here."

"Oh, *goot.* She is quite the little helper. She makes me wish for another girl. She is much less trouble than my boys have been."

"What has Jeremiah tried to swallow today?"

"My sewing bobbin. I can't take my eyes off him for a minute. Thankfully, the baby isn't much trouble yet, but I'm sure he'll be just like his brother when he is old enough to get into mischief."

Lizzie held out her arms for Jeremiah and was delighted when he grinned and reached for her in return. She propped him on her hip and followed Katie into the house. They were settled at the kitchen table when Elam came in. He hung his hat on a peg by the door.

Jeremiah, who until that moment had been quiet seated on Lizzie's lap, started whining to get down. Elam plucked him away from Lizzie.

"Charming the girls already, are you?" Elam took a seat at the table and allowed the little boy to sit on his lap.

"Indeed, he has been," Lizzie replied.

"My wife tells me you are interested in working for us. Have you any experience at basket weaving?"

"None, but I would be interested to learn. I can help with the children, of that I'm certain."

"Well, then, come down to the shop and let me show you what you will need to know. You may decide the work isn't for you. It can be tedious."

He handed his son to his wife, and Lizzie followed him outside and into his shop. It was part of the barn, but had been walled off to separate it from the rest of the structure. The moment Lizzie stepped inside the room, the aromatic scent of cedar and wood shavings enveloped her. The walls had been painted a bright white. Tools hung from the pegs neatly arranged on one wall. A long table sat in the middle of the workshop, and a small stove in one corner held a simmering vat of something reddish-brown. Around the table sat three women, each with partially completed baskets in front of them.

Elam said, "This is Mary, Ruby and Sally. They all work for me part-time."

Sally put down the basket she was working on. "Lizzie, how nice to see you again."

Lizzie met the other women, who, as it turned out, were Elam's sister and sister-in-law. After seeing how they turned the thin strips of poplar wood into beautiful baskets, Lizzie realized this was something she would like to learn. She thanked the women for their demonstrations, asked a few questions and then followed Elam back to the house.

Katie was setting out mugs of coffee. Everyone took a seat at the kitchen table. "Well, what did you think?" Katie asked.

"I think I have a lot to learn, but it looks like something I would enjoy."

"How soon would you be able to start?" Elam asked.

"Today," Lizzie said quickly.

Elam and Katie exchanged amused glances.

"I'm afraid I don't have a room ready for you yet," Katie said.

"Why don't you start tomorrow? If you think you'll like the work, let's give it a two-week trial," Elam suggested.

Lizzie grinned as excitement bubbled up inside her. She took a sip of coffee. "Tomorrow will be fine."

Carl secured the last panel into place with a length of wire and glanced out the barn door to see Lizzie returning. Even from across the yard, he could see the grin on her face. She caught sight of him and jumped down from the cart. "I got the job," she yelled.

He couldn't believe how relieved he was. She wouldn't be going back to Indiana. She had a job and a place to stay in the neighborhood. He would see her again. Even if only from a distance.

Joe came up to stand beside him. "What did she say?"

"She said she got the job."

Joe gave a disgusted humph and walked away, but Carl wasn't fooled. Joe might not admit it, but he didn't want her to leave, either.

A few minutes later, Lizzie came out of the house and raced down the lane with something in her hand. Intrigued, Carl watched until she slipped whatever she was carrying into the mailbox and raised the flag to let the mail carrier know there was mail to pick up. Was it a letter to her sisters? Probably.

Carl hoped everything would work out for them, but he knew what people desired was not always what God had planned for them. His poor little sister's short life was proof of that.

Turning back to his work, Carl began getting ready to shear. He had three days of hard work ahead of him. He wouldn't get much done if he couldn't stop thinking about Lizzie. He didn't need the constant distraction of having her near, but...oh, how he desired it.

After spending much of yesterday in her company, he had retreated to his hut, thinking that the distance would help him stop thinking about her. It hadn't worked.

The mixture of foolish longing and painful reality swirling through his brain left him feeling hopelessly muddled.

Lizzie had a way of turning him inside out with just a smile. How was he going to get through another day, let alone the years ahead, if she stayed in Hope Springs?

Lizzie could barely control her excitement as she walked back from the mailbox. Everything was falling into place. The letter she mailed to Mary contained a second letter to her sisters explaining everything: Lizzie's job, Clara's job and her fervent hope that they would all be together soon.

In with the letter, Lizzie had put all of her money. It was enough for a one-way ticket for Clara. She prayed that Clara would come. Together, they would soon earn enough to pay for Betsy and Greta to join them and keep the younger women from being forced into marriage instead. It wasn't a foolproof plan, but it was all Lizzie had to offer.

What they needed now was a place to stay. The Lord had provided jobs. Lizzie was sure He would provide them with a home, too. She just had to have faith.

Bubbling with happiness and optimism, she went to the barn to watch the men at work. A small group of sheep had been gathered in a pen inside the barn. The air was filled with sounds of their bleating as they milled around. A narrow passageway had been built from the large pens outside to a smaller one where Carl was preparing to start the work.

A large piece of plywood had been put on the

ground outside the gate of the smallest pen. Carl was down on one knee on the board tying on wool moccasins. When he finished, he reached for the clippers and affixed them to his right hand.

Moving closer, Lizzie said, "Why the special shoes?"

"They keep my feet dry and keep me from slipping on the oils from the fleece."

"Are you going to shear the rams first?" She eyed the four big fellows separated in a pen by themselves.

"That's right." Carl didn't look at her but kept his eyes downcast.

"Why?"

"They're bigger and harder to work with. It's best to get them out of the way so the rest of the work goes more easily. We only have four rams. It doesn't normally take long."

"And you said two hundred ewes." It sounded like a tremendous amount of work for one man and her elderly grandfather.

"That's right."

"I vaguely remember watching the shearing when I was little. A man used electric clippers. He brought his own generator with him. I thought it was very worldly at the time. Doesn't it take longer to clip the fleece by hand?"

Unlike the clippers she remembered, Carl had what looked like a giant pair of scissors strapped to his hand. The blades hooked together at the handle ends instead of in the center.

"It takes me about six minutes per sheep instead of four minutes if I were to use electric clippers. Joe likes them shorn the old way."

"In keeping with our faith. That's understandable."

"He likes it because the fleece isn't cut so close to the skin. Hand-sheared sheep are left with a short coat instead of looking naked. It gives them better protection against foul weather. It's also less stressful for our pregnant mothers without the buzzing sound of the clippers and the smell of gasoline fumes from a generator."

"Are the two of you gonna keep yacking or can we get some work done?" Joe shouted from just outside the pen where the sheep were milling.

Carl waved. "I'm ready."

"What do you need me to do?" she asked.

"There needs to be a clear flow of sheep entering and leaving the shearing area. This barn is divided into two parts. Where the sheep come in and where they go out. The catch pen, the small one here, is connected to the outside corrals by movable panels."

"I see that." The narrow alleyway was just wide enough for one single ram to walk down to the actual shearing pen.

"After I'm done shearing the sheep, I'll turn him into this second alley. I need you to close the gate behind him so he can't run back into this area."

"Got it."

"Once I'm done with all of them, you'll need to close that big gate by the barn door and open the smaller gate beside it so the ewes go out to a separate corral."

"So you just want me to chase them outside for you?"

"Basically. Don't get in with the rams. They can be mean."

"I will remember that."

"Joe may need help giving the animals their worm medicine while I have them still. He'll take care of the fleece that's cut off, too. You can make notes in our logbook for us. Each sheep has an ear tag with a number on it. Joe will tell you what to write."

"Sounds easy enough."

"It is if the sheep cooperate. The only thing they do without protest is grow wool. Ready to start?"

"Sure."

Lizzie quickly learned that sheep were not the cute, cuddly animals of her memory. They were much stronger than they looked, horribly stubborn, smelly and incredibly loud. The bleating grew to a deafening din inside the barn.

Duncan nipped at the heels of the rams as the reluctant animals filed into the catch pen.

Carl opened a small gate and pulled out the first struggling ram. Grasping the heavy wool, he tipped the sheep backward until it was sitting. The second the sheep's feet were all off the ground, it stopped struggling. The animal looked as if it were being held still by the force of Carl's will.

With the ram braced between his legs, Carl quickly set to work clipping first the belly fleece and then around the entire animal until the wool came off in one large piece.

Joe pulled the fleece aside, folded it and placed it on a nearby table. He made a few quick notes in a ledger, gave the animal a dose of medicine and then went to move the next ram into the catch pen with Duncan's help.

Lizzie watched how it was all being done as Carl sheared his second ram. She noticed the first ram had come back inside to be with the others. While Joe was busy rolling up the fleece, she went to shoo the fellow outside.

The ram balked and wouldn't leave. She opened the gate to go in and move him along. In the next second, she realized her mistake. The ram, seeing a new way out, bolted past her, knocking the gate wide open.

Lizzie cried out a warning, but it was too late. The ram didn't slow down. He plowed into Joe and sent him flying before charging through the open barn door beyond. She stared in horror at her grandfather's crumpled figure as Carl raced to his side.

Chapter 7

Lizzie drove the buggy as fast as she dared. Carl sat in the back cradling Joe, but with every bounce and jolt, her grandfather moaned in pain. The sound made her cringe with remorse. It was all her fault. In her foolish need to prove she could be useful, she'd simply proven she was careless.

After what seemed like an eternity, the outskirts of Hope Springs came into view. Thankfully, there was very little traffic on the streets. She was able to follow Carl's directions and they arrived within a few minutes at the front doors of the Hope Springs Medical Clinic.

Carl lifted Joe out of the buggy and carried him inside. The tiny, elderly receptionist behind the desk jumped to her feet. "Oh, my. What has happened?"

"Joe's been hurt bad," Carl said.

"Bring him this way. I'll get the doctor."

Carl and Lizzie followed her down a short hallway and into an examination room. Carl gently laid Joe on the bed. "It's okay, Joe. You're going to be fine."

A young man in a white lab coat hurried into the room. "I'm Dr. Zook. What seems to be the matter?"

"Where is Dr. White?" Carl asked.

"He's not in today. I'm his partner. Is that a problem?"

Carl shook his head.

"Are you related to Bishop Zook?" Lizzie asked.

"Very distantly, if at all. Zook is simply a common name in these parts."

Outside the door, the receptionist asked, "Should I call for an ambulance, Doctor?"

"Give me a few minutes to see how serious this is, Wilma. Have Amber finish with Mrs. Lapp and then ask her to join me. Can someone tell me what happened?"

"It's my fault." Lizzie clasped her hands together. "I left one of the gates open and a ram got out. He ran into Grandfather and knocked him down. Grandfather hit his head on one of the steel fence posts. It was bleeding terribly."

The doctor began to unwind Lizzie's apron from around Joe's head. "Head wounds are notorious for bleeding a lot. Has he been unconscious long?"

Carl took a step back from the bed to give the doctor more room. "He's been in and out for the past half hour or so. He complains that his right leg hurts. I think it's broken."

The doctor looked kindly at Lizzie. "You might want to step out and let us get him undressed. I'll let you know the extent of his injuries as soon as I've finished examining him."

Lizzie nodded and left the room. She found her way back to the waiting area. Taking a seat on one of the upholstered chairs that lined the wall, she put her head in her hands and prayed.

A short time later, she heard a door open and she looked up. It wasn't the doctor. It was a blonde Englisch woman in a pale blue smock. She walked beside Faith Lapp.

"Everything looks good with your pregnancy, Faith. I'll see you back in two weeks. Sooner if you have any problems. You know I'm available day or night. I'd love to stay and chat a little longer, but I'm needed for another patient."

"*Danki,* Amber. I will see you in two weeks," Faith said. She turned to leave and caught sight of Lizzie. Her eyes widened with surprise. "Lizzie, what are you doing here?"

"Grandfather has been hurt."

"I'm so sorry to hear that. Is it serious?" She sat down beside Lizzie and took her hand.

Her comforting gesture was all that was needed to push Lizzie's shattered emotions over the edge. She burst into tears.

Faith wrapped an arm around Lizzie's shoulder. "There, there, don't cry. He is in God's hands, and God is good."

Lizzie nodded but couldn't speak. She was too choked with tears and worry.

Faith stayed with her until the doctor finally came out to talk to her. She could tell by the look on his face that it wasn't good news. She rose to her feet. "How is he?"

"He's resting comfortably at the moment. I've given him something for pain. The head wound was not serious. It required a few stitches, but he did sustain a minor concussion. The problem is that Joe has a broken hip. We can't treat that here. He needs to go to the hospital. He'll need surgery to pin the broken pieces together."

"Surgery? Is that dangerous at his age?" Faith asked.

"All surgery comes with risks, but I'm afraid there's very little choice. The fracture won't heal unless it can be immobilized."

"Do what you think is best, Doctor. Can I see him now?"

"Of course. I'll make arrangements for an ambulance to transport him to the hospital in Millersburg."

Faith laid a hand on Lizzie's arm. "I'll let Bishop Zook know what has happened. Don't worry. Everything will be taken care of."

Lizzie nodded and walked down the hall, but hesitated before going into the room. What could she say except that she was sorry? She wiped the tears from her cheeks and opened the door.

Joe lay on the same bed with his eyes closed. A sheet was pulled up to his chin. A white bandage stood out starkly on his forehead. He looked pale and helpless.

Carl sat in a chair beside him. He glanced up as Lizzie peered in. "It's okay. He's awake."

"Of course I'm awake," Joe growled. "Who could sleep with all this commotion?"

"Oh, Daadi, I'm so sorry. I was only trying to help. Please forgive me."

"Things happen. That old ram has had it in for me since I bought him. Carl, it will be up to you to get the shearing done. It'll be hard to do it all yourself."

"I can handle it, Joe. You just rest and get better."

"You won't be able to manage the lambing alone."

Lizzie stepped closer to the bed. "I'll help. I know I made a mess of things today, but I want to make it up to you."

"What about your new job?" Carl asked.

"I'm sure when the Sutters hear what's happened, they will understand if I can't start work for a few more days."

"It will be a few weeks."

"Oh."

Joe shifted uncomfortably on the bed. "The girl won't be any use to you, Carl."

"She'll be better than no one."

It wasn't much of a recommendation, but Lizzie was thankful that he spoke up for her. "Faith Lapp is out in the waiting room. She said she'll let Bishop Zook know what has happened."

Joe pushed up on one elbow, his eyes blazing. "I don't want that busybody Esther Zook in my house, do you hear me?"

Lizzie was stunned by his outburst. Carl rose and eased Joe back on the bed. "I thought you liked the bishop. You told me he was a good man."

"He's a good man married to a shrew of a woman.

She'll turn her nose up at everything I own and tell folks what a pity it is that I've let the place go to ruin. I don't want her to set foot inside my door."

Lizzie moved to stand beside him on the other side of the bed. "I won't let her in. I promise."

The outside door opened and the nurse entered. "The ambulance is here. I'm going to have you both step into the waiting room while they get Mr. Shetler ready for transport. Which one of you is going to ride with him?"

"I will," Lizzie said quickly.

"*Nee,* you go home. I want Carl to come."

Lizzie had to concede. Of course he wanted his friend, not the careless granddaughter he barely knew who put him here in the first place.

The nurse gestured to Lizzie to come with her. When they were outside in the hallway, she said, "We haven't met. I'm Amber White. I'll make arrangements for a driver to take you to the hospital."

Embarrassed, Lizzie shook her head. "I have no money to pay a driver."

"Don't worry about that. We have a fund set up for just such an emergency. All the local Amish churches donate to it. The driver will make sure you get to the hospital and that you get home when you are ready. Just let the receptionist have your name and address."

"I don't know how to thank you."

"Of course you do. Someday, you will see a person in need, and you will help them. That is all the thanks I require." Amber went back to the room and Lizzie went to speak to the woman behind the desk.

* * *

Carl rode in the back of the ambulance strapped into a small seat out of the way of the crew, but situated where he could see Joe. His friend's color was so pale that Carl began to worry something else was wrong. At the hospital, Carl stood aside and tried to keep out of the way as they admitted Joe and readied him for surgery.

When a lull in the activity finally occurred, the two men were alone for a few minutes.

Joe looked over at him. "With that long face, you make a man think you're on your way to a funeral."

"It will be a long time before anyone plants you in the ground, Woolly Joe."

"I hope so, but a man never knows what the good Lord has in store for him. Could be that I'm on my way to see Him now and just don't know it."

"Lizzie feels bad enough. If you decide to die, she's gonna feel awful."

"She should go stay with the Sutters instead of staying on the farm."

"If you are worried about her safety or anything else, don't be."

"No, it isn't that. I know you'll watch over her. I have no worries on that score. It's just that a sheep farm isn't any place for a woman."

"You don't give Lizzie enough credit. She can handle the work and then some."

"I bought the place a year before I married Lizzie's grandmother. My wife, Evelyn, hated it. She hated the sheep. She hated the smell of them. She hated the long hours and the hard work during the lambing season.

I thought she would grow to love it as I did, but that never happened. After a few years, I realized it wasn't the farm. She was never happy with me."

"I'm sorry to hear that."

"The Lord didn't bless us with a child until we were close to thirty. I thought having a baby on the place would make a difference to Evelyn, but it didn't. She died when Abigail was only two. I didn't want the girl to grow up hating the place the way her mother did. I sent her to live with my wife's sister until she was fourteen. I visited her every week, but I'm not sure it was enough. Maybe if I had kept her with me from the start, she would've felt differently about leaving the way she did. Maybe she thought I didn't care about her, but I did. I loved my little girl."

Carl laid a hand on his friend's shoulder. "Joe, if you give Lizzie half a chance, she will grow to love you as I do."

Joe shook his head. "It's better to be alone. You take care of my sheep while I'm laid up, you hear me?"

"I hear you. The sheep will be fine."

"I know they will be with you looking out for them. You and I, we get along okay. We don't need anyone else."

Carl had spent the past five years believing that was true, but now he wasn't so sure. He was learning that a life spent alone could be painfully lonely.

A nurse in surgical garb entered the room. "Mr. Shetler, your granddaughter is here. Would you like to see her before we take you to surgery?"

"*Nee*, let's get this over with."

The nurse looked surprised, but said, "I'll show her where the waiting room is."

A few minutes later, more people came in. Joe was wheeled from the room. Carl followed them to a large set of double doors.

One of the nurses gestured toward a side hall. "The waiting room is the first door on the left. The surgeon will come talk to you as soon as he is finished."

Carl laid a hand on Joe's arm and leaned close. "God is with you, my friend."

"I know. I just hope He is with the Englisch *doktor,* too."

Carl managed a smile. When they took Joe through the double doors, he walked down to the waiting room.

Lizzie was seated alone by the window. Her hands were clasped together and her eyes were closed. He knew that she was praying. As if she sensed his presence, she looked up and rose to her feet. "How is he?"

"They just took him into surgery."

She sank back onto her chair. "He didn't want to see me."

"Don't dwell on it. When he gets out of here, you can ply him with more of your wonderful cherry cobbler."

"I don't think my cooking can undo the damage I've done today. Do you?"

He didn't have an answer for that.

They waited together in silence until the surgeon finally came in to tell them Joe's surgery had gone well. Later, when Joe was moved to a room, he refused any visitors. Carl, knowing Joe wouldn't change his mind about seeing her, convinced Lizzie to go home.

By the time the driver delivered them to the farm, it had grown dark. Carl stood on the bottom porch step as Lizzie opened the front door. She looked back at him. "I wish there was more that I could do for him. I feel so bad about this."

The urge to take her in his arms and comfort her was overpowering. He clenched his hands into fists at his sides to keep from reaching for her. "We are to take care of his sheep. That is all Joe wants from us. Get some rest, Lizzie. Tomorrow will be a long, busy day."

In the days to come, she would be working by his side. The joy the thought brought him was bittersweet. They would have a few days together, maybe a few weeks if she stayed through the lambing, but she wouldn't stay with him forever.

Carl wasn't surprised to see Lizzie just after dawn the next morning. He hadn't slept well and he doubted she had, either. She came down to the barn dressed in a faded green dress with her hair covered by a matching green kerchief instead of her usual black *kapp*. She carried a basket over one arm. When she drew near, he could see the puffiness in her eyes. She must have cried herself to sleep.

He longed to offer a comforting hug, but knew she wouldn't welcome such a gesture.

She held out the basket. "I have some cold biscuits and sausage with cheese and a thermos of coffee. It's not much."

"It's fine. I'm not that hungry."

"Neither am I."

"Save them for later."

She set the basket aside and pulled on a pair of her grandfather's work gloves. "I promise to do only what you tell me and exactly what you tell me. Where do I start?"

"You can start by not being so hard on yourself."

"I have put my grandfather in the hospital and made twice as much work for you. I'm not being hard on myself."

"Okay. First, we need the floor clean around where I'm working. You'll need to keep it raked and swept to prevent hay and other bits of debris from getting into the wool."

She grabbed a broom and began cleaning the old wooden floor of the barn with a vengeance.

Carl smiled at her eagerness. She was determined to be as much help as another man. He knew she felt badly about the accident, but she was going to wear herself out if she kept trying so hard. "Pace yourself, Lizzie. We have a lot more to do."

When they had the floors cleared, Carl brought in the rams that hadn't been shorn the day before. He wouldn't let Lizzie help until they were done and outside in their own separate enclosure.

He kicked the fleece aside and said, "Now we can move the first bunch of ewes into the catch pen. I'll need you to catch a sheep and bring her to me. When I pull her out and hold her, you need to squirt a dose of medicine into her mouth and then make note of it in our record book."

"I'll do whatever you need me to do."

She made a grab for the first animal and tried to pull it to where he stood. It was amusing to watch a one-hundred-and-twenty-pound girl trying to pull a two-hundred-pound animal with four splayed feet and a lot of determination across the pen. Finally, she gave up and the ewe scampered away from her.

Carl started to laugh until he caught sight of Lizzie's face. There were tears in her eyes. "I can't do any of this," she wailed.

"Sure you can. You just have to learn how to control sheep." He caught a ewe in the corner and said, "Come here. You place your hand firmly under her jaw and around her nose like this." He demonstrated. "Then you lift their nose up. This move will keep an ewe still if you press her against a wall or fence so she can't spin away."

Lizzie wiped her cheeks with the back of her hands. "So how do I get her to you?"

"You keep her nose up, put a hand on her hind end, and you walk her backward like this." He demonstrated moving the reluctant ewe to the shearing gate. "They won't all come easily, but most of them can be convinced this way."

He proceeded to give the sheep her medicine and then said, "Now I want you to hold this one here while I step out."

Lizzie looked dubious, but she did as he asked. The sheep, sensing a weaker hand, began to struggle, but Lizzie leaned into her, pushing her against the wall and holding her still.

"Good girl."

He stepped out of the shearing gate, grabbed the sheep from her, took it down to the ground and began to snip away. "While I'm cutting the fleece off, I want you to look up the ear-tag number in our flock record book and mark that she has been wormed. You'll see a place for a checkmark for the medication, a place to write a note if the animal needs a closer checkup because she's sick or acting strange."

"Okay." She flipped through the pages of the book and quickly made a note.

By the time she finished making the entry, he had the fleece off and allowed the ewe to regain her feet. Bleating loudly, she scampered down the runway and out into the corral beyond.

"Ready to bring me the next one?"

"Aren't you going to roll up the fleece?"

"I'll wait till we have a few piled here, and then we will clean and bag them."

From the group milling in the small pen, she grabbed the next one and moved it within Carl's reach. He pulled it from the pen and proceeded to shear it. In this way, they went through the morning. Sometimes, Lizzie managed to have one ready for him. Often, he had to step in and help her. By midmorning, he made the catch pen smaller so the sheep had less room to evade her.

At noon, Lizzie dusted off the front of her apron. She was breathing hard, but looked pleased at her accomplishments. "That was the last one."

"Twenty down, one hundred and ninety left to go."

Her eyes widened. "One hundred and ninety more?"

"Give or take. There will be a half dozen or so that we will cull, so they won't be sheared."

"What will we do with them?"

"I'll take them to the sale barn later this spring.

Some will be purchased for slaughter, but a lot of them become fluffy lawn mowers. It's not a bad way for a sheep to live out its days. Come, I'll show you how we take care of the fleece."

He laid the first one from the pile on the table. "We pick off the really dirty wool and any grass or hay that might be stuck in it. Then we fold them up like this." He demonstrated and carried it to a gigantic plastic bag that was held upright by a large wooden frame with boards a few feet apart like a ladder on the sides of it.

"I've been wondering about this thing. It looks like a windmill without a top."

"The slats are so that I can climb up and get inside the plastic bag to tromp down the wool."

"That sounds like something I can do for you. It's got to be easier than wrestling sheep."

"It is easy, but, honestly, you don't weigh enough to pack down the fleece."

She looked for a second as if she wanted to argue with him but quickly thought better of it. "I'll fold the fleece, and you stuff the bag."

"It's a deal."

"Is it time for me to bring in more sheep?"

"It's time for a rest and some lunch. After that, I'll sharpen my shears, sweep off the platform and we'll start all over again."

She grimaced as she rubbed her hands together. "I had no idea their wool could be so greasy."

"It's lanolin. It gives you soft skin." He held out his hand. She ran her fingers across his palm. In a heartbeat, his mouth went dry. He inhaled sharply as his heart beat faster.

She must've sensed something, because her gaze locked with his. He wanted more than the brief touch of her fingers. He wanted to hold her hand. To reach out and pull her close. He wanted to learn everything there was to know about this amazing woman.

She quickly turned away. "I'd better get something ready for lunch. I hope cold sandwiches will be okay."

"That will be fine."

"Goot."

He watched her hurry away and wished he had a reason to call her back.

Lunch and the rest of the afternoon passed in an awkward silence. Carl tried to keep his mind on his work, but he was constantly aware of where she was and what she was doing. Her boundless energy began to lag in the late afternoon. He called a halt to the work even though he hadn't finished nearly as many animals as he had hoped to.

He went to clean up while Lizzie returned to the house. An hour later, he came in to find his supper waiting for him. Lizzie was seated in her usual place, but she was fast asleep, slumped over the table with her head pillowed on her arms.

Carefully, so that he wouldn't wake her, he picked up his plate, meaning to take it outside. Instead, he found himself frozen in place watching her sleep.

He studied the wisps of wild red curls that wouldn't be contained beneath her scarf, the high cheekbones of her face, the way her eyebrows arched so beautifully. He had never seen a more lovely woman.

Once, he would have had the right to court her. To drive her home after a Sunday singing or to slip away with her after dark to attend a barn party or simply take a long walk in the woods. Once, but not now.

Such a thing was impossible. He had failed God with his weak faith. He should have died alongside his sister. He should have accepted the fate God willed for him and for one small girl and joined them in Heaven. Instead, his cowardice made him break his covenant with God.

Any future he might imagine with Lizzie was nothing but a wisp of smoke pouring from the barrel of a fired gun. A puff of white mist lost in the wind that could never be called back.

Lizzie squirmed into a more comfortable position and sighed deeply. He had no future with her, but he had this moment to remember all his days.

His food was cold by the time he let himself out the door. Duncan was lying on the porch waiting for him. The dog sat up. "Stay. Guard," Carl told him.

The big dog moved in front of the door and lay down. Knowing Duncan would alert him to any problems, Carl walked down the hill to his cold and dark hut.

Chapter 8

For Lizzie, the following day started out much like the day before, except she ached from head to toe. There wasn't a muscle in her body that didn't hurt.

She wasn't used to such physical labor. She kept house for her uncle and sisters and did all the cooking, canning and most of the laundry. Twice a day she helped with the milking, but she didn't have to wrestle the Holsteins into their stanchions.

Sheep were stubborn, smelly and loud. She had no idea why her grandfather thought so much of them. But he did, and she would help Carl care for them until Joe was able to do so himself. For however long it took.

By midmorning, she was working some of the kinks out of her shoulder when she spotted a wagon turning into the drive. She looked at Carl. "Are you expecting someone?"

He finished clipping the ewe he had between his knees and then straightened to look out the barn door. "No, I'm not expecting anyone. Joe doesn't get visitors."

A buggy turned in behind the wagon. "I hope it's not the bishop's wife." Lizzie had no idea how to prevent the woman from entering Joe's house if she wanted to.

Together, she and Carl walked out of the barn. On the front seat of the wagon, she recognized Adrian Lapp and his son, Kyle. Several young Amish men she didn't know jumped down from the wagon bed behind them.

The buggy pulled in with Katie Sutter and Sally Yoder on the front seat. They got out and began pulling large picnic hampers from the back.

Lizzie glanced at Carl. He just shrugged. "It looks like we've got some help."

Adrian and his young men approached them. Adrian said, "I've heard that your animals don't spit when you shear them. I thought I would come see this wonder for myself."

He gestured to a gray-haired man in blue jeans and a plaid shirt behind him. "This is Sheldon Kent. He's not Amish, but he says he knows how to get the wool off a sheep."

The man held up a pair of hand shears identical to the ones Carl used. "It's been a few years, but I reckon I still know my way around a fat woolly," he said in a thick Scottish brogue.

Carl broke into a wide smile. "Fat woollies I have aplenty. This way and thanks for the help."

Lizzie turned to Katie and Sally. "How did you know?"

"Faith Lapp told Bishop Zook about Joe's accident. He knew Sheldon Kent from over by Berlin and went to see if he could help shear. It's a blessing that Sheldon was free and could come. The bishop stopped by to tell us yesterday about his plan. We found a few more volunteers to help and here we are. Where would you like this food?"

"In the house, I guess. Is the bishop's wife coming?"

"Not today. Why?" Katie asked slowly.

"For some reason, Grandfather doesn't want her in the house."

Katie and Sally looked at each other and burst out laughing.

"What's so funny?" Lizzie asked.

Katie struggled to control her giggles. "Esther told my mother-in-law that she wouldn't set foot on Woolly Joe's property."

"The bishop's wife said that? I wonder what it's all about." Lizzie knew her grandfather wouldn't explain even if she asked him.

"We may never know. Grab that box off the backseat, Lizzie. We'd best get ready to feed our men." Katie marched ahead into the house.

Sally waited until Lizzie extracted the box and then walked beside her to the house. "Tell me, have you found out anything about your grandfather's hired man?"

Lizzie looked at her sharply. "What do you mean?"

"He is something of a mystery around these parts. No one knows where he came from. He rarely speaks to anyone except the children. Some people think he's ex-Amish. Some people say he's a weird Englisch fellow that's soft in the head."

Lizzie bristled. "Carl is not soft in the head, but he was raised Amish."

"I'm sorry. I didn't mean to insult your friend."

"We're not friends. He lives and works here, that's all. He works hard, and he's a good shepherd. He cares about the sheep. My grandfather respects Carl's privacy and I do, too."

"You are right to do so. I was being nosy. Forgive me."

Lizzie realized she had spoken too harshly. "There's nothing to forgive. I'm tired and short-tempered today and worried about my grandfather."

Sally smiled. "Of course. I think a hot cup of tea is called for. Come in and rest."

With so much help, the shearing was finished by the end of the day. Carl thanked the men who had come. Joe would be happy to learn the job had been finished in record time. When the wagon finally rolled out of the yard in the late afternoon, Carl looked at Duncan sitting beside him. "This will give us a few more days to get ready for the lambing."

He knew how to do that, but he didn't know how to take care of a convalescing patient with a broken hip. Or a young woman who was so determined to make a place for her family.

Would Lizzie stay and help take care of her cantankerous grandfather, or would she move to the Sutters' farm as she had planned? It was something they should talk over. Perhaps now Joe could be convinced that he needed his granddaughters to come stay with him. Lizzie would be thrilled if they could all stay together.

Carl went to his hut and changed out of his grimy work clothes. Wrapping them and a few other items in his sheets, he carried them all to the back porch. It was his intention to do his own laundry, but Lizzie heard him filling the machine with water and came outside.

"I can do those for you, Carl."

"I can manage."

She took the box of laundry soap out of his hand. "You have been working all day, while I wasn't allowed to do anything harder than brew a pot of coffee."

"You've been working nonstop since you arrived. I think you deserve a few hours of rest."

"And now I've had them. Supper will be ready in a little while. I'm going to walk over to the telephone booth and call the hospital to check on my grandfather."

While the Amish did not allow telephones in their homes, Carl knew that Joe's congregation allowed a shared telephone that was located centrally to several farms. "I'll walk over with you when you go."

Was he being too bold? Hadn't he convinced himself last night that he didn't deserve her interest? Even so, he held his breath and waited for her answer.

She smiled and nodded. "I would be glad of the company. *Danki.*"

He grinned, giddy with relief. "I'm anxious to hear how he is doing, too."

The phone booth was a half mile from the end of the lane. To Carl's knowledge, Joe had never used it.

Carl had used it only once. A year ago, he had called the Englisch bakery where his sister Jenna worked to let her know that he was okay. He knew she would relay his message to their parents. Jenna begged him to come home, but he couldn't face his family yet. Not until he believed he had earned God's forgiveness. In a moment of weakness, he gave Jenna his address.

She had been writing to him every week since that day. He had read the first two without answering them, but he couldn't bear to read them after that. It was too great a reminder of his shame and his loss.

He thought a lot about that phone call as he walked beside Lizzie. He missed his family just as Lizzie missed hers. Although he knew he might never see his home again, he wanted Lizzie to have the people she loved around her.

It had been a long time since he'd given a thought to what someone else needed. He said, "The doctor told Joe that he was going to need extra help when he came home."

"I've been thinking about that. I reckon I should tell Katie Sutter that I won't be able to work for her and that she should look for someone else."

"Actually, I was thinking that your sisters might be able to come help care for him."

She shook her head. "They don't have the money to get here. I sent all that I have, but it is only enough for one of them. I don't know if Clara will come without Greta and Betsy."

"Have you written to them about their grandfather?"

"I haven't. I don't know how to explain what a mess I've made of things here."

"Perhaps knowing that you need help taking care of him will convince Clara to come."

"I hadn't thought of that. You may be right."

"It happens sometimes."

She gave him a puzzled look. "What happens sometimes?"

"Sometimes it happens that I'm right. I was making a joke, Lizzie."

She pressed her hand to her mouth and giggled. It was the cutest sound he'd ever heard. They arrived at the phone booth all too soon for him.

He waited outside the door until she came out. "How is he?"

"The nurse said he is doing very well except for a small fever. She said he is cranky, and he's been complaining about the food."

"That doesn't surprise me. If he wasn't complaining about something, I'd be really worried."

"She said to expect him to stay there for a week or so depending on how well he does with his physical therapy."

"I almost wish they would keep him longer."

"Why?"

"Once the lambing season starts, I'm not going to have time to look after him. Knowing Joe, he's going to want to be out helping."

She sighed. "We must be thankful that he is recovering. If he allows me to stay, I will take care of him while you take care of the lambs."

"I hate to see you give up a paying job that means so much to you."

"It's my family that means a lot to me. Grandfather

is part of my family even if he doesn't want to be. I'll stay until he's fit, and then I will find a job. Clara's wedding isn't until the first week of May. I have time yet to earn the money my sisters will need to join me."

"Knowing that you'll stay until Joe is mended takes a load off my mind."

She blushed and smiled sweetly. "I'm glad."

"What else did the nurse say?"

She updated Carl on what was said as they walked home. He tried to slow the pace to make the trip last longer, but Lizzie wasn't one to drag her feet. Was her haste because of the work she had yet to finish, or was it his presence that she was eager to escape?

He couldn't blame her if that was true. He didn't belong in the company of an Amish maid. Most Amish people would frown on even this harmless activity because of his exclusion from their faith. Those who didn't know that he had been placed in the Bann could criticize Lizzie for spending time alone with an outsider. Either way, he was putting Lizzie's reputation at risk. Today, the community had rallied around her. He wanted it to stay that way. The less time he spent with her, the better it would be for her.

He stopped walking. "I've got a ram out in the upper pasture that I need to check on. I noticed an abscess on his back when I sheared him."

She shot him a perplexed look. "But it's almost suppertime. Can't it wait until tomorrow?"

"I'm not hungry. Go ahead and eat without me. Don't look for me tomorrow, either. I've got a lot of lambing pens to get set up."

"You have to eat, Carl."

"I've got food at my place. It's not as good as your cooking, but I'll make do."

"I'm not going to let you go a whole day without a hot meal and that's that."

"Okay, you can feed me supper tomorrow." He started backing away.

"Are you sure?" She sounded reluctant to see him go.

That was all the more reason for him to leave, but he couldn't believe how difficult it was to walk away. "I'm sure. Have a good night, Lizzie."

"*Guten nacht,* Carl."

He stopped a few feet away from her and turned back. "My place is only a quarter of a mile away if you need something."

She smiled softly. "I know."

"Right." He gestured toward the pasture. "I should get going."

"Be careful around those rams. I have no idea how to run a sheep farm."

If anyone could do it, she could. "I don't think it would take you long to learn."

Although Lizzie's thoughts and prayers frequently turned to her grandfather and to her sisters while she worked the next day, she was amazed at how often they strayed to Carl. A dozen times during the morning, she stopped what she was doing to look out the window in the hopes of catching a glimpse of him. Each time, she was disappointed.

Was he avoiding her, or did he really have so much work to do that he couldn't even stop in for a cup of coffee? She kept a pot warm on the stove just in case. In the early afternoon, she poured herself a cup, took one sip, grimaced and poured the rest down the drain. It was strong enough to float a horseshoe. She was glad that Carl hadn't had a chance to sample it.

She finally caught a glimpse of him and Duncan walking across the pasture toward his hut around six o'clock. She realized if she made another trip to the phone booth that their paths would pass close to each other in front of his home. That way, she could pretend she hadn't set out to meet him deliberately.

Quickly, she changed her stained apron for a clean one. She patted any stray hairs into place and went out the door, but she was doomed to disappointment. She didn't meet Carl or Duncan on her walk. Had Carl seen her coming his way and changed directions?

She continued along the path feeling let down and more disappointed than she should have been. When had she come to depend so heavily upon Carl's presence to cheer her?

Today, like yesterday, the sun shone brightly in the sky. The same flowers bloomed in the grass along the roadside and the trees pushed the same green leaves open. A lark sang a happy song from the fence off to one side. The sights, sounds and the smells of spring were still all around her, but they seemed muted without Carl's companionship.

The realization troubled her.

As soon as her grandfather was able to live on his own again, she would have to leave. She had grown far too fond of Carl in the short time that she'd known him. She couldn't delude herself into thinking otherwise. Wasn't she out here hoping that he would join her? Such feelings were a recipe for disaster, for both of them.

When she reached the phone booth, her call to the hospital only added to her worries. The nurse she spoke to seemed reluctant to share much information. She did relay the fact that Joe still had a fever and that he was undergoing more tests.

On the way back to the farmhouse, Lizzie picked up the mail. It was too soon to expect an answer from Mary, but Lizzie was disappointed anyway when there wasn't anything for her.

Her grandfather's newspaper was there. She wondered if the hospital would supply him with a copy. Tomorrow, when she called again, she would ask. She thumbed through the rest of the mail. There were a few pieces addressed to her grandfather and a letter for Carl that caught her attention.

She studied it briefly. Was it from the same person that had written to him last week? She hadn't paid attention to the previous letter, so she had no way of knowing. The return address on the one she held was Reedville, Pennsylvania. Was that where he was from? The sender's name was Jenna King.

A sister or his mother? A wife? The block printed letters of the address had a childlike quality. His child perhaps? He could be married with a half dozen *kinder* for all she knew. It was an unsettling thought. The envelope in her hand sparked far more questions than answers about the man. She was curious to see what Carl would do with this letter.

She didn't see him until she rang the bell for supper that evening. He came in and washed up without looking at her. Was he still upset with her for causing Joe's accident? She couldn't think of anything else she had done to make him avoid her.

Maybe he sensed her interest and wanted to stem it. She blushed at the thought.

"Have you heard anything about Joe?" he asked.

"I called the hospital again. They told me he was running a fever. I got the feeling the nurse wasn't telling me everything."

He leaned a hip against the counter as he dried his hands. "You think Joe is worse than they are letting on?"

"I don't know what to think."

"What did the nurse say?"

"That he is still running a fever and they are doing more tests."

"Maybe I should go see him."

"Would you? That would be wunderbar."

"If it will ease your mind, I'll see if I can get a ride with Samuel Carter tomorrow. He's a local English fellow who uses his van to drive Amish folks when they need to travel farther than a buggy can go."

She bit her lower lip, then said, "You must not do it as a favor to me."

"Right. No favors. Okay. It will ease *my* mind to see how he's doing firsthand."

"Goot." The small distinction seemed silly, but it relieved her conscience.

The sound of a car pulling up outside and Duncan's mad barking made them both glance outside. "Who is that?" she asked.

"I have no idea."

Lizzie opened the door and saw Dr. Zook get out of a dark blue car. He wasn't dressed in his white coat this evening. He was wearing a light gray sweater and a pair of faded blue jeans.

He nodded to her. "Good evening, Miss Barkman. I thought you might like an update on Joe's condition."

Lizzie stepped back from the door. "Of course. We were just talking about him. Please come in. Can I get you a cup of coffee? We were about to have supper. You are welcome to join us. Several of the local women have left desserts with us. I understand that Nettie Imhoff's peach pie is quite good."

"It is. I've had it on several occasions, but I don't need anything tonight, thank you. I can only stay for a few minutes. I wanted to let you know that your grandfather isn't getting along as well as I had hoped. Unfortunately, there have been some complications."

Lizzie pressed a hand to her heart as fear made it thud painfully. "What type of complications?"

"His blood work shows that he has an infection. We believe it's in the surgical site."

"Is it serious?" Carl asked from the kitchen.

The doctor turned to include Carl in the conversation. "It can be, but at this point it's not life-threatening. It is, however, something we need to keep a close eye on. What this means is that Joe will have to remain in the hospital for at least another week of IV antibiotics. I'm sorry. I know this is not what you want to hear."

No, Lizzie had been hoping to hear that Joe would be home soon and up and around in no time.

Carl held out his hand to the doctor. "We appreciate you stopping by in person to give us the news."

"It was on my way home from making rounds at the hospital. We'll let you know if there's any change in his condition. I also wanted to visit with you about his care when he does get to come home. He's not going to be able to live alone for at least six weeks."

"Six weeks?" Her heart sank at the news. It was only six weeks until Clara's wedding. She wouldn't be able to get a job and make enough to pay Greta and Betsy's way here.

"Will that be a problem?" Dr. Zook asked.

Lizzie raised her chin. "*Nee*, I'll be here for as long as he needs me."

"And I'll be close by," Carl added.

"I know the Amish take care of one another, but I've also heard that Joe is something of a recluse. The nurses at the hospital tell me he's turned away all his visitors, including the bishop."

"He can be cantankerous," Carl admitted.

"That's what worries me. I don't want him trying to do things by himself too soon."

"I'll see that he behaves. He'll listen to me." Carl's tone reassured Lizzie and the young doctor.

"Good. Joe's caseworker will come to visit with you about his needs before he comes home. If you have any questions, feel free to stop by my office or give me a call." With that, the young doctor nodded goodbye and went out the door.

Lizzie pressed a hand to her forehead. "Daadi has to be all right. I've only just gotten to know him again. I can't bear the thought of losing him."

Carl looked worried, too, but he said, "Joe is a tough old goat. He's going to be fine. We have to believe that."

He was trying to reassure her and she was grateful for his effort. "You're right. I'm borrowing trouble to worry about something I can't change. All things are in God's hands."

"I'm sorry that I can't do more to ease your worries." His tone was soft and filled with regret.

"I appreciate that." Lizzie looked away from the sympathy in his eyes. It was becoming much too easy to accept his kindness when she knew she shouldn't.

She indicated the packet of mail on the table. "Would you go through this and see what needs to be taken to Joe? There's a letter for you, too."

"Thanks." He picked up the bundle and leafed through it. He separated one letter, carried it to the stove and dropped it into the fire. She knew without asking that it was the one addressed to him.

It was none of her business what Carl did with his correspondences, but she was still shocked. Her curiosity about him rose tenfold. Who was the woman who wrote to him, and why did he burn her letters?

Chapter 9

After a hectic week, Lizzie expected a day of rest on Sunday, since there was no church to attend. Amish congregations gathered for worship every other week. The "off" Sunday, when there was no preaching service, was reserved for quiet reflection, visiting and family time.

At home, it would have been the day for reading quietly or perhaps going to visit a friend or neighbor. Because she and her sisters didn't have the extended family so common among Amish communities, they seldom visited anyone but a few close neighbors. Her uncle wasn't a popular man. It was rare that anyone came to visit them.

The morning passed much as she expected, but a little before noon, Elam and Katie Sutter drove in.

Sally Yoder sat in the back holding Jeremiah while Rachel leaned out the window with wide round eyes.

Glad for the distraction that would prevent her constant worry about her sisters, Lizzie went out to greet them. Three people emerged from the back of the buggy. As she was being introduced to Levi and Sarah Beachy and Naomi's daughter, Emma Troyer, several more buggies turned into the lane. Lizzie looked around for Carl, but he remained out of sight. The second buggy held the Lapp family, and the last vehicle belonged to a couple she hadn't met. Faith introduced them to her as Joann and Roman Weaver.

Joann, a plain woman with amazing green eyes, said, "I think I remember you. Didn't you go fishing with your grandfather when you were little?"

"Now that you mention it, I do remember going to a lake with him, but I remember throwing rocks into the water, not fishing. Are you the little girl who could skip stones so well?"

Joann laughed. "I don't know that I did it well, but I did it often, until I learned that it scared the fish away. I'm so happy to see you again. I feel like I have discovered a long-lost friend."

Her husband wore a sling on his left arm. "I believe you have. Just remember, I'm still your number-one fishing buddy."

"Like I could forget that." The smile the couple shared made Lizzie wish that someone would smile at her that way.

It was a silly thought. She never expected to be courted. She never wanted to be courted. So why would she long for such closeness with any man?

"Newlyweds," Sally whispered in Lizzie's ear as she walked past. "They only have eyes for each other."

The children ran past her and greeted Duncan. Then they immediately went down to the barn to look at the sheep. The next time Lizzie glanced their way, she saw Carl was with them. He was holding Rachel and letting her pet one of the ewes. She squealed each time she touched the animal's soft wool, making Carl laugh at her antics. Joann and Roman went down to visit with Carl. Were they friends of his? Did they know his history?

Sally bounced down the steps of the porch and stopped beside Lizzie. "Good, those two have gone to make sheep's eyes at the sheep instead of at each other. For two people who couldn't stand one another just a year ago, they certainly get along well now."

Lizzie watched Carl explaining something to Joann and wondered if there was someone in his past that he loved, or was loved by in return. Were the letters he burned from his mother or a sister? Or were they from a wife that he'd left behind? How many letters had he ignored? More important, why?

Katie soon claimed her attention, and Lizzie went inside to discover a lunch had been laid on her table with enough food to feed an army.

She passed an amazing day with her new friends. They laughed and told stories about each other and about her grandfather. They made Lizzie feel as if she had always been a part of their circle of friends.

Their closeness reminded her of her sisters. Katie was a lot like Clara. They were both quiet, deep think-ers. Greta, with her love of animals, would find a kindred spirit in Faith. Sally was only a little older than Betsy, but Lizzie could imagine them as friends and confidantes, boldly speaking their minds and giving the local boys a heartache or two.

If only she could get her sisters to Hope Springs, life would be so much better for all of them.

The afternoon passed quickly, and when the last of her visitors had gone, Lizzie walked out onto the porch and took a seat on one of the two green metal chairs along the side of the house. From the scuff marks in the railing's white paint, she suspected that both Carl and her grandfather spent evenings here with their feet propped up.

She had been sitting only a few minutes when she saw Carl leave the barn. He glanced in her direction. She raised a hand and waved. He hesitated, as if torn between coming to the house or going to his hut. Duncan had no difficulty making a decision. He loped across the yard and up the steps to sit between the chairs. Lizzie reached down to pet him. He licked her hand in doggy gratitude.

When she looked up, Carl was coming her way. He silently climbed the steps and took a seat. She almost giggled when he tipped his chair back and propped his feet on the rail in front of him. "You've had a busy day."

"I have been overwhelmed with visitors, that's true. You will be amazed at the amount of food that is on the table. They insisted on leaving everything. I may not have to cook for a month."

"That would be a shame. You're a mighty good cook."

She blushed at the compliment. "It seems that Grandfather has many friends. I had no idea. Do they visit often?"

"Not since I have been staying here, and that's almost four years now. Naomi Wadler comes a few times a year, but she never stays long. She keeps Joe's larder stocked with jars of garden produce, jam and fruit from her orchard and puts up the stuff he grows, too."

"Really? I wonder why. Are they related?" It was common practice for Amish families to care for their elders.

"Not that I know. I always thought she was sweet on him. I'm glad she does it or we would end up eating nothing but muttonchops and crackers."

"Sweet on my grandfather? Are you serious? He's old!"

Carl chuckled. "He may be old, but he can keep out of her way fast enough. She may be chasing, but he isn't ready to be caught."

"Naomi wasn't here today, but I met her daughter, Emma. I like her very much."

"I've never met her, but if she is anything like her mother, she is a formidable woman."

"I noticed you talking to Joann and Roman Weaver. Are they friends?"

"Don't you mean do they know I have been shunned?"

"*Nee,* I meant no such thing." Maybe she had been wondering that, but she wouldn't admit it now.

"Joann and Roman like to go fishing at Joe's lake. I speak to them now and again. A few times, they have left their catch with us. Joann is something of a bookworm. She was telling me today that llamas make good guard animals for sheep, plus, you can sell their fleece."

"Do they spit?"

He chuckled. "Worse than an alpaca."

"Let's stick with Duncan. He never spits." The dog wagged his tail at the mention of his name. She reached down and stroked his head.

"Is this what the off Sundays are like where you come from?" Carl asked.

"*Nee.* We seldom have visitors. Uncle Morris doesn't like it when our friends come over. He complains that we can't afford to feed everyone. What about you? What were Sunday afternoons like when you were growing up?"

"A lot like this. My mother has twelve brothers and sisters, and my father has five, so we were always inundated with cousins, aunts and uncles or we were traveling to visit them."

"You must miss that."

"Sometimes, but I like my privacy." He shot her a pointed look.

She ignored it. "Do you keep in contact with your family?"

"No."

"How sad. I thought perhaps the letters that came for you are from someone in your family. I saw the name on the return address was Jenna King. I know it's not my business…"

"You're right. It's not," he said abruptly.

She took offense at his attitude. "If you intend to be rude, I'm going inside."

He quickly stretched his hand toward her. "No, wait. Don't go yet. I'm sorry. It's just that I don't like to talk about my past."

"Talking helps, Carl."

"It can't change what has happened."

"No, but it can show us that we aren't alone in our troubles."

"In case you haven't noticed, Lizzie, I like being alone."

"In case *you* haven't noticed, Carl King, *you* don't." She rose and stomped into the house.

Duncan whined, sensing the tension that Carl tried hard to control. Lizzie enjoyed needling him. He reached out and ran his hand over the dog's silky head. "We used to like being alone, didn't we?"

Until Lizzie showed up and constantly made him aware of how barren his life was. Working, eating, sleeping and watching over the sheep had been satisfying enough for him until a week and a half ago. How could such a little slip of a woman turn things topsy-turvy in a matter of days?

Maybe he was drawn to her because she reminded him so much of Sophia. Like his youngest sister, Lizzie's enthusiasm sometimes outweighed her common sense. Still, he liked that about her. She saw what she wanted, and she worked to achieve it. But no matter how hard she worked at prying into his past, she was going to find herself up against a dead end. His crime was his own. He wouldn't share the story of how he fell so far from grace. He couldn't bear to see the look on Lizzie's face if she found out he had murdered someone.

The door opened and Lizzie came outside again. Her normally sweet expression was cold. She thrust a foil-wrapped plate into his hands. "Enjoy your supper...alone. I won't be cooking tonight."

She turned on her heel and marched back into the house. She didn't quite slam the door, but she shut it with conviction.

Duncan lifted his nose toward the plate. Carl held it out of his reach. "Oh, no, you don't." He raised his voice and shouted, "This is mine, Duncan, and I'm going to enjoy it alone!"

Somewhere in the house, a door slammed. Feeling slightly gratified at having had the last word, he walked down the hill toward his hut. At the door, he paused. As much as he hated to admit it, Lizzie was right.

There was a wooden chair outside his front door. He grabbed it and carried it toward the small creek that meandered through the pasture. He stopped beside an old stump that he could use for a table. From this vantage point, he could see the house up on the hill. Somehow, just knowing she was up there was a comfort.

He settled down to snack on cold fried chicken, carrot sticks and biscuits that were flaky and good, but they didn't measure up to Lizzie's. Not by a long shot.

The next day began with a flurry of work. Knowing that her grandfather would be unable to put in his garden or do such chores for several weeks, Lizzie attacked his garden plot with a vengeance. The weather had turned cold again. The taste of spring had been just that, a taste. March wasn't going to go out like a lamb.

It was nearly noon when she noticed Carl standing outside the fence watching her. Finally, she couldn't bear his stoic silence any longer. She thrust her spade into the ground. "What are you staring at?"

"I have some composted manure and straw I need to get rid of. Shall I haul it over here? I don't want to do you any favors."

"Shall I go in the house so you can do it alone?"

He struggled to keep a grin off his face and lost. "I reckon I deserved that. I'm sorry I was cross with you yesterday."

"And I am sorry for being a nosy busybody. Your life is your own, Carl. It was wrong of me to pry. Can we be friends again? I really dislike eating alone."

"So do I, but can we be friends?"

She smiled. "I don't see why not. You are invaluable to my grandfather, and I wasn't joking when I said I didn't know how to run a sheep farm."

"You have been a good learner. Next year, you'll be able to wrestle the sheep to me with barely a thought. I may even teach you how to use the shears." He opened the garden gate and carried in a spade. He took a spot beside her and began to turn over the dirt.

"Next year. I hadn't thought that far ahead. I've been so focused on getting my sisters here. Will I even be here a year from now? So much depends on my family."

"Have you heard anything from them?"

Lizzie shook her head. "I only sent them my letter

a week ago. I should hear something soon. I have another letter that I need to mail today. I had to explain how my foolishness has landed our grandfather in the hospital. I want them to be prepared for what they will find when they arrive."

"Did you tell them about me?"

"Only that you live on the property and you take care of the sheep."

He stopped digging to look at her. "Nothing else?"

"Nothing else."

He nodded and began to spade up the soil again. Working together, they finished half of the garden before Lizzie called a halt to the work. "I want to get my letter to the mailbox before the mail carrier goes by. We can finish the rest tomorrow."

Carl stepped on his spade, driving it deep into the earth. "I thought I would call the hospital and see how Joe is today."

"Let me get my letter and I'll walk with you part of the way. That is, if you don't mind?"

He chuckled. "I don't mind. Is there any coffee left from this morning?"

"I have tried keeping some on the back of the stove, but it just gets bitter. It won't take me long to make a fresh pot. You must tell me what vegetables Grandfather will want planted this spring."

"He's fond of kale and radishes, I know that. He likes cucumbers and the squash casserole Naomi brings over in the summer."

"I'll check with her for the recipe and see what variety of squash she uses." Lizzie walked through the garden gate ahead of Carl, happy to be on good terms once more.

The day became a pattern for the rest of the week. Over a cup of coffee in the midmorning, they discussed what work needed to be done and made plans to get as much done as they could before the lambs began to drop. Carl finished building the sheep pens while Lizzie continued to work on the garden until rainy weather put a stop to her outdoor activity. In the late afternoon or early evening, they would walk together to the phone booth. Normally, Lizzie was the one who spoke to the nurses and relayed the information to Carl. Joe refused to take phone calls in his room. It was permitted by their church in such circumstances, but the hospital staff respected his wishes.

As the days passed, Lizzie began to worry that she hadn't heard from Mary or from any of her sisters. It was likely that Uncle Morris had forbidden them to contact her, but she hoped and prayed they would find a way. It was during those worry-filled times that Lizzie came to rely on Carl's words of reassurance.

It was strange that a man who had been shunned by others could be such a comfort to her. More than ever, she wanted to help him find his way back to the community that meant so much to each of them.

One evening, after hearing from the nurses at the hospital that Joe was doing better, Lizzie and Carl stopped at the mailbox on the way back to the house as had become their habit. Lizzie opened the front panel and pulled out the mail. Excitement sent her pulse racing when she saw an envelope with her name on it. She clutched it to her chest. "Finally! It's a letter from my friend Mary. Please, Lord, I hope she tells me that Clara is coming."

She handed Carl the rest of the mail and quickly tore open her letter. As she read, her excitement turned to shock.

She felt Carl's hand on her shoulder as her knees threatened to buckle. "Lizzie, what's wrong?"

She managed to focus on his face. "Mary writes that Uncle Morris was furious at my running away. He and Rufus have decided to push the wedding up. The banns were read at last Sunday's church service. The wedding will take place two weeks from today." Lizzie pressed a hand to her cheek.

"I'm so sorry. I don't know what to say."

Tears welled up in her eyes and trickled down her cheeks unheeded. He pulled his hand away. She missed his comforting touch immediately.

"What does Mary say about the money you sent? Clara may decide to come now that she knows how little time is left."

"She can't. Mary hasn't been able to see them or get my letters to them. Uncle Morris has forbidden her to visit. They don't know where I am or that I haven't abandoned them. Two weeks! I can't even return for the wedding. I sent all the money I had to help Clara leave. It was all for nothing. For nothing!"

She fled down the lane and rushed into the house, leaving Carl standing alone behind her.

Lizzie went through the motions of fixing a meal, cleaning the house and readying the garden for planting. The work kept her busy, but it couldn't take her mind off the fate of her sisters. She felt marooned in the ramshackle house with no hope of seeing them again. Even Carl's softly spoken words of reassurance and quiet strength couldn't lift her spirits.

She often felt his eyes on her. She tried to put on a brave front, but inside she was miserable. When she went to bed at night, she prayed fervently for the Lord's intervention and for the courage to accept her failure as His will.

Late one afternoon, she came in from feeding the chickens and saw an envelope on the kitchen table. She picked it up. Inside was several hundred dollars. For an instant, she thought her prayers had been answered, then she realized who had left the money.

It was the answer to her prayers, but it was one she couldn't accept.

Her hands trembled as she placed the envelope back on the table and turned away.

Carl was standing outside the screen door watching her. She realized in that moment how much she had come to care for him.

"You have not taken it from my hand," he said quietly.

"But I know it's from you."

"Your grandfather would say this way is acceptable."

"It is a wonderful gesture, but I can't take your money, Carl."

He pulled open the door and came in. "Tell me how to make it acceptable to you and I'll do it. It's all I have. Please, take it."

"I could not accept such a favor."

"Would you accept it from me if I had not been shunned?"

"But by your own admission you have been. I must hold true to the vows I spoke before God." Her grandfather once said shunning was a difficult and painful thing. Until this moment, she hadn't realized how right he was.

Carl's shoulders slumped in defeat. "You won't accept it even if it means never seeing your sisters again?"

"Even if it means that."

"You live your faith, Lizzie Barkman. God will surely smile on you."

"Just as He smiles on all His children," she said quietly.

Carl stared at the floor. "I could not hold true to my faith as you do. He has turned His face away from me."

She moved to stand in front of him. "That isn't true, Carl. God never turns away from us. It is we who turn away from Him. We give in to doubt and fear, but He knows our hearts. He knows we need His love. Forgiveness and acceptance are ours for the asking."

He shook his head. "I have asked for forgiveness many times, but I have not received it. I don't know that I ever shall."

"If anyone knows you, they must surely see your goodness. Your desire to help me means more than I can say. I know now what my grandfather sees in you. You have such a generous heart."

He raised his eyes and stared at her for a long moment. "And you are a strong, brave woman."

"Not at the moment." She picked up the envelope and held it out to him. He took it from her and left the house. She sat down at the table and wept.

Chapter 10

Lizzie stood by the mailbox waiting for the letter carrier to reach her. She spotted the white van stopped at a farm down the road and knew he would come her way next.

She couldn't let go of the hope that Mary would write and tell her something had changed. It had to change. Clara couldn't marry Rufus. It was unthinkable.

When the van pulled up beside her, she waited impatiently as the man in the gray uniform behind the wheel sorted through the stack in his hand. "Looks like only one today."

He held it toward her. "I haven't seen Joe for a couple of weeks. I hope he's okay."

She glanced at the letter and saw it was addressed

to Carl. She put it in her pocket. "My grandfather is in the hospital with a broken hip."

"Man, that's tough. I'm sorry to hear that. My son and I were planning to stop in and buy a club lamb from him later this spring. Should we rethink that?"

"I'm afraid I don't know what a club lamb is, but Carl King is here. I'm sure he can help you."

"Great. A club lamb is one that's raised by a kid in 4-H or FFA, Future Farmers of America. Carl was the one who helped my son choose a lamb last year. It took second place at the county fair. My boy is hoping for first place this year."

"I'm sure Carl will be happy to help you again."

"He's really good with kids. My son learned more about how to take care of his lamb from Carl than he did from his 4-H leader. Well, give Joe my best." He nodded and drove away.

Lizzie started toward the phone booth next. Was it only two days ago that she strolled along this path with Carl at her side? It seemed as if a century had passed since then. So much had happened. So much had changed. Her mad scramble to get her sisters to Hope Springs had come to a painful stop.

As had her growing friendship with Carl.

Her refusal of his gift put his shunning front and center between them. As it should have been all along, she acknowledged.

Leaving the security and close-knit circle of her family had put her adrift in a sea of change. Nothing was as she imagined it would be. Nothing worked out as she had hoped. Carl's quiet, reserved strength had offered her shelter from the storm of events taking place around her. It was no wonder she grew to cherish his friendship so quickly.

He was a good man. She didn't doubt that, but he no longer believed as she did and that was unacceptable. He knew it, because he had stopped coming by the house. She had seen him out and about on the farm, but he didn't come in for coffee in the morning or for lunch, or for supper, for that matter.

In short, he left her alone.

And she missed him terribly.

She reached the phone booth and saw Duncan lying outside it. Her traitorous heart gave a happy leap before she could put her hard-won resolve into place. A few moments later, Carl emerged. He stopped short at the sight of her.

"*Gutenowed,* Carl." She was pleased that her voice sounded composed with just the right touch of reserve.

"Good evening." He looked haggard and worn, as if he hadn't been sleeping well.

"Were you checking on Joe?" she asked.

He hitched his thumb over his shoulder toward the phone. "Yes. He's doing much better today. He's been up walking with a walker. There's no sign of fever. Looks like the antibiotics have done the trick."

"That's wonderful news."

He shifted uncomfortably. "It is. He should be home in a week. Look, I've got to go. Are you doing okay?"

"I'm fine, and you?"

"I'm managing. Have a nice night." He tipped his hat and walked past her.

She watched him until he disappeared around a bend in the path that led to his hut. He never looked back. She wanted to call out to him, but she couldn't think of a reason to do so. She didn't want him to know how much she missed having him around.

Should she have taken the money he offered? It would have been enough, more than enough. She could have taken it, confessed later to the bishop and accepted his forgiveness. There were ways around the rules, but they weren't just rules to her. They were the glue that bound her Christian community together against the forces that would break it down, both from the outside and from within.

Because of the Ordnung, every Amish man and woman knew what was expected of them. They knew their purpose in life. The rules of their society weren't made to be broken or ignored. They were made to guide and to guard against the disruptions of the world that could come between the faithful and God. Accepting the Amish faith came at a great price. It was never done lightly.

She might regret not using Carl's gift, but she knew she had done the right thing.

If only she had her own money or something she could sell, but she owned nothing of value. She had little more than the clothes on her back. Her heart ached as she thought about the life Clara would be forced to live with an abusive husband.

It would be their mother's life all over again.

Lizzie remembered all too well the desperate attempts to keep peace in the house, waiting in agony for the simple spark that would set their father's temper ablaze. He was always sorry afterward, but his repentant behavior never lasted, yet their mother forgave him time and again.

Lizzie shuddered at the memories. Clara deserved better.

Lizzie was lost in her thoughts and didn't realize a buggy had stopped on the roadway until someone called her name. Sally Yoder waved and beckoned Lizzie to her side. Lizzie didn't recognize the woman seated beside her. She wore dark glasses and looked to be several years older than Sally.

"I'm so glad we ran into you. We were just on our way to a quilting bee at my cousin's house. Have you met Rebecca yet?" Sally asked.

Lizzie shook her head. "I don't believe so."

The woman in the dark glasses leaned around Sally. "Hi, I'm Rebecca Troyer. It's a pleasure to meet you, Lizzie. Everyone has been talking about the sudden appearance of Woolly Joe's relative. Almost no one knew he had a family. How is he doing?"

"He's better. He may be home in a week."

Sally smiled in relief. "That's wonderful news. The reason I wanted to see you was to ask if you would like to ride with my family to the church service on Sunday."

"That's very thoughtful of you, Sally. That would be great as long as it's not out of your way."

"Not at all. We will go right past your lane. How are you doing living by yourself out here?"

"It's very quiet, but there's no one to interrupt my work during the day. Grandfather's house is getting the scrubbing it deserves. I found some half-empty paint cans on the back porch, so I plan to spruce up the kitchen."

"That sounds like a monumental task. Are you free this afternoon? Would you like to come to the quilting bee with us? We are making a quilt for my aunt's fiftieth birthday."

"We would love to have you join us," Rebecca added.

"I'm afraid I have limited skill with a needle. Rebecca, did I see one of your quilts for sale at the inn in Hope Springs?"

"Yes, my Lone Star quilt. Naomi sold it yesterday. I'm always amazed when someone buys one."

"You shouldn't be," Sally said. "You have a wonderful talent. People recognize the value of your work. We should get going. Lizzie, we'll pick you up at eight o'clock on Sunday morning."

"I look forward to it." Lizzie waved as they drove away, but her mind was already reeling. She did own something of value. Something of enormous value to her, but was it valuable enough to buy one-way bus tickets for three young women from Indiana to Hope Springs?

She had her mother's beautiful wedding-ring quilt.

The very idea of parting with the only thing she had to remember her mother by was painful to contemplate. What if she sold it and her sisters still didn't come? Then she would have less than nothing.

She walked the rest of the way home and wrestled with her choices. She could break down and use Carl's money, sell her mother's quilt or accept that she could do nothing. None of them were good choices, but there was only one she could live with.

When she entered the house, she was surprised to see Carl in the kitchen with a box of oatmeal in his hand. He gave her a sheepish look and set it on the counter, like a little boy caught with his hand in the cookie jar. "I'm out of oatmeal. I knew Joe had an extra box. Do you mind if I use it?"

"Is that what you've been living on?"

He stuffed his hands in his front pockets. "I like oatmeal."

"So do I, but not for three meals a day. I'm having chicken and dumplings for supper. There's plenty. You're welcome to have some."

He hesitated, glanced at the oatmeal box, then said, "Thanks. Don't mind if I do."

She turned aside to hide the surge of happiness that engulfed her.

It was just supper. She had to make sure she didn't let her emotions get out of hand again. "I may have discovered a way to earn the money I need to send for my sisters."

"Have you found another job? I can manage without you until Joe comes home."

"*Nee,* I saw Sally Yoder and Rebecca Troyer a little bit ago. They were on their way to a quilting bee. It reminded me that Naomi sells quilts for local women at the inn. She sold one of Rebecca's recently. I have a wedding-ring quilt. I thought I would take it to her and see if she could sell it for me."

She busied herself putting plates on the table and

avoided looking at him. She didn't want him to see how hard her decision had been.

He was a difficult man to fool. "A wedding-ring quilt is often a part of a young woman's hope chest."

"I don't plan to marry, so I have no need of the quilt." She tried to sound offhand but failed miserably.

"I thought marriage was the goal of every young Amish woman."

She turned to face him and wrapped her arms tightly across her middle. "It's not the goal of this Amish girl. Every family needs a maiden aunt to help care for the elderly and to help look after the children. That's the life I want."

"I can't see you living a life without love in it. What has given you a distaste for marriage?"

"I didn't say I have a distaste for it. I just said it's not the life I want." She stuffed her hands in the pockets of her apron and encountered the letter she'd forgotten to give him.

She held it out. "This came for you. I'm sorry I didn't remember sooner."

He took it from her, stared at it for a long moment, then put it in his shirt pocket. At least he didn't toss it in the fire this time. Was that a good sign?

She finished putting supper on the table and they ate in silence. She was afraid he would resume his questions regarding her feelings about marriage, but he didn't. It was fully dark by the time supper was over. Low clouds had moved in, bringing with them a chilly wind.

Carl put on his cowboy hat and coat and took a lantern from a hook by the door. He raised the glass and used a match to light the wick. "I have one ewe out in the hilltop pen that I need to check on. I may have to move her into the barn if she isn't better by morning."

"All right. Is there anything I can do?"

"No, I'm just letting you know so you don't worry if you see a light out in the field. Good night, Lizzie."

"*Guten nacht,* Carl," she said and watched him go out. She carried the dirty plates to the sink and glanced out the window. Carl had stopped at the corral gate. He set his lantern on the fence post and took something out of his pocket. Was he going to read his letter? She held her breath.

He brought the envelope to the top of the lantern chimney. After a few seconds, it caught fire. He held it between his fingers, turning it slightly to keep from being burned until there was only a tiny bit left. He dropped the piece to the ground and watched until the fire consumed all of it. Then he picked up the lantern and walked out into the field.

Lizzie turned away from the window. Her heart ached for Carl and for the woman who wrote him every week. How she must love him to keep writing in the face of his continued silence.

Who was she?

It wasn't his intention to take supper with Lizzie when he went to the house earlier. He really did need the oatmeal. Even a large box didn't last long when a man ate it three times a day. Cereal was his only reason for being in her kitchen.

At least, that was what he told himself as he crossed the dark pasture with a lantern in his hand. He might have been able to convince himself of that fact if he had actually taken the oatmeal with him when he walked out.

It was still sitting on the counter where he'd left it. He was hungry, but not for food. He craved Lizzie's company. He longed for a glimpse of her smile, to see her look upon him with kindness and maybe something more.

Duncan came out of the dark to walk beside him. He glanced at the dog. "I'm a fool, you know."

Duncan's only response was to lope away.

"So much for venting my troubles to a friend." Carl walked on. The dog couldn't help him with his dilemma. It was something he would need to come to grips with on his own. Although he had only known Lizzie Barkman for two weeks, he was falling for her in a big way.

He'd tried staying away from her, but his efforts had been futile. He was drawn to her in a way that had nothing to do with a home-cooked meal and everything to do with the way she made him feel when she smiled. He was drawn to the warmth of her soul.

He hadn't questioned the wisdom of staying in Hope Springs since the day Joe offered him a place to live. Until she showed up, the farm had been a sanctuary for him. A place where he could retreat from the world and the harm he'd caused. Only, now his self-imposed solitude had abruptly lost its appeal.

Lizzie's rejection of his offer to help hurt deeply even though he had half expected what her reaction would be. It was his inability to help that hurt the most.

It kept him awake at night and made him realize how truly separated he had become from those of his faith.

As it turned out, she didn't need his help. She'd found a way without breaking her promise of faith.

He stopped walking and looked back at the house. The light from the kitchen window went out. He watched as the faint light of her lamp passed through the living room and vanished briefly before it reappeared in the window of her second-story bedroom. Would she sleep beneath her wedding-ring quilt tonight? He recognized the distress she tried to hide when she talked about selling it. The decision hadn't been an easy one for her.

He watched her window until the light went out. It was one thing to be alone when it was his choice. It was another thing when he ached with the need to comfort Lizzie but could only watch her struggles from afar.

A new thought occurred to Carl as he stood beneath the brilliant stars strewn across the night sky. Was Lizzie's arrival the way the Lord had chosen to call him back to the faith he'd grown up in?

The next morning, Lizzie finished her chores and left a note for Carl telling him she had gone into town. After that, she climbed the stairs to her small bedroom and stared at the quilt on her bed. It was all she had to remind her of her mother. It was the only thing of value she owned in the world.

She pulled it off the bed and wrapped it around her shoulders. It wasn't the same as being hugged by her mother, but it was as close as she could come until they met again in Heaven.

Tears filled her eyes. She would never feel her mother's arms again, but she could have her sisters' embraces to comfort her. She would have to sell her heirloom to make that happen. In her heart, she knew her mother would understand.

Laying the quilt on the bed again, she folded it carefully. Then she placed it in the box and tied it shut with a length of string. With it tucked firmly under her arm, she walked down the stairs and out the door with a purposeful stride.

It took her over an hour to reach Hope Springs. At the door of the Wadler Inn, she hesitated. She took a moment to gather her courage, then she opened the door and walked in.

Naomi Wadler wasn't behind the desk. An elderly Englisch gentleman greeted Lizzie. "Good morning. How may I help you?"

Lizzie laid her box on the counter. "I have a quilt that I would like Naomi to sell for me."

Naomi appeared in the doorway of a small office behind the counter. "Did I hear my name? Lizzie, how nice to see you again. How is Joe getting along? We have all been praying for him."

"The doctor told us that he developed an infection, but he has improved with the antibiotics they are giving him. He could come home in a week, but he'll still need care and physical therapy."

"I'm glad to hear that. What can I do for you, child?"

"I have a quilt I would like you to sell for me."

"Is this it?" She motioned toward the box.

"*Ja,* it's not a new quilt." Lizzie broke the string and opened the box. She pulled out the quilt and tears stung her eyes again at the sight of the intricately pieced fabrics in muted blues, pinks and soft greens.

"This is lovely. Was it all done by one person? My buyers prefer quilts done by a single hand rather than the ones done at a quilting bee."

"My mother made it by herself. It's very dear to me, but I have no idea what it is worth to someone else."

Naomi's eyes softened. "Are you sure you want to sell it?"

"I don't want to, but I must." Lizzie choked back tears. "It's the only way I can afford to pay for my sisters to move here. It is desperately important that they come. I know my mother would understand and approve. That makes selling it a little easier."

Naomi came around the counter and slipped an arm across Lizzie shoulders. "Surely your grandfather would loan you the money."

"I can't ask him now. He has hospital and doctor bills to pay. His accident was my fault. Besides, you know what a recluse he is. He doesn't want us here."

"Doesn't want you here? You must be mistaken."

"I wish I were. I left my home and traveled here with the hope that my grandfather would take us in. Things have become very…difficult at home. He refuses to help."

"I thought Joe would do anything for Abigail's children."

"I know he is old and set in his ways. A house full

of women would be disruptive for him. I try to understand and forgive him. Can you sell the quilt for me?"

Naomi smiled sadly. "Absolutely. I know someone who might treasure this as you would."

Lizzie stroked the quilt one last time. "*Danki.* I hope it will be useful to them. Do you know how soon I could expect it to sell?"

"A quilt of this quality will be snatched up in no time. Don't worry about that. I'll send my son-in-law out to the farm with the money for you as soon as I can. Take heart, Lizzie. Something good will come of this, you'll see. Our Lord is watching over you and your sisters."

Lizzie nodded. If only she could be sure this was the path He wanted them to travel.

Naomi began folding the quilt, but her sharp eyes were fixed on Lizzie's face. "Tell me, how are you getting along with Carl King? He's an interesting young man, isn't he?"

Chapter 11

Lizzie hoped she wasn't blushing as she looked away from Naomi Wadler's pointed gaze. "I think Carl is doing well enough. Frankly, I don't know what my grandfather would do without him. He's been a tremendous help with all the farmwork. I know that grandfather trusts him to take care of the place and everything on it," she added with a rush, all the while wondering if she had given away too much of her own feelings about Carl.

"I was more interested in how you are getting along with Carl."

"Me? I have barely seen him the past few days. He has a lot to do to get ready for the arrival of our lambs." It wasn't a lie. Carl had been making himself scarce. She didn't need to explain why.

"I've always liked that young man. It is a pity he

no longer follows our Amish ways. I know that Joe is terribly fond of him."

Naomi was one of the few people that had visited the farm with any frequency. Lizzie couldn't pass up the opportunity to see if she knew something about Carl's past. "Grandfather told me a little about how they met. Did he ever tell you?"

It was Naomi's turn to look uncomfortable with the conversation. "Joe and I don't really talk a lot when I visit. Even when Abigail lived at home, Joe wasn't one to make idle chitchat."

"You mentioned you were a friend of my mother's. I would love to hear about her when she was young."

Naomi spoke to the gentleman behind the desk. "Charles, Miss Barkman and I will be in the café if you need me." She handed him the box with Lizzie's quilt. "Put this in my office, please."

Naomi came around the counter and hooked her arm through Lizzie's. "Let me treat you to some of the best shoofly pie you've ever had. My daughter makes it. I can tell you so many funny things about your mother."

Lizzie smiled at her. "What was she like when you knew her?"

"She came to live with us when she was only two and I was fifteen. I became her little mother. Did she ever tell you that I was the one who chipped her front tooth with a baseball bat when we were playing ball? Of course, it was an accident, but I felt so terrible about it every time I saw her smile."

"She never told us that." Lizzie allowed Naomi to

lead her through a set of French doors to the Shoofly Pie Café that adjoined the inn.

Carl peeked in through the front window of the Wadler Inn. He didn't see Lizzie inside. He'd waited more than an hour after she left home to come into town, as well. He was sure she would have come straight here. He didn't want her to know what he had planned, but he was determined to help her reunite with her sisters.

When he stepped inside the lobby, the elderly Englisch gentleman behind the counter smiled brightly. "Welcome to the Wadler Inn. How may I help you?"

"I understand that you have quilts for sale."

"Yes, we certainly do. You will find our area quilters are some of the very finest. Their creations are true works of art, although the Amish do not view them as such. The ones around the fireplace are the only ones we have at the moment, but more come in all the time."

"I'm actually interested in a wedding-ring quilt that was brought in this morning."

The man looked perplexed for a moment and then said, "Let me get Mrs. Wadler to help you. That quilt is not on display."

Carl relaxed. It hadn't been put on display, so it must be still available. The man went into the café next door and returned a few moments later with Naomi. Her eyes widened in surprise. "Why, Carl, what are you doing here? Joe is doing okay, isn't he?"

"As far as I know, Joe is being his cantankerous

self with the hospital staff who get paid to put up with him. I'm here to buy a quilt."

Naomi's eyebrows inched higher. She glanced over her shoulder into the café and then back to him. "Did you have something special in mind?"

"It's a wedding-ring quilt."

She steered him toward the fireplace. She took a seat and he sat across from her on a plush sofa. "Do you know who made it?" she asked.

"I'm not sure who's stitched it, but Lizzie Barkman, Joe's granddaughter, would have been the one who brought it in."

"I see. It's a shame you didn't buy it from her before she left the farm this morning. It would have saved you both a lot of time."

He was going to have to admit why he was here. "I don't want Lizzie to know that I'm the one buying it."

"Why not?"

There was no way he was going to reveal his entire reason, but he said, "I know it means a lot to her, and I don't want her to feel beholden to me."

"I can understand that, but I'm sorry to tell you the quilt is no longer available."

"Do you mean you sold it already?"

She kept her gaze on the door to the café. He wondered if he had interrupted her lunch. "I haven't actually sold it, but I am holding the quilt for someone. If they choose not to purchase it, I will be sure and let you know."

He rubbed his palms on his thighs. "Lizzie has an urgent need for the money the quilt will bring. Please, let me know as soon as possible."

"By Monday. I will let you know by Monday. And now I must get back to my guest." She rose to her feet and he did the same.

"Thanks for your help." He had done all he could. One way or the other, Lizzie would get the money she needed.

Naomi tipped her head slightly to one side as she stared at him. "Joe has placed a lot of faith in you, Carl. Please don't let him down."

"Don't worry. His sheep are safe with me."

"I wasn't actually thinking about the sheep."

He was too stunned to reply. She gave him a wink and walked to the desk. "Charles, would you please arrange a driver for me on Sunday evening?"

"Yes, ma'am."

She waved to Carl. "I'll be in touch."

Sally and her family picked up Lizzie on Sunday morning and they joined the long line of buggies traveling single file along the country road. The line moved only as fast as the slowest horse. No one would dream of passing a fellow church member on the way to services. Such a move would be seen as rude and prideful. Even the young men with their high-stepping horses and topless courting buggies held to a sedate pace.

Lizzie found her gaze drawn to Carl's front door when they drove by the pasture gate. The door was closed. There was no sign of him. No smoke came from the chimney even though the morning was crisp.

Surely he must miss being part of a community that made God the center of their lives. Lizzie knew that she couldn't live cut off from her faith. She prayed that she never had to find out how it felt.

Like the previous prayer service, Lizzie was captivated by the simple but eloquent sermon delivered by Bishop Zook. He had a rare gift for preaching the word of God.

About an hour into the service, she noticed Katie Sutter was having trouble managing Jeremiah and the new baby. Both of them were fussing. Katie got to her feet and came to the back of the room where a set of stairs led to the upper level. When Jeremiah saw Lizzie, he reached for her and began hollering at the top of his lungs. Lizzie immediately got up from her seat and took charge of him.

"Bless you," Katie whispered. "I think he needs changing, and the baby wants to eat."

Lizzie wrinkled her nose. "He does." She followed Katie upstairs to one of the bedrooms. After she changed Jeremiah's diaper, she took him to the window to entertain him while Katie nursed his baby brother.

She pointed to a cardinal in the branches of the tree. "See the bird? Can you say *bird?*"

He babbled happily, but none of his words sounded the least like *bird*. He pointed a chubby finger at something and jabbered louder. Lizzie looked to where he was pointing and saw a dog. She realized it was Duncan. He was lying under the last buggy parked at the end of the row.

Lizzie leaned closer to the window. Was that Carl standing at the rear of the buggy?

It was. She straightened. What was he doing here?

When the next hymn began in the room beneath her, she realized that Carl was singing, too. She couldn't hear him, but she could see the rise and fall of his chest and the movement of his lips.

She pressed a hand to her heart as pity welled up in her. How often had he stood apart from the worshippers and worshipped from afar? How sad that he wouldn't allow himself to return to what he clearly loved. More than ever, she wanted to find out what had driven him away.

Naomi softly opened the door to Joe's hospital room. The blinds were drawn. The room was dark. He was sitting up in bed, but he had fallen asleep with the newspaper spread over his chest. He wore a hospital gown. It was the first time she had ever seen him in something other than his blue work shirt or his black Sunday coat. He looked…helpless and alone.

The sight only strengthened her resolve. She walked to the side of the bed and took a seat in the single chair beside him. He slowly opened his eyes and focused on her. For a second, she thought she saw a glimmer of happiness before he frowned. He yanked the bedspread up to his chin. The newspaper went flying. "What are you doing here?"

"I came to see you."

"I'm not in the mood for company."

"That's hardly surprising. You haven't been in the mood for company for the past twenty years."

She laid the package she carried on his lap. "I brought you something."

He looked at it as if it might contain a snake. She

almost laughed. It would be funny if it weren't so sad. "Go ahead, open it."

"You have no call to bring me presents."

"I declare, you can make a mountain out of a mole-hill faster than anyone I've ever met. Just open the package."

"I always knew you were a bossy woman."

"And I have always known that you are a stubborn man."

He lifted the lid of the box and gazed at the fabric with a perplexed expression on his face. "I don't have need of a quilt, but thank you. The stitching is quite fine."

"Abigail made it."

That shocked him. "Abigail? You don't mean my Abigail?"

"Yes, Lizzie brought it to the inn. She wants me to sell it. It's the only thing she has to remember her mother by. Abigail made a quilt for each of her daughters before she passed away. Lizzie was in tears when she handed it over."

Joe ran a hand lovingly over the fabric. "My Abigail always had a fine hand with a needle. You taught her well."

They both fell silent as thoughts of a shared past overwhelmed them. Naomi drew a deep breath. "She also had a stubborn streak. I suspect she got it from you."

"Why would Lizzie sell this?"

"Because she is desperate to bring her sisters here. Joe, we are old friends. What is Lizzie so afraid of?"

"Morris is making Clara marry a man that Lizzie feels is unsuitable. Harsh, even. That's why she came to Hope Springs. She was hoping I would take them in."

"And why have you turned your back on them? The truth, Joseph," she demanded when she saw the belligerent glint in his eyes.

His expression slowly softened. "Lizzie is so much like her."

"But she is not Abigail. I know your daughter broke your heart when she married that man. She broke my heart, too. I saw what he was long before she would admit it. But hearts mend, Joe. Love mends a broken heart."

"I haven't any love left in me."

"You can't fool me, you old goat. Your heart is full of love for that young man you've taken in and for Abigail's daughter. You're just afraid to admit it. You're afraid of being hurt again."

"What if I took them in and they turned against me the way she did? I couldn't bear it."

"So you think it's better not to care at all? That's selfish. Has trying not to care for Lizzie made you happy, Joseph? The truth, now!"

"*Nee,* it has not."

"Then I see that you have two choices. Risk loving that wonderful child and her sisters and enjoy the best of what God has given you, or turn your back on His gift and keep on being a miserable shell of a man. What's it going to be, Joseph Shetler?"

"You shouldn't speak harshly to me, woman. I'm a sick man."

She leaned forward and laid a hand on his cheek. "Not so sick that you can't see how much I care for you, I hope."

He looked away. "I don't know what you're talking about."

"I had such a crush on you when I was young."

"A *maedel*'s foolishness. I'm almost twenty years older than you."

"Fifteen years. And while that was a lot when I was eighteen, it's not so much now that I'm sixty."

"You've gone soft in the head or something to be talking like this. You married a good man. The right man."

"Yes, I did, and I loved him dearly, but he's been gone for eight years now. Did you really think I brought all those canned vegetables and preserves to you out of Christian duty for the past five years?"

"Well...*ja,* I did."

"You silly man. I was trying to get your attention. I see now that the only way to accomplish that is by plain speaking. I'm right fond of you, Joseph Shetler. I would know now if you feel the same way."

"You can't expect a man to answer a question like that when he's under the influence of Englisch pain medicine."

"When I heard you had been taken to the hospital, I realized what a fool I have been to stay silent for so long hoping that you would speak first."

"You could have your pick of upstanding fellows. There's no reason for you to chase after a rickety old sheepherder. I can't even walk. What kind of husband would I be? Besides, a sheep farm is no place for a woman."

"Nonsense. So Evelyn hated sheep. So what? I like sheep. And I happen to like rickety old shepherds. Are you going to make me ask the question?"

He scooted up uncomfortably in bed and smoothed the spread over his chest. "What question would that be?"

She shook her head and began to gather up her things. "I reckon I'm a foolish old woman who thought that maybe, just maybe, I could have a second chance to love a man and be loved in return. I see I was wrong. Good night to you, Joseph. May the Lord bless and keep you." She rose and headed for the door.

"Wait," he called out.

She kept her gaze fixed on the doorknob. "I have been waiting, Joseph. I'm not going to wait anymore."

"All right, all right, have it your way."

Joy surged through her. She turned slowly to face him. "What does that mean exactly?"

"I'm not going to come courting in some fancy buggy."

"I don't need a fancy buggy."

"Well…it'll be lambing season soon. Any plans you've got will have to wait until summer."

She smiled broadly, walked back to his side and took his hand. "A quiet little summer wedding sounds wunderbar."

Worry filled his eyes. "Are you certain about this, Naomi?"

She bent down and kissed him. Then she whispered in his ear, "I've never been more certain of anything."

"I think I'm too old to be this happy." He wiped a tear from the corner of his eye.

"The good Lord didn't put an age limit on happiness, darling. Will you buy Abigail's quilt? If not, I will put it up for sale in my shop."

He looked down at the soft fabric. "I wish I knew what my daughter would want me to do."

Lizzie was raking up the previous year's litter from the vegetable garden when she saw a buggy coming up the lane on Monday. She didn't recognize the man driving, but she walked out to meet him. He drew up beside her and tipped his hat. *"Guder mariye."*

"Good morning and welcome."

"Are you Lizzie Barkman?"

"I am."

"I'm Adam Troyer. Naomi Wadler is my mother-in-law. She wanted me to deliver this to you." He leaned forward and held out an envelope.

"What is it?"

"I believe it is payment for your quilt."

"My quilt has been sold already? I only left it there on Saturday."

"I'm afraid I don't know the details, but it must've sold."

Lizzie opened the envelope. She looked up at Adam in shock. "This can't be right. There's far too much money here."

"Many of the quilts we sell fetch fine prices. The Englisch don't seem to care what they have to pay. I've seen some of the larger quilts at auction go for thousands of dollars."

Overwhelmed with gratitude and excitement, Lizzie realized she had more than enough to buy bus tickets for all her sisters.

"*Danki.* Please tell Naomi that I am eternally grateful for her help. Now I have to get this in the mail." As Adam turned the buggy around, Lizzie sprinted toward the house.

There is still time. There is still time. The refrain echoed in her mind.

"Carl! Carl, where are you?" She knew he had gone to town earlier, but she had seen him return. She wanted to share her joy and she wanted to share it with him. She raced up the steps, yanked open the screen door and ran full tilt into him.

Carl wrapped his arms around Lizzie to keep her from falling as they both struggled to catch their balance. Fear clutched at his heart. "What is it? What's wrong?"

She looked up, grinning from ear to ear. She patted his chest with both hands. "Nothing's wrong. Everything's right and God is good."

She didn't seem to notice that he was holding her. He noticed. She was close enough for him to see the flecks of gold in her bright hazel eyes. She was close enough to kiss. More than his next breath, he wanted to taste the soft sweetness of her lips.

Duncan nosed open the screen door and joined in with exuberance. He jumped up and planted his front feet on Lizzie's side, barking wildly. Carl slowly lowered his arms and reluctantly released her.

She turned her beautiful smile on the dog. "Yes, everything is fine, and you, Duncan, are a *goot, goot hund.*"

She took hold of his front feet and turned in a circle as the dog hopped to keep up with her. Laughing, she grabbed his face and ruffled his fur. Duncan dropped back to all fours, but continued to wag his tail as he fixed his eyes on her.

Carl folded his arms over his chest and tried not to be jealous of a dog. "Have you had good news about Joe?"

"I haven't heard anything about Grandfather today, but my quilt has been sold. I have money, Carl. Enough money to bring my sisters here and some left over."

"That's great news. Are you sure your sisters will come? They haven't written to you."

"I pray that they will. I pray with all my heart that they will find the courage to leave my uncle's house. I used to think that everyone's lives were like ours. That words of compassion were spoken at church but not practiced at home. Since coming here, I realize there are kind and generous people who live their faith as our Lord commanded and do more than pay it lip service. I'm so glad that I came."

"I'm glad that you came, too."

She blushed at his words, but nothing dimmed her happiness. "I have to get this in the mail to Mary. What will you do if three more women show up on your doorstep?"

"I'll hide."

She laughed as she rushed up the stairs. She didn't believe him. If only she knew the truth. The last thing on earth he wanted was a house full of women to look after.

Just the thought of it made his blood run cold.

Chapter 12

Lizzie carried the coffeepot to the sink and began filling it with water. It had been two days since she put her quilt money in the mail to Mary. It should arrive today or tomorrow. How soon would she hear something?

Joe would be home before long. Would that mean less time working beside Carl? She enjoyed his company. She glanced out the window and noticed a speck of white in the green grass on the hillside beyond the barn. She leaned closer.

"A lamb. That's a lamb. Oh, my goodness, they're coming." She left the pot in the sink, ran out the door and raced down the hill to Carl's hut.

The door was open. He was seated on the edge of his bunk pulling on his boot.

"Carl, I saw one. I saw a lamb!"

A slow grin spread across his face. Why wasn't

he as excited as she was? "We have been expecting them, Lizzie."

"You don't understand. It's out there all alone. The mother isn't with it. What if she has abandoned it?"

"Then you will get to bottle-feed one, but let's hope the mother is nearby."

Lizzie waited impatiently for him to pull on his other boot. "I don't see how you can be so matter-of-fact when a baby has been left all alone out in the wilds."

Her patience gave out. She turned and ran back up the hill toward the pasture. She was out of breath and panting when she reached the baby sleeping quietly in the grass. She held her aching side as she sank to her knees beside it.

It was so small and so precious. She wanted to scoop it up and cuddle it in her arms, but she was afraid to touch it.

She heard a noise nearby and realized the mother was less than ten feet away on the other side of a bush. Her second lamb was busy nursing and twirling its tail.

"You didn't leave your baby. What a good mother you are."

Lizzie was still gazing at the beautiful sleeping creature when Carl joined her. He had a large navy blue bag slung over his shoulder. Duncan trotted at his heels.

Carl leaned down and picked up the lamb. It came awake with a start and struggled in his hands. Its frantic cries brought the ewe running back. She immediately began bleating loudly in protest. At a word from Carl, Duncan went out to distract her.

"What are you doing?" Lizzie demanded.

"When a lamb is born, some processing is required."

"What does that mean?"

"First, I checked to see if the lamb is healthy, and this one looks like she is. Then I put iodine on the navel to prevent infection. I give her a numbered ear tag because we will need to know which babies belong with which mothers. The numbers are easy enough to see when the lamb is standing still, but when they are running about, it's a lot harder, so I mark them with these waxy crayon sticks. I put the ewe's number on like so."

He demonstrated by marking the number forty-two on the lamb's left side with a yellow marking stick.

"If it's a single birth, the lamb will get marked with one stripe across its back from side to side. If it's a twin, two stripes and so on. Always mark them on the left side."

The mother continued to bellow her displeasure and lowered her head in a threatening gesture. Lizzie took a step away from Carl. "Are we done? She's very upset."

"Almost. I just have to put this rubber band over the tail. It's a bloodless way to dock the tail. The part below the rubber band will simply die and fall off in a couple of weeks. A shorter tail allows for cleaner sheep."

"I could've gone my entire life without knowing that fact."

He chuckled as he put the lamb on the ground. She quickly scurried to her mother's side. The mother stopped protesting and nuzzled her baby before moving away with it only to go through the entire process all over again when Carl caught and marked her other lamb.

He gave Duncan the command to gather, and the dog began herding the sheep and lambs toward the barn.

From that moment on, Lizzie had very little time to think about her sisters coming, about Joe getting out of the hospital and about how much she enjoyed working beside Carl. She was too busy with the newborn lambs.

Things went well until the weather took a turn for the worse. April began with an unusually cold and rainy week. It was a potentially disastrous combination for the newborns.

Some of the newly shorn mothers sought the shelter of the sheds and the barn, but some chose less suitable birthing places, such as dense thickets and groves of trees in the pasture.

Carl worked tirelessly to move the reluctant mothers and their newborns into the sheds. He built additional pens inside the barn and even moved the horses out so that he could turn their stalls into sheep maternity wards. Lizzie divided her time between bottle-feeding a pair of orphans every three hours and making sure Carl had food, hot coffee and warm, dry clothes.

When he wasn't assisting an ewe with a difficult birth or checking on the condition of the lambs, he combed the pastures for the few expectant mothers who had wandered away from the flock.

After three days of nonstop birthing, Lizzie could

see how tired Carl was. "Please, let me help more. Tell me what to do."

"You're doing enough."

"I can do more."

"Lizzie, that's the trouble with you. You always think you can do more."

"Try me. If I can't manage, what have you lost?"

"Very well. In the smallest shed are the ewes that lambed three days ago. I need you to take hay to them and make sure they have plenty of water."

"I can do that. What else?"

"Add fresh straw to the pens if they look dirty. That will keep you busy for the next hour."

It didn't take her an hour to complete the tasks. She was back at his side as soon as she was able. He had delivered a set of twins from one ewe and was helping a second one deliver a lamb that was breech. "I've given them hay and water and new straw. Now what?"

"Check on number fifty-four. She had twins, but she wasn't letting one of them nurse a while ago. Let me know if they're both doing okay."

Lizzie walked down the aisle looking into the small pens where the mother sheep stood with their new babies until she saw the one whose ear tag was fifty-four. One of her babies was up and nursing. The other lay in a small huddle in the corner. Lizzie stepped into the pen and tried to rouse the little one, but it seemed too weak to stand. She rushed back to Carl.

"One of them is lying down and won't get up."

"Can you check his temperature for me?"

"If you tell me how." She felt so stupid. How could

she be of help to him if she had to constantly run to him for information and instructions?

He grabbed a thermometer from his box of equipment and explained what she needed to do. "A lamb's temperature should be about 102°. If he's colder than that, take him to the warming boxes I have set up by the stove in the house." He extended the thermometer to her. She hesitated, then took it from him. This wasn't about Carl's shunning. This was about saving as many lambs as possible.

The lamb was much colder than he should have been. She bundled him up in a blanket and carried him up to the house. Carl had set four boxes around the stove in the kitchen. She put the lamb in one and made sure there was plenty of wood to last the night before going out to the barn again. She paused and groaned when she stepped outside. The bitter-cold rain was mixed with snow. How much worse could it get?

Carl's second ewe had successfully delivered her lambs. Both were trying to get to their feet while their mother nuzzled them. He gave Lizzie a tired smile. "These will be fine. I'm going back out to the hilltop pen. I saw two more ewes laboring up there an hour ago."

"Carl, it's snowing."

"Let's hope it doesn't last. Go back to the house. I'll be in shortly."

She did as he asked, but he wasn't back soon. She moved a lamp to the window to let him know she was still up in case he needed her, then she sat down in her grandfather's chair to wait. Carl would need some of the warm soup she had simmering on the stove when he came in.

Sometime later, she was jolted awake when the kitchen door flew open. Carl came in along with a flurry of wet snow. His black cowboy hat and coat were dusted with white. She hurried toward him. "You must be chilled to the bone."

He had something buttoned up inside his coat. Crossing to the stove, he knelt there. "I need your help. Bring me blankets, old ones if you have them, or towels."

He opened his jacket enough for her to see he had two tiny wet lambs bundled against his body for warmth.

Lizzie sprang into action. She raced up the stairs and pulled towels and blankets from the linen closet. Returning to Carl's side, she waited as he extracted one lamb and handed it to her. "Dry her good. She might make it. I'm not so sure about her brother."

"Did their mother reject them?" Lizzie knew it sometimes happened. She wrapped her baby in a towel and handed a second towel to Carl.

"Yes, she had triplets, but she would only nurse one."

Lizzie put the little one down for a minute and put several of the towels in the oven to warm. She went back and dried her charge as best she could. When the towels in the oven were warm, she wrapped the lambs in them.

"They'll need colostrum," Carl said. His baby remained lethargic.

Lizzie had learned it was the first milk the ewes

produced and was essential to the newborn's health. A supply was kept frozen in a small propane-powered freezer in the barn. "I'll get some and warm it up."

She handed him her lamb and jumped to her feet. Carl caught her hand as she walked by and looked up at her. "Thank you. For everything you've done. I don't know what I would have done without you."

"I'm glad I was here to help."

"So am I."

He slowly released her hand and she missed the comfort of his touch more than she imagined was possible. "You're an amazing man, Carl. I don't know how you do it. I admire your dedication, your skill, your selflessness. This has been a time I will never forget."

After that, the following days became something of a blur for Lizzie. Two more orphans joined the collection in the kitchen. Each morning at five o'clock, Lizzie rose, made a mug of strong tea and checked on the orphaned lambs. Most times, Carl was already there feeding them their breakfast before getting his own. It was amusing to see him seated on the floor with a baby bottle in each hand and lambs climbing on his lap in the hopes of being next.

After the babies were fed, she and Carl walked together to the pasture looking for lambs that had arrived during the past few hours or for ewes that were in obvious distress. When they found lambs, they would carry them back to the barn with their anxious mothers following alongside.

During the peak lambing season, the new arrivals came fast and furious. The ewes delivered late at night, in the early hours and throughout the day. At times, it seemed to Lizzie that there were baby sheep in every nook and cranny on the farm.

Through the rough parts, it seemed to her as if Carl never slept. She knew, because she slept very little herself. But no matter how tired or busy she was, she always made time to run down to the end of the lane and collect the mail. Every afternoon she hoped for a message from her friend or her sisters, but none came. Slowly, her hope began to fade.

The bad weather finally broke on Sunday morning and the sun came out. Lizzie had never been so glad to lift her face to the warming rays and simply soak them up. It was the off Sunday, so there was no need to travel to church.

Carl opened the gates of one shed and let the ewes with lambs several days old out into a larger enclosure. The ewes, thrilled to be back outside, got busy eating the new green grass where the sun had melted patches free of snow. The lambs, not used to being ignored, discovered each other.

They gathered in a bunch and began butting each other. Suddenly, they broke and ran, jumping and leaping for the sheer joy of it over the ground until they noticed that they had strayed too far from their mothers. In what looked like a race, they all came galloping back. Only an occasional mother even raised her head from the green grass to check on them.

Lizzie leaned on the fence beside Carl and watched it all with a feeling of deep contentment. "'This is the day which the Lord hath made; we will rejoice and be glad in it.'"

"Psalm 118:24," he said quietly.

Her heart turned over as she looked at him. "Isn't it wonderful how God brings us joy in the simplest ways? It's a sign of His endless love."

She didn't turn away from the warm look that filled his eyes. "You almost make me believe that, Lizzie."

Drawn to the change she sensed in him, she stepped closer and laid her hand over his heart. "Then I'm happy to be His instrument. The Lamb of God gave up His life on the cross so that we might know salvation. It is up to each of us to cherish or to deny that gift."

He looked away. "It's more complicated than that."

She let her hand fall to her side. "When you come right down to it, it's not."

Bracing his forearms on the fence, he stared at the ground. "There are other people involved."

"God didn't create us to live alone. There are always people who touch our lives, for better or for worse. None of them can change God's love for you or for me. It is eternal."

"So they say, but it doesn't feel like it to me. I'd better finish checking the pens in the barn. We have a dozen mothers-in-waiting left."

He walked away, leaving her aching for his pain. He was so lost. If only there was some way to help him.

When the last pregnant ewe gave birth, Lizzie gave a huge sigh of relief. After more than a week of non-stop work, the worst was finally behind them.

On Friday, just like clockwork, another letter arrived for Carl, but this time there was a letter from

Mary, as well. Lizzie had been on the verge of giving up hope. Clara's wedding was less than a week away.

She quickly opened her letter and read the bitter news. Mary had been unable to see her sisters, but she would keep trying to get Lizzie's money to them.

Lizzie nearly screamed with frustration. She wanted to hear from her family so badly, while Carl ignored letters from his. It wasn't fair.

Back in the kitchen, Lizzie started supper, but she was drawn to Carl's letter. She picked it up and spent a long time looking at the envelope. Was Carl ignoring an olive branch extended by his family? Lizzie had no way of knowing unless she opened the letter and read it.

It was so tempting. Carl would never know if she burned it for him. She laid the letter on the kitchen table with the rest of the mail and went to the stove. Turning back quickly, she snatched the envelope up and held it in the steam rising from the eggs she was boiling to make egg-salad sandwiches. The steam burned her fingers before the glue on the envelope gave way.

Ashamed of herself, she put the letter back where it belonged and continued fixing supper. A dozen times, she glanced at the table as she worked. Finally, she covered the distraction with a kitchen towel.

It was not her letter. It was not her life. To read or to destroy the correspondence was up to Carl. She removed the towel and put the letter under the newspaper.

It was nearly dark by the time he came in. She was

seated at the table with a cup of coffee in her hands. "Do we have any sick ones?"

He hung his cowboy hat on a wooden peg beside the door. "Not yet. At least, none that I've found, but I think we're missing one."

"An ewe or a lamb?"

"A lamb. Number eighty-three had twins, but she's only got one lamb with her now."

"Maybe one of the others stole it." An ewe without a lamb of her own would sometimes try to steal another's baby.

"Maybe. Is there any coffee left?"

"In the pot. It's fresh."

He poured a cup, blew on it to cool it and took a sip. "Before you leave, will you please teach Joe how to make good coffee? I can't go back to drinking the shoe polish that he makes."

She chuckled. "I will do my best."

He looked around the house. "This is nice."

She looked around to see what he was referring to but didn't see anything unusual. "What's nice?"

"Coming into a clean house with supper simmering on the stove. You have no idea what a difference it makes after a long, hard day of work outside."

"I'm happy that I can ease your way, for you work very hard. Supper will be ready in about twenty minutes." She pointed to the pile of mail on the corner of the table. "The paper came today, if you want to read it while you wait."

"After supper."

Lizzie bit her bottom lip to keep from mentioning

his letter. Maybe this time he would open it. She got up and began to set the table.

When they finished the meal, Carl took the mail into the other room while Lizzie cleaned up. She was putting away the last plate when he walked past her, opened the firebox of the stove and dropped the letter in.

"Supper was good. Thank you. I'll see you in the morning." He walked to the pegs by the door and put on his coat and hat.

Her heart sank. Someone was desperately reaching out to him, and he was just as desperately keeping that someone at bay. She couldn't remain silent any longer. "If you mark them Return to Sender, perhaps she will stop writing."

He paused with his hand on the doorknob, but didn't look at her. "I tried that once, but it didn't work."

Lizzie heard the pain in his voice and wanted to throw her arms around him and hold him close. It was impossible for her to do so, but knowing that didn't lessen her desire to comfort him. "I think only someone who loves you very much would remain so persistent."

He walked out and closed the door behind him without a word.

Carl continued toward his hut in the dark. He knew the path by heart. He didn't need to see where he was going. Duncan walked beside him. He looked down at the dog, who had been his best friend for a long time. "Lizzie is like a dog with a bone about those letters.

In fact, she's worse than you are. She's not going to bury it and leave it alone."

She was every bit as persistent as Jenna was. He wished now that he'd never told his sister where he was staying.

He sat down on the chair outside his door and stared out over the pastures. The white sheep dotting the hillsides stood out in stark contrast to the dark ground. They looked like little stars that had fallen from the sky. Duncan lay down beside Carl and licked his paw.

Only a month ago, Carl would have enjoyed the peaceful calm of a night like this, but tonight he didn't appreciate the pastoral serenity. Tonight, he was restless and edgy.

Lizzie was eager to find out more about him. He saw it every time she looked at him. He heard it in her voice each time she mentioned his letters. She cared for him. He saw that in her eyes, too, even as he struggled to keep his feelings for her hidden.

If he gave in and told her the truth, what would he see in her eyes then? How would she look at him when she learned he had killed a man? Would he see horror? Revulsion? Pity?

He leaned his head back against the wall. Maybe it was time for him to move on. It would be best to go before he fell deeper in love with the amazing little woman with smiling eyes. A woman he could never hold.

Duncan suddenly sprang to his feet and growled deep in his throat. The hair on his neck stood up as every muscle in his body tensed.

Carl stared out into the darkness, trying to see what

had riled his dog. It took a bit, but finally he saw a darker shadow streaking along the hillside on the opposite side of the creek. He stood up to get a better look. Was it a coyote or a dog?

He realized as the animal crested the hill that it carried one of his lambs in its mouth. A second later, it was lost from sight. Duncan took off after it at a run.

Chapter 13

The day Joe came home from the hospital was the day of Clara's wedding.

Carl watched Lizzie try to keep a brave face as they waited for the van that would bring Joe home, but he could see the strain she was under. The days since she had mailed her quilt money had gone by without a single word from her sisters. He had no idea what had gone wrong with her plan, but she wore the look of a woman who was barely hanging on to hope.

He wondered how long it would be before he saw her smile again.

Outside, the sun was shining. A soft breeze turned the windmill beside the barn and stirred the new grass in the pastures in small, undulating waves. Carl had moved the entire flock close to the house, but he was still losing a lamb every other night.

Lizzie became as nervous as a June bug in a henhouse when the van finally rolled in. And well she should be. She was the reason Joe ended up in the hospital in the first place. Carl knew Joe had forgiven her, but he was worried that Joe might not let her forget it anytime soon.

When the driver got out and opened the door, she rushed down the steps with an offer of help. To Carl's surprise, Joe calmly accepted Lizzie's offer and allowed her to help him out of the car. He walked haltingly with a walker, but managed well enough.

With Carl on one side and Lizzie on the other, they were able to help Joe up the steps and into the house. Once inside, he looked around and sighed deeply. "You have no idea how good it feels to come home."

"I have your room ready, Daadi. Would you like to lie down now?"

"No, I'm sick of being in bed. I would like to sit in my chair for a while."

"Of course." She hovered beside him as he crossed into the living room and sank with a deep sigh of relief into his overstuffed chair. She quickly arranged a footstool and pillows so he could elevate his legs. She had been paying close attention to the home-care instructions the hospital had mailed to her.

Carl was delighted to see his friend looking so well, if a bit weak and worn-out. "You have two hundred and seventy-eight new lambs."

"How many ewes did we lose?"

"Only two."

"And how many lambs have we lost? Every day I watched the rain running down the windows of the hospital I was thinking about my poor babies out in such weather."

"We didn't lose any to the weather."

"Are you serious?"

"Lizzie has been busy bottle-feeding six of them."

"That's a lot of work," Joe said, looking at her with admiration.

"I don't mind. They're adorable, but any praise must go to Carl." She turned her earnest eyes in his direction and he saw admiration in them, but also something more. He saw an echo of the way he felt about her.

"Carl worked day and night to make sure the sheep had the best possible care. He went out in a snowstorm to look for lambs. He brought back two that lived because of his dedication."

Carl decided the bad news could wait until after Joe had rested.

Joe looked around the room. "Where's Duncan? I didn't see him when we came in. He normally raises a ruckus when there's a car around."

"I have him on guard duty with the flock."

Lizzie knelt beside Joe. "We can talk about this later. Daadi, you need to rest."

"Coyotes?" Joe's sharp eyes drilled into Carl and ignored Lizzie.

"A big one."

"How many has he gotten?"

"Four."

Joe pushed himself up straighter in the chair. "You know what has to be done?"

"I won't touch a gun, Joe. You know that."

"A gun?" Lizzie's eyes widened with shock. "You aren't thinking about shooting it, are you?"

Joe gave her an exasperated look. "A coyote that starts killing sheep won't stop. It has to be put down."

"Isn't there another way?"

"What other way?" Joe asked.

"I don't know, but it doesn't deserve to be shot without trying something else. We could trap it."

Carl remained silent. Each word of Lizzie's protest cut like a knife. She couldn't bear the thought of him killing a wild predator. How appalled would she be if she knew the truth about his deed? He grew sick at the thought.

Joe patted her hand. "Women! Soft hearts and soft heads. My rifle is in my room, Carl. You know I wouldn't ask you to do this if I could do it myself. The sheep can't defend themselves."

Carl nodded. Lizzie's eyes begged him not to do it. He looked away. He didn't want to kill anything, but better that she hate him for thinking about shooting a coyote than to know the truth. Maybe this way she would see that he wasn't worth trying to save.

Maybe he could stop loving her if she stopped looking at him as if he was her hero.

Lizzie couldn't decipher the expression on Carl's face. It was as if he had suddenly turned to stone. There was a lack of life in his eyes that troubled her.

"I'm surprised your sisters aren't here," Joe said, pulling Lizzie's attention away from Carl.

"I have not heard from them," she said. Her disappointment and worry were too heavy to hide.

"Oh. I thought they had the means to join you. Naomi Wadler stopped in to see me and she mentioned that you were selling a quilt to pay for their bus fare. Did you change your mind?"

"I sent them money. However, it may have been too late or my uncle may have intercepted it. Clara's wedding was moved up after I left. The ceremony was to take place today."

He sank back in his chair. Lines of fatigue and pain appeared on his face. "So she is married to him, the man you don't like and don't trust. I'm sorry for her. And for you."

"It must be God's will for her. Perhaps her kindness will change his heart and make him a husband she can respect and admire."

Joe laid a hand on Lizzie's head. "I have been a fool and so I must pay the price, but I'm sorry you must pay it, too. What will you do now?"

"I love it here. The people of this community are so warm and loving. I even like the sheep now much more than I did when we had to shear them."

"But you aren't going to stay," Carl said softly.

"I can't leave them there. I have to go back." She tried to gauge his reaction to her decision, but she couldn't. Tears blurred her vision.

"You can't go until I'm fit," Joe grumbled.

She rose to her feet. "Of course not. I promised I would stay as long as you need me. I should go feed the orphans. Carl will stay with you to make sure you don't overdo it."

"I don't need a babysitter."

Lizzie escaped out the door before she heard Carl's

reply. He was used to handling Joe. She knew he would manage without her. She gathered the baby bottles and milk replacer and went down to the barn where the orphans lived now. After only a week, they had outgrown their warming boxes. They slept now in an empty stall at the back of the barn.

She sat down on the hay among them, and as they pushed and shoved for her attention, she held their soft bodies close one at a time and gave in to her tears.

She was responsible for her own heartbreak. She knew better than to fall for Carl, but that hadn't stopped her from embracing every dear quality he possessed. It was so easy to love him.

In the long years ahead, she would look back on their days together and remember what it was like to share the joys and pains of everyday life with him. She would never forget the way he made her feel.

If only she knew he would find his way back to his faith, she wouldn't mind leaving so much.

After she finished feeding the orphans, she returned to the house and went up to her room. She pulled a sheet of paper from the small desk by the window and sat down to write a letter. She raised her pen to her mouth and nibbled on the end of it as she considered what to say. Finally, she started writing.

Dear Jenna,
You don't know me, but I am a friend of Carl King's. He lives and works on my grandfather's sheep farm here in Ohio. I have only recently moved here, but I soon became aware that you write to Carl every week. I hesitate to tell you

this, but Carl burns your letters without reading them. He does not know that I am writing to you.

When I first met Carl, he told me he is in the Bann, but he will not say why he has been shunned. His situation weighs heavily on my heart for I have come to care for him a great deal.

Lizzie lifted her pen from the paper. She didn't just care for Carl. She loved him. She always would.

A tear splashed onto the page as she began writing again.

Carl keeps all rules of our faith, except that he will not attend our services. I have seen him standing outside of our place of worship, close enough to hear the preaching and singing and yet not be a part of it. His separation from God is painful to see, for I know that it is painful to him, too.

It is my hope that with some understanding of Carl's past, I can help him to return to the faith he clearly loves. He refuses to tell me anything. I'm hoping that you will. I value Carl's friendship and his trust. I risk losing that which is most dear to me by writing to you, but what Carl stands to gain is so much more important.

Please forgive me if you find this intrusion into your affairs offensive. I mean no harm. I don't do this lightly, but only with the very best of intentions. If you do not answer this letter, I will not bother you again.

Your sister in Christ,

Elizabeth Barkman

When she finished the brief missive, she folded it and slipped it into an envelope before she could change her mind. Carl was stuck in limbo. He couldn't move forward with his life until he had received forgiveness from someone in his past. If that person was the author of his letters, then perhaps letting her know how much Carl desperately needed her forgiveness would spark their reconciliation.

She didn't delude herself into thinking Carl would approve of her actions. He would be furious with her.

She composed a second letter. This one was to her sisters telling them that she would be returning in a few weeks. As much as she longed to see them, she dreaded returning to life in her uncle's home. How would she bear it after knowing a better way existed?

She took her letters down to the mailbox in the early afternoon when she knew the mailman was due to go by. If there was a letter from Mary or from her sisters and they were coming, Lizzie wouldn't send the ones she had written, for it meant she would be staying in Hope Springs.

The postman handed over the mail. "I see you have a new crop of lambs out there. How did it go?"

"Busy. Joe is home from the hospital now. You are welcome to bring your son and pick a lamb whenever you like."

"We're going to be gone on a family vacation for a week, but we'll do it sometime after we get back. Do you want to mail those letters?" He pointed to the ones in her hand.

She finished looking through a handful of junk

mail. There was nothing from her family. She nodded. "I guess I do."

Her conscience pricked her all through the day and kept her awake until long into the night. She had no right to interfere in Carl's personal affairs. It was prideful on her part to think what she said would matter.

Where was Clara tonight? Was she at the home of her new husband? How was he treating her?

Lizzie pulled her pillow over her face to shut out her fears. It didn't work.

Carl attributed Lizzie's long face to her grief at not being able to help her family. She didn't say a word as they finished the morning chores and turned out the youngest lambs with their mothers. She barely spoke to the orphans as they clamored for her attention.

On the way back to the house, he said, "You're awfully quiet today."

"Am I?

"Do you have something on your mind?"

"A lot of things."

"Such as?"

"Number ninety-four doesn't seem to have enough milk for her triplets. We may need to supplement one of them with milk replacer."

"Just what we need, another mouth to feed in the orphan pen."

"I'll take care of moving him this afternoon," Lizzie said as she walked up the steps ahead of him. She opened the front door and stopped so abruptly that he almost ran into her. She shrieked, dropped the bucket she was carrying and charged into the room. Carl rushed in behind her to see what was wrong.

Suddenly, the room echoed with shrieks as three women rushed to embrace Lizzie. They were all laughing, crying and hugging each other. Joe stood leaning on his walker on the far side of the room.

Carl skirted the women and moved to stand beside him. "I take it these are the rest of your granddaughters?"

"They are. Have you ever heard such a noisy bunch? They're worse than a barn full of sheep."

Although Joe tried to hide it with his gruff words, Carl heard the happiness in his voice. Carl was happy, too, that Lizzie's dream had come true. Now she wouldn't be leaving.

Lizzie had tears of joy rolling down her face but she didn't care. "How did you get here? I thought the wedding was yesterday. I didn't know when I would ever see you again."

Greta said, "The wedding *was* yesterday, but the bride failed to show up for it."

Clara grasped Lizzie's hands. "I don't know how I can ever thank you. We would have come sooner, but we didn't know Mary had the money you sent until the morning of the wedding. Uncle Morris wouldn't let us have visitors until then."

Betsy wrapped her arm around Clara's waist. "Mary showed up at the house demanding that she be allowed to attend Clara on her wedding day. There were already people at the house, so I think uncle didn't want to look bad in front of them by saying no."

Greta took up the tale. "The moment Mary was in the room with us, she gave us your letters and then handed each of us a bus ticket and said that her buggy was waiting for us outside."

"We climbed out the window and drove into town as fast as we could. We barely made it to the bus station on time," Betsy added with a dramatic flourish.

Lizzie pressed a hand to her heart. "Oh, I wish I had been there to see it."

Clara shook her head. "If you had been there, none of us would be here now. You showed us the way. Your courage gave us courage."

"I prayed that you had guessed what I was trying to do and that you didn't think I had simply run away."

The three sisters exchanged glances. Greta laid a hand on Lizzie's shoulder. "We knew."

Joe came forward with his walker. "Now that all the screaming is over, I hope a man can have his lunch in peace."

Lizzie drew a deep breath. "*Ja,* Daadi. We will have your lunch ready in no time."

She caught sight of Carl as he was slipping out the back door. She left her sisters and caught up with him on the back porch. "Where are you going? You must stay and meet my family."

"Another time." His voice held a sad quality that made her want to fold her arms around him.

"But I want them to meet you. Stay for lunch with us."

"Half the table won't be big enough for all of you, Lizzie." It was a pointed reminder that he could not eat with them.

"They don't have to know. I won't say anything. They will think you are an Englisch hired hand."

"But I will know, and you will know, Lizzie. I'm glad your plan worked. I'm really happy for you."

"Will you be in for supper?"

"I don't think so."

It was then that Lizzie realized the arrival of her sisters spelled the end of her time alone with Carl. "You have to eat."

"We've had this conversation before. You like to feed people."

"It's what I'm good at."

"Fix me a sandwich, then. I'm going to camp out in the pasture and try to keep that coyote from killing any more lambs.

"Will you shoot it?"

"Not if I don't have to."

"*Goot.* That makes me feel better."

"It's a wild animal, Lizzie."

"Every life is valuable, Carl. We are all God's creatures."

She saw him flinch at her words. Maybe she was being too hard on him. The lambs were God's creatures, too. She didn't want any of them to die. "You'll do the right thing. I know that."

He nodded and walked away, but she had the feeling that she had somehow let him down.

Lizzie spent the rest of the day surrounded by her sisters. They were eager to hear about everything that she had done since leaving home. Her stories about shearing alpacas and sheep had them all laughing. Her grandfather sat on the edge of their group and added a few stories of his own. When she recounted Naomi's stories about their mother, she caught a glint of tears in Joe's eyes.

She made up sandwiches for Carl, but he never came to the house to pick them up, so she left them in the refrigerator for him and left a note telling him where they were on the kitchen table.

The next morning, he came in while her sisters and Joe were all seated around the kitchen table. Carl's face was grave. He held a bloody bundle in his arms. Lizzie jumped to her feet. "Are you hurt?"

"No, but this poor little girl is." He unwrapped part of the cloth to show them a lamb with a gaping wound on its hind leg.

Lizzie immediately came over to examine the animal. "It's a deep laceration. She's going to need stitches. We should get her to a vet right away. She may go into shock from blood loss. We need to keep her warm." She lifted the lamb out of Carl's arms and moved to stand close to the stove with it.

Greta filled a hot-water bottle and gave it to Lizzie, who tucked it in with the lamb. She looked at Carl. "Was it the coyote?"

"Yes. It came within fifty feet of me. It has no fear of humans. I think it's a coydog. A coyote and dog cross. That's why it's so big. It's not killing for food. It's killing the sheep for fun. Duncan drove it off but not before it had a chance to kill one and maim this poor little one. I'll go hitch up the wagon."

Joe said, "Take the buggy. My trotter is faster than the pony. Greta, you and Lizzie take the lamb to the vet. Carl, you and I need to figure out what we're going to do about this."

"We should notify the sheriff. The animal is big enough to start attacking cattle, too, if it hasn't already."

"All right. Go call him. Then take my gun out and practice with it. I'm not going to lose my whole lamb crop. I can't afford to lose even one more."

Carl knew Joe was right, but the last thing he wanted in his hands was another gun.

Chapter 14

Sheriff Bradley came to the farm, and Carl filed a report with him. The sheriff suggested Carl put a notice in several of the local newspapers with a description of the coydog in the unlikely event that it was a pet and not a wild animal. After an entire week passed without another attack, Carl joined Lizzie and Joe in the living room.

Carl leaned forward and propped his forearms on his thighs. "Maybe the sheriff was right and the coydog isn't wild. Maybe the owner read about his pet in the paper and decided it was time to keep Fido in his kennel at night."

Joe nodded. "Another explanation is that someone else took care of the problem for us."

"I'd rather think that he's home and safe with his family," Lizzie said.

Carl looked around. "Speaking of family, where are the girls?"

"Clara has gone to meet Adrian and Faith and see if she wants the job they have to offer. Sally Yoder took Betsy to meet the Sutter family."

He frowned at her. "Wasn't that the job you were going to take?"

"I would have been happy to work for them, but I think Betsy will be happier."

"You just want to stay here and boss me around," Joe grumbled.

"You're right. That's exactly why I want to stay. It's time for you to do some more walking. You can't sit around all day like a king on his throne."

Joe muttered under his breath, but he stood up with his walker. "I'll be outside with Greta. I've never seen anyone so happy to be hoeing in the dirt. My garden will be twice its size when she's done. Lizzie, I meant to tell you what a good job you've done with that crippled lamb. She's almost as good as new."

"Danki." Lizzie was smiling as she watched Joe make his way out the door.

"Is this what you imagined it would be like when they came?" Carl asked.

By mutual consent, they had avoided spending time alone in each other's company. She kept her eyes lowered modestly. She rarely looked him in the eyes anymore. "This is so much more wonderful than I dreamed. It fills my heart with joy to see them meeting new people and going to new places."

"It does my heart good to see you happy, Lizzie."

She turned her face aside. "You should not say such things."

"I know it's not proper, but I wanted you to hear it anyway. You didn't used to be so proper."

"Things were different then. Now I have my sisters to think of."

He'd done a lot of soul-searching while he was patrolling Joe's pastures over the past few nights. Soul-searching and longing for a life within the community that had welcomed Lizzie and her sisters with such joy and kindness.

He had arrived at an answer. He hoped. He would go home and beg forgiveness for Sophia's death and the killing of the soldier from his parents, his siblings and his church. If they granted him what he sought, then the past would stay in the past. When a sinner was forgiven, the sin need never be mentioned again. Lizzie would never have to know what he had done.

"I'm going away for a while, Lizzie."

She looked up and locked eyes with him. "For how long?"

"I'm not sure."

"But you'll be back."

"It is my dearest hope to return to you as soon as possible." He couldn't say too much, but he longed to tell her of his love.

"Are you going home, Carl?"

"Ja."

She smiled. *"Goot.* I miss you already. When are you leaving?"

"The day after tomorrow."

She reached out and laid her hand on his. "Then I wish you Godspeed."

He left the house feeling hope for the first time in five long years. Lizzie had brought hope into his life. She was the sign he had been waiting for.

"Is that a car I hear?" Joe asked from his chair. The crippled lamb, now known as Patience, was asleep on his lap. Greta was out checking the pasture with Carl and Duncan. She expected them back at any time.

Lizzie looked out the living-room window. "It is a car. Maybe it's one of your therapists."

"I don't have physical therapy scheduled for today."

She pointed a finger at him. "That doesn't mean you get to skip your exercises."

"Nag, nag. Don't worry, I'll do them. I don't intend to be glued to a walker for the rest my life. Don't just stand there. Go see who it is."

Lizzie brushed off the front of her apron, straightened her *kapp* and went to the door. An Amish woman and an ebony-skinned girl of about thirteen dressed in Englisch clothes emerged from the backseat.

The girl darted away from the car and came running up the steps. "Is Kondoo Mtu here? Where is he? I want to thank him for the good life he has given me."

Her thick accent kept Lizzie from understanding who she was looking for. "You must have the wrong house. There's no one by that name here."

The Amish woman came and stood behind the girl with her hands on her shoulders. "*Kondoo Mtu* means 'Sheep Man.' When Carl would say, *'Ja. Ja,'* to her, it sounded like 'Baa. Baa.' Hence, Sheep Man. Hello, I'm

Jenna King. And this bundle of energy is my adopted daughter, Christina. Her English is improving, but she still has trouble with many of our words. Are you Elizabeth Barkman?"

"I am." Lizzie wasn't sure what else to say. She had expected a letter in response to the one she wrote, not a face-to-face visit.

"Who is it?" Joe shouted from the living room.

"I'm Carl's sister," the woman said with a knowing smile.

Lizzie went weak in the knees with relief. Not a wife. A sister. "Oh, I'm very glad to meet you. Come in and meet my grandfather."

"Where is Carl?"

"He's out checking the lambs. He should be in soon. He still doesn't know I wrote to you."

"I'm very glad you did. When you wrote that Carl had burned my letters, I was hurt. I knew I had to come see him in person. Besides, I wanted to meet the woman who cares so much about him. "

Lizzie's face grew hot. "I do care about him. He's a good man."

"Then perhaps together we can help him find his way back to his family and his faith. You said Carl hasn't told you why he was shunned. Is that still true?"

"He won't speak of it."

"It's a tragic story, but one I think he must share with you himself. If he isn't ready to do that, then my coming here may have been a mistake."

Was it a mistake? Lizzie prayed she hadn't done the wrong thing by writing to Jenna. "I don't think it was a mistake for you to come here. Carl told me yesterday that he planned to go home."

Relief brightened Jenna's eyes. "That's good to hear."

"Please come inside while you wait for him."

"Danki." Jenna held out her hand and Christina dashed to her side. Together, they entered the house.

Lizzie scanned the hillside, looking for Carl. There wasn't any sign of him. A sick feeling settled in her stomach. What was he going to say when he found out what she'd done?

In the living room, Jenna and Christina took a seat on the sofa. Lizzie introduced them to her grandfather. Christina couldn't sit still. She was up and down a dozen times to pet the lamb in Joe's lap and look out the window. Jenna gave Joe an apologetic smile. "I'm sorry. She's just so excited to see Carl again. She hasn't seen him since they came back from Africa."

"Carl was in Africa?" Joe was clearly shocked.

Lizzie leaned forward knowing she was finally going to learn about Carl's past.

Jenna nodded. "We had a younger sister named Sophia. She was drawn to missionary work. She chose not to be baptized and left home to work with a Mennonite group in Africa. She fell in love with a young man working there and they decided to marry. Sophia wanted someone from the family to attend her wedding. You can't blame her. My mother's health wasn't good. I didn't want to go, so Carl went."

Christina beamed. "He came to my village. He made us all laugh. He made Sophie happy. We liked him."

Jenna's eyes grew sad. "The wedding never took place. The village was raided by rebel soldiers and everyone was killed, including Christina's parents. Carl and Christina were the only survivors."

Christina left the window to stand in front of Lizzie. "The bad men came and shoot, shoot, shoot. Kondoo Mtu, he saved me."

Jenna leaned forward. "Christina, no! We don't speak of this."

But the excited child continued, "He get gun and kill the bad man who killed my father. He shoot him dead. We hide. Then more soldiers find Sophia and my mother. They kill them, too."

Lizzie went rigid with shock. A loud buzzing filled her ears. No Amish man would raise a gun to another human. She couldn't believe what she was hearing.

Jenna jumped to her feet and put her arms around Christina. Regret was etched deeply in her face. "I'm so sorry, Lizzie. This isn't how I wanted you to find out."

Lizzie couldn't draw a breath. It was as if the air was gone from the room. "Carl killed a man? He shot him?"

"Yes, I did," Carl said from the doorway.

Lizzie turned to stare at him, but she couldn't speak. Never had she imagined such horrible things could happen to someone she knew.

Christina dashed across the room. She threw her arms around him. "Kondoo Mtu, do you remember me?"

"Yes, I remember you." He kissed her cheek and she beamed at him.

"Thank you for bringing me to Jenna. She is good lady."

"I know. Why don't you go down to the barn and tell the lady there that you would like to feed the lambs? Tell her that I sent you. Her name is Greta."

When the child did as he asked, he looked straight at Lizzie. "Now you know."

What should she say? She hadn't been prepared for anything like this.

After a long minute, he looked down and gave a deep sigh. Then he turned and started to walk away.

Behind her, Lizzie heard Jenna call his name. He stopped. He spoke without turning around. "You shouldn't have come here, Jenna. Why did you?"

"She's here because I wrote to her," Lizzie admitted. Why wouldn't he look at them?

"You shouldn't have done that, Lizzie." He shook his head sadly. "I knew this was too good to last."

He walked away without another word, leaving Lizzie in shock and wondering what to do next.

Jenna put her arm around Lizzie's shoulders. "I'm so very sorry."

Lizzie managed to speak without breaking down in tears. "Don't be. It's Carl's choice to remain apart." Apart from her and the love she would so willingly give him.

"Come, sit down and I'll tell you the rest of the story."

Lizzie followed her back to the sofa.

When they were seated, Jenna said, "Carl returned to our family a broken man. He was haunted by his actions and Sophia's death. At night, he would wake up screaming. We did all we could to console him, but it didn't help. He refused to ask for forgiveness. He didn't believe he deserved it. He stopped going to church services and eventually our bishop had no choice but to place him in the Bann until he repented. Instead, Carl left without telling anyone where he was going."

Joe sighed heavily and straightened his leg with a grimace of pain. "He didn't have a destination in mind. He told me he'd been walking the back roads and getting odd jobs to get by. It wasn't until he found a starving puppy that he decided to stay in one place. The Lord blessed me when He led Carl here."

Jenna smiled at him. "Our family is grateful for your generosity. Carl didn't contact us until two years ago. He called the business where I work. I thought it signaled a change for the better, something we had all been praying for. I wrote him every week thinking that reading my letters would help him see that we still loved him and wanted him to come home."

"He would have gone home if I hadn't interfered." Lizzie bit her lower lip, rose from the sofa and went outside.

After hearing Jenna relate the entire sad story, she finally understood a little of what Carl had gone through. She gathered her shattered emotions and went to find him and beg his forgiveness.

Following the path that led to his place, she tried to imagine what she would say to him. Nothing formed in her mind. It was as if a dark curtain had been pulled across her emotions. She paused in the open door of the shepherd's hut. He had his back to her. He was stuffing his clothes in a black duffel bag.

"Carl, I must speak to you."

He stopped what he was doing and straightened, but he didn't turn around. "Don't bother. I already know what you have to say."

She took a step inside the door. "I don't think you do."

"You know what I did. You don't have to say anything. I'm leaving. All I ask is that you take good care of Duncan for me."

"All I ask is that you turn around and look at me."

His shoulders slumped. "Don't make this harder, Lizzie."

If he wouldn't turn around, she would just have to apologize to his back. "It is not my intention to make anything harder, but my good intentions have not turned out as I hoped. I'm sorry for interfering, Carl. I shouldn't have written to Jenna without your knowledge. I betrayed your trust, and I'm truly sorry. I wanted you to confide in me."

"When is the right time to tell the woman you love that you're a murderer?" He closed his eyes and bowed his head.

In two quick strides, she crossed the room and cupped his face with her hands. There were tears on his cheeks. "I cannot begin to comprehend the horror and the terror you faced. Under such ghastly circumstances, a man does not know how he will react until he is in the situation."

"Our faith tells us what a man must do, no matter what circumstances he faces. 'Thou shalt not kill.'"

He pulled free of her touch and resumed packing. "I made a choice. I decided another man's life was less valuable than mine, or Christina's. I became his judge and jury, and I snuffed out his life in the blink of an eye. In his fellow soldier's fury to avenge him, I brought a terrible fate upon my sister and the women with her. They all died because of me. I'm the one who should have died, not Sophia and her friends. I see them in my dreams. I can't get their faces out of my head. I never wanted you to know what I did."

"Don't torture yourself. I know your sister has forgiven you."

"Go back to the house, Lizzie. I don't want to see you again. I can't bear the way you look at me now. Tell Jenna to go home. I don't want to see her, either."

"But you told me yesterday that you intended to go home."

"I was wrong to think I could. I see now there is no reason to go back. Nothing has changed for me."

Lizzie struggled to find the right thing to say, but she was at a loss. She didn't know how to help him deal with his crushing burden of guilt. "I was shocked by what I heard. I'll admit that."

"Can you say your feelings for me haven't changed?"

"Give me some time to come to grips with this."

"That's what I thought."

"Please, do not judge me harshly. I'm not sure how I feel, but I do care about you. I forgive you for what you did. There's no question about that in my heart. Have you forgiven yourself?"

"I don't know how to do that."

She couldn't get through to him. "Where will you go?"

He stopped packing and raised his face to the ceiling. "Away." Then he began stuffing his clothes into his pack again.

"Carl, don't shut me out."

"Go away, Lizzie. Please."

Lizzie felt as if the ground had vanished from beneath her. She couldn't reach through the prison walls he had erected around his heart. With no other choice, she left and went back to the house. When she reached the porch steps, she broke down and sobbed as if her heart were breaking.

Because it was.

Carl stood in the hut after Lizzie left without moving. It hurt to breathe. He had no place to go. He was adrift without a compass of any kind. What now? Where could he find a hole deep enough to hide in so that he never had to face himself again? Where would he find peace?

Nowhere. So why was he running away? What was he running to?

He raked a hand through his hair. It wasn't right to leave while Joe was crippled. He owed the man too much.

If he left, he would never see Lizzie again. She didn't hate him, but had he lost her love?

He fell to his knees with his hands at his sides and gave vent to his pain. "God, why are You doing this to me? Because I dared to love her? You made her the way she is. How could I not love her?"

He had no idea how long he knelt slumped on the stone floor. His legs grew numb. His eyes burned from the tears that streamed down his face. All he could say was "God, help me. I'm sorry. I'm sorry. Forgive me."

Gradually, his despair faded and a gentle calm replaced it. He felt something rough on his face. He realized that Duncan was licking his tears.

He wrapped his arms around the dog and held on. "Am I forgiven? Have you been the sign from Him all along but I refused to see it? Was Joe the sign I had God's forgiveness? Is it Lizzie? How many signs do I need to tell me that life is good if I choose to live it as He wills?"

As He wills, not as Carl King would have it.

For the first time, he understood that he couldn't hide from what he had done. He had to accept his failure, not wallow in it, and go forward. He would face other tests in his life. Some great and some small, but all were by the will of God. He prayed for the strength to meet them with humility and peace in his heart.

Struggling to his feet, he walked to the door, surprised to see it was almost dark. Duncan growled low in his throat. The sounds of frantic sheep cries reached Carl. Looking east, he saw part of the flock scattering in a terrified panic just across the creek. The large coydog raced among them.

Joe's gun sat just inside the door. Carl picked it up. The feel of the cool wooden stock made him sick to his stomach. He tightened his grip. He owed it to Joe to protect the sheep. It was just a wild animal, not a man. He'd done much worse. He could do this. He just hadn't expected God to test him so soon.

He tightened his grip on the gun. He wouldn't let Joe down.

He made Duncan stay inside and closed the door, then he sprinted toward the sheep in trouble. The frenzied bleating of a lamb guided him to his target. The coydog had a lamb down at the edge of the creek. He saw Carl and stood over a struggling lamb with his head lowered and his teeth bared.

Carl raised the gun and sighted along the barrel. His finger curled over the trigger but he couldn't pull it. He drew a shaky breath and lowered the gun.

He couldn't do it. Not even to save the lambs. He couldn't take a life, even that of a predator.

He stepped closer and yelled. The coydog flinched, but stood his ground.

"I won't kill you, but maybe you'll think twice about going after sheep again."

Carl sighted carefully. He let out a sharp whistle. The coydog lifted its head and perked its ears. Carl fired. The bullet hit the rocks in front of the animal, peppering him with bits of stone. He yelped and took off, shaking his head as he ran.

Carl crossed the creek and hurried to the downed lamb. It struggled weakly as he picked it up. Its injuries appeared superficial. It was suffering from exhaustion and shock as much as anything. "Joe's going to have to invest in a few more guard animals to keep the rest of the flock safe in case that big fellow didn't get the message. I've heard llamas make excellent guardians."

He picked up the lamb and cuddled it close. "Don't worry, little one. I reckon Lizzie will have you fixed up in no time. I only pray that I can mend the harm I've caused her."

He started toward the house with long, sure strides.

He had wounded Lizzie as surely as the coydog had wounded the lamb in his arms. If it took him the rest of his life, he would show Lizzie how sorry he was. If she gave him a second chance, he'd never shut her out of his life again.

Surrounded by her sisters and her grandfather, Lizzie sat at the kitchen table and tried to gather up the pieces of her broken heart. Jenna and Christina had gone to the inn in Hopes Springs for the night. They would travel home tomorrow.

Lizzie propped her chin on her hand. "I've made such a mess of things."

Clara laid a hand on Lizzie's shoulder. "You were trying to help."

"My interference didn't heal a family breach. It has driven Carl farther from those who love him." Including her.

"He'll come back," Joe said. "In time, he'll see that you meant well. Everyone makes mistakes."

"I've made more than my share lately." She looked out the window as the lights of a car swept into the yard and stopped.

"Now who is here?" Joe asked.

"I don't know. I don't recognize the car. It's not the one that brought Jenna earlier."

She had her answer a moment later when her uncle Morris and Rufus Kuhns stormed through the door.

Chapter 15

"Onkel, what are you doing here?" Lizzie demanded. Her voice trembled with fright.

"I have come to take you and your wayward sisters home. How dare you defy me in this fashion?"

"How did you find us?" Betsy had tears in her eyes.

"Lizzie wrote a letter to you, but you were already gone. When I saw the postmark, I knew you had come here. You will be disciplined for this disrespect of your elder. Get your things and get in the car." He slapped a thick wooden yardstick on the table, making them all jump.

Rufus advanced on Clara. She shrank back in fear. He raised his fist and shook it at her. "You have made me the laughingstock of our community. You will come back and wed me." He grabbed her arm.

"*Nee,* I will not."

He struck her across the face. The women shrieked in outrage. Lizzie grabbed Clara and moved to put her own body between Rufus and his victim. "Leave her be."

Joe rose to his feet. "Get out of my house."

Morris pushed him back into his chair. Joe fell and grimaced with pain.

Rufus glared at Lizzie. "I'll teach you to interfere between a man and his betrothed." He raised his hand to hit her. She cowered before him.

"Enough!"

Everyone turned to see Carl in the doorway. He held a rifle in one hand and a lamb in the other.

Rufus eyed the gun. "This is a family matter, Englisch. It's none of your concern."

Carl set the gun against the wall and ignored the red-faced man. "Are you all right, Joe?"

"Right as rain. What's the matter with my wee woolly?"

Carl spoke softly to Lizzie. "He's been mauled. I need your help. We need to clean his wounds."

She was frightened, but his calm words gave her courage. She moved away from Rufus, pulling Clara with her. "Go get some towels, Clara. Greta, put some water on the stove to heat. Betsy, would you fix some milk for him? It's in the barn. We need to get fluids into him."

"Sure." Betsy started for the front door.

Morris smacked the table with his stick again. Clara and Betsy flinched, but Clara went up the stairs and Betsy went out the front door.

Lizzie heard Duncan barking in the distance and hoped he would stay away. Her uncle wasn't fond of dogs.

She took the lamb from Carl's arms. It cried pitifully. "It's all right. We'll fix you up."

"Stop what you're doing and get your things. We're leaving," Morris shouted.

Lizzie looked into Carl's serene eyes. "I think he may need stitches."

"You know best. Should we take him to the vet?"

Rufus and Morris exchanged puzzled looks. Lizzie knew they weren't used to being ignored.

"Obey me, you ungrateful child." Morris raised his stick and stepped toward Lizzie.

She closed her eyes and tried to shelter the lamb. She knew what was coming. Suddenly, Carl's arms were around her, shielding her. She felt him flinch with each blow her uncle struck, but he never made a sound.

A crash followed by screaming made her open her eyes. Duncan had charged through the mesh of the screen door and launched himself at Morris. Her uncle fell in his attempt to evade the dog. He was lying on the floor, trying to beat the dog off and screaming for Rufus to help him.

Rufus aimed a kick at Duncan. The dog easily evaded it and turned his attention to his new attacker. Darting in and out, he sought a hold on Rufus's leg and found it. Rufus hollered in pain.

Morris saw his chance and made a dash for the front door. Duncan, seeing his prey on the run, charged after him. Morris barely made it out, slamming the wooden door behind him. Rufus made a limping run for the back door. Carl spoke quickly. "Leave it, Duncan. Down."

The dog dropped to the floor and lay panting as he watched his master for his next command. Outside, the car engine sprang to life and the vehicle roared up the lane. Lizzie had to wonder what the Englisch driver must think of the evening's events.

She realized she was still in Carl's arms. She relaxed against his chest and drew several shuddering breaths. He lifted her chin with his hand and gazed at her face. "Are you all right?"

"I should be asking you that."

A tender smile pulled at the corner of his mouth. "At this moment, I've never been better in my life."

"Then maybe I can stay here a little longer?"

He pulled her close and tucked her against him. "You definitely should."

The front door flew open. Betsy stood there gasping for breath. Clara ventured down the stairs with towels in her arms and Greta moved to Joe's side to check on him. He patted her hand. "I'm fine."

Carl smiled at Betsy. "Duncan was shut in my hut. How did he get out?"

She was still panting. "I opened the door for him because it sounded like he wanted out. Onkel Morris doesn't like dogs. I thought they should meet."

Clara dropped to her knees to hug Duncan. "You are a wunderbar guard dog."

He wagged his tail happily. Joe said, "Bacon for that boy tonight for sure."

Everyone began to talk at once except Lizzie. She

was content to rest in Carl's arms. She never wanted to move. It seemed her grandfather finally noticed.

He cleared his throat loudly. "We should get that lamb fixed up."

Carl reluctantly released her as her sisters came to take the lamb from her. He said, "We need to talk."

She pressed a hand to his cheek. "The past is over and done. It need never be mentioned again."

He flicked her nose with one finger. "It's not the past I want to talk about, Lizzie Barkman.

"After this baby is fixed up, would you care to drive into town with me? I need to see Jenna and Christina. I have a lot of explaining and apologizing to do. To all of you."

Naomi Wadler greeted them with some surprise as they came into the lobby of the inn. Carl approached the counter. "My sister Jenna King is staying here. Would you let her know that I'd like a word with her?"

"She and Christina are in the café. I'll show you the way. How is Joe getting along?"

"Fine. You should come by for a visit," Carl said with a slight smile for her.

She blushed. "I'll do just that. Tell him I'll be by with some canned goods on Sunday."

He and Lizzie followed her to the café doors. Lizzie caught his arm. "If you want to speak to your sister alone, I can wait in the lobby."

He covered her hand and gave her a reassuring squeeze. "I want you by my side."

The smile she gave him warmed his heart. The Lord had truly blessed him when He brought her into his life.

They found Jenna and Christina seated in a booth in the corner. Christina saw him first and jumped up to hug him. "Kondoo Mtu, I thought I would never see you again."

Lizzie took a step to the side as he hugged the child in return. Jenna looked uncertain about what her response should be. He kept one arm around Christina, but he held out his free hand. Jenna scooted out of the booth and threw her arms around him.

He choked back the tears that threatened to keep him silent. "I'm sorry, Jenna. I'm so sorry for the hurt I've caused you and everyone. Can you forgive me?"

"All is forgiven. All is forgiven. Come home, Carl. We love you. We miss you so much."

He looked over Jenna's head at Lizzie. "I don't deserve such unselfish love."

"Yes, you do," Lizzie said softly.

He read in her eyes what she wanted to say. She loved him, too. Soon he would be able to tell her how he felt, that he loved her with his whole heart and soul. For now, he had to believe she could see his love for her shining in his eyes.

After everyone's tears were dried, Naomi brought them slices of pie and cups of coffee with a mug of hot chocolate for Christina.

Jenna took a sip of coffee and sniffed once. "What are your plans now, Carl?"

"I thought since you have already hired a driver that I would ride home with you."

"Mamm and Daed with be so happy to see you. It will be a wunderbar surprise."

"I'd like to see the bishop first thing and explain myself."

Jenny reached across the table and took his hand. "You know that he and everyone in the church will rejoice that you have returned."

"I know. The thing is, I'm not going to stay, Jenna. I'm coming back here."

She glanced between him and Lizzie, who was blushing bright red. "Although we will hate to lose you again so soon, I think everyone will be happy for you."

"I won't be happy," Christina said with a pout.

He ruffled her hair. "I'll come visit a lot. You'll come to visit me here, too."

"Can I feed the lambs again?"

They all chuckled. He nodded. "Sheep Man said you may always feed the lambs."

When they were finishing their pie, Naomi approached again with a large box in her arms. "Lizzie, I have something for you."

Lizzie's eyebrows shot up. "For me? What is it?"

Naomi laid the box on the table. "Open it and see."

Lifting the carton lid, Lizzie squealed in delight. "It's my mother's quilt!"

Naomi smiled at her. "The buyer thought you should have it back."

Lizzie's eyes narrowed as she met his gaze. "Carl, did you do this?"

He held up both hands. "I tried, but someone beat me to it."

"Who?" Lizzie looked at Naomi.

"I promised not to tell."

Lizzie pulled the quilt from the box. "But it was so

much money. I need to pay someone back. I can't accept such a gift."

Naomi fisted her hands on her hips. "You can and you will."

Lizzie's eyes narrowed again. "Naomi, did you do this? Do I owe you money?"

"*Nee,* it wasn't me. I'm just glad the quilt is back where it belongs. Your mother made it as a wedding gift for you. I know, and the buyer knows, that she would want you to have it. She would be so pleased that you used it to help your sisters find a safe home."

Lizzie held the quilt to her face and closed her eyes. "Please give my thanks to the buyer. I can't believe it came back to me."

Naomi patted Carl's shoulder and winked at him. "Now all that is needed is a wedding."

On the last Sunday in April, the congregation of Bishop Zook found itself in for a few surprises.

Carl had gone to meet privately with the bishop a few days before. Lizzie didn't know what they talked about, but she knew Carl planned to join their church if the congregation would ultimately accept him. It had to be a unanimous vote of all baptized members, so she knew Carl would be under close scrutiny for the next few months.

He looked very handsome in his dark coat and flat-topped black felt hat. He spent a lot of time running his hands up and down his suspenders. She could tell he wasn't used to them after wearing jeans for more than four years. There were a lot of surprised looks when the bishop introduced him after the service.

Faith Lapp had delivered a healthy seven-pound baby girl the week before. She brought her to church for the first time and everyone, including the Barkman girls, took turns admiring her. Adrian stayed by his wife's side, playing the role of proud papa with ease.

Lizzie, like everyone else, dropped her jaw when the banns between her grandfather and Naomi Wadler were read aloud by the bishop as the last item of the morning. She turned to her sisters. They all shrugged. None of them knew anything about it. Joseph, in his usually abrupt manner, left early after church and avoided a ton of questions. Naomi climbed into his buggy with him and they drove off, leaving people to speculate wildly on their whirlwind romance.

Only Sally Yoder said, "I knew something was up between them all along."

Later that afternoon, when Lizzie and her sisters arrived home in Carl's new buggy, they all piled out and rushed into the house.

Naomi held up a hand to forestall their questions. "He was supposed to tell you."

Joe looked defensive. "The time never seemed right. It's my decision to wed. If it doesn't suit any of you, too bad."

The sisters surrounded him with hugs and best wishes. No one objected to having a new grandmother in the family.

After supper that night, Carl asked Lizzie to come for a buggy ride with him. Her heart raced as she agreed.

They had been careful to keep things low-key during his transition from an Englisch to an Amish sheepherder. His presentation to the church was the next-to-last step on his road back to the faith of his heart. It opened the way for him to court Lizzie without damaging her reputation.

Carl drove them out to the lake. It was an old stone quarry that had filled with water a century before. It was a favorite fishing spot for some of the locals, but they had the place to themselves that evening. They got out of the buggy and found a large flat rock to sit on by the water. Lizzie got up and threw a half dozen stones into the lake to ease her jitters.

Carl rested back on his elbows and watched her. "Can I ask you a question, Lizzie?"

"Of course." She came to sit beside him.

"On the night your uncle showed up, what did you think when I walked in with a gun in my hand?"

"I saw the gun and lamb at the same time. I thought you had been out protecting the flock from the coy-dog."

He studied her intently. "You didn't think I would use the gun?"

"On my uncle? *Nee,* that never crossed my mind. Can I ask you a question?"

"Sure."

She hesitated a moment. "Did you shoot the coy-dog?"

"*Nee,* I could not."

She grinned with relief. "He hasn't been back. I'm grateful for that."

"I found out who owns him."

"Did you? Who does he belong to?"

"Our postman."

"He's the mailman's dog?" Lizzie laughed.

"He and his son stopped in to buy a club lamb a few days ago. He had the coydog with him. He said the boy wanted the dog to get used to sheep so he wouldn't bother the one they took home."

"Oh, dear. Did you tell them that he can't be trusted around the lamb?"

"I had to tell them he's been killing our sheep. They offered to pay for all the damages. They felt bad about it, especially the boy. Joe wouldn't take their money."

"He's too happy these days to worry about money."

"Naomi is making a new man of him, that's for sure."

"Speaking of new men, you look very Plain in your new suit."

"I am a new Plain man, and I'm in love with a beautiful Plain woman." Carl leaned close and Lizzie knew he was about to kiss her. She had never wanted anything more.

His lips touched hers with incredible gentleness, a featherlight caress. It wasn't enough. She cupped his cheek with her hand. To her delight, he deepened the kiss. Joy clutched her heart and stole her breath away. She had been waiting a lifetime for this moment and she didn't even know it.

He pulled her closer. Her arms circled his neck. The sweet softness of his lips moved away from her mouth. He kissed her cheek and then drew away. Lizzie wasn't ready to let him go. She would never be ready to let him go.

"I love you, Lizzie," he murmured softly into her ear. "You have made me whole again. I was broken, and you found a way to mend me. I lived a life of despair, ashamed of what I had done. I thought I was beyond help. And then you came into my life and I saw hope."

"I love you, too, darling, but it is God that has made us both whole."

"And the two shall become as one. I never understood the true meaning of that until this very moment."

He kissed her temple. "Will you marry me, Lizzie Barkman?"

Lizzie had never felt so cherished. The wonder of his love was almost impossible to comprehend. This man, who had seen so much of the world, wanted her to be his wife. Emotion choked her. She couldn't speak.

He drew back slightly to gaze at her face. "Am I rushing you? Please, say something."

"Can't you hear my heart shouting *yes?*"

"No, for mine is beating so hard that I can't hear anything."

"Yes, Carl King. I will marry you."

Suddenly, he lifted her off her feet and swung her around, making her squeal with delight.

"I love you, Lizzie. I love you. I love you. I will never get tired of saying that."

When he stopped spinning, her feet touched the ground again. She gazed into his eyes. "And I will never grow tired of hearing it. I can't believe this is real. I'm afraid that I'm dreaming."

"Shall I pinch you?"

"Don't you dare."

"Then I will simply have to kiss you again. If I may?"

She put her hands on his chest. "You may. For as often and as long as you would like once we're married."

"Then say it will be soon."

"November will be soon enough."

He growled and pulled her snugly against him. "November seems an eternity from now."

She wavered. "It does, doesn't it?"

"I think we should have a June wedding."

"June will be too soon, but I think October will be about right."

He leaned close. "As you wish, but this is the last kiss you will get until our wedding day."

She gave him a saucy smile. "Then you had better make it a good one."

He proceeded to show her just how wonderful a kiss could be.

* * * * *

HARLEQUIN
PLUS

Announcing a **BRAND-NEW** multimedia subscription service for romance fans like you!

Read, Watch and Play.

Experience the easiest way to get the romance content you crave.

Start your **FREE 7 DAY TRIAL** at
<u>www.harlequinplus.com/freetrial</u>.